# STOCKDALE

# STOCKDALE

A novel by Priscilla Lalisse

iUniverse, Inc.
New York  Lincoln  Shanghai

# STOCKDALE

Copyright © 2005 by Priscilla Ann Thomas Lalisse

All rights reserved. No part of this book may be used or reproduced by any means, graphic, electronic, or mechanical, including photocopying, recording, taping or by any information storage retrieval system without the written permission of the publisher except in the case of brief quotations embodied in critical articles and reviews.

iUniverse books may be ordered through booksellers or by contacting:

iUniverse
2021 Pine Lake Road, Suite 100
Lincoln, NE 68512
www.iuniverse.com
1-800-Authors (1-800-288-4677)

ISBN-13: 978-0-595-37244-7 (pbk)
ISBN-13: 978-0-595-81641-5 (ebk)
ISBN-10: 0-595-37244-9 (pbk)
ISBN-10: 0-595-81641-X (ebk)

Printed in the United States of America

## Acknowledgments

During the writing of *Stockdale*, the following people provided much needed support, advice, criticism, encouragement and enthusiasm, for which I will always be more grateful than they could possibly know:

Angela Berneur, Robin Bates, Jeannette Cezanne, Mark Clement, Rodney Conwell, Agnés Cotelli, Deirdre Dressie, Jennie Wren Duke, Bruno Germaine, Lajuana Hill-Zanoni, Insight Design Solutions, Dorothy Johnson, Forrest Johnson, Forrest Johnson, Jr., Janay Johnson, Audrey Jones, Houston Jones, Madison Jones, Patrice Jones, Juliet Lac, Danny Love, Gabrielle Luthy, Philippe Megange, Stefan Naumann, Michelle Parks, John Parrish, Michaela Porte, Gerry Tatham, Lewis Tatham, Patricia Seldomridge, Leslie Serour, Susie Smeriglio, Barbara Ulbrich, and Aaron Watson.

In addition, a special thank-you to my P.R. Manager, Carolyn Moncel and Mondave Communications; my editor, Arlene W. Robinson; and finally, my son Zachary, who inspires me every single day, and is truly my greatest gift ever.

In Loving Memory

Harry Heard, the best grandfather I could have ever asked for,

Mattie Stockdale Groce, my great-aunt, so gracious and caring,

Celestine S. Moore, my godmother, who brightened everyone's life,

and Jon Payne, my high-school friend and band-mate, who left us far too soon.

Dedicated to my grandmother,

Beatrice Stockdale Heard

Affectionately known as "Mombee"

May 25, 1914–November 27, 2004

Mere words could never express…

I Celebrate myself;

And what I assume you shall assume,

For every atom belonging to me, as good belongs to you.

Walt Whitman

# Chapter 1

▼

It was 1975, the end of our school year, and the beginning of one of the worst summers of my life. I was a seven-year-old kid in the second grade and it was the last day of school. My best friend at the time, a white girl named Kerrie, often pretended with me that we were Charlie's Angels. Kerrie, a.k.a. "Jill Monroe," was bigger than I was, tall, with the classic pale skin, blonde hair and blue eyes. I was "Sabrina Duncan," the dark-haired angel. Kerrie actually looked like Farrah Fawcett—at least I thought she did until we got to high school—but then again, with my café au lait skin, dark brown eyes and black curly hair, I've *never* looked like Kate Jackson.

We Angels were head-over-heels in love with Starsky and Hutch. Not David Soul and Paul Michael Glaser from the television series, but two boys in our class named David and Charles. David was "Hutch," and that name naturally fit him; he was, in reality, tall with almost-yellow hair. Charles was dark-haired and shorter, with chubby cheeks and long eyelashes, and he was my Starsky. We gave each other gum and sat beside each other in the lunchroom every day. I even let him borrow my crayons. So, by the end of second grade, I was sure Starsky would accept my red cut-out heart that I had personally colored just for him.

What followed sticks in my mind like Krazy Glue gone mad. We were walking out to the yellow school buses that we took every day to get home. Charles and I were almost to the part of the sidewalk where he would turn right to go to his bus, and I would turn left to go to mine. It was then or never. I took a deep breath and reached inside my coat, retrieved my cut-out heart, and offered it to him. He took it, looked at it, and then gave it back to me.

"Why don't you want my heart?" I asked, shuddering in the rain.

"I can't, Cassie," he answered.

"Why not?"

"I just can't take it," he said, and stepped back from me.

"Aren't we boyfriend and girlfriend?"

"No, we can't be."

"Why not?"

"Because I'm white and you're black, Cass."

And then he walked on off to his bus and left me standing there.

Crushed. Just like that, the cutout heart and mine were broken. I dropped it on the ground and stepped on it. It was a rainy mess. In pieces. My first heartbreak. He was the first boy I ever really liked.

Bye-bye, Starsky.

\* \* \* \*

When I got off the bus at my house, I went straight inside and sat down near the living room window. Still wearing my raincoat, I was looking outside at the rain rolling down the driveway when my mother appeared carrying a box of my father's clothes. *The last box.*

I saw my father's favorite flannel shirt hanging out of it. Somehow, in his rush to leave that morning, he had forgotten it.

"Cassandra Taylor, what's wrong?" Mama asked me.

"It's the last day of school," I lied.

"Oh, honey," she said with a relieved sigh. "You'll see your friends again next year." Then she opened the door and set the box outside on the front porch. I knew then that she wasn't going to let my father come back home.

I reached into my schoolbag, pulled out my box of Crayola crayons and started inspecting all the colors, from yellow to brown to black. My mother was right. I would see my friends again the next year. But I was sure it would never be the same.

\* \* \* \*

Deacon Jacob "Jackrabbit" Jenkins didn't look like he was eighty years old. He didn't talk or walk like he was eighty years old, and he certainly didn't drive like he was eighty years old. Or at least he liked to think he didn't.

About a month after I'd experienced my first heartache, "Mr. Jackrabbit," as we kids called him, was on his way home after having spent all Sunday long at the

New Ebenezer Baptist Church Convention in a nearby town. They say he usually drove way under the speed limit whenever he drove his 1973 Oldsmobile because it was his "baby."

Those who had attended the same church service would later say that Deacon Jenkins might have been thinking about the good sermon Reverend Sanders had just preached. The newly "called" preacher had shown out, which means he had jumped and shouted, sang and ran down the church aisles commanding Christians and heathens alike to stand up and clap for Jesus. They said he had a wonderful singing voice too, so he was everybody's kind of preacher.

Some dared speculate that Deacon Jenkins had eaten too much at the after-church dinner, particularly too much of Miss Fannie Joe's turkey and dressing. They hypothesized that he just might have nodded off at the wheel from having a full belly. But whatever Deacon Jenkins was thinking about that humid summer afternoon, no one would ever know. No one knew why or whether it had been he who'd run the stop sign on the final stretch to his home, a road that he had journeyed down several, several years.

Deacon Jenkins was killed on impact, and so was everyone in the station wagon he hit when one of them ran that stop sign: Mr. and Mrs. Peter Smith and their two children, Robert and Lizzie, who were apparently playing Uno in the backseat.

This was a tragic event on every level. Deacon Jenkins, a.k.a Mr. Jackrabbit, was well loved by everyone who lived on his side of town in the black community. The Smiths were well known and loved by everyone in the white community. Even though we all lived in *one* town, it was as though we actually lived in *two*, separated only by a set of defunct railroad tracks.

The white townsfolk blamed everything on Deacon Jenkins, and the black folks blamed everything on Mr. Smith. No one, not even the police, could determine the true nature of the crash…or at least they wouldn't say.

For a whole week, mad over what they called "the messing up of a good deacon's reputation," black workers threatened to quit work and called in sick at the town's chicken plant, panty factory and pajama factory. But in the end, they all went back to work, pointing out that anger couldn't feed them, and that besides, they still had to pay their church dues. The bosses were so happy they didn't have to shut down their plants, they gave the workers a ten-cent raise.

Deacon Jenkins' and the Smiths' funerals were all held all on the same day, one week later. The town was still in an uproar over all the deaths, with blame still shooting out from every direction. Mr. Jackrabbit's funeral was on our side of town at the Mount Zion Missionary Baptist Church, with the very same Reverend Sanders preaching his eulogy. The Smiths' funeral was held across the railroad tracks on the opposite side of town at Chapman's Funeral Services, for immediate family only.

During Mr. Jackrabbit's funeral, which I attended with Mama, my grandparents, and my kid sister, Kelly, Reverend Sanders sang one of our old beloved hymns: "A Charge to Keep I Have, a God to Glorify," which made the whole church deeply steeped in grief. Reverend Sanders preached for over an hour, stressing the obligation of love and forgiveness, saying that we had to forgive whoever was to blame for the accident and pray that God would welcome them all home. Hands clasped firmly and looking down at my new white-patent-leather Sunday shoes, I joined in with the rest of the congregation and prayed for the souls of Mr. Jackrabbit and the Smiths. I listened to the hallelujahs and the amens and the thank-you-Lords, and dared even whisper a few words for my lost love Starsky as well.

"Dear Lord," I prayed, "bless Mr. Jackrabbit and those Smith children, their mama and daddy. Please let my daddy come back home to us. Don't let him stay far away. And Lord, please let Starsky know that I still want to be his girlfriend, and that I ain't black. I'm yellowish-brown."

That was my 1975 summer in Stockdale, Alabama.

# Chapter 2

People think that Catholics are the only tortured souls. Not so, I tell you, not so. When I was fifteen years old, I had a crush on a boy named Max, as did every other girl in my class, both black and white. Max was a dark-skinned boy with smooth skin and what we called "good hair." He also had big brown liquid eyes, and to top it off, was the number-one football and basketball player in our high school. His skills demanded respect from white and black people alike. We may have been different colors and lived on different sides of town, but everyone wanted the Stockdale High School team to be the best team in the district and make it to the playoffs. Therefore, everyone was equal on the field. Max was only a sophomore and was already making newspaper headlines. I totally fell for him.

We had a few classes together; we talked and got along well. The thing that bothered me about Max, though, was that he had a wild reputation and was sleeping with half the girls in our class. Of course, when he was with the white girls, it had to be done on the sly—in places like cars after games, quick-like before anyone could guess or find out. I tried not to believe what was going on, but I knew Max was what my grandmother called mannish.

Even though I wasn't a blonde-haired blue-eyed cheerleader, I was still friends with the most popular people in school. Because of his athletic ability, Max was a part of the in-crowd too. Maybe that's why I thought we would be perfect for each other. Who knows.

One night when I was babysitting for one of my cousins, I asked her if Max could come over and watch TV with me. The baby's father, my cousin's husband, had been killed in a car accident, and she was just starting to date again.

Everyone knows everyone in Stockdale; Max's family went to church with my family, and on and on and on, so there was no problem. He came over, just as he had been invited to, without hesitation. I don't remember what date it was, or even the month. I know it was hot and maybe summer, because I remember the little white fan my cousin had in her two-bedroom apartment that made so much noise I worried if the baby would be able to sleep.

Half an hour or so of rocking later, the baby was finally sleeping in his crib and Max and I were watching television on the sofa. I couldn't think of much to say to him because I was still surprised he was actually there. Without any warning, he turned to me, asked if I wanted to have sex with him, and sat there waiting for my response. I said I couldn't do it, that I wasn't ready, and he said, "Well, we can't talk then." He grabbed his keys off the coffee table and left, slamming the door behind him, and I'll be damned if he didn't wake up the baby too.

I was depressed for one month.

* * * *

My sister Kelly and I had a job with Grandmama. Kelly's three years younger than I am, and was only twelve then, but it didn't matter. She was a big help for her small size. Our job? We cleaned the houses of elderly white people. I liked having my own pocket money, and never felt ashamed to do this sort of work. Neither did Grandmama or Kelly.

We went every Saturday morning to the home of a widower who paid us twenty dollars for the work, which, between the three of us, took about two-and-a-half hours. It was an old house, in need of painting and remodeling. His wife had died some years before, and there were rooms in the house the owner couldn't bring himself to enter. I felt spooked just going into them myself, but they were a part of my duties. I had to vacuum these rooms, dust them and arrange all the dusty books and newspapers. Kelly had to clean and mop the bathroom floor. Grandmama did the kitchen, and never took her part of the money. Instead, she gave me half of it and Kelly the other half.

I used to see various postcards that the widower received from his daughter, who was traveling. He had cards from such far-off places as New York City, Hawaii, California, Mexico, Spain, France, and once, even from Egypt. While I cleaned and dusted, I always pretended that I was going to New York City, or Spain or Italy…or France. I let myself daydream every Saturday because even though I was only fifteen years old, I never quite felt that I was a true Alabamian.

I always felt there was another world outside of Stockdale waiting for me too, just like there was for the widower's daughter.

On one of these Saturdays, after we cleaned his house, Kelly and I went to the neighboring town of Jefferson with my grandparents. This was something we did frequently after work on Saturdays. Stockdale did have a grocery store, but we didn't like to shop there; the owners were rednecks. Black people from Stockdale drove the full thirty minutes to the neighboring town for their weekly groceries, not only because Jefferson was larger with more choices, but also because it apparently had a larger black population. Mama never bought our groceries in Stockdale, ever. Even if it meant borrowing a carton of milk from my grandparents until she could get to the Piggly Wiggly in Jefferson, she'd wait.

Our pockets were full with our ten dollars from working, and we swore that we were rich as we went through our weekly ritual: heading to the mall where our grandparents did their shopping and left us to ourselves for a while to do ours. Once inside the mall, we went to a delicatessen called Piccadilly's. We chose our usual—a small side salad and strawberry cheesecake. We didn't have enough for a soda, so we took water. We had spent half of our ten dollars, but we knew it was going to be good. We sat down and ate our food as if we were in the best Manhattan restaurant.

Suddenly, Kelly stopped eating and pointed past my shoulder. I turned my head around and there he was: Max, at the cashier's stand, holding a to-go container. I hadn't really talked to him since the night he stormed out of my cousin's apartment, indignant that I wouldn't have sex with him. By this point, I didn't care about him in that way anymore; I had convinced myself that he was way too mannish for me. Still, I was curious, and I strained to hear what he was saying to the cashier.

"Look, if you don't have enough money, you'll have to put something back," the pink-faced cashier was saying. "Maybe you can go and find your parents and then come back."

"I thought I had enough money, but—wait, let me look again. Maybe I can put back the strawberry shortcake. How much is that?"

"You are really holding up the line," she said, "and I have to let these other people pay and be seated."

I couldn't take it anymore. He looked mighty ridiculous. And there was, in fact, a white church group waiting in line behind him, wearing frowns and wondering what the holdup was. From the look on his face, I thought he might even start crying.

I made my way up to the cashier's counter. "Hey, Max. What's up?"

"Hey," he answered, looking up sheepishly at the cashier.

"Listen, me and Kelly are here," I said. "Are you okay? You need some money?"

"Well I ah, I ah, well, you know…my parents are in J.C. Penny's and ah…"

"Here's two dollars. You can pay me back Monday at school."

He took the money, frankly relieved, and paid the cashier. I returned to my seat, and Kelly and I looked on as he made his wobbly way out the restaurant, all the while looking at us with an embarrassed smile and nodding his thanks. Kelly and I laughed hysterically once he was out of sight. Kelly was happy he had gotten his food to go, but I really didn't care one way or the other. All I thought about was that Max was such a popular football player and basketball player, a lady's man all over Stockdale, and yet he didn't even have enough money to buy himself a piece of strawberry shortcake. Whoever said revenge isn't sweet has never heard of Piccadilly's strawberry shortcake.

We finished our food and joined our grandparents at our normal meeting-place. They had their bags from Sears and JCPenny. We had our full stomachs and laughter.

These types of Saturdays were just how we liked them, and this one with Max not having enough money at the cashier's counter was the funniest and best of all. My grandparents, especially my grandfather, always thought it funny of us to spend our money at Piccadilly's every week. For him, it was much cheaper and better to just get an ice-cream cone from McDonald's. But for us, eating at Piccadilly's was pure luxury. In the end, they really didn't mind at all, just as long as we kept a tiny bit of money left over for Sunday school and church the next day. But then again, if we *had* spent it all, Grandmama would have slipped us a quarter anyway.

# Chapter 3

The years went by quickly for me up until the eleventh grade. I never forgot about my dad, but I sort of let him fall to the backburner for a while. I still thought about him, where he was and why he didn't come back to Stockdale, but my obsession to find him wouldn't take over again until a few years later. I was still going to church, to three or four services a week, doing pretty well in school when I wanted to, and still dreaming of being in some place other than Alabama. I still wanted to see the world. I still had the same friends, both black and white, and I still enjoyed my popularity at school. I was in the Drama Club, Beta Club, English Club, Spanish Club, and whatever else; you name it, I was a member. At church, it was the same thing: youth group, usher board, choir member and Sunday school secretary.

Things seemed to be getting better because I was almost out of school, and to be almost out of high school for me meant one thing: freedom. I was going to college, and I knew that would be in another city. Maybe I wouldn't have enough money to go out of state for the first two years, but I was at least going somewhere bigger than Stockdale.

Near the end of my junior year, Max and I were still the only black kids from our class who'd been admitted to the popular crowd. I had been brought into and kept in the crowd by the head cheerleader because she loved the way I dressed. Imagine that.

My aunt had given me a ton of her old clothes once. In this lot was a pair of shiny black pants. They were slinky and soft. They might have even been silk. One day I wore them to school with a pair of white socks, black shoes, a white shirt and black jacket. I thought I'd been pretty successful in copying Michael

Jackson's "Off the Wall" look. Heather, the cheerleader, commented on how great my look was. She said that I was brave to wear that kind of pants to school, and that she loved them. She called me a rebel. What I didn't know up until then was that I was actually wearing black lounge pants. I was almost in pajamas, for crying out loud. Pajamas. Oh well, I guess you could say my passion for Michael Jackson got me into the in-crowd.

Mama played a large part in it too. If IZOD was the new trend, she kept me in IZOD. If Aigner was the purse all the girls were carrying, she got me one. If Reeboks were the new sneakers, well, she got me those too. All it took was one mention of what Heather or some other popular girl was wearing at school, and I had it—even if Mama had to put it on layaway first, and she rarely did.

The main thing she insisted on was that Kelly and I spoke correct English. She said that would help us gain respect. Moreover, with her being a junior-high English teacher—and the only black teacher on staff—how could we not? We weren't allowed to talk like most of the other people in Stockdale, both black and white. We weren't supposed to say, "He gone git it when she git home." Instead, we had to say, "He's going to be in trouble once she gets home." Of course, there were times when we lapsed back into the old town-talk, but we tried not to, because our advantages would be taken away if we did. That meant no extra money, no treats and no IZODS.

There were several cute boys I liked in my eleventh-grade class, but I never had a chance with them. Same old problem: They were white and I was black. It never even came up. They never asked me out, or even hinted in that direction. Sure, there was a little flirting going on from some of the braver ones, but that was it. Although he and I later became excellent friends and I was his most trusted confidant, Max was still out as a possible boyfriend. The other black guys in my class were totally uninteresting, uninterested in me, skipped school, or I just simply didn't like them. I wanted to see plays, they didn't. I wanted to write poetry, they thought that was weird. I wanted to visit Russia, and they thought I was insane. I wasn't "a stuck-up black girl" like they accused me of being, I just had nothing in common with them.

I really began to like one of the white guys who was on the football team with Max. He seemed to be interested in many of the things I was—traveling, foreign languages, theater. In fact, this was the David who was better known as Hutch when we were in second grade, only at that time, I had my eye on Starsky. David flirted with me in classes, and we laughed a lot together. I think he would have tried to date me had the "rules" been different. Too bad.

Max, however, didn't have the same problem that I had. Well, not exactly. He kept doing his thing undercover with the white girls he liked, but that was just it—he could only see them behind closed doors. He couldn't date them openly or take them to the prom.

Soon, the tables sort of turned for good. Things got infinitely more complicated.

Heather Hughes, the cheerleader who'd seen fit to tell me that I was at school in pajamas, was five-feet-five-inches tall, had shoulder-length blonde hair, startling green eyes, and a year-round tan. She was one of my best friends, and by far the most popular girl at school. She hung out in our black neighborhood and never judged it, or us, and she sat at the "black lunch table" at school. Most of the other girls, especially the white cheerleaders, only associated with white kids. Heather associated with everybody.

Heather was also having an affair with Max.

I hadn't actually thought they were that serious about each other, but I was wrong. Near the end of the year, she pulled me aside at the lockers and gave me some news I hadn't been at all expecting.

"You're what?" I asked her, almost screaming it in a mild whisper.

"Yeah, I'm three months' pregnant and I am not sure who the father is."

*Okay!* I thought.

Heather was a smart girl, straight-A student, beautiful, pleasant, and open-minded. She had her sights set on an Ivy League school and her parents could definitely afford it and were ready to send her. I couldn't believe what I was hearing. What had she gotten herself into?

This wasn't such a *complete* shock to me, though. While I knew she was seeing Max on the sly and had been for a long time, I also knew that her out-in-the-open boyfriend was a white guy named Roger. Roger was a nice guy, but a little more on the redneck side, and not so open-minded when it came to having black friends, much less black boyfriends. That was going to be the problem. This girl's parents weren't so open-minded either. There was no way she could have had an open relationship with Max, much less have his child. If the baby were, in fact, his, as I suspected it was.

"You know, I think there's more of a chance that this baby is Max's than Roger's," I said, voicing my thought. "You've been having sex with Max every chance you get. You told me yourself that you and Roger only have sex together once a week or even less."

For me it was logical. For her, it was not, or she didn't want it to be.

"This baby is Roger's!" she said, gritting her teeth and trying to keep her voice to a whisper. "There's no way it can be Max's. And besides, I've already told Roger, and he's ready to marry me."

I raised my eyebrows and glanced around to see if any teachers were within earshot, then turned back to her. "Are you crazy? Are you nuts? What if you marry this guy, and then six months later in the delivery room, you deliver a little mixed baby? What are you gonna do then? He'll divorce you right then and there when he sees a baby that's half-white and half-black."

I sensed that neither of us could keep our voices down much longer, so I grabbed her arm and moved her down the hall, out the double doors and into the gym.

"It won't happen like that," she said. "I'm sure it's Roger's. I'm gonna stop seeing Max, marry Roger, and everything will work out just fine. It has to, Cassie!"

"Go home and think about it before you talk to Roger though, and definitely before you tell your parents!" I yelled the words at her as she ran down the hallway, and just stood there shaking my head from side to side. Not so much shocked at her problem, but at how she planned to handle it.

I went home thinking about Heather's predicament. The way I saw it, that baby was definitely Max's. I paced the kitchen floor in the house wondering what to do, who to call, who to tell or if to tell. After I'd walked about a mile around the kitchen, I couldn't take it anymore, and decided to go to Heather's house. I had to convince her that she would be in a heck of a mess if she went through with her plans.

I drove Mama's Honda Civic across the railroad tracks, past the merchants, past dozens of well-groomed lawns and trees, past the peaceful town lake, and finally pulled up to the Hughes family's white two-story house and parked on the street. I got as far as the partly open kitchen door when I heard the whole ugly thing going on inside.

"So you have just gone and messed up your whole life, haven't you?"

It was her mother. I recognized Mrs. Hughes' voice, but not from the way I was hearing it. I stopped, frozen, not able to move or breathe.

"Yes, Mama," I heard Heather say. "But it was an accident. I forgot to take one of my pills. I didn't mean it."

I forced myself to move closer and stooped down beside the door, hoping no one would see me.

"We're going to Atlanta, and you are going to get rid of that baby this week." Mrs. Hughes' voice was calmer than before, as if she'd made the decision seconds before saying it.

"But it's okay, Mama," Heather said. "Roger knows, and he's going to marry me."

I could see Heather turn her back on her mother and walk around the kitchen bar.

Her mother stomped her foot. "You little tramp. Do you think I don't know what you've been doing all these months? Do you think I don't know you've been pulling up your skirts for that little boy Max all this time? The black football star of Stockdale? Are you insane? I've known it from day one. I never said anything because…I mean, look at him, the boy is good looking. I didn't think there was any harm in you seeing him as long as it never got out. But I never expected you to go and get your stupid self pregnant by him!"

She walked over to Heather and spun her around like an old Raggedy Ann doll. Now standing directly in front of her, she jabbed her finger in her daughter's face. "Now you listen, and you listen good. We have our family to think about. We have a reputation in this community. We didn't work hard to become successful lawyers for nothing! And how is this going look to your little sister? You're supposed to be an example to her, for Christ's sake. It's simple: There will be no black babies born around here, young lady. There will be no mixture in the Hughes bloodline!"

Heather kept her head bowed. Her mother continued her rant. "And you had better be glad your father doesn't know about this, or he would just plain kill you! Now do you understand? Look at me! Do you?"

She was shaking Heather by the shoulders. I was sure Mrs. Hughes was going to shake the life out of her.

I pulled my head away from the door. My face felt hot and my stomach was churning. I wanted to push open the door, but I was stopped in my tracks by Heather's voice.

"I don't have to marry Roger," she said, "because I've already talked to Max too. He *knows*, Mama. He knows and he loves me. You hear me, Mama? He loves me. It's not just sex. I was just using Roger for show. But I want to be with Max. I can marry him and have this baby. We can be happy together, I know it."

I strained to hear what I knew was going to be horrible, but I heard nothing. With no other choice, I looked back inside. Heather's mother was grasping the kitchen counter. Her face had turned stark white. I thought she would surely faint. No one and nothing in the house moved. I continued holding my breath, all the while thinking two things: *Please don't let her hurt Heather*, and *Please don't let her use the n-word.*

Finally, Mrs. Hughes woke up from her mad trance and said, "Are you kidding me? Are you joking?"

"No. I want to marry Max. I love him, and I'm tired of hiding it. I don't care if he's black. It doesn't matter."

Mrs. Hughes slapped Heather with such force that she almost fell over from it. Then she said, "You are my child today. But if you even think about marrying that nigger, you will be disowned."

Damn. She'd done both. She'd said the n-word and she'd hurt Heather. And there I was all the time, thinking she wouldn't possibly go that far.

"Do you hear me? Disowned," she spat. "You will not have a sister anymore. You will not have a mother, a father, grandparents. *No one*. No one in the family will claim you ever again. And if you think I'm not serious, you try me. You try me, Heather. You want to marry this black boy and ruin your whole life and put a stain on ours, too? You go right ahead. Pack all your stuff tonight and leave. But if you leave, you won't ever get to come back. You hear me? Ever."

Mrs. Hughes continued, her voice becoming more and more uncontrolled with each sentence. "I'm going to your grandmother's house right now. If you're gone when I get back, so be it. If you're still here, then I'll assume your relationship with this boy is over and done with for good."

She walked out of the room and slammed a door somewhere.

Heather crumpled to the kitchen floor, looking like a beat-up doll. The whole scene reminded me of a play we'd been in together. Was it *Hamlet*? It had to be. But this was worse. This was real. Too real.

I heard a car door slam and an engine starting up. When I saw the car coming out of the garage, Mrs. Hughes at the wheel, I hunkered down even more. As soon as she drove out of sight, I made my way into the kitchen.

"Heather. Heather. I'm here."

She looked at me, her eyes wide in disbelief. Her lips were still quivering. I don't think she recognized me at first, but when she did, the tears flowed faster and freer than ever.

"She's a monster," she sobbed. "How can she? I love him. Didn't she hear me? I love him. Why can't I be with him?"

I almost couldn't answer her. Really. I mean, how many times had I spent the night in their house? None. How many times had I joined her and her mom at a restaurant? None. I had heard Mrs. Hughes praise Max several times on his skills, his looks, how far he would go, what a promising career he would have. None of that mattered, though. He just wasn't acceptable as a husband or even a boyfriend to her daughter. Same old story, just a different chapter.

"I have to tell you something, Cassie."

Her words were the only thing that woke me out of my daze. I looked at her.

"I haven't had sex with Roger in over four months," she said. "I know for sure that this baby is Max's. I want to be with him. I want to marry him. What am I going to do?"

I had no words, no advice, nothing.

"I don't want to walk around with Roger anymore," she said. "I can't do it. I won't do it. I won't let them do this to me. I won't let them take me away from Max."

"Heather listen, just try to calm down," I said. "Maybe your mother didn't mean it." I regretted the lie the instant it came out of my mouth, but I forged ahead. "I mean, maybe she'll change her mind. When she gets back, she'll be much calmer. You'll see. You have to talk to her again."

It was all I could manage, and all of a sudden, I wanted to get out of there. I never wanted to set foot in that house again. But at the same time, I felt an immense sadness and powerlessness for Heather. "Just what are you going to do, Heather?" I said. "What are you going to do? Are you going to Max's house? Do you want me to drive you? Do you need me to stay here with you?"

But she just sat there, rocking herself and staring past me. But then, it was as if she'd come out of her own trance. "No, I'm fine," she said. "Really. Go on home. I'm going to call Roger and explain that I can't marry him. Then I'm going to call Max and tell him that I can't marry him either. I'll just have to do what my mother wants. I mean, she's my mom, for God's sake. I have no other choice."

I didn't buy her newly calm attitude. "Are you sure you don't need me to stay here with you, girl?" It was more like a plea than a question.

She pulled herself to her feet. "No, I feel okay. You go on home. You probably don't want to see Mama when she comes back here, now do you?" She forced a laugh.

I didn't know what to do or what to think, so I did the only thing I could: I left. Of course, I assured her she could call me day or night, and blah, blah, blah. But Heather, well, she wasn't listening. She was already gone.

# Chapter 4

About nine that night, I called Heather's house, and her mother greeted me with the same cheery voice as usual, as if nothing in the world were different. I was appalled. I tried to conceal it and kept talking, saying, "Yes, Friday's game should be really good…. Un huh, yeah, they're going…. Okay, talk to you later. Bye."

Thank God when she finally put Heather on.

"Hey, Cassie, how ya' doin'?" she said.

She was asking how *I* was doing? Then I started thinking that maybe her mother was nearby, and she couldn't talk.

"I'm fine," I said. "But I'm worried about you. Are you okay? Did you talk to her again?"

There was a brief silence. Was she crying? Then she said, "Everything's fine. I've made my decision and I'm happy with it. I'll explain everything tomorrow at school. And Cassie, thanks for being such a great friend. I'll never forget it."

She sounded somewhat better, and I believed her.

We hung up, but I couldn't stop thinking about it. Something was bothering me to no end, but I couldn't figure out what it was. Even so, I had to get some sleep. My head was about to explode from all the drama. The last thought I had as my head hit the pillow was that well, she *did* seem to be doing better.

\* \* \* \*

The next day was a Friday, game day. "Go Stockdale!" and "Beat Cubs!" signs appeared in nearly every store window and was written all over cars. Students came to school with our school colors painted across their faces. Mind you, in

Stockdale and practically anywhere else in the southeastern region of the United States, football rules. Games are not to be taken lightly. Besides, there wasn't really any other form of entertainment in Stockdale, so games were doubly important.

I went to the lockers, saw no sign of Heather, and went on to homeroom. She didn't come by the time the bell rang, so I thought maybe she was going to be late for school. Then I went on to first period. Still no sign of Heather. Now, I was worried. The attendance rules were strict. If she didn't come to school at all, she couldn't cheer that night, and she loved to cheer. Plus, it would be an opportunity to see and talk to Max.

By lunch, I'd started to have all kinds of notions. Like, had she run away to California or somewhere? I started asking around. No one had seen her and no one had heard from her. By the sixth and final period, I picked up the payphone near the principal's office and called her. No answer.

The after-school pep rally came. Still no Heather. There was also no Max, no Roger, and no Heather's little sister. I started panicking, but tried to keep myself contained until I could get home to my own phone and call nonstop until I got her.

I was headed to my bus when a friend of ours, Rachel, pulled me aside and asked me to ride with her. "What's up?" I asked her as we got into her car. "You look horrible. Are you sick?" *Maybe she's pregnant too. Oh, no.*

She couldn't seem to look at me, and just started crying and talking at the same time. "Cassie, Heather is..."

I sighed. "Go ahead and tell me. She's gone, isn't she?"

Rachel cried even harder, but somehow pulled herself together and finished. "Her car went off Lake Creek Bridge this morning on the way to school. She's dead, Cassie. She's dead!"

I looked at Rachel in wonder, convinced that she was completely insane. "There is no way this is true," I managed. "Who told you this? How do you know? I just spoke to her last night. Someone's just playing a mean joke on you." I had almost started to believe it myself.

Rachael shook her head. "You know I work in the principal's office during final period, and I heard him asking her mother questions and saying how sorry he was. It's true— I tell you it's true! And even the secretary was crying. She had a car accident. She's gone. She's dead."

As Rachel completely melted into tears, I sat, stunned, wondering how on earth I let Heather get to this point. I told her I was there for here. I told her she could call me day or night. Maybe I should have gone back over to her house again? But no, she wasn't dead. She couldn't be! There was a simple explanation to all of it. Someone was playing a joke on the principal, had to be.

I got Rachel together and told her we had to get going. "Girl, please take me home." Somehow, she managed to do that.

As soon as I got there, Mama was waiting at the door. This was something she rarely did. As I entered the house, I saw two of my aunts sitting at the kitchen table, talking in lowered voices and avoiding eye contact with me. They said hello slowly and sadly. My worst fear was being confirmed.

Mama followed me into my bedroom. I could tell she wasn't going to speak, so I did the talking. "Is it true?"

She looked down at the green carpet and told me the same things Rachel had already told me in the parking lot at school. Stockdale is so small, news travels faster than CNN.

"It sure is bad," Mama said. "She...She was a nice girl...bad accidents like that...they happen sometimes. I'm really sorry."

She turned and walked out of my room. I could tell that if she stayed, being the sensitive person she was, she would have given way to tears. Thus, I was left alone in my grief.

I sank down on that cool, clean, carpet next to my bed. I couldn't scream. I couldn't cry. I couldn't even talk. I just thought and thought and thought. About what a good friend Heather was. About how her parents must be feeling. About Max and Roger. About what was, and what would never be again. I pictured her as she was the night before, inconsolable, and then strengthened. I wondered how her car could possibly have given her trouble, because it was brand-new. She'd been given the car for her sixteenth birthday, and it was absolutely fine. *Maybe the brakes failed,* I told myself. *Or maybe she was still too upset to drive from the fight she'd had with her mama the night before. Maybe there was an animal in the road.*

*Wait a minute...*

The hair on my head stood up like the Heat Miser's in *The Year Without a Santa Claus,* and it wasn't even Christmas. You see, Lake Creek Bridge, the bridge that Heather's car went off, was *twenty miles away* from both her house and our school.

I was shaking so hard when I pulled myself up from the floor, I had to grasp onto my grandmother's handmade quilt that covered my bed. When the shivering slowed, I decided I had to have some answers. I reached for the phone and with sweaty, trembling fingers, dialed Heather's number.

# Chapter 5

▼

No answer. Hang up. Redial. Busy. Hang up. Redial. Still busy.

I was a wreck by then. Why in the hell was she on Lake Creek Bridge? Something inside me assumed the answer, but I couldn't go there. It was impossible. She was too smart for that.

Redial. Finally, it was ringing. Someone answered.

"Hello, this is Cassie, Heather's friend," I said quickly. "Is Mrs. Hughes there"?

It was Heather's mother. I hadn't recognized her voice. I asked her if I could come over, and she told me to come right away. I felt strange about it, but got Mama's permission, crossed the railroad tracks and drove right over there. When I pulled up, only one car was there: Heather's mother's. I was surprised, because Heather had a huge family and many friends.

It was creepy being in the house again. It had only been twenty-four hours. How could so many things happen in twenty-four hours?

I don't know how long I was standing out there, numb and trying to think, when Mrs. Hughes opened the door and ushered me on into the house. Then she offered me some lemonade. I thought she was crazy and looked it. When she started talking, or rather explaining things to me, she sounded crazy, too.

"Cassie, Heather was an angel. She didn't always make the right decisions, but she was a good girl. I don't know what I'm going to do without her."

I couldn't speak. I knew that if I did, I'd break down. I let her keep talking.

"My aunt died in a car accident," she said. "It was a horrible thing. The whole family suffered. But I never thought a car accident would take my child."

I felt my neck stiffen. *Did she say car accident? Dare I ask a few questions?*

I was still pondering that when she continued her speech and thereby answered my questions.

"I don't know where she was going but she shouldn't have been skipping school." She laughed, but it sounded bizarre, false. "She could have stayed at home today if she was sick. She must have been going to Atlanta to shop and didn't want me to know about it. She did that sometimes, you know, run off shopping the whole day without telling anyone."

*I see. She doesn't know that I know what was on Heather's mind last night when she went to bed.* I didn't know whether to feel angry or sad. What was she trying to prove? Was she doing damage control? Did she believe that? My head started swimming. I didn't know what to believe, what to think. I knew I didn't quite trust Heather's mother after what had happened yesterday. But then again, she was her mother.

She put her hand on my shoulder. "I wanted you to come over here because you have something here. I was in her room and saw where she had put a Post-it. I guess she was going to give it to you today at school, but since she skipped, she didn't take it with her."

She led me into Heather's room. My palms were sweaty and my knees felt like bricks as I followed her down the hall. When we entered Heather's bedroom, it was the same as I had always known—four-poster bed, blue comforter, large pillows, white desk and dresser, posters of Wham! on the walls, and teddy bears everywhere. Heather had left some jeans strewn across a chair, pom-poms on the floor next to the chair, and books all over her desk. All normal.

Mrs. Hughes walked over to the desk and picked up the first book on the pile. It was my English book. The Post-it said: "Give to Cassie. Cassie's book."

I almost cried. I had lent it to her two days before, telling her that if she lost it, I would never speak to her again because I had written many notes in the margins on Poe. How trivial Poe seemed at that moment. I needed to leave.

"Thank you, Mrs. Hughes," I said. "I lent it to Heather. I'm gonna leave you alone now. If there's anything I can do…I mean, Heather was my best friend. Everyone's gonna miss her. If you need anything… Bye."

I put the book under my arm and didn't look back as I left the bedroom with Mrs. Hughes following me. I had just put one foot outside the kitchen door when I heard sobbing behind me. I just kept going.

\* \* \* \*

The funeral was held three days later at Heather's family church. It was the second time I'd been there. The first time I tried to attend services with her, I'd been turned away. Her pastor had politely and most delicately escorted me back out the front door and explained to me that it was better in the eyes of Our Lord and Savoir if blacks and whites worshipped him separately, in their own way and in their own churches. I cried all the way back home and vowed never to step foot in there again. But now, because of my dear friend, I was back and frowning at the same-looking petrified pastor, who seemed very much put out by my presence.

Heather's mama and daddy buried Heather in her red-and-black cheerleader suit—right down to the pom-poms, sneakers and socks. Her nails were painted, her face was made up, and she was wearing all of her gold necklaces and bracelets. It was a horrible sight. Her parents had even put her bullhorn in the casket. I thought I was going to throw up when I saw her there, lying in that pink casket, all puffed up like a blonde-cheerleader doll. I couldn't be made to look at her again when they opened the casket one last time at the cemetery. No way. That wasn't the image of Heather I wanted to remember. I had nightmares about her in that pink casket and cheerleader suit for years afterward.

\* \* \* \*

My other friends were having a hard time too. Max cried with me in person and on the phone. Every time we saw something about her death in the days following—in the town newspaper, the school newspaper or the town over from Stockdale's newspaper—we would cry for her all over again. Max had been present at the funeral too, but he hadn't stayed. I couldn't blame him. I think he felt as if her whole family was watching him. They were. And of course, the pastor was watching us both. Max also felt like it was his fault somehow, as did I. I was the only one with whom he could talk about her. He knew I knew everything about her being pregnant and wanting to run off with him, but he, too, thought that accidents just sort of happened that way, and that, ultimately, we could do nothing about it. I wondered if he was right.

\* \* \* \*

When people die, things change, and whatever is comfortable is no longer comfortable. In the days after a funeral you have everyone at your house, and then a few days after, you have no one and you are all alone because people no longer know what to say to you or what to do for you. It had only been about a month since Heather's funeral, but it seemed like a year. I hadn't been eating. I'd barely spoken to any of my other friends, except Max. I hadn't spoken to Heather's mother or family either. I moped around so much that my family was talking about sending me to my aunt's house for a change of scenery.

I was, however, sleeping a little better. I wasn't having as many nightmares or dreams about her. And I, like Max, had finally decided that Heather's death was just a terrible accident that we had to get over.

And now, I needed to get back to my schoolwork. I was hanging by a dangerous thread since Heather's accident. At the beginning of the school year, what now seemed like years before, we'd been assigned a reading list in our English class. One of the assignments was now due. I had already read the Poe poem many times. I knew it by heart. I loved it. Heather didn't know it and had borrowed my book after someone stole hers. On this particular night, I decided to read the story again. Perhaps Edgar Allan would help take my mind off things.

It was the first time I'd opened the book since I retrieved it from Heather's house. It was tough, but I managed to open it and started flipping pages.

I got to the page of Poe's poem "Annabel Lee." I could see the few notes I'd written there in my usual black ink. But another ink color now assaulted my eyes—blue.

My stomach began turning into knots again: Only Heather had borrowed my book, and although I'd asked her not to write in it, I knew it was her.

I slowly lowered myself to my bed, feeling the same feeling I'd had the day she died—panic—took a deep breath and forced myself to look at the page.

*Dear Cassie,*

*I don't know when*
*You will find this*

*but I hope you will.*

*Thanks for letting me
Borrow your English
Book.*

*By the time you
get this I should be
somewhere else.
I just wanted to say 'bye'
And thanks for being my
Good friend, my best friend.*

*Don't Look for me or
be sorry
That I left. I'm doing
What I want to do.*

*I won't Be made to
live a lie. Mama and Daddy
think that they can control
Me and my life and even
the life of my baby
but they can't. I won't
let them.*

*One more thing,
Don't show Them
this note Cassie, not ever.
In fact, Don't show
it to anyone,
Not even Max. If I was
Really your best friend,*

*then you will do
this for me. Love always,*

*-Heather*

*P.S. good luck with your ACT test—I know you're gonna do good and Get into the U. of A. Roll Tide forever. Think about me.*

There it was in blue and white. Mind you, I was a good Christian, in the church all the time, but at that moment all I could think of was *Oh shit*. That, and Heather had sent me a secret message, and I didn't like it.

My first instinct was to show it to my sister Kelly or our mother, just show it to somebody. But she had asked me not to. Had almost begged me not to.

Stuck, I read it again. The second time didn't help much more than the first time had. I had to read it again, a third time. This time I was looking for clues. Did she do the unthinkable? "*Did* she drive her car off that bridge on purpose?" I muttered.

I had posed the question aloud for the first time since her death. No matter how many times I read it, I still couldn't be sure.

I closed the book, but by this time, I'd just about memorized the note. I couldn't get it out of my head and I couldn't stop asking myself the same question: Was it an accident or was it suicide plain and simple? Is that why she used the past tense when she referred to me as her friend?

That night, the nightmares started again. This time, Heather asked me to skip school with her and go to Atlanta. I agreed, and when she came to pick me up that morning, Max was in the car too. My sister Kelly came out of the house and asked if she could go. We let her. After driving a few minutes, we all noticed we weren't on the road to Atlanta. Instead, we were on Lake Creek Bridge.

Heather started laughing like the Wicked Witch of the West and drove the car over the rail into the water, all the while laughing. We tried to get out of the car but we were sinking, sinking deeper and deeper into dirty brown water while Heather was laughing her head off.

After a few nights like that and similar nightmares, I started sleeping with the light on. I still couldn't get to sleep at all for thinking and analyzing. And when I did fall asleep, the nightmares came, and I woke up drenched in sweat, then stayed awake the rest of the night trying to get back to sleep. I never could.

I tried thinking of the typical lottery dream—you know, winning the lottery and what you would do with the money, and you usually fall asleep pretty quickly because you're content. Didn't work. And then, I couldn't go to school the next day because I was too tired and sleepy.

I stayed locked in my room for three days. My mother thought I had the flu. Finally, I decided I was either going to go crazy and end up in a mental institution, or confide in someone, even show the note to someone if need be. Either no one else had suspected suicide, or they simply hadn't told me. I wanted to talk to Heather's mother. She would know, wouldn't she?

I waited until Saturday to go over there. Mrs. Hughes smiled when she saw me and we hugged for a long time. This time, there were worry lines in her face. Her hair looked grayer and she'd lost at least ten pounds. So I temporarily forgot about the racial slurs she'd made earlier, and how she might have driven her daughter away, or worse.

"Cassie, I'm so glad to see you," she said. "No one has been to the house in a while." She was getting glasses out of the kitchen cabinet, the tall lemonade glasses that had little lemons around the edges. I took a seat at the bar. She kept talking.

"I guess you came over because you were worried about us. We were just as shocked as everyone else in Stockdale. Another child lost. But what was wrong with that girl? Heather wasn't close to her. Were you? Would you like some cookies to go with your lemonade?"

I had no idea what she was talking about, and told her so. She looked at me as if I had just come back from outer space. "Honey, didn't you know that Antonia Kitchens killed herself out there in their trailer while her parents were asleep? It happened two days ago." She stopped talking to take a sip of her lemonade, then picked right up from where she'd left off. "They say she was depressed. I don't know what happened really. They just said they heard a shot in the middle of the night and her dad went into her bedroom and there she was with a shotgun in her mouth. Dead."

She was eyeing me, and came around the bar to stand in front of me, just like she'd done to Heather that day.

Finally, I was able to speak. "What did you just say, Mrs. Hughes?"

She started telling me the story all over again. It's true I'd heard her the first time, but I was just too stunned to say anything else. I *had* known Antonia Kitchens, and I guess she had every right to be depressed. She was different, extremely different, and people in Stockdale didn't really understand her or appreciate her differences. She was white, with short brown hair and glasses that covered her green eyes. She was shy, a loner, and also a tomboy. She always wore dirty-like jeans and t-shirts with black Army boots. She went hunting. All her friends were male; girls didn't like her and called her a dyke. The boys she wasn't friends with called her the same thing. I had no problem with her. I, too, thought she was a tomboy, but it didn't bother me. I had worked as her science lab partner once, and after I got to know her, found her actually nice and cool. She told good jokes too.

"…and they say that her mother is just devastated," Mrs. Hughes was saying. "As well she should be, because I don't know what I would do if Heather had taken her own life. Why, there's just no way I could deal with that. And why would Heather have done that anyway? She would never have taken her own life…even if she wasn't happy. Not saying that she wasn't, because that girl had everything to live for. No, Heather would have never…I just don't know what I would do if I were in that mother's position." She spoke slowly now, and was wringing her hands so hard, they were red.

"Are you…? Ummm." I tried again. "So you don't think Heather was like that at all? I mean, she would have never…ummmm…taken her own life?" I looked down at my glass.

It seemed like an hour passed, but it was only a few seconds before she finally answered. "Of course not, Cassie, and you know it. What are you saying? Are you okay? Well, you knew Heather. My God, child, you know she wasn't like that Antonia girl."

I could tell that Mrs. Hughes was on the verge of rage; one side of her mouth started twitching, and her face had become as red as her wrung hands. I stumbled some quick apologies, told her I'd been ill for the past three days and hadn't slept. This calmed her, and soon she was offering me more lemonade and updating me on Heather's little sister.

I sat on the barstool in her kitchen sipping lemonade and looking straight at her while she was talking, but I was totally somewhere else. She had answered my question, and she hadn't. I'd been rereading "Annabel Lee." Rereading the margins and the note Heather had left me. Clearly, Mrs. Hughes thought her daughter's car going off the bridge was an accident, or she refused to even consider otherwise.

The answer I sought wasn't here. It was time for me to leave. My palms were getting sweaty again and my stomach felt like it was going to turn itself inside out. "I'm sorry, but I have to get on back home," I said. "I just wanted you to know I was thinking about ya'll."

She thanked me, reassured me and hugged me, and then walked me out to my car. There was no menace or ill-feeling in her goodbyes.

I watched her as she went back into the house. What else could I have done but leave? Even if I'd shown her the note, she never would have believed Heather committed suicide. I didn't know what to believe myself, and I was the one who had it.

I cranked up the Honda, and in the words of the late Deacon "Jackrabbit" Jenkins, asked myself, "Damn, Heather, why did you have to go and do a fool thing like that for?"

# Chapter 6

I still had the dreams, or rather, the nightmares, and was still on the verge of telling people about the note at different times, but I never did. At times, I broke down crying at school and had to run to the bathroom. Or, when Sundays came, the most depressing day of the week for me, I cried in my room and reread her note and/or "Annabel Lee." Perhaps it was irrational, but I always ending up blaming my absent father for it—he who wasn't there and didn't even know Heather Hughes, or me for that matter.

But that was just the thing—he wasn't there, and he didn't know me. I needed someone to talk to, someone to tell me that everything was going to be all right, and he had let me down once again. Sure, I had Mama and my grandparents, but they were busy with work and their own lives. But my father…well, he was off somewhere in another state with no other children, so I was told, and he had ditched me. I continued to wonder how a man could walk away from his children for years on end without anything—no letters, no calls, and no visits. Even though I begrudged him this, I knew the time was coming when I needed to face him and ask him one simple question: Why?

* * * *

Exams kicked in, ACT and SAT tests, recommendation letters—all the stuff you have to do to get into college—and that helped take my mind off things a little. That wasn't the thing that yanked me out of my gloom, though. It was my cousin, the nail-biting Natasha, and it all started with a party.

Natasha and I were neighbors as well as cousins, and she lived exactly three houses down the street from us. We went to church together, we fought and got beat up together by bullies, played together and spent the night at each other's houses on a regular basis.

One Friday, Natasha told me about this event that was going on in the town over from Stockdale. It was going to be wild, she said. It was, in fact, a talent show, and talent shows were important. High-school kids formed groups to sing or dance, or both. The ones with the most talent won prizes. Kelly and I even had our own group, and had won a couple of local contests ourselves. I told Natasha I would go with her, and that I'd drive.

Once we were in the car, she confessed exactly why she wanted to go to this show. "I met a fine guy, Cassie. I met him at last week's talent show. Remember? I tried to get you to go, but you were depressed or somethin'," she said, turning up her mouth at me. As she spoke, she was biting her nails and spitting the pieces out the window. "Anyway, he is sooooo fine. And guess what? He got a twin brother who looks exactly like him. Both are fine. And they have a friend named Aaron. He's white, but just as fine. You can have your pick between his brother and his friend. I told them you were comin'."

I looked at her and frowned. *Now* I knew why she was dressed nicer than usual. Her short denim skirt was rolled up even higher around her waist. She had on a white shirt, and the sleeves were rolled up; they were always too short for her long arms.

"Girl, why didn't you tell me all that?" I said. "Here I am wearing just anything. And anyway, I don't feel like meeting anybody tonight. You are just *wrong* for that. And stop spitting that out the window, it's just gonna blow back in here."

She would not be moved. "Cassie, you need to meet somebody. Look at you. You been locked up in your room for I don't know how long. You don't even hang with me no more. Every time I call you, Kelly say you can't even talk on the phone. Tonight you gone have some fun, girl. Imagine us with twins, girl. Twins!"

I rolled my eyes at her, and looked at myself in the rearview mirror. No makeup, hair a mess and in need of a retouch, and a faded black denim shirt. Nice.

Once we got to the community center where the talent show was being held, I felt a little better. There were a lot of our friends there from other schools, some cousins, and also people from Stockdale. Max was there, too. He usually didn't miss talent shows, and I suppose he needed to get out so he could stop thinking about Heather. He had stopped talking about her; I think it was the only way for him to get on with his life. I was the only one still walking around with a load on my chest, so it seemed.

I walked over to say hello to him, but slowed halfway there when I noticed he wasn't alone. He spotted me and waved me over, then gave me a big hug. "Hey, Cassie. I'm glad Natasha got you out of the house tonight."

"Hey. She tricked me, that's what she did." I looked in the direction of his friend, a thin white girl with long black hair wearing a Jefferson High cheerleader sweater. Definitely Max's type.

"Well, I'm gonna see you guys later on," he said. "Taco Bell maybe?"

"Yeah, Max, catch up with ya' later." I walked back over to where Natasha was, thinking, *Max and his damn cheerleaders*. I was mad at him for making me think about Heather again.

Natasha was tapping her feet, and didn't seem to appreciate my holding her up. We made our way inside the modest community center, a medium-sized white building used by the neighborhood for arts and crafts, workshops, kid's activities, you know, stuff like that. But Friday and Saturday nights, it was used for talent shows. We got good seats in the front row, luckily, because had we not, I think Natasha would have been mad at me all night for stopping to speak to Max.

"So what's your boyfriend look like?" I asked her.

"Girl, he is *fine*," she said, playfully hitting me on the leg.

"I know, you already said that. What does 'fine' mean in this case?"

"Well, he's light-skinned. I think he's part-Spanish. And he has green eyes. Green eyes, girl! He's got black wavy hair, and he's a little shorter than me. He's just fine. Wait until you see him."

"This guy is *shorter* than you?" I said. In general, she didn't like guys who were shorter than she was. She was already six feet tall and wore a size twelve shoe.

"He's so fine I couldn't help it."

"So you really like this guy, huh? What's this boy's name?"

"Blake."

I shook my head and grinned.

\* \* \* \*

We watched the show and it was as funny and as entertaining as usual. There was a girls' group that performed the song "Your Smile" by René and Angela. René Moore and Angela Winbush—now *those* are some real divas. Another group performed "Mr. Telephone Man" by the group New Edition. I can still remember the lyrics even now. This group of four or five boys was dancing and doing their thing on stage, and everyone was up on his feet and dancing along to the song. Except for Natasha. She remained seated with a darkness growing about her eyes as she bit her nails. Her source of stress? This was the last group, and her guy had never shown up.

We did our usual thing—went to Taco Bell and had tacos after the show. But Natasha had an attitude and didn't want to eat. "He told me that he was gonna be there," she said. "They were supposed to dance tonight."

I was getting full on my tacos, and hers too, since she didn't eat them. "Yeah, he could've called you," I said. "He knew you were coming, didn't he?"

"Well you know, they don't have no car, and maybe Aaron had to work." Then her lips curled up into a smile. "I know where they live. Let's go by there. Then you can meet him and his twin brother too. Come on girl."

I was enjoying my tacos but I was getting sleepy, and was just about to suggest we head back to Stockdale. I looked at my watch. She knew what I was going to say and cut me off.

"It's not too late. They don't go to bed until real late."

Suspicious, I said, "You saying their parents let them stay up all night and let them have friends over at eleven at night? You must be joking. You're gonna get us embarrassed going over there. It's too late. Maybe we can come back tomorrow."

Natasha started fixing her hair. "Girl, you don't know them, I do. They ain't got no daddy. And they mama? Well, she don't even live with them. They live with their grandma. They can do what they want. Let's go."

*What type of family* is *this, then?* I thought. *No parents. No rules. No curfews.* Sounded interesting…at least a little.

We got into the car and started driving back in the direction of Jefferson. I figured we had about one hour—thirty minutes to hang out over there, and then thirty minutes to get back home. Any longer than that, and I was going be in trouble. I did have a curfew, and so did Natasha.

We had made it to the center of Jefferson when she told me to turn toward the east side of town.

"What do you mean, the east side?" I blurted. "They live over there? Why didn't you tell me?"

"It's okay. I've been over here before. Just lock your doors."

"'Just lock the doors.' Are you nuts? It's *dangerous* over here, Natasha."

"Come on, girl, it's not that bad. Plus, we're almost there already."

I should have turned that Honda Civic around.... But I didn't. We kept going about five more minutes and just as she had said, we were there.

She pointed. "It's that blue house on the right."

The house itself looked okay. It was the other houses around it that were dilapidated. We had a couple of shacks on our street in Stockdale, but nothing like the houses we were looking at now. We were clearly in a poorer 'hood than ours back home.

I looked over again to make sure my door was locked, but Natasha was already getting out of the car. Before I could blow the horn, she was already on the porch. *Fassie!* I thought. *Fass* and *fassie* were words used, especially by my grandmother, to describe girls who are too forward or aggressive. And that's exactly what Natasha was acting like just then—*fassie!*

Natasha knocked on the door while I kept the motor running. *Good!* I thought after a moment. *Nobody's home.* I smiled and hoped she would get her *fass* tail back in the car.

Just as my hopes were soaring, the front door of the house opened. I could only make out a figure and a blue light coming from within the house. *Hmm. Blue house, blue light. Okay.*

Then I saw Natasha signaling me. Did she want me to get out? *Here? Dang.*

I waited until she came to the car to get me and rolled down my window, but only halfway.

"Cassie, they here," she said. "Git on out."

"It's already late and we don't have much time. Who's all in there anyway? And what's that smell coming from your clothes, girl?"

She tried to open my door but it was still locked. "Girl, git out and just meet them and we'll go."

Neither of us said anything for a few seconds. There she was, all happy, oblivious to everything except getting inside that house. I saw a spot of red taco sauce on the front of her blouse, from where she'd eaten that one bite of her taco. I thought about mentioning it, but likely, that wouldn't slow her down.

"I don't want to go in there," I said. "Tell the twins 'bye' and come on."

She stepped back, folded her arms and rolled her eyes at me. "We came all the way over here. I just want you to say hi, that's all. Then we can go. They waitin' and I left the door open."

I sure wish I'd stayed in the car, but you know I'm going to tell you I got out.

Sure enough, she'd left the door halfway open. I could hear Al Green coming from inside the house. I let her go in, then followed. At first, I couldn't make out anything except a blue light coming from the ceiling and smoke. But as my eyes adjusted to the room, I could see there were three people in what appeared to be the living room, and voices, female voices, coming from another room.

The smoke was everywhere, and I almost started coughing. It smelled vaguely familiar, too: pot. I'd once walked into our school gym's bathroom and surprised a couple of what our principal quickly called "juvenile delinquents" smoking it. Ohhh, if my pastor could see me now!

From the kitchen area, I could hear grease popping in a skillet. Someone was cooking fried fish. Nobody got up and nobody said a word. I just stood there looking at the three guys until Natasha broke the silence. "This is my cousin Cassie."

The three boys nodded, as if saying "What's up?"

"Hey," I said.

Natasha continued with a nervous fervor in her voice, "This is Blake, and this is his brother J.R. They call him J.R. 'cause he's always watching *Dallas* and thinks he's ruthless like J.R. Ewing."

I tried to laugh. It didn't come out right. I could see J.R. clearer than the others because he was sitting closer to the room a regular light was coming from. Natasha hadn't lied. J.R. was very easy on the eyes. He was also making himself a new pot-filled cigarette.

"The other guy is Aaron," Natasha said.

I felt like I had to be cool, so I said, "What's up?"

Aaron, the white guy, offered me his cigarette, and J.R. laughed out loud, a circus laugh. When he wasn't rolling the cigarettes, he was eating Doritos, drinking a Budweiser, and laughing. The other guy, the other brother, said nothing, just looked at me. Or rather, stared at me. He had one hand wrapped around a Budweiser as well, but he wasn't smoking, or eating any of the Doritos.

J.R. told us to sit down, and we did. I took the seat closest to the door, a thick brown leather chair. Natasha almost missed and fell down as she sat beside her friend Blake on the matching brown leather sofa filled with black throw-pillows. The leather furniture smelled new, and indeed looked brand-new, but you could barely tell with all the smoke-smell.

With the blue light still flashing, I looked around at the room and noticed the walls were painted in some shade of pale blue. There were matching end tables with tiny black lamps sitting on them, and a small black coffee table in the middle of the floor. African art hung high on the walls—a mother and her baby, three children walking in a field.

At the same instant I noticed the picture, I felt a slight disturbance on my feet, like a fly that's buzzing by your ear and won't leave you alone. I looked down.

Below, crawling around on the stained burgundy carpet beside my feet and on my feet, were a few roaches. I tried to shake them off discreetly, but now, I was absolutely ready to go. I looked at Natasha and tried to give her an eye signal. She was too busy staring at Blake, who in turn was too busy staring at me.

My stomach was queasy now. I can't stand roaches and had already decided I didn't like the smell of marijuana, especially marijuana mixed with fried fish. I was about to stand up and leave when J.R. said to Blake, "Yo' bro', we 'bout to git on up out of here and hit that party down on Madison. You stayin' here with the broads or you hanging with us?"

I glanced at Natasha, thinking, *Did he just call us broads?*

Blake didn't break his stare, but answered "No, you go on. I'm gonna catch up with ya'll cats later. I'll git Tasha to drop me off down there."

J.R. and Aaron went out the front door. Seconds later, we heard a rattling noise outside, and then someone howling with laughter. Blake jumped up and ran to the door with us behind him.

"Oh shit. I fell, bro'. I fell and I tore my ass up." J.R. was lying in the grass beside the porch.

"Ain't the first time *bro'*, and won't be the last," Blake said.

"Yo' man, when you gone fix them steps, bro'?"

"I'm gittin' to it. I'm gittin' to it." Still laughing, Blake turned around and went back into the house, with the two of us still in tow. I still wished we were leaving too. Natasha, on the other hand, was as happy as a clam.

"Why didn't you come to the talent show tonight?" she asked, looking at me to second her. "I thought you were dancing. It was a good show, wasn't it Cassie?"

Blake shrugged. "We couldn't make it. Is Cassie your real name?"

He was talking to me. I hesitated, but then said, "No, it's Cassandra, but nobody calls me that, except my mom sometimes. Usually when she's mad."

"Then I'm gonna call you Cassie, then. You wanna beer or something, Cassie?"

I couldn't stop the grimace on my face. *Lord, please don't let my grandparents find out I was here in this den of sin.* "No, I don't drink, and you shouldn't either."

"Whoa now, Miss Cassie. You don't have to take it. Nobody's forcin' you. But I won't drink one either if you don't want me to." He put the beer back down on the coffee table. "What grade you in?"

"I'm going to the twelfth."

"Me too. You know a dude name Max, don't ya'? I know he play ball for Stockdale."

"Yeah, he's one of my good friends. I know him."

Natasha chimed in, "*He* was at the show tonight."

He ignored her and kept talking to me. "So you don't smoke or drink, huh?"

"Nope. Never have and never will."

"I can admire that. All right then."

He wouldn't stop looking at me, and during this time of small conversation or whatever it was, I could see what Natasha had been describing to me before. The boy was fine, even finer than his brother. I didn't know if he was Spanish or of Native American origin or something else, but he was mixed with something extra. Grandmama told me that all of us black folks are "mixed," but his mixture was more immediate—one of his parents must have been something other than black. He had the smoothest skin, and it was light brown. It was *lovely*. And his eyes were green, whereas his brother's were brown. They were a real complement to his skin. He had the same wavy black hair as his brother's, and it looked as though he spent quality time on maintaining it. Maybe he used DAX or TCB hair grease or hair sheen. I don't know, but something. His clothes were of the same immaculate quality—crisp gray shirt, new-looking Levis and white sneakers. In short, he was gorgeous...and I was definitely ready to leave.

While this was going on, I could also see that my cousin was biting her nails again, and it looked like she was ready to leave too. I stood and said, "Well, we have to get on out of here and get back to Stockdale."

Natasha and Blake stood too, and Blake said, "Can you drop me off on the way at that party?"

I didn't want to do it, but Natasha opened her big mouth. "Yeah. You ready?"

But before we could leave, a small light-skinned woman came rushing out of the kitchen. She was wearing an old tattered apron and huge eyeglasses. She didn't speak to us or even acknowledge we were there. She only spoke to Natasha's friend.

"You leavin' now? Did J.R. already leave? You tell him I know he took that twenty dollars out my purse, and I'm gonna whup his ass when he git back here."

She left just as quickly as she had appeared, and then the voices in the kitchen started up again. I headed for the door and was ready to leave any and everyone who wasn't in my car by the time I got there. But I guess they were on to my agitation or were agitated themselves, because we all got in about the same time.

I did a double take when Blake got in the front with me. I first thought it was because he was going to get out first, but I soon understood it was for a different purpose.

"So Cassie," he said, "you wanna go in this party for a while? You might as well since you're dropping me off anyway."

I tried to change the subject. I didn't like him leaving Natasha out. She was sitting in the backseat like a puppy that had just been left at the kennel. "Was that your mama back there?" I asked. "She was mad."

"Nah, that was my grams. She been cookin' for a fish fry all night and she just talk like that when she tired. By tomorrow she won't even remember it."

"Where's your mama?"

"She's not living with us right now," he said, and turned his head away from me.

*Okay. Just let me shut up and get rid of this boy at his party.*

But *he* wouldn't shut up. "Yeah, we were supposed to dance tonight, but J.R. and Aaron got high. We gone do it next week though. You comin'?"

"I…don't know."

"So you a churchgoing girl?"

I let out a long sigh and sped up the car.

"My bad. I don't mean no disrespect. Anyway, you comin'?"

I'd had enough of him neglecting Natasha and paying too much attention to me. "Ask Natasha."

End of the conversation.

We got to his party place and he got out. I put the Honda in reverse, but he turned around and asked me to get out of the car for a minute.

"Why? What do you need?" I said, looking in the backseat at Natasha.

"Let me talk to you for a minute, girl."

"You can talk to me right here."

"Come on now, I don't have much time either. They waitin' for me. Just one minute."

I looked at Natasha and Natasha looked at me. "What do you think?" I whispered.

"See what he wants," she replied. But I could tell by the way she turned up her lips that she didn't like it. Neither did I.

Still, I got out, and he pulled me a few steps away from the car before saying, "Look, I wanna see you again. You wanna come by tomorrow?"

I turned up my eyebrows. I hadn't expected this, even if he *had* been staring at me all night long. "What? Are you insane? You're my cousin's boyfriend. What do you think I am?"

"What? What the hell you talkin' 'bout? I ain't Tasha's boyfriend. We friends, but that's it. Who told you that? She told you that?"

I glanced over at the car and sure enough, she'd gotten out and changed positions. Natasha was now sitting in the front, watching everything.

"Yes, she told me that," I said, "and we can go right on over there and ask her if you want to."

"Yeah, let's clear this up right now," he replied, "'cause I never told her we was goin' together. I know her, that's all. I met her at a show and she been tagging along behind me every since."

"Yeah, right."

"Don't get me wrong. She a nice girl, but she just a friend. I wanna talk to *you*. You hear me? I wanna talk to *you*. So let's go on over to the car and git this over with. After that, maybe you'll come by my house?"

He was serious *and* waiting for an answer. I looked over at the car again and Natasha was still sitting there. I didn't know what to do. On one hand, I wanted to go over there and rid her of her illusions. I had seen it all night. This boy was not interested in her at all. I had a feeling that he was a bad boy too. On the other hand, she'd be crushed if I went over there with him. I couldn't imagine her embarrassment when he told her his true feelings about her.

"Just leave her alone," I said at last. "There's no reason to hurt her feelings like that." I headed back to the car.

"Are you sure? Because I really wanna see you again."

"Yeah, I'm sure. I have to go. It was nice meeting you."

We drove off while he stood in the yard, watching our car. Neither of us said anything to each other until we were halfway to Stockdale. There wasn't much traffic, and the sky was pitch-black. I put in my New Edition tape to lighten the mood in the car, but then turned it off when it reminded me of the talent show and Blake again. I didn't want to tell her *Hey, your boyfriend is lousy and he doesn't really like you.* I was sure she'd seen this for herself. I was wrong, though.

"You know, he's really shy sometimes," she said. "That's why he didn't talk to me much in front of you. But when I call him tomorrow he'll be talking a lot."

I wanted to stop the car and pull over on side of the road. "What? Are you serious?"

"Yeah, he's shy."

"Natasha, he didn't even say bye to you," I sputtered. "He hardly even looked at you the whole time we were there in that smoked-up house. Put some glasses on if you can't see what's going on."

She shrugged, unaffected. "You just jealous 'cause he's so fine, Cassie. But I ain't mad at ya'."

"Jealous? I'm not jealous. That boy is *bad*, Natasha. He's bad news and you need to stay away from him. Yeah, he's cute and all, but he's a pothead too. You saw the smoke. And his grandmother was there in the next room and didn't even care. And you know they don't go to church either."

"He don't really smoke that much. It's his brother and his friends. You saw him tonight. He didn't even smoke anything."

I chuckled. "That's because we came just when he was about to light up."

"Why do you have to be so negative?"

"Why do you have to be so *dumb*?"

She reached over and turned the radio on, then leaned her head against the car window.

"Look I'm sorry, Tasha. I just don't want you getting hurt."

"I won't, girl. I won't. But you should have talked more to J.R. He liked you, I could tell."

"Really? Ya' think?" I could scarcely contain the sarcasm in my voice.

Which she missed entirely. "Yeah. Maybe we can see them again."

By then I had nothing left. It was enough just keeping my eyes open going through the thick white fog that always seemed to gather during the early morning hours. I tried several different settings on the car's defroster, trying to clear the windshield. I always forgot which one did the trick, but none of them seemed to work tonight.

When we got back to Stockdale I dropped Natasha off. The last thing she said was, "He really likes the O'Jays. I'm gone get him somethin' tomorrow." And then she slammed the door.

*What's she talking about?* I thought. I always knew that…well, even though she was my cousin and I loved her, Natasha wasn't the smartest girl in her class. Now, I wondered, *Is she just plain stupid? Or am I? Has he really been dating her?*

I kept wondering, but always came back to the same point—he treated her like crap tonight, so how could they be in a relationship?

One good thing came out of it. This became my new obsession. For the next few days I didn't have to think about Heather and her note, or how Max was holding up. I simply had to ponder the relationship this boy named Blake had with my cousin.

Back at home, and the next day, I told Kelly about him, and about everything that had happened.

Kelly was at the sink, taking her turn at washing the dishes. Her answer came quickly. "It sounds like he liked you and he didn't like Tasha."

I sighed. "Well, it doesn't matter, because I don't want to see him anymore. And if she asks me to take her over there, I'm not gonna do it."

Kelly frowned, told me she wanted to see for herself what this boy looked like since everyone kept saying how fine he was, and then went on washing dishes.

\*     \*     \*     \*

A few weeks passed, and Tasha and I were still as close as ever. Or so I thought. I didn't talk about her so-called boyfriend, but she did. But one day after school, I did ask, "So, have you seen Mr. Blake?"

"No. He ain't called me."

"Why don't you call him instead?"

She looked down at the ground and rubbed her white sneakers along the pavement like she was trying to scrape something off of them. "They don't have a phone."

"Oh, then how do you call him?"

"I call next door at the neighbor's house, and she goes out there to git him."

Since she wasn't looking up at me anyway, I started staring at her shoe on the pavement, too, and said, "I see."

One of her friends drove up, and Tasha got into the car with her. That was a relief. I needed a break. All that analyzing over Natasha and Blake and Blake and Natasha was getting tiresome.

# Chapter 7

One Saturday a couple of weeks later, I was outside hanging clothes on our clothesline. We'd already been over to clean the elderly widower's house, and were back from shopping in Jefferson. The strawberry shortcake had been delicious as usual. It was 70 degrees and sunny, so Mama preferred to hang out the clothes rather than use the dryer and heat up the house. I preferred the dryer, but then, I didn't have a choice. I was trying to get my chores done, hoping that would impress Mama enough so I could borrow the car that night.

There were windows on the back of our house facing the clothesline, so I heard the telephone when it rang. A moment later, Mama yelled out the window. The phone was for me. I'd been expecting a call from Natasha, to know if she would be able to go skating the next night in Jefferson. Sunday nights were skating-rink nights. Stockdale had no exciting Sunday activities going on...except church.

I finished hanging the last sheet, grabbed the clothespin bag and hurried back into the house, breathless by the time I answered the phone.

"Is this Cassie?"

I knew who it was, but I didn't believe my ears. "How did you get my number? Who gave it to you?"

"Are you mad 'cause I got it? I got it from Tasha."

"From Tasha? From Tasha, my *cousin*? Stop lying. Tasha would never give you my number."

"How many times do I have to tell you that me and that girl don't go together? She is *not* my girlfriend."

"Call me back in ten minutes," I said, and hung up the phone, intending to call Tasha and find out what was going on. By the time I'd dialed the number, she walked in the front door.

I hung up the phone and glared at her. "What did you do? Did you give Blake my phone number?"

She nodded. "He called me and asked me for it."

"Why does he want to call me? And why would he call you and ask you for the number? You got some boyfriend, girl."

Mama was creeping through in the direction of the washing machine, so we went outside and sat on the porch.

"I think he like you," Tasha said. "He probably gone call you."

"He already *has* called me, Tasha, and that's what I'm talking about. I don't want him calling me!"

She stood and walked off the porch to stand in the yard, biting her nails. "Whatever, Cassie. Whatever."

"*Whatever?* What does that mean? What am I supposed to do here? And why don't you stop biting your nails. There's nothing left to bite on anyway."

"You do whatever you want to do," she said, and looked at her fingers as if what I'd just said about her nails might be true.

"He's supposed to be *your* man, Tasha. I can't help it if he's after me. I didn't ask for this."

She kept studying her fingernails. "You gotta choice. Either talk to him or don't, but I don't care."

"You mean to tell me that you wouldn't care if I talked to him?"

"I gave him your number, didn't I?"

"Yeah, but that doesn't mean anything. I saw your face that night when he was talking to me."

"Girl, I don't care nothin' 'bout that boy, for real. If you like him, then you should go for it."

"Are you serious?"

"Yeah, I'm serious. I gave him your phone number, didn't I? I mean, he fine and all that, but I been thinkin' 'bout it, and really...I don't think he my type."

She started walking out of our yard and in the direction of her own, while switching her hips a little bit too hard and singing some song about leaving again. I looked at her and shook my head, knowing her disinterest was fake.

Inside the house, the phone rang again. My heart lurched. *Dang, that's him. I know it.* I ran in and grabbed it before anyone else answered.

"Hey it's me," he said.

"Look, you got some nerve calling here. Tasha just left."

"Let's talk about you and me."

"There isn't anything to talk about. Why are you calling here?"

"Are you goin' skatin' tomorrow night? I'm gone be there."

I knew I was going, but I didn't want to tell him. "I don't know. Tasha and I were *supposed* to be going together."

He didn't respond at first. But then he said, "Let Tasha stay at home. You just make sure you there. I gotta go now. I'll see you tomorrow, Cassie. Be there, all right? Bye." And click, he was gone.

The next day: church all day and skating at night. Before church, I'd called Tasha to see if she was still going, and she had told me yes. But when night came, her mother was singing a different tune.

"Cassie, she said I can't go."

"Why not?" I said. "You *gotta* go, girl."

"She said no. You wanna ask her?"

"Yeah, put her on." Her mother was notorious for her mood swings and anger. I knew I couldn't change her mind, but it was worth a try. I didn't want to show up there by myself with Blake on the loose.

"Helloooh."

I felt defeated as soon as I heard the monotone voice. Still, I couldn't give up. "Mama said I could drive over to the skating rink tonight, and I was wondering if Tasha could go with me." There, I'd said it.

"Tasha's staying at home tonight, Cassie, and that's the end of that."

She passed the phone back to Tasha, who said, "See, she in one of her moods tonight and I can't go nowhere. Listen, Blake will be there, so find him and talk to him."

"I'm not tryin' to find him or talk to him, Tasha. I told you already. I gotta go and finish getting ready. I'll see you tomorrow at school. Bye."

"Bye," she said, and her dejection was clear.

After we'd hung up, I stood there for a moment looking out the window. I so wished Natasha was going. For one thing, she could put a leash on Blake if he was there. And even though he'd ignored her before, I felt guilty that I might come face-to-face with him without her presence. It wasn't fair that her mother was taking out her depression on Tasha. But then again, she always did.

I pulled myself away and finished getting ready. Kelly was already done and waiting on the porch. I, too, wanted to get out of there before Mama could change her mind about letting us go. We talked about Tasha and the situation with Blake all the way over to Jefferson, but with no resolution except to make the best of the situation.

There were cars everywhere in the parking lot of Rainbow Skate Center. This skating rink probably wasn't the largest in the state, but it was the largest one in the county, and the only one considered cool because they allowed R&B music on Sunday nights—"black night." People skated until midnight, and then there was a dance contest. If white people showed up, it meant they were "down," or their parents didn't know they were there, or that they simply liked New Edition too. But usually, there were never more than three or four white people there.

I was always disappointed by that. I never looked for Spanish people or Mexican people to be there, or any other ethnicity, because there really weren't any living there. But I did wish for more diversity. I had often mentioned the skate party and dance to several of my white girlfriends, but none of them ever wanted to go. Well, none of them except Heather. She'd come with us plenty of times, and it wasn't just to be with Max. She really enjoyed the skating and dancing after. She could even dance a little bit. *Heather...*

Kelly and I were waiting in the long line to get in. I asked her if she remembered the last time Heather came with us and fell down in the middle of the floor while trying to skate backwards. She said she did, but by the way she said it, almost whispering it, I knew she didn't really want to talk about Heather, so I dropped the subject.

After about twenty minutes, we were in. Inside, the people were already wall-to-wall, and outside there was still a long line of people waiting to get in. Rainbow Skate Center was already playing our favorite song, "Planet Rock," the song to play if you wanted to get everyone moving. People were dancing on the side of the skate floor, in their skates on the floor—wherever they could find enough space to move.

There were the usual groups there—the Jeri curl group, the people who wore drippy curly-perm liquid down their shirts and left wet stains wherever they sat and rested their heads. But boy, could they skate! They came every week, and always wore matching red outfits. There were also the rougher girls from Jefferson. These girls were wearing tight jeans in red, green and white, with huge gold earrings, and huge overdone red hair. It was the '80's in full effect all right, like a mini fashion show but with ghetto-like style. The preppy crowd was there, too—the khaki-and-polo crowd. Kelly fit in this group, since she always wore Levis and IZODS, or khakis and Polos. The ripped-jean group was there, as well as the Madonna look-alikes.

I myself was wearing my basic gear: all black. I started this trend during my junior year, and I was the only one in Stockdale and, I dare say, Jefferson, doing it. My family hated it. People always came up and asked me if I were from New York…or Miami. I loved it. How I wanted to say yes.

We got our skates, put them on and got onto the floor. Considering the size of a town like Jefferson, the skating rink was pretty large. There was gray carpet surrounding the skating floor, and near the front, game machines. In the back there was a snack bar serving sodas, chips, and nachos. The DJ knew how to get everyone excited. They were still playing the remix of "Planet Rock," which meant that it would last for a long time.

I warned Kelly to stay close to me. The floor was really crowded, and with all the dancing going on and people skating backward, I was a little afraid for her. She could skate as well as I could, though, and reminded me of that. I never could dance really well, but I had a few moves in me, and we made our way around the floor, implementing our little dance moves like everyone else, under the air current filtering through the ceiling to cool people off. The part of the song came up where Afrika Bambaatta tells everyone to scream, and everyone in the whole building let out a long one.

After the song was over, we got a couple of drinks and sat on the side of the floor near the main exit. On the other side, the far side, there were nook-like openings where two or three people could sit. One of these nooks was directly across the rink from us. I don't know how long he'd been looking at me, but he'd already begun when I spotted him across from us, sitting in the nook.

"Kelly, it's him," I whispered.

"Who?"

"Blake. Tasha's boyfriend."

"Where? Where is he?" she said, looking from left to right.

"No, he's across the floor there." And for the first time, I saw that he wasn't alone. He was sitting with a dark-skinned girl. Short, boyish hair. Cute. Because of what she was wearing, a long black dress, I knew she wasn't from around there.

"Well, if that's Tasha's boyfriend," Kelly said, "he sure ain't actin' like it. That sure ain't Tasha over there."

"Yeah I know," I said, shaking my head.

I felt a hand on my shoulder and looked up. It was a boy from Jefferson High School. I used to see him every now and then at church. He sang tenor in a gospel singing group with his father and two brothers.

"Hey, Cassie," he said. "What's up girl?"

"Nothing. What's up with you?"

"You know, just chillin'. Yo', I got a message for you."

I straightened up on the bench where we were sitting. "What's that?"

"My friend Blake…well, he over there, and he wanna talk to you."

"You know him?"

"Yeah, you know that's my homey."

"Yeah, well, he's my cousin's boyfriend."

"See, it ain't even like that. Who you talkin' 'bout? Tasha?"

"Yeah, exactly."

The boy's face turned serious. "They ain't together, girl. Yo', Blake told me about that. That girl got some problems. She need to stop goin' around spreadin' that lie on my man."

Kelly and I just looked at each other. Was he serious? Or was this some sort of conspiracy?

Kelly was already standing up and looking in Blake's direction. Something told me not to go over there, so I stalled. "So, you guys singing next month in Stockdale?"

"Yeah we gone sing. But you need to go talk to my man."

"Look, he isn't alone. I'm not going over there."

"That's just a friend of his from out of town. She visiting her grandma next door."

"Yeah, whatever. Look, we're going to skate some more. We'll talk to you later."

I stood up to join Kelly. When I saw her frown, I shot another glance over in Blake's direction. Sure enough, he was still looking in ours.

I grabbed her hand and pulled her onto the floor. When we got to the side where Blake was, I simply sped up and refused to look at him, although I knew he was looking at me. We continued like this for the rest of the night—skating, getting something to drink, and resting a little. The one time I allowed myself to deliberately look over there again, I realized that Blake was no longer there. I was glad.

An hour later, they started playing slow dance music, indicating that the skating part of the night was ending. Kelly and I took off our skates, then headed off to play Ms. Pac Man. Kelly had beaten me about three times when I gave up and we turned back around to face what had now become the dance floor. They were playing, "Your Smile" by René & Angela, and we stood on the edge of the carpeted floor, bobbing our heads to the music.

Suddenly, someone grabbed my hand and pulled me toward the dance floor. I looked up, but I already knew it would be Blake. It was.

I pulled my hand away. "What do you think you're doing? Wait. Just wait."

"What's wrong? I just wanna dance with you, girl. You scared?"

"Scared of what, of you?" I said, crossing my arms and rolling my neck.

"I don't know. You actin' like it. You wouldn't even come over there and say what's up earlier."

"You looked busy to me."

"Nah, it ain't even like that. She from North Carolina. Her grams lives next door to us. I couldn't leave the poor girl at home. She knew we was comin'."

"Yeah, right. Where is she now?"

"Oh, she gone home. She couldn't stay for the dance."

"Too bad for you." I turned around to where Kelly was standing and introduced them.

"Hey Kelly, what's up?" he said. "Why don't you tell your sister to dance with me?"

To my disappointment, she did just that. "Go ahead, Cassie. I'll wait for you right here."

I grudgingly started walking toward the dance floor with him.

"See, it wasn't that hard now, was it?" he said. "Why you bein' so mean to me? You playin' hard to git?"

"I'm playin' my cousin's cousin, that's what I'm doin'," I said, letting the Stockdale town-talk creep into my sentence.

"You still hung up on that? How many times I gotta tell you?" He had stopped whatever it was he was doing, because we weren't really dancing. We were just standing out there taking up space on the dance floor. "Either you like me and believe me, or you don't."

I ran my hand through my hair and looked around to see if anyone else had heard that. There were plenty of people watching us, partly because we weren't dancing, but the girls around us were only looking at him and smiling, trying to get his attention. But he was only looking at me, and waiting on some sort of answer.

I guess that darn René & Angela song got to me, because the next thing I know, I was dancing with him. Slow dancing. And this time I was staring at *him*. At how nicely he was dressed again: starched Levis, blue tee-shirt, and a new pair of brand-new white Reeboks. I have to admit, thinking back on it all, the boy sure was fine—the finest boy I had ever seen before in my life.

This little dance continued for two or three songs. By the end, my back felt slightly damp where his hand had been and that sharp pain in my head was coming. I had migraine headaches pretty often, but I could tell this one was going to be the headache of all headaches. I could feel it. I needed some air.

"Look, I gotta go," I said as I walked away. "I need to find Kelly and git outta here. I mean, ah, I have to go."

"Why you gotta rush?"

Oh, great! He was following me. "Because we live in Stockdale and I have to drive back. It's already late."

"Can I come with you?"

I stopped and turned around to face him. "No. No way."

"Just for a little while?"

I repeated my refusal, but he grabbed my hand and started rubbing it, then said, "I think you want me to."

A group of girls were walking by. I knew they went to his high school because one of them, the obvious leader of the pack, was wearing a Jefferson football player's jacket.

"Hey, Blake sweetie. How you doin'?" She was smiling so big I thought her face was going to break. The one talking was wearing a V-neck tee-shirt that revealed large pushed-together breasts. I glanced down at her tight jeans and found myself wondering what size she wore.

"Hey there, now. You girls be safe tonight." And with that, Blake had dismissed them. They walked away with their mouths turned up and rolling their eyes at me.

I watched them until they were at a safe enough distance away from me. I didn't want them trying to pull my hair out from behind. Girls from Jefferson High School weren't the same type of girls that you could find at Stockdale. They were bigger, tougher and always ready to fight.

I saw Kelly and started walking over to her, calling, "Look, I'll talk to you later," over my shoulder at Blake.

She and I met under the exit sign and headed out to the car. Blake was following us all the while, but we kept walking. When we reached the car, I turned around and let out a long sigh. "We have to go. What do you want from me, huh?"

"A kiss before you go."

Kelly was already in the car. I laughed a high-pitched laugh that didn't even sound like my voice. "You're crazy."

"One kiss."

"No, you'd better—"

Before I could further protest, he'd pulled me off the car and was kissing me. At first, I had my hands down at my sides, frozen rigid with my eyes wide open, my mind racing with thoughts like, *Who's watching us? Does Kelly see this?*

Finally, I softened against him, moved my hands up along his muscled arms, and started running my fingers through his black wavy hair. It was so soft, and he smelled good too. It was the first time I had ever kissed anybody. At that precise moment, I knew I was finished, but at that precise moment, I knew I didn't care.

# Chapter 8

▼

The next day I knew I had to face Natasha at school, talk to her as soon as possible, to explain everything. I spotted her walking down the hallway and gently grabbed her by the arm. "Hey, girl. We sure did miss you last night at the rink."

"Really? I bet."

"Of course we missed you. Why are you saying that?"

"Well, I heard you had a good time. I heard you had a *real* good time."

"Girl, what are you talking about?"

"Cassie, don't try to play games with me. I know everythang." She moved over to the side of the hall to let other people pass by, then leaned against the cold gray lockers. I did the same.

"Tasha, yeah, we had a good time," I said. "It was fun and all. I did want to talk to you about something though."

"I already know."

"You already know what, Tasha?"

"I know you was locking lips with Blake outside the rink."

My eyes widened. "Who told you that?"

"My cousin told me. She was there."

"Which cousin? Who?"

"Look, that's neither here nor there. Point is, I *know*."

"I didn't kiss him. He kissed me. I never meant for any of this to happen."

"It don't matter. I gotta git to class. I'll talk to you later." She walked away before I could protest, and left me standing there alone against the lockers wondering what I'd done.

Kelly came by, tore me away from the lockers, and pulled me down the hall. I managed a smile, but lost it with her next words.

"Girl, everyone knows what happened with you and Blake last night."

"What? How? I just got through talking to Tasha, and she knows. And it was just a kiss. That's all."

"Her cousin Babygirl saw you. And you know she has a big mouth. She's already told half of Stockdale."

I didn't go to the lunchroom that day. There were too many people rolling their eyes at me when I walked down the halls.

After that day, Natasha and I didn't talk as much. She still spoke to me, but every time I brought up Blake's name, she acted as if she was cool with it. So I fell into the trap. I started seeing him—not all the time, but whenever I could. I went to his house, and sometimes brought him home with me. My nerves got worked up each time, with Tasha living just three houses down. But after a while, it didn't seem to matter. She came over sometimes, and talked to us as if we were all great friends.

Blake met Mama and hung out with my friends and me. We spoke on the phone some and wrote letters to each other. We went to the movies. Kelly adored him. All of my friends adored him. Everything was fine—in the beginning.

\* \* \* \*

Months later, spring had rolled around, and it was time for the senior prom. I went over to Blake's house to find out what the deal was.

"Are you going with me?" I asked him.

"I don't know if I can."

"Why not? Can't you get a tux?"

"Yeah, that ain't the problem. The problem is somethin' else."

"What?"

"Umm…You know I'm a man, right?"

"I hope so." I laughed, but couldn't see where this was going.

"Well, a man has needs Cassie. A man has *needs*. You see what I'm sayin'?"

I wasn't laughing anymore. I looked at his face: no smile. "What are you saying?"

"I'm saying that I have needs. I need some sexual healing, Cassie. You know, like Marvin Gaye says? I need some sexual healing, girl." He leaned back on the sofa, looking at me with a soft smile.

"Yeah, I hear what you're saying, but I'm not listening."

"What's wrong? Don't you need some sexual healing too? We been goin' together for months now. You been gittin' it from somewhere else?"

"No, but I'm sure *you* have," I said, but hoped it wasn't true.

Silence, and then he leaned forward and stared me down. "You still a virgin?"

"That's none of your business."

"I figured you were. Ain't no shame in that game. Look, I'll go to the prom with you. I was just teasin' you, girl."

By this time, I wasn't sure if I wanted him to go with me. But what he'd said stung a little, too. I thought about all my friends. None of them was a virgin anymore. I was the last one.

I asked, "Why do you want to go to the prom with a virgin?"

"Because I love you. I do. I love you, girl."

I looked at him. I watched him. I studied him. I held my position. He maintained his. He didn't turn his gaze away from me, but instead looked me straight in the eyes before saying it again. "I love you."

\* \* \* \*

A month later, I had questioned nearly all my friends about the art of having sex, as well as my cousin Daniel in St. Louis. He was older than me and despite the distance, more like my big brother.

I thought I was ready to go to the prom. I wore a long black dress, with black sequined shoes and matching bag that I had borrowed from Mama's fashionable sister, Aunt Betty. Blake wore the standard black tux-and-white shirt combination. His hair was all shiny, and so were his shoes. He came to my house and picked me up in a car he'd borrowed from his friend Aaron, and we went to the prom.

Stockdale High's senior prom was like most proms: boring, bad music and over early. It's the after-prom stuff that really counts. Since Blake didn't have a lot of money, we ate at Taco Bell. After we'd stuffed down countless tacos, the moment I'd been dreading came.

"So, do you want to go back to my house for a little while?"

"For what?"

"You know what for. So we can be alone for a little while. Ain't nobody there right now."

"I need to get on back home," I said, looking in the direction of Stockdale.

"No, you don't."

"Yes I do."

"Just for a little while, Cassie. Come on."

I said yes. I prayed that God would forgive me, and had half convinced myself that since I was in love and could really end up marrying this guy, it was all right. That maybe I wouldn't burn in hell.

\*     \*     \*     \*

It was true; Blake's house was empty when we got there. We sat down on the sofa and started kissing. I knew where it was going, but I had decided to go with the flow. After a brief make-out session on the couch, Blake stood up and pulled me into his bedroom. When we got in there, he started taking off my prom dress. It fell to the floor. I didn't really know what to do, so I started helping him to take off his tux. We were facing each other butt-naked in his dark bedroom, with only the hint of a light coming from the kitchen. It was so quiet you could hear neither cars, nor traffic, nor people, nor roaches running around in the kitchen.

"Look, Blake, uh, I'm not sure if this is the right thing for me to do," I said, stepping away from him a little and covering myself with my hands.

"Yeah, it's right. It feel right. Don't it feel right? You know I love you. And you love me too, don't you?"

I had never said it to him. "Yes, I love you. I love you a lot, and I have for a long time."

"Why didn't you tell me, girl?"

"I thought you knew."

"Yeah, I figured you did." He pulled me back up against him. "Don't worry, I ain't gone hurt you."

I could feel his hardness against me, but it was my stomach that was transforming itself into knots. I stepped back again. "Well, you know, everyone I talked to says the first time really hurts."

"It don't have to. I'll be gentle. But we can go if you aren't ready to do it."

I softened, struck by the sympathy in his voice. I answered by kissing him. This was the only cue he needed. He pulled me down on the bed.

"Ouch! That hurts," I said a minute later, and pushed him off me.

"It's almost in. Just hold one more second."

It felt like a tampon gone terribly, terribly wrong. It reminded me of an emergency at church I'd had once in which I needed a fix. My "friend" had started and I wasn't equipped. A lady from the choir came in with the solution, but it was a tampon, not the nice cushy diaper (i.e., pad) I was accustomed to wearing. I went into the bathroom and tried to put it in and ended up getting it in only halfway.

For the rest of the afternoon I could hardly walk or sit down in the pews. Deciding that only a man could invent something like that, I swore off tampons for good. What Blake was doing to me felt almost the same, but worse.

"Is it in yet?" I asked.

"Almost."

*This is definitely not what it is cracked up to be. This sucks.*

Finally, it was in and it seemed to get better for just one second…right before someone opened the bedroom door and tried to turn on the light in the bedroom. Busted.

"Blake, what in the hell's goin' on in here? I didn't even know you was here it's so dark up in here. Why don't this light work?"

"It's just us, Grandma," he said, trying to cover us up.

"What ya'll young folks doin' in here? Why don't this light work? It blown?"

"No, it ain't blown, Grams."

"Oh, you slick, ain't ya', boy? You took that light out again didn't you? Y'all git up from there and git ya' clothes on. I got company comin' over here."

My face was twisted in agony along with the lower half of my body. I could hardly crawl out of bed. Blake, on the other hand, laughed.

"Why are you laughing? It's not funny!" I made my way around in the dark trying to find my clothes. "We just got busted."

"Don't worry 'bout it. Don't worry 'bout her. Just git your clothes on so I can take you on home."

"What did you do? Did you have this planned all along? Did you do something to the lights?"

"Look, girl, I just unscrewed the light bulb in case she came in here, that's all."

"I guess you've done this before. Take me home right now."

On the way, I refused to speak to him. I don't really know if it was because of the embarrassment of his grandmother walking in on us, his attitude about that, the pain coming from between my legs, or guilt that I'd waited until I was eighteen and given over my virginity to someone that perhaps I couldn't really trust.

When I got back home, I slowly and delicately walked into the house, as though I'd break into a thousand pieces if I moved in the wrong way. Mama was still up, watching a foreign film on HBO. Any other time I'd have joined her, but I couldn't that night. I stood there for a second reading the subtitles. It was a French movie. Some guy had killed himself because the woman he loved had tricked him. *But wait a minute. What am I doing? I've gotta get out of here before she starts asking questions.* So long, Mr. Frenchman.

The thought never occurred to me to actually talk to my mother about what had happened. That was nuts to me. Instead, I started running bathwater in the tub. She heard that, came to the bathroom door, looked at me curiously, and then left. I thought she wanted to ask me about the prom or something, but just didn't.

After I took a bath, I felt much better and decided to call Daniel in St. Louis.

"Hello?" By the way he answered, I could tell that he hadn't been asleep. He was twenty-six and liked to party, and it was Friday night.

"Hey, it's me."

"Hey, my favorite cousin." I could hear him smoking a cigarette. "What's up? How was the prom?"

"I did it, Daniel."

"You did what?"

"I had sex, or almost did."

"You did what? I thought you were going to wait, Cassie."

"I did wait. I was the last one out of all my friends, so don't give me a hard time. I'm eighteen years old."

"Calm down, calm down. I'm just surprised, that's all. Did you just get home?"

"Yeah. I came home and took a bath. But I had to tell somebody."

"You came home and took a bath? At this hour? Did you tell your mom? Is she up?"

"Are you crazy? No, I didn't tell her. I came home and she was watching TV and I took a bath. She came in there, but she didn't say anything. She doesn't know."

"Cass, she does know. You came home and took a bath in the middle of the night. You never did that before, did you?"

"No."

"Hon', you can be sure she knows now."

"Dang."

"Don't worry about it, little cuz. If she wanted to say something, she would have when she came in the bathroom. Just be careful from now on, if you don't want her to know."

I sighed. "Okay. I have to go to bed, before she comes in here asking me questions."

"Call me tomorrow."

"All right. Bye."

"Bye, Cassie. Be good."

What was he talking about, *be good*? It was already too late for that, and I knew it. I got into bed and closed my eyes and prayed. *Lord Jesus, forgive me for not waiting until I got married.*

# Chapter 9

▼

Two months came and went. We were sitting outside on Blake's porch one day, when the conversation about his mother came up for the first time since the night we met.

"So, is she coming to your graduation?" I asked him.

"Nah."

"Why not? It's an important day. I can't wait to graduate."

"She ain't, that's all."

"Why not?"

"'Cause I quit school."

"You did what? You quit? In your senior year, you quit?"

"Yeah, really ain't no big deal."

"You're crazy. This is the end. Why do you wanna quit now?"

"Just couldn't deal with it no more."

"What's your grandma gonna say? What's your mama gonna say?"

He laughed. "Nothin'."

"Nothin'?"

"Nothin'. Should've quit a long time ago."

He really *was* insane, I decided. Quitting high school in his senior year! "Where exactly *is* your mother?"

"She's in LA."

"LA? Los Angeles?"

"Yeah." He looked down at his new black Nikes and examined the shoelaces.

"What's she doing out there? That's far."

"She had to git up out of here for a while…. She'll be back soon, though."

"What happened? You didn't want to go with her?"

"I…couldn't go with her."

"Why not?"

"Look, why you askin' me so many questions girl? Quit fishin'."

I bit my lip and got up so he wouldn't see that my eyes were starting to water. I headed for my car.

"Where you goin'? Come back. All right. Shit." He rose up off the porch and started walking behind me. "I'll tell you. Just sit back down. Take it easy, all right?"

Since curiosity already had the best of me, I did just that. He put his hands in his pockets.

"My mom's…she had some problems."

"What kind of problems?"

He shot me a glance as if to say, *"Shut up or I'm not going tell this story."* I stopped talking.

"She was involved with someone and…ummm…it got ugly. She had to leave town."

"What?"

"Cassie, my mom's— She's— She was involved with someone and his wife didn't like it."

"What? You mean…your mama…she—"

"Yeah. She was creepin' with another woman's man, girl."

"Holy cannoli!"

"Holy what?" He chuckled. "Girl, you so corny."

I ignored that. I wanted the rest of the story. A husband-stealer? Blake's mother? No way. "So what happened?"

"She caught them together. They were gittin' their groove on."

"Somebody call *The Young and the Restless*."

"Yeah, they were in bed together and this lady walked in, saw them, ran out, got her gun and threatened her."

"Holy cannoli!"

"You already said that. Anyway, Moms was scared for weeks and since the man's wife was still, you know, threatin' her, she had to leave town for a while."

"That's why you live with your grandma?"

He nodded.

"Don't you miss your mama?"

"Hell, yeah. But you know, she calls and stuff. But we big boys, me and J.R. It ain't no sweat."

The idea came so quickly, it was out of my mouth before I knew it. "Come to church with me tomorrow. It can help you."

He let out a loud, mocking laugh, looked at me to see if I was serious, and then started laughing all over again. Near the end, it turned into an uneasy laugh. I knew he was faking it.

"Nah, I can't make it tomorrow."

"Well, what about the next Sunday?"

"Look, girl, I don't feel like goin' to no church, okay?"

"You should. You need to pray…. You could ask Jesus to help—"

"Git the hell out of here with that, girl." He stood, jammed his hands back into his pockets. "You thank that's the answer for everythang, don't you? Shit. I'm outta here. I'm gone to git me a beer."

It was time for me to leave. My English was all out of control again and I had that intense headache coming on again. Blake looked like he could possibly cry a fountain. But then again, you could never tell about him.

I thought the conversation had brought us closer together—the part about his mother, especially. I thought I had it sewn up tight: his heart and confidence, that is, and it was a good thing because I'd bitten the bullet. Lost the battle. I was in love. I thought he was, too. I mean, he had to be to share something as personal as that with me, right?

Wrong.

\* \* \* \*

Graduation night. Stockdale Gym. The place was filled from bottom to top, all the seats on the floor taken. My mama, grandparents, cousins, uncles and aunts were all there. Even Aunt Betty had flown in from DC just to see me walk across the stage. But for all the pomp and circumstance, for all the emotions, excitement, relief, money envelopes, congratulatory cards and cameras, there was no Blake in sight. He had actually stood me up for my high school graduation.

I thought they believed I was crying because I was happy to be graduating, but they weren't fooled. They knew what was going on. The advice of my friends and family? Forget about Blake. Go to college and get yourself a guy who's doing something.

Maybe they were right. I *was* beginning to listen. But then again, I had to know why he hadn't shown up, because that made two people who weren't there who were of great importance to me: Blake and my father.

I went to his house after much pleading and reasoning with my fellow graduates and friends. They didn't think he was worth it. I wanted to know. I *had* to know.

They waited in the car with the doors locked, listening to Hot94 FM. I knocked on his door, walked in and saw him dressed only in his boxer shorts, completely passed out on the sofa with five or six Budweiser bottles littering the floor beside him.

That wasn't the only thing I saw. Wrapped up in his arms next to him, and completely naked, was the voluptuous, ebony-skinned girl I'd seen flirting with him at Rainbow Skate Center the first night we kissed. Her boyfriend's Jefferson Panthers jacket was draped across the leather chair next to the sofa.

I picked up one of the beer bottles and thought about prodding him with it, waking him up so he could know that I knew. But there were so many empty bottles lying around, they couldn't have been woken up…sorry, I mean *awakened*, even with a bullhorn. They were completely obliterated. The girl was even snoring.

I heard a noise coming from the back of the house. It was a creaking sound…opening. Something was opening. Of course, it was the screen door to the back door. And then I heard Blake's grandmother's voice. She was complaining, as usual.

I threw the Bud bottle in the leather chair and ran out the front door, tears sliding down my cheek and onto my shirt. I was trying to get out of there so fast, I fell off one of the steps. With a *Damnit, why don't they get these things fixed!* I pulled myself to my feet, got in the car and drove off at crazy speeds.

"Think of it this way, Cass," Rachel said. "Now you can go to Panama City Beach with the rest of us seniors tomorrow and have all the fun you want."

While my friends high-fived each other, I sniffled, blew my nose and tried to keep my heart from falling out and into my lap.

# Chapter 10

Graduation parties and Panama City Beach were over. Time to get down to work. I had chosen The University of Alabama at Birmingham, otherwise known as UAB, because I loved the campus and thought it was a great school. Birmingham was a great city, and much larger than Stockdale and Jefferson put together. I made some new friends, got used to the city, and finished the eight weeks of summer school. There was a break before fall classes started, so I decided to go home so I could see my family, go to my own church, and okay, so I could see Blake too.

I hadn't seen or spoken to him since he stood me up on graduation night and I walked in on him and his naked ebony princess. He'd called my dorm several times, because that crazy cousin of mine, Natasha, gave him the number. But luckily, I was never there when he called. That, or the dorm girls were too lazy to walk around to my room to see if I was there. In any case, I never called back. I was too mad and too humiliated.

It was Friday, and my grandparents and Kelly came to pick me up because I didn't have my Honda at UAB yet.

"What courses you takin'?" Grandmama asked, turning around to look at me in the backseat.

"Just the basics for right now. I had English and history this summer."

"Good. Did you know Miss Allie?"

"Miss Allie? I don't remember her...."

"You know Miss Allie. She used to press out my hair every Saturday 'fore she got sick."

I had to say yes or she would have kept saying, "You know Miss Allie." "Yes, ma'am," I told her. "I think I remember her."

"Well, she died yesterday. Funeral gone be Sunday. You and I can leave after church and get there on time. They burying her down at Shiloh. Jacksons' got the body."

My grandparents lived at funerals. They knew the day, the time and the name of the undertaker, sometimes even before it hit the papers. Even if the person wasn't a relative, they went. For them, it was a question of respect, of saying your last goodbyes, and finally, seeing how the person was laid to rest. If in any case they were unable to go—say, like there were two funerals on the same day or in totally different places or if they were sick—someone always brought them back an obituary. I once counted all the obituaries at my grandparents' house, which they kept in the cabinet in the formal dining/living room. I stopped when I reached five hundred. I'm not kidding.

Miss Allie was ancient. She was my grandmother's cousin on her great grandfather's side, and they hadn't seen each other since she and Grandmama worked in the fields together at age ten. We still had to go to the funeral. Usually, I didn't really mind going to the funerals. It was time spent with them, and if it were just Grandmama, she let me drive. She even let me wear jeans and wait for her in the car if I didn't feel like going in on that particular day. Maybe this would be the case with Miss Allie.

"You know we weren't allowed to get as much education as you, girl," my grandfather said. He was doing the driving. He loved to drive. Even though he drove like a snail, in his pickup truck and Oldsmobile alike, we didn't mind. Music was coming from the eight-track tape deck. He was still playing the same group—The Mighty Clouds of Joy. "We wanted to go to school, but we had too many other things to do. Sow the fields. Milk the cows. Take care of the younger children. And when we *did* get to go to school, we had to walk six miles there and six miles back. My Lord. If you didn't have any shoes, that was a long walk."

We liked his stories about growing up, but they were often very hard to listen to. We felt badly for our grandparents. You could look at their old wrinkled hands and know their life hadn't been IZODs and Reeboks. They had to make their own clothes and grow their own food, while we lived off Taco Bell and other places. They didn't just eat chicken back in their day. They had to chase the chicken, kill the chicken, and cook the chicken, all by themselves. Compared to them, we were spoiled and we knew it.

"My daddy told me that there ain't nothin' better than an education," he said, looking in the rearview mirror at Kelly and me. "Sometimes you just got to teach yourself. That's what your grandmama and I did. Lord have mercy. But we made sure that all our children went to school and got an education. An education is priceless. Not one of them is without a degree. A *degree*. And most of them have master's degrees. Thank the Lord Almighty. You hear me, Cassie?"

"Yes sir."

"You don't want to end up at the chicken plant, do you?"

"No sir."

"Well, you do the best you can and make somethin' out of yourself over there at UAB, and you can have a master's degree too."

"Yes sir, I will."

"How you gone get back to school?" my grandmother asked.

"Mama's bringing me back."

"Huh?"

"Mama's going to bring me back," I said a little louder.

"What you say, girl?" Granddaddy asked.

Kelly jabbed me in the arm.

*Oh.* "I say Mama gone brang me back o' *hey*-re."

"Alrighty, then."

Sometimes, with my grandparents and other elderly people in Stockdale, especially on our side of the railroad tracks, we had to speak with a little bit of dialect.

\*    \*    \*    \*

Our house was still the same. Same flowers. Same wicker furniture on the porch. I don't know what I'd been expecting. It had only been two months. Nothing had changed. Except my mother's face. She was standing up against the refrigerator and didn't smile or say hello to me when I walked into the house. Then I knew why.

"You got a letter yesterday. It's on the kitchen table."

I walked over there and saw an official-looking letter in a white envelope marked URGENT across the top with my name and address on it.

I looked at her. "Why is it open? Who opened it?"

"Just read it, Cassandra."

I took the letter out of the envelope, looked at Mama one last time, and started reading it.

To Whom It May Concern:
   It is our duty as officials of the Jefferson County Health Office to notify you that someone that you have had intimacies with is infected with a sexually transmitted disease. Please bring this letter with you to our heath office at once, or to your local health office, in order to be examined and treated if necessary. STDs can be very dangerous when not treated and…

I dropped the letter onto the white-tiled kitchen floor and backed up against the table.

So *this* was what Mama had been dreading.

I forced myself to look up at her. I couldn't speak to her, though. My mouth and tongue were completely dried up. *How could he? That jerk. And now Mama knows? And to think that I wasted my virginity on him! This is what he does to me? I'm going to get him.* I couldn't say those words aloud, but I couldn't keep myself from crying either.

"Get your bag," Mama said. "I've already made you an appointment and we're going over there right now."

She was gathering her things. Purse, car keys. A bag containing bath towels that she wanted to return to Sears. I was so glad that Kelly wasn't in the room.

*Kelly!* "Mama…does Kelly know?"

"No, of course not. Kelly doesn't need to know. Now get in the car. We're going to be late."

I followed her outside to the car. I didn't know if I should apologize, explain, or what, so I said nothing all the way to Jefferson, and neither did she. She pulled into an office building parking lot.

"Is this where the clinic is?" I asked her.

"We're not going to the Jefferson clinic. You're going to see a private physician."

I let out a long, deep sigh of relief. At a public clinic, I ran the risk of seeing someone I knew. I had friends who had told me stories about the public clinic, and how you almost always ran into someone you knew.

\*   \*   \*   \*

A couple of days later, I found out the results of my test: negative. I didn't have any terrible diseases. My mother was so relieved, she didn't give me half the lecture I was expecting. But I couldn't escape it all together.

"Cassie, you need to stay in school, focus, and leave Blake alone."

"Okay." *What else could I say?*

"You need to study, you hear me? And another thing…I've noticed that your English is slipping a little. What's happened? You always do so well. You're in college now, so please pay attention. It's more important now than ever."

"Mama, everybody in Stockdale talks crazy. Black folks period talk crazy."

"Do I talk like that? Do your aunts talk like that?"

"No, but—"

"Cassandra, just because all these other kids talk like they don't have any sense whatsoever, that doesn't mean you and Kelly have to. I know you know better too."

"What about when I talk to Grandmama and Granddaddy?"

"That's different. And that's not what I'm talking about."

"All right."

"I want you to stop talking like you are uneducated, when you are. Do you understand? Just one more reason to stop seeing Blake."

"Uh huh."

"Girl, what did I just get through telling you? Do you want to end up at the chicken plant?"

"I mean, yes. I understand. And no way am I working at the chicken plant."

"Well, act like you have some sense, then. If I've told you once, I've told you a hundred times: Education is the *key*."

\* \* \* \*

I was relieved, but not one hundred percent. I still had to confront Blake about what he had put me through. As soon as I had the opportunity, I drove to his house. When I got there, there was a car parked in front I'd never seen before. A new Cadillac. Black. It was fiercely shining in the sunlight. I was still looking at the car and had just put my hand up to knock on the door when it opened.

"May I help you?"

It was a tall woman, lean, like Blake's grandmother. Maybe forty. She had long black hair pulled back into a ponytail and the same green eyes as Blake. She wore a pair of yellow slacks with a yellow off-the-shoulder blouse, and had several gold chains around her neck. I looked down at her feet and saw white leather-like house shoes. She smelled like baby powder.

"Hi. I'm, ummm…. I'm Blake's…umm." What *was* I? Had we broken up? Officially?

"Oh, I know. You're Blake's girlfriend. You're Cassie, aren't you? College student at UAB?"

"Are you—?"

"Yes. I'm Blake's mother. You can call me Chris," she said in a very proper accent.

"Nice to…ummm…meet you, ma'am."

"Would you like to come in? Blake should be back soon."

She pushed the door open wider so I could go through. I sat down on the leather sofa, the same place where I'd seen Blake lying half-naked with the girl from Jefferson. My body involuntarily shivered.

"Would you like a Coke?"

"Yes ma'am. Ummm…if it's not too much trouble, I mean."

She smiled and walked out of the room. I looked around. The decor had slightly changed. There was a new rug, oriental looking, that covered the floor. Some of the African art had been taken down. The coffee table was different too. This one was made of all glass, and in the middle of it were various letters, some personal, some business related, all unopened and made out to a "Christine Reynolds."

"Here you go, hon."

"Thank you," I said, nervously taking the Coke from her hand and shifting my eyes from her mail. She took the leather chair across from me, picked up her mail and began nonchalantly looking through it. Maybe she had seen me eyeing it, but she didn't let on.

"Blake should have already been back by now," she said, putting the letters back on the coffee table, facedown, and then crossing her legs and leaning back into the chair.

"Where is he?"

"He went with Mr. Monroe to look at a car."

"Who's Mr. Monroe?" I asked, and put the Coke carefully on the floor beside me. Then I thought about the new rug and started to move it when she stopped me.

"Don't worry about that, dear. Leave it there. Mr. Monroe is one of Blake's school counselors."

"Oh yeah. I met him, once." *Did she know Blake quit school?*

Apparently not. With a strange look, she said, "So you've seen him?"

"Yes. He was very nice."

She stood up. Was that sadness on her face? A frown?

She turned her back to me and said, "He's a good man. He does a lot for Blake. He's like a…a mentor."

I guessed he was one of her friends who looked in on Blake and his brother while she was in LA. *Yes, that has to be it.* And when she turned back around to face me wearing a warm smile, I forgot about my uneasiness, and looked down at my Swatch watch. Just as I thought: It was time to drive Grandmama to Miss Allie's funeral.

"I have to go, ma'am." As I said the words, I was already standing and heading for the door. "I have to drive my grandmother to Shiloh."

"Call me Chris, dear."

"Thank you. Will you tell Blake I came by?"

"Of course. Be careful going down those steps. I'm having them fixed next week."

"Thank you. Bye."

"'Byeeee," she said, ever so sweetly, but before I could get off the porch she had already slammed the door behind me.

# Chapter 11

▼

I turned up the Honda's radio and rolled down the windows, then looked at my watch again. 2:45 p.m. Grandmama and I were supposed to leave for the funeral at three o'clock. I knew I was taking a chance in going to Jefferson after church. I knew Grandmama would be wondering why I was late. But it had been my first opportunity to get over there to see Blake. I sped up, hoping she wouldn't be outside waiting on me when I did get back to Stockdale.

Although I was slightly preoccupied with being late, overshadowing that fear was the encounter I just had with Christine Reynolds. Oh, excuse me: Chris. *How long has she been back?* I wondered. *And why did she come back? Was the woman who was chasing her still around? How long has she been away, anyway?*

My mind was racing just as fast as the Honda was switching lanes on the old highway back to Stockdale. Meeting her gave me a feeling in the pit of my stomach I couldn't explain: I'd call it dread. There was something in the way she talked, the way she looked at me as if she knew many things that I didn't, even something in the way she glided across the room and said, "Call me Chris, dear."

I was so wrapped up in my thoughts, I have no idea how long he'd been following me. I heard him before I *saw* him: a loud, screeching noise that just annoys people to death. Policeman don't need guns; they could protect themselves with just that terrible noise riding on the tops of their cars.

I looked in the rearview mirror. Sure enough, blue lights. State trooper. Caught. *Damn.*

I pulled over at the nearest possible place and prepared to hand over my license. I'd never gotten a speeding ticket before. He was a caramel-colored officer. Maybe he would let me go? Fat chance.

"Miss, may I see your driver's license, please?"

"Yes sir." I gave him the license.

"Are you aware of how fast you were driving, Miss? The speed limit here is fifty-five. You were doing eighty." He bent down, looked through my car window at me.

"I'm sorry, sir. I didn't know I was going that fast. My grandmother is waiting on me and I have to get to her house."

"Is your grandmother sick?"

"No. I have to drive her to a funeral and I'm late." *Surely he'll let me off.*

"Young lady, if you don't slow this car down they're going to be having *your* funeral."

Then he starting writing my ticket. Just what I needed. Meet the mysterious mother of my boyfriend. *Or ex-boyfriend?* Get a speeding ticket I cannot afford, and then drive all the way to Shiloh to Miss Allie's funeral and listen to people I never met before cry their eyes out.

On the other hand, maybe I would fit right in. At that moment, I was definitely ready to cry my own eyes out.

\* \* \* \*

Months came and went. I didn't hear from Blake again, and I hadn't gone back to his house after the day I got the speeding ticket trying to leave it. Whenever I went home on the weekends—and that wasn't too often, because I was happy to have finally escaped from Stockdale—I steered clear of his house, his neighborhood, and anyone who knew him. He'd cheated on me, and his mother was a riddle. Their whole life was too mysterious for me. But I still kept the pictures of Blake and me, and looked at them every once in a while.

In the end, I wagered that it was better to be happy and alone, than unhappy in someone else's face. At least that's what Aunt Betty from DC told me, and I figured she was probably right.

# Chapter 12

It was a Saturday night at the beginning of a new semester, and I was following Pam, my dorm roommate from Atlanta, down the hall. Pam was an aggressive girl on the outside, and most of the other girls in the dorm and especially on our floor were intimidated by her. She was aggressive, in fact, because she was depressed. Her parents had made her go to school in Alabama instead of where she wanted to go, which was Spelman College in Atlanta. They thought if she were near Morehouse, where her boyfriend was going, she would surely flunk out.

Being her roommate, I came to find out that, rather than being tough, Pam was quite warm and tender. Coming from Atlanta, she had the greatest hair and hairstyles, and the coolest clothes, too. And she appreciated me. It was I who heard her crying in our room at night because she missed her boyfriend. It was I who consoled her each time she came back from Atlanta after having spent a wonderful weekend with him, and then had to come back. And when she couldn't get there to see him, or he couldn't get to Birmingham, she was incredibly miserable. I knew all her secrets, and she knew most of mine.

At this moment, Pam wasn't on a mission to Morehouse; she was on a mission to the common kitchen on our floor. Someone was cooking Korean food again. I knew it had to be Yumiko, whom we called "Yumi" for short. I was in a class with Yumi. She was half Korean and half Japanese, but grew up in South Korea. I loved hearing about her culture. She was just as normal as we were. She just liked her rotten cabbage, that's all. "*Kimchi*," she called it. One day when we were alone in the kitchen, I tasted some of it, and it wasn't all that bad, actually. But as soon as I smelled the food and saw Pam throw her book down and rise from her bed, I knew there would be trouble, and decided to go with her.

Yumi wasn't there when we got to the kitchen, but about ten girls were, complaining. Most of them were black. The white girls never had enough nerve or time or will to complain about the smell. Pam was outraged at that alone, because she said they had to know how bad it stunk. It smelled bad to me too, but I did respect the rights of the Asian girls to cook their own food. I mean, how would they feel if we started cooking chitterlings, or worse yet, cleaning them? I didn't even want to imagine that smell. One day, someone would decide they just couldn't live without a chitterling sandwich, and they would be right there in the common kitchen cleaning and cooking chitterlings. It was inevitable.

I tried to get this point of view over to the others, but they weren't hearing it. "It smells really bad, but it's their right, guys," I told them. "They have to eat."

"Cass, for heaven's sake, that shit smells horrible," Pam said, with her hands on her hips and her neck rolling around, in full diva mode. "She stankin' up the whole dorm."

"Yeah, well, just open all the windows. The girl's got to eat."

"Why can't she take her stankin' ass over to Captain D's, then? Hell, that shit smells less fishy than whatever the hell she's cookin' up in here."

The others were shaking their heads in agreement and adding their "For reals" and "Un huhs." I was quickly running out of arguments, and the last thing anyone wants to be is an enemy on a floor with fifty girls, including my own roommate.

So I said, "Look, I'm sure she doesn't mean any disrespect to anyone here. I'll go to Yumi's room and talk to her about it."

Pam heaved a sigh. "Yumi, do me, I don't care what you tell her, but please do somethin', Cass, cause we just can't be livin' up in here with that mess. Tonight we all gone be smellin' like we just came out some rice patties and shit."

Everyone hollered in laughter. It wasn't funny to me, but all I wanted was a truce. I didn't want Pam leading the whole pack down to Yumi's room to confront her about her eating habits. I'd try to think of something to help Yumi out later on.

The girls who weren't standing in the kitchen talking about Yumi were running back and forth from each other's rooms, borrowing clothes for the step show that night. There was nothing better than a weekend campus party, especially if it was an "Alpha" party. Alphas ruled our campus. They were the largest black fraternity at UAB, and gave the best parties and step shows. I was an Alpha Sweetheart, so I was going to the party for sure: Alpha Sweethearts, little sisters to the Alphas, got in free.

I had already been to Yumi's room and was on my way back to my own to get ready. I had simply told Yumi that her food was ready and that she should check on it. I'd think of a way to explain to her the woes of the floor on Monday. It had to be done with tact, and I wasn't about to come up with it tonight. I had to get ready for the step show.

I had just passed the payphone when it started ringing again. There was one payphone for the whole floor. The thing was, if you answered the phone, you had to walk around to whoever's door to let her know she had a phone call. The floor was so big, most people just didn't feel like it, so they often let the phone ring unless they were expecting a call. I wasn't, but I answered it anyway.

"Fourth floor."

Nothing.

"Hello, fourth floor?" I repeated.

"Yeah, ummm...is this the dorm?"

I knew this voice. Or did I? "Who do you want to speak to?"

"I need to speak to Cassie in Room 407."

*How did he know that? Tasha again? Max? Did he call Stockdale?*

"She's not here," I lied, and started twisting the silver phone cord around in my fingers.

"Hold up. Is that you, Cass?"

My cover was blown. *Now, do I speak to him or to hang up? Well, let's get it over with.* "What do you want, Blake?"

"Hey, girl, I knew that was you. What's goin' on, baby?" He was slurring his words. There was loud music coming from the background and other male voices. Nothing had changed.

"Are you drinking? Where's your ebony princess? Is she drinking with you tonight?"

Silence on the other end.

"What are you calling me for? Did she dump you for another? Did she cheat on you like you cheated on me?" I was already heated up, shouting into the phone. The people in the kitchen had calmed down and hung onto my every word now, though to look at them, you'd have thought they were really into that *Soul Train* show playing on the kitchen's television.

"What you talkin' 'bout, girl?"

"I'm talking about you sleeping with that girl from Jefferson High. Don't act like you didn't do it because I know you did. I saw you." I would have sworn steam was coming out of my ears. Or it could have been coming from the kitchen. From Yumi's kimchi.

"I didn't sleep with nobody, girl. Is that why you don't call me? You think I cheated on you? I loved you, Cassie. I still do."

"You need to get yourself saved and stop lying. That's what you need to do." And then, like a madwoman, I yelled into the phone, "Go to church!"

"Oh, here we go. Now she talkin' 'bout some church shit again. Girl, you gone start believin' in *me*?"

"Believe in you? I don't even know why I'm wasting my time talking to you. But let me just tell you this: I know what you did. I saw you. I saw her. Naked on your couch. Is it clear for you now? Is it clear, *liar*? Now don't you call me here again. You got that?"

Silence. Though he could have been talking and I wouldn't have heard anything. I was breathing heavily with anger and shaking by then.

One of the girls from the kitchen came over and handed me a Kleenex. *Am I crying? Please God, don't let me be crying.* But I could already feel the moisture on my face.

"Cassie, look, nothin' happened, okay?"

*Is he insane? Still lying. Now's the time to hang up in his face.*

I was ready to do exactly that when he started explaining again. "Look, I'm not perfect, Cassie. But the point is, I love you and I need you, girl. J.R. moved off, and my grams is real sick. They don't think she gone make it, girl. You hear me?"

"I need you, Cass. I love you, girl. All them other girls I slept wit when we was together don't mean nothin' to me. When I saw them, it was just for a piece of ass. That's it."

"What did you just say? *All those other girls?* There was more than one? There *is* more than one?"

"Well...I...um...You know I got needs, Cassie."

"No wonder. You jerk. Do you know what you put me through? You know what I'm talking about. I got a nice surprise in my mailbox last summer. My mother knows about it too." I wanted to threaten him and make him feel ashamed, but I couldn't. No use in letting the whole dormitory know I'd gotten a letter from the public health office.

On the other end of the phone, Blake laughed. "Ah girl, that wasn't shit. Don't even worry 'bout that. Everythang cool."

"Blake, I hope your grandma gets well." For a moment, I thought about the funny old lady that was his grandmother and what a character she was. Then I thought about my own.

"All right then, sweetie. I knew you would come around—"

Then I snapped out of it. "I *do* hope your grandma gets better. But don't ever call me again."

"Well forget you too, then, girl. Shit. I don't know why I called yo' ass fo' no way."

"Then don't make the mistake again." *Click.*

I ran down the hall to my room before anyone could see just how much I was crying. As soon as I got the door closed behind me, I could no longer hold in the sobs.

*Should I call Mama? No, she'll say 'I told you so.' Should I call grandma? No, too late. She's in bed. I can't really tell her anyway, can I?*

There was no one to call. I wished I could call my father. *Where is he?*

Pam had already left for the step show. It was better that way. I wouldn't have to explain to her that all I really wanted to do was crawl under my comforter and go to sleep.

The familiar pain in the left side of my head was coming again. I could feel it. I took off my new black Esprit shirt that I'd intended to wear to the step show, slumped onto the hard floor and continued sobbing into my hands. *Sleep*, I told myself. *Just get in bed.* I thought about a song: *It will be all over in the mornin'.*

But of course I couldn't sleep. The dreams about Heather had started again. Heather Hughes, Cheerleader. Heather Hughes, Best Friend. Heather Hughes, Suicide? This time in the dream, Heather was still in her car but on the passenger side. Blake was the one laughing and driving. Driving them off the Lake Creek Bridge. And my father was sitting in the backseat.

# Chapter 13

Months later. A Saturday. 1:45 p.m. Michael pulled up onto the ramp right in front of my dorm to pick me up in his new red BMW convertible. There were girls, mostly black ones, standing around in the dorm lobby, staring through the clear glass, and all eyes were on me as I hopped into the car, reached over, and hugged him really tight. I could almost hear their *oooohs* and *ooo-wees!* while I was squeezing him. We ended the show of affection and headed for the Galleria Mall, leaving the dormitory girls rooted to their spots, still looking.

You see, Michael was white.

\* \* \* \*

For years, I'd wanted to learn to swim. So, I decided to take a swimming class. Mama was afraid of water, so Kelly and I didn't learn when we were little. Something I always regretted.

When I arrived at the class the first day, I met Michael. He was a great-looking guy by anyone's standards. Blonde hair. Blue eyes. Nice square jaw. Tall. Lean. He looked like a model, and should have been one. I also noticed and learned something else about Michael that first day. Michael was completely and unabashedly gay. I must admit I was a bit disappointed, seeing how we got along and seeing that he didn't take this race thing seriously at all. But what are you going to do? Be really good friends, that's what. That's all you can do.

So in the beginning, I had a tiny crush on Michael. Michael had a crush on our swim instructor, and it seemed that our swim instructor had a crush on me. He used to call me "Miss America." I closed my eyes in agony every time, and when I came out of the locker room and he said things like, "Here's the lovely Miss America. How are you today?" I wanted to evaporate.

I was the youngest girl in the class. The rest of the women were in their mid-forties and older, just taking the class independently, not regular fulltime students. The teacher, a man in his mid-thirties who looked like a Native American, often winked at me too. Whenever he spoke, he seemed to always focus his attention on me, and when I left the pool at the end, I could feel his eyes burning a hole through my backside. When I turned around, *bam!*—just as I thought, he was looking, waving, and smiling from ear to ear. Michael thought it was hilarious. I thought it was horrible.

I realize now that I should have complained to someone in the administration. I wish I had. What I did, quite simply, was quit. My nerves were too bad to even try to swim. I assumed there would be inappropriate touching and feeling. There was no way I could continue. Michael quit right after I did, saying the class was no longer fun for him without me, and that we would both drown together. We were close friends from that day on.

Special note to all male swim instructors: Don't stare at us or our swimsuits, don't gawk at our butts, and whatever you do, don't make stupid comments like, "Here comes Miss America" or wink at us. Our future swimming or drowning depends on it! Thank you.

"So what are you going to get at the mall today?" I asked Michael as we sped along the interstate.

"I need a new outfit for tonight. Jeffery and I are going out for dinner at that new restaurant in Vestavia Hills, honey. I need to look good." He was looking at me through his black Ray-Bans.

I smiled at him. "Wow, that sounds good. He sure does like you, this Jeffery."

"Honey, yes he does. I think he's going to introduce me to his sister this weekend."

"Really?"

"Girl, he just about has to. We've been dating for over three months now."

He changed lanes to pass an elderly lady driving an old yellow Thunderbird.

"Is he still thinking about moving to California?" I asked.

He nodded. "I'd love that. Don't get me wrong, I like your little old Alabama just fine," he said, taking on an Alabama accent, "but I grew up in California. I'd have still been there had my father not taken the chief of staff position down here at UAB Hospital. But, great surgeon and man that he is...well, if Jeffery does move to Cali, I'm outta here. I can always visit Mom and Dad. And you."

"Do you think he'd ask you to move out there with him?"

Michael pulled into a parking space in the parking deck at the mall.

"Look at me, Cassie. I'm twenty five, and I look pretty good. He's forty, and has already lost a lot of his hair. Do you think he could really do better than me?" He burst out laughing so loud, he scared the family that was getting out of their car behind us.

"You know Michael, you are so right," I said. "You're in there."

He gave me a quick hug and we went into the mall.

\* \* \* \*

After doing Structure, the Limited, Macy's, and Rich's, we finally left the Galleria. The topic on the way back to the dorm was all together different, however.

"Did you hear anything back from the Red Cross, Cassie?"

"No. Nothing. I don't think they can find him." I looked away. "It's been over ten years."

"Nobody in your family knows where he is? Where he went when he left?"

I sighed. We'd covered this ground before. "Big Mama…my grandmother, his mother…told me he went to Atlanta. She went up there one time, when I was like nine. Mama wouldn't let me go. When I was old enough to drive, I asked Big Mama where he lived. She couldn't tell me. She didn't know anymore."

And then, inspiration hit. "You know, maybe…maybe I can ask my aunt this time. His sister. I never thought to ask her. Maybe she knows, and she'll be willing to tell me."

I vaguely heard Michael speaking. Inside my head, I was already forming a new plan, a plan to get a concrete lead. A plan to finally find my father.

\* \* \* \*

Michael pulled onto the ramp right in front of my dorm again, retrieved my Limited bag from his trunk and handed it to me. We gave each other a long, tight hug, he kissed me on the cheek, then he got back into his new BMW and headed to his apartment to get ready for his big date. I entered the lobby of my dorm, knowing I, once again, was the subject of the day's discussion. The girls whispered and pointed at Michael as he drove away, while glancing back over their shoulders at me. As used to this type of behavior as I was, it still managed to shock me.

*Birmingham. Big city. Bigger city than Stockdale.*
*Still in the Deep South, though.*

*Conclusion: Same Old Book. Different Chapter.*

*   *   *   *

The only kink in the plan, and it was minor, was that my aunt Vernadean lived in Italy. Her husband was in the Army, and he'd been stationed over there as far back as I could remember.

I looked through all the telephone books until I found out what the time difference was over there, set my alarm clock for 3 a.m. one Sunday morning, and headed for bed. At 3 a.m. my time, it would still be early morning in Europe, and I could catch them before they left for church, assuming they still went in Italy. I didn't know how much the telephone call was going to cost, but I hoped to keep the conversation as short as possible.

"Hello? Hello?" I said, still trying to wipe the sleep from my eyes.

"Yes?"

"Hello, this is Cassie calling. Will's daughter?"

"Well, hi there, girl. How are you doing? I haven't seen you since you were a little girl."

"Yes, I know. It's been a long time. How are you?"

"We're all doing just fine. Mama told me you asked for our number, and I was hoping you would call. Are you still trying to find your daddy?"

"Yes. Yes I am. I was wondering if you could help. If you had any addresses or phone numbers for him, you know. From that time you all went to see him?"

A long pause. "That was so long ago, Cassie. I wasn't even married then. And you know we've moved so many times, being military and all—"

"Yes, I know. And I understand. But if there is anything you might remember…" I was starting to lose hope. Again.

"Listen, tell you what I'll do," she said. "I'll think about it, and I'll look around in some old boxes and see what I can dig out. Okay, sweetie? Give me your number."

I gave it to her, but without any enthusiasm. I would never find him. I would never know my father, or what he looked like now and if it were true that I looked just like him.

My pity party almost caused me to miss what my aunt was saying.

"…It sure was a crazy trip. The lady he was staying with was real nice, though. She had an odd name…. What was it? I'll look through my stuff, but what was that lady's name…?"

"A lady? He was staying with someone?"

"Yes, your daddy was living with a la—"

I fought sudden tears. "No one ever told me that. No one. I've searched for his name in phone books, through the phone company. And now I find out that—The phone is in this lady's name? Is it her house?" I wanted to throw the phone against the wall, but it was Pam's.

"Cassie, I'm really sorry, honey. I thought you knew. I thought someone—"

"Nobody has told me anything! It's almost impossible to know or understand anything in this family." I regretted saying that immediately, because she'd always been nice to me. But it was too late.

"Cassie, I know it's hard for you," she said. "I wish you could have gone with us when we saw him years ago, but your mother didn't want you to. But now you're older. You *will* see him soon. I've got a good feeling about it."

"Well, thank you, Auntie," I managed. "I appreciate it."

We finished the call, and I hung up chanting, *Long, deep breaths. Long, deep breaths. Long, deep breaths.* I wished he'd been trying to find me half as hard as I was trying to find him.

I had to write this latest development in my journal. He had been staying with a woman. The phone wasn't in his name. The house was hers. It all began to make sense. All those wasted calls. All that wasted time.

I secured the journal from its hiding place in the back of my underwear drawer, sat on my bed and began writing. I wished Pam was there, but she'd been in Atlanta since the previous week, staying at Morehouse in her boyfriend's dorm more and more since he'd finally managed to get a private room. He went to classes; she slept all day until he got back. Sometimes I didn't see her for a full week. When I asked her what she was going to do about her own classes, she told me not to worry about it. "Okey dokey," I'd said. What else could I say?

We had a phone in our room now, but not many people had our number. When it rang, I thought it was Pam calling to check on her messages again.

"Cassie? It's your auntie, honey. I remembered that name."

"The name?"

"The name of the lady your father was staying with when we went to visit him."

Buzzing sound on her end of the phone.

I found my voice. "What is it?"

"Deee-boe-ice. I told you it was a funny name. I can't pronounce it."

"Can you spell it, then?"

"Yes. I even wrote it down. D-E-B-O-I-S. Dee-boe-ice."

"Debois."

"Is that how you say it?"

"Yeah. Thanks, Auntie. Thank you so much. I have to go now. I'll call you. Bye."

*And so it comes down to this Debois woman.*

I finished my journal entry, dropped it back in my underwear drawer, and started planning.

*Will Taylor. My father. Staying with a lady named Debois.* I had to get there, to Atlanta, to find him once and for all. If I didn't, my life would continuously be "off." Something would be missing. I wouldn't be whole. I knew this. My closest friends knew this. But my mother didn't know this. She couldn't and wouldn't understand. So I did what I thought was best: I didn't tell her.

# Chapter 14

Only the people involved with the mission were told. Michael. Pam. Lashaundra. It didn't take long before we were off for Atlanta, Georgia.

Having a name made things easier. I called information, and was barely on hold two seconds when the operator called off her number. Then, after nervously watching the phone for almost half an hour, I got up the nerve to call.

"Debois residence."

She'd answered the phone on the first ring. I thought it was all falling into place too easily. After years and years of searching and wondering—

"Yes, hello. I'm looking for...I mean, I'll calling for a Mr. Will Taylor, please. I'm not sure if I have the right number, but...is this Mrs. Debois?"

"Yeah. This ain't Will's family, is it?"

"Yes. Yes ma'am. It's his daughter."

"Well, bless my soul. The Lord is good."

"Is he there by any chance? Does he still live there?"

"Yeah, chile, he do, and you need to come up here and see 'bout him. Somebody do. He in a bad way." She let out a prolonged sigh. "Are you still there, chile?"

"Yes ma'am."

"Can you come up here and see 'bout yo' daddy, chile?"

"I...umm...I can try."

"Take a pen and I'll give you my address. It's 123..."

I grabbed a pen off the desk next to my bed and took down the address. "Thank you, Mrs. Debois. I'll call before I come."

"All right, honey. Just try to come as soon as you can 'cause he sho' needs it."

"Okay. Bye."

"Bye-bye, doll."

And that's how easy it was.

*So he needs me. He needs me. After all those years of me needing him.*

But what for? What was wrong with him? Why hadn't I asked? Why hadn't she or he tried to contact us? Why should I go?

Why? Because I had no choice. I had to go.

This was the moment I had waited on for years. I would not end it here. I was going to Atlanta. I planned to leave the following Sunday.

\*   \*   \*   \*

"Who in the hell would want to run off to Atlanta and not see her man if he was there?" Pam said. She was in a bad mood, having given up her weekend with Mr. Morehouse to accompany me. Her mood didn't improve when I told her we wouldn't have time to swing by her boyfriend's dorm, not even for a minute.

"Just get in the car, Miss Pam," Michael said. "We're already off schedule."

"Are you sure you want to miss studying, Lashaundra?" Pam asked her.

Lashaundra was a new friend I'd shared French 101 with.

Lashaundra gave Pam's arm a friendly pinch and got in the backseat of Michael's car. "I can miss a few hours, Pamela. No problem. Besides, I'm ahead anyway."

"Well if you fail anything, don't go blamin' it on us now," Pam said, getting into the back with her.

"Don't you worry about it. Mike, how long will it take us to get there?"

"About two hours, I think," Michael answered.

Two hours. Two hours away from finally seeing him. My Lord!

I looked down at what I was wearing, already second-guessing my choice of clothing: UAB colors. Green tee-shirt, yellow shorts, sneakers. Would he be proud to see me in UAB colors? Would he even notice?

"Are you ready, Miss Cassie?" Michael said, bringing me back around.

I jerked my head up from looking at the upside-down UAB on my shirt. "What?"

"Are you ready to go?" He fastened his seat belt.

"I—I guess so," I said, got in the front next to him and fastened my seat belt. "Let's go!"

\*     \*     \*     \*

What can I say about Atlanta? Atlanta sucks! I've never liked it, and I especially didn't like it that day. It had been holding my father hostage all these years, and now I was going there to find out why. We got there easily enough, though. It was a straight shot on Interstate 20. Everybody had talked a lot on the way there, and I was glad of that. It gave me less time to think about what was to come. Michael talked about Jeffery and his possible move to California. Pam talked about Mr. Morehouse and how she might still talk her parents into transferring to Spelman. Lashaundra talked about her grades and what law school she wanted to attend. I was happy listening. Even so, I still had to make an effort to control the churning rise and fall going on inside my stomach.

When Mike announced that we were nearing our destination, everyone sat up, stiff from the long drive. We'd exited off I-20 and made a left turn. That left turn made all the difference. Suddenly, we were in the projects. The ghetto of Atlanta. The black ghetto of Atlanta. All the buildings looked the same: red brick.

We pulled up to Mrs. Debois's building number in Michael's red BMW convertible, and could feel eyes on us when we got out of the car and knocked on Apartment 123.

*Apartment number 123*, I thought as we stood there waiting for someone to answer the door. *Easy as 1-2-3. 1-2-3. A-B-C.*

It had to be some sort of lurid joke. Apartment number 123. *Nothing* was as easy as 1-2-3.

"Well, well, well. If the good Lord sho' ain't good. Ya'll here to see Will, ain't ya'? Ya'll come on in."

At some point during my near-nervous breakdown over the possible significance of the numbers on her door, Mrs. Debois, a short gray-haired lady, medium brown in complexion and wearing a brown flowered dress to match, had opened the door and was now standing directly in front of us.

"Thank you. We're happy to be here," Michael said. He took my hand and squeezed it.

I squeezed his hand much harder than he squeezed mine. It was better than pinching myself. I still couldn't speak.

"Ya'll come on in and make ya'selves at home here."

The four of us piled into her apartment. The living room held a massive yellow sofa and two large matching armchairs, all covered in transparent plastic. Old school. Tall, brass-like lamps sat on matching wood end tables. The coffee table held a white vase and red artificial roses. There was a poster-sized Jesus Christ hanging over a modest-sized television in the corner. Above the sofa, a mural held three photographs: John F. Kennedy, Martin Luther King, Jr. in the middle, and Robert F. Kennedy on the right. I'd seen similar pictures in the homes of my grandparents' friends.

"Hello, Mrs. Debois. Thank you for letting us come today," I finally said, taking a seat on the yellow sofa and listening to the rustle of the plastic beneath me as I tried to slide back. My friends were still standing.

"Doll, you know it ain't no problem. 'Sides, it ain't for me, it's for him. It's for Will, 'cause honey, he sho' is in bad shape. I'm just glad you kids is come."

She was looking at me but reaching for a pair of bifocals, which were on the wooden coffee table next to the sofa. I passed them to her.

"You the one I talked to on the phone, chile?"

"Yes, ma'am."

"Well o' course. Just look at ya'. He gone be so happy."

She could not, would not know what agony I was in.

"Is he…?" I stumbled.

"Chile, let me go git him. Ya'll make ya'selfs at home. I be right back." She walked hurriedly down the hallway.

As soon as I thought she was out of earshot, I said, "You guys sit down. You're making me nervous."

Pam sat on the sofa beside me, but Michael kept looking outside the window at his car. Lashaundra was doing the same.

"Cassie, how are you feeling?" Pam said.

"I don't know. I just don't know." I clasped my hands in my lap.

"Well, he'll be here any minute now, and we—"

We all looked up to see that Mrs. Debois had come back into the room. She was alone. She didn't speak, but she didn't have to. Lashaundra stifled a gasp. I just looked up at her in abject horror. We had driven all that way, and my father wasn't even there.

# Chapter 15

"Now I know what ya'll thinkin' but don't ya'lls worry ya'selfs none. I know where to find him. Come on." Mrs. Debois was already unlocking the screen door, and we all followed behind her, not knowing where in the world she was taking us.

We walked around her building and headed toward another one. The path we took was a narrow sidewalk, enclosed, like the ramp we used to have at our school to walk to our buses in case it rained. While walking and wondering what I would do if he wasn't there, I saw a tall figure at the end of the sidewalk, leaning against the red brick wall of the building we were heading toward.

"There he is, chile. There yo' daddy, straight ahead. Ya'll just keep walkin'. Okay?" And with that short introduction, Mrs. Debois turned around and left me standing there, looking at the lone figure.

"I can't see anything," Pam said.

"Do you have your eyes open, girl?" Lashaundra said. "He's right there."

"I still don't see him."

Michael gave a frustrated sigh. "Let's just keep walking and then everyone will see him. Come on, Cassie." He took my hand and the four of us continued down the sidewalk.

I couldn't tell whether he was awake, asleep, or dead. He was indeed leaning against the wall, but his eyes were closed. No one moved. No one breathed, and no one said a word. I figured it was up to me to do something. What? I had no idea. There I was after years of waiting, standing two feet away from my father, the man I had cried for, wished for and needed my whole life. And there he was, standing against a red-brick project wall with his eyes closed.

Besides looking comatose, he looked like a missing Bee Gee. A member of the Jackson Five. Marvin Gay-ish. He was wearing blue jeans with huge bell-bottom legs. I had never, and have never since, seen bells as large as that. He wore a purple shirt with a large collar. An orange hat on top of a big black afro. His shoes were brown and had buckles on them. Other than that, I looked into his face and saw that he looked just like me.

I cleared my throat and said, "Excuse me."

Nothing. Dead calm. No one moved.

"Excuse me," I said again, much louder than the first time.

He opened his eyes, and then he closed them, and reopened them, noticing the four of us staring at him with our eyes wide open.

"I knowed ya'll was comin,'" he said as he threw himself from against the wall to stand up on his own. "Ya'll want some tomatoes? I got a lot of them."

For the first time, I noticed the red, ripe tomato in one of his hands. *My Lord!*

We all backed up a few feet away from him.

"No, thank you," Pam said.

"Which one of ya'll's my daughter?" he asked, coming closer to us.

*What is he saying? Did he say what I think he just said?*

None of us said anything aloud. We just stood there, glued to the sidewalk, huddled all together like chickens in a chicken coop.

"I know." He pointed his long, skinny finger. "You's Cassandra."

He was standing right in front of Pam.

Pam shook her head no.

He passed on in front of Lashaundra, who was standing next to Pam, and uttered, "You's Cassandra."

"No, sir."

He stood in front of Michael for a second, and kept going. I was the last one.

"You's Cassandra," he said.

He then grabbed me and hugged me before I could stop him. I didn't want him to hug me, though, and when I resisted, it made him drop his ripe, red tomato onto the sidewalk. I took it as a sign: Maybe I shouldn't have gone in search of Will Taylor.

\*   \*   \*   \*

After we led him back to Mrs. Debois' house, she explained to us that my father was sick. He'd been renting a room from her for years, and she had seen his condition go from bad to worse. She said that he would die if he didn't stop drinking and get some professional help.

I assured her that I would notify all the right people, but that I was only a college student. I promised to tell my grandmother, his mother, and my aunt. I assured her that someone would be back for him.

She gave my father hot coffee to drink as we talked. Though he said nothing, after about an hour, he seemed to come around. She tried to make me feel better about his not knowing me. She blamed it on the alcohol, and said that he was drunk. I should have known when we saw him leaning against the wall. What was I thinking?

It didn't matter to me, though, this explanation. I hadn't returned my father's hug before because I was furious. Here I had traveled miles to see him, to finally meet him, only for him to not even recognize me or know who I was. I was nothing to him. I never had been. Maybe Kelly had been right to turn me down when I'd asked her to come.

Will Taylor passed out before we finished arranging for someone to come back and pick him up. He lay there on the sofa with his afro sticking high in the air and his bell-bottom jeans ringing the carpet below. My friends and I could only stare at him with our mouths open. Time to go. There really was nothing else to say. Besides, my head was beginning to hurt.

"Thank you so much, Mrs. Debois. I'll call you very soon," I said, shook her hand and walked outside onto the porch. She was saying goodbye to my friends and I was looking at the various people who had gathered in the yard in front of me when I spotted a light-skinned lady, age impossible to tell, wearing a red mini-skirt and matching shirt and red high-heeled shoes, standing next to Michael's red car. She almost blended in. Almost.

Michael had seen her too, and though he seemed cool, his voice betrayed him. "Who is she and what does she want?" he asked me, whispering, as we walked over to his car.

The lady in red smiled and stepped back and even held our doors open for us. We had no idea who she was or what she would do, or when. She made her move though, as soon as she saw us fastening our seat belts.

"Are ya'll headed to Birmingham?"

She had seen the UAB sticker on his car. Or maybe my shirt. Or the car tag? I wasn't sure.

I figured it was my duty to answer her since she was hanging onto my car door. "Yes. We go to school there."

"Can I go with ya'll?" She had her head inside my window and kept looking from me to Michael and from Michael to me.

"We don't have enough room in here," I said. "I'm sorry."

"Look, I got some gas money. We can scrunch up in the back there."

"Hell-to-the-no, Cassie," Pam said between gritted teeth. "Michael, get us out of here."

"Come on, ya'll. Help me out. I gotta get away from these projects."

Then we had an intervention. Mrs. Debois came out to the car. "Chile, git away from these here chullen and let them git on their way. You know you cain't go with them and you ought to be 'shamed of yo'self for botherin' them. Now come on here."

She grabbed the lady in red by the arm and started pulling her toward her porch.

"Michael, crank it up. Crank it up and get us out of here," Pam yelled from the backseat.

By then, seven or eight people had formed a circle around the car.

"Boy, you better get us going, for real," Lashaundra said, eyeing them.

Michael cranked the car, put it into reverse and gently pressed the gas, blowing the horn at the same time so the people who had gathered behind the car would move. The lady in red saw us reversing, jerked her arm away from Mrs. Debois and ran toward the car.

Michael turned the car around and started going faster. She ran alongside the car, her red pocketbook in hand swinging against her body, screaming, "My ride! Stop! My ride. I'm missin' my ride. Ya'll wait on me!"

When I last turned back to look at her, she was still running behind the car watching us drive out of sight.

No one spoke a word all the way back to Birmingham. What could we have said? What could *I* have said? Nothing. I was too embarrassed that my father hadn't even known who I was. Too embarrassed that he was living like a drunk, and in fact, he *was* a drunk, still wearing clothes from the 1970s, complete with a huge afro.

Anger. Frustration. Disappointment. I couldn't feel any relief yet. That would have to come later, when I managed to have a conversation with him and ask him the one question that had been haunting me my whole life: *Why?*

\* \* \* \*

That night, when everyone had said their goodbyes and gone their separate ways, I dreamt about Heather again. Heather and my father were riding along Lake Creek Bridge. They were both singing along to the radio—it was Anita Baker's "Sweet Love." My father had a big black afro, far bigger than I'd seen that day in real life. The stranger thing is that Heather had an afro, too.

## Chapter 16

"Come on, Cassie, help git him in the car," Big Mama said. Along with her eighty-year-old boyfriend Kenny, she and I had gone back to Mrs. Debois' in Atlanta to pick up my father. I was on the lookout for the lady in red and couldn't quite concentrate on getting him into the car.

"Okay, I'm coming." I slowly walked over to the car, all the while looking around for our would-be hitchhiker. She was nowhere in sight.

*Wait a minute,* I thought. *Why do I have to help him get into the car? Why did I ever agree to come with them to pick him up?*

I suddenly started thinking of all the possible repercussions. Like, what would happen when Mama found out that I'd helped bring Will Taylor back to Stockdale, Alabama, where he hadn't been seen for twelve years?

But it was too early to start worrying about that. Or perhaps too late. My father was now inside the car and on his way back to Stockdale, where he would live on the black side of the tracks like the rest of us.

I tried not to look at him during the ride back, but found I couldn't help myself. There he was, in the flesh, my father. My daddy. *Yep, ladies and gentleman, here he is. The one, the only, Mr. Will Taylor.*

I noticed how much I really *did* look like him. Everything my paternal grandmother had told me about that was true. We were the same height, the same slim build, the same complexion. Amazing. What I also noticed was that he was much too skinny for his own good. He almost looked like a stickman. When I'd seen him before, he was wearing baggier clothes. But on this day, he was wearing more fitted clothing. Still the '70's look. But anyone could see just how sick and thin he really was.

I'd made up my mind that although I could look at him, I wasn't ready to talk to him yet. But he had different plans. As we got closer to UAB's campus—where they were dropping me off because there was no way I was going to be seen with them in Stockdale—he looked over at me and spoke.

"It's really good to see you, Cassandrie."

*Cassandrie? He doesn't even know my name, for crying out loud!*

"Cassie," he said, shortening it when I looked at him with my eyebrows turned up in a frown.

I shook my head in annoyance and felt anger rising from my stomach. I couldn't restrain myself any longer.

"Why didn't you ever call me?" I said. "Why didn't you ever come back to see how I was, or where I was, or what I was doing? What were you doing there in Atlanta all these years, not even writing me or sending one birthday card or Christmas card? Nothing. Why?"

There, it was out. Years of pain and suffering and questioning and doubting, and now it was out. I sat back, begging myself not to cry, and turned my face to the window.

We would arrive at UAB's campus any minute to drop me off. My grandmother and Kenny were arguing over the directions in the front, so they weren't paying attention to us in the backseat. Suddenly, I turned back around and faced him. I wanted my answer. He was looking down at his hands, which were slightly shaking.

"I—I thought you was happy, Cass," he muttered. "I just thought you was happy."

"Yeah, but you never even bothered to check, did you?" I shouted. "Did you? And what about Kelly? Did you think she was happy too?"

Big Mama turned around and frowned at me, but I didn't care. I kept going. "You should have checked. You really should have checked. Because you know what? I was *not* all right. I was *not* happy."

We had arrived in front of my dorm. I got out and slammed the car door hard behind me before saying one last thing. "You should have checked."

And then I stormed off inside, not even saying goodbye to any of them sitting inside the car, looking at me with their mouths wide open.

\* \* \* \*

I cried myself to sleep that night. Sure did. There were just too many things happening at once for me.

After I had slammed the car door on my past and future, I had a couple of other shocks to deal with. The first was with Pam.

I'd just entered the dorm lobby, still steaming from the confrontation with my father, when I saw her there with suitcases. Pam's parents were there too, and they were taking things out of the dorm and loading them up in a van parked outside in front, something I'd been too angry to notice on the way inside.

"Pam, what are you doing?" I asked, approaching them. "Where are you going?"

"I left you a note upstairs," Pam said with her head down.

"What's going on?"

"I'm...going back to Atlanta"

"Why?" I gave a confused half-smile. "Oh, are they letting you go to Spelman?"

"No. Not quite. You see, I—"

"Girl what is going *on*?"

"I flunked out, Cassie.... I flunked out."

"What?" I looked over at her parents.

"UAB showed me the door. I'm out for one year, Cassie." She broke into tears.

I managed to say, "How long have you known about this?"

"I just found out a few days ago. I didn't want anyone to know. Not even you. You don't know how embarrassing it is. I—I am so ashamed. Mama and Daddy are so mad at me."

I hugged her. "Look at this way. Maybe you can get into Spelman and finally be close to Mr. Morehouse, no?" I forced a small smile.

"With my grades? I'll never get into Spelman now. And besides, it doesn't even matter now." She started to cry even harder.

"Maybe you can. Have faith, Pam." Then, it hit me. "Why do you say it doesn't matter now?"

"'Cause he broke up with me, Cass."

"Mr. Morehouse broke up with you?"

She nodded. "When I told him about the letter. When I told him about the letter saying that I...umm...had to leave UAB. That I had failed. He told me that he—he needed someone successful. Because he's going to be a doctor and everything." Her sobs came harder. "He said he...he'd met a girl from Clark."

I was glad her parents had gone back outside. "Maybe you can win him back, Pam. You'll be right there in Atlanta with him. But is he really worth it?"

She kept crying, and I let it drop. My anger for her sake remained. She'd flunked out of UAB because she stayed in Atlanta days at a time while Mr. Morehouse was on the fast track to becoming a successful doctor. I couldn't ignore the irony, though. The very thing her parents didn't want to happen happened anyway.

The second thing I had to deal with came from home. I'd called my mother to tell her that Pam was gone, to express my grief. She listened and said that was sad, but she couldn't talk long because she had to find Kelly.

*Find Kelly?* "What's wrong with Kelly, Mama?"

"Your cousin Natasha just called and said that Kelly's boyfriend was hurt and they've rushed him to the hospital."

"Kelly's *boyfriend?*" There had to be some mistake. Kelly and I were tight, and she hadn't told me anything.

Mama sighed. "We didn't know it either. But look, I have to find out where she is, if she stayed at the gym or went to the hospital."

"But what happened? Who is this guy and what happened?" I said, starting to lose it.

"Kelly's going with a white boy from Stockdale High named Jimmy. They were at the gym watching a game, and a group of white men jumped Jimmy and beat him up. Tasha said they told him it was for dating a black girl. And she said the boy was hurt pretty bad. One of the coaches called the rescue squad for him. Honey, I hate to go, but I've got to find Kelly. I'll call you when I get back."

She had already hung up and I didn't even have time to say goodbye.

*Kelly, Kelly, Kelly.* I couldn't believe she hadn't told me. Who was this Jimmy? And Mama had said that a group of men beat him up? As in *grown* men? I couldn't believe it. I just couldn't believe it.

I lay down on my bed, put the telephone beside me, and looked over at Pam's bed. No covers, no stuffed animals. Nothing. The room was completely dark except for the streetlights on 18th, and I was utterly alone. Nothing to block out the thoughts racing in my head.

My father. Pam. Kelly. And now, a seventeen-year-old white kid named Jimmy who lay beaten up in the emergency room, beaten by a group of grown white men.

Yep, same story, different chapter. *Stockdale, Stockdale, Stockdale. Will you ever change? Will you ever unlearn your prejudice? Your hatred?*

I wanted to pull my hair out and run down the dorm halls screaming, but instead I just said a prayer: *Lord, please have mercy on us foolish people.*

\* \* \* \*

The phone was still beside me when it rang the next morning. I sleepily reached over and picked it up, wary of whom it would be and what they'd want.

"Hey," Kelly said.

I sat straight up.

"Mama told me you called last night."

"Well, thank God *somebody* told me. What's going on?"

"He's okay. He's out of the hospital now. But it could have been a lot worse."

"You're of course talking about your new boyfriend, right? The one you forgot to tell me about? What's his name? Jimmy?"

"Yeah. I really like him. More than like."

"More than like? How long has this been going on?"

"A few months now, but Mama just found out."

"Is she angry?"

"A little bit… She told Grandmama and Granddaddy about it."

Sudden anger brought my next words. "Where were you when all of this was happening? What if they had beaten you up too?"

"Cassie, they were just a group of stupid rednecks."

"*Dangerous* rednecks. They made your boyfriend go to the ER."

"Are you saying that I should stop seeing Jimmy? Just because of a bunch of sorry rednecks?"

Her voice, defensive and hurt at the same time, made me take a deep breath and temper my next words. "No, of course not. No way. You know me better than that. But be careful."

"I will. *We* will. His brothers said they're going with us to the rest of the games, and that they'll kick anyone's butt who lays a hand on him or me."

"So his family's cool with you guys seeing each other?"

"Yep. And his mama has already called ours to tell her so. She told her that she was sorry for what happened, and that I was always welcome at her house. But…Mama said I could go see how he was doing, if I didn't stay too long. But then Granddaddy said I didn't have no business going down there, so Mama changed her mind."

"I guess they're in shock over all of this, Kelly. You didn't even tell *me*."

"Look, I wasn't trying to keep it a secret. I just hadn't told you yet, that's all."

"But yet you weren't exactly hiding it. You were walking around the game with him."

"It's a free country."

"It's Stockdale, honey. It's Stockdale."

"Well, Stockdale or not, nobody's going to keep me away from Jimmy. Nobody."

And then, I remembered. "Kelly. I— Our father is going to be in Stockdale again."

"So."

"Kelly, did you hear me? He's in Stockdale. Now's our chance to talk to him."

"Finding him was your dream, Cassie, not mine. He doesn't exist to me. All that matters is Jimmy. That's it, and that's all I want to talk about."

How could I blame her? And as for her new love, I should have known then that a lot more was going to happen with Kelly and Jimmy. But I didn't know. Or at least, I didn't think about it right then.

# Chapter 17

Two weeks later I made it a point to go to Stockdale, and I had two reasons for my stomach to dance. One, Kelly and the situation at home with her new boyfriend Jimmy. That wasn't going to be easy. The second reason: By this time, Mama and the rest of our family probably knew about Will Taylor being back in Stockdale—not to visit, but to live. I also figured they were probably aware that I was the one who'd gone to Atlanta to find him. In short, I knew that if they knew this last detail, I was going to be in trouble for sure.

It didn't take me long to find out that my worst fears were real.

"Hey, I'm home," I yelled when I walked in the front door.

No answer.

I walked to the back of the house, to the bedroom Kelly and I shared. No one there, either.

And then I heard voices at the front door.

"The Honda's outside. She's here." Mama came in the door, carrying a bag of groceries.

"Hey," I said, as lightly as I could. "Need any help?"

"You *are* mighty helpful, aren't you?" Mama looked at me sideways as she put the groceries down on the table. She then headed right back out the door.

Before I could react, Granddaddy came in carrying a twelve-pack of Cokes.

"Hey, Granddaddy. I made it. You need some help?" I tried taking the Cokes from him. He wouldn't budge though. *Hmmmm...*

"There are only a couple of bags left," Mama said when she came back in. The problem was, she wasn't looking at me. And neither she nor Granddaddy acted as if they were happy to see me. That's when I knew I'd have problems. They'd seen my father, or someone had told them he was in Stockdale, and they knew I had played a hand in bringing him there.

"So, where's Kelly?" I said, trying for a change of subject.

"She's at band practice. I have to go pick her up right now."

"I'll go get her."

Mama nodded. "Go now, because I'm already a little late in getting down there."

I walked out the front door, knowing it was going to be a long weekend. Not the four-day kind—the stressful kind.

*If they know…Well, what's the big deal anyway?* What if I *did* go up there and find him and cause Big Mama to drag him out of Atlanta? *What is it to them?*

But it had been two weeks, and they hadn't mentioned it. Maybe they didn't know? No, they knew. For sure, they knew. I could see it in their eyes and hear it in their voices. They were angry about it. They were crying out louder than Anita Baker's "Sweet Love" on my car stereo as I drove to pick up Kelly from school. Well, at least she could fill me in.

Kelly was already standing outside and looking at her watch when I pulled into the parking lot. I could tell from her face that she was happy to see me, and not just because I was picking her up. Maybe she was relieved to have an ally.

"When did you get home?" she said. "I didn't know you were coming."

"I just decided at the last minute. Sorry we're late in getting you. Mama just got back from Jefferson and getting groceries."

I started the car and drove in the opposite direction of our house.

"So what's up?" Kelly asked, putting on her seat belt.

"You tell me, girly-girl. Still seeing your little boyfriend?"

She didn't like me saying "little," but I found it a bit amusing. And besides, she was my younger sister and this boy was younger too.

"Yeah, we're still seeing each other," she said. "But we haven't seen each other much since…since that last game."

"How's he doing?"

"He's fine now. But Mama doesn't want him coming over to our house, and she doesn't want me going to his now." Kelly spoke with a massive frown on her face. For a moment, I thought she was going to cry. She turned her head to the window as I headed in the direction of Jefferson's mall.

"What else did she say?" I knew the answer before I asked the question. I asked it anyway, just in case.

"Nothing."

"Okay."

"Cassie, what am I going to do? I want to see him. I have got to see him." Her voice was barely audible. "You've got to help me. Help us."

There it was—that sentence I'd been dreading, but knew was coming as soon as she opened up the car door and got in. Another decision to make. Another hard decision to make.

I turned the car around and headed back toward our house. I'd subconsciously decided to save the gas. But I guess, somewhere in the back of my mind, I already knew what my decision would be. Racism could not, would not win. I wouldn't let Kelly's boyfriend become another Starsky. And besides, he was already crazy about her. Still crazy about her and wanting to see her, even after he'd been sent to the ER. For me, there wasn't a choice. Even though I feared for her because I thought she was a little young, and dreaded our mother's reaction, I would help Kelly see her Prince Jimmy that weekend.

\*     \*     \*     \*

At seven o'clock, Kelly and I left the house headed for *Over the Top* with Sylvester Stallone. I had a huge crush on Sly. He could do no wrong in my eyes. He was so tough and cute. Anyway, back to Kelly. She had persuaded me to go to the movie, which wasn't hard, and to take Jimmy with us. That was a little bit harder. Near the conclusion of the deal, I thought about what I'd say if we were caught. That is, if someone saw us at the movies together and told Mama. I would be in even more trouble than I was already.

Jimmy's house was close by, albeit in the white neighborhood on the white side of the tracks. Of course. We're still talking about Stockdale. As soon as I tapped the horn twice, the front door of the house opened and a skinny little pale kid with bushy blonde hair walked out smiling and carrying something that looked like a flower under his arm. There was a woman with the same type of hair, surely his mother, standing in the door waving at us.

*Wow.* I had never witnessed such a thing in Stockdale before. I was happy that things were at least starting to change: that whites and blacks were coming together.

I looked at Kelly and Jimmy, who'd gotten in the backseat, and smiled a huge smile. I was proud of them—the first official black and white couple I knew of in Stockdale, Alabama. Maybe The Doctor's dream and mine was finally coming true, slowly but surely.

I drove off, giving a two-horn beep to Jimmy's mother and waved at her. The action had great meaning in our family. We normally reserved the two-horn beep for family members and close friends when driving off to God-knows-where in our cars. And since tomorrow isn't ever promised to any of us, it's actually pretty special. Always has been, always will be. Jimmy's mama had accompanied Jimmy to the door and smiled sweetly at us and waved, so surely she deserved the honor.

That night came and went, but only four people knew we'd been to the movies together—that I'd acted as a nice little chaperone to my younger sister and her white boyfriend. Nobody saw us at Jefferson's movie theater; neither did we see anybody from Stockdale that we knew. Kelly was ecstatic that she'd had a real date with Jimmy. He was pretty ecstatic too. He held her hand all night long. I was just happy to have helped out. At least I was that night.

* * * *

A few months later, back at UAB, the Alphas were having another step show. I was excited about going; I'd met a guy who belonged to the group—Langston, who was named after the famous African-American poet. He was extremely handsome, funny and sophisticated. He could dance. He could step. He had it all going on. What more could a girl ask for? Well, I got more than that. Langston drove a Jaguar, and his parents were both doctors. He was at UAB to become a doctor as well. In short, I thought he was an excellent-looking black man with lots of dating potential, and not some pot-smoking, not-wanting-to-go-to-college-or-better-himself Blake.

I thought Langston had actually noticed me at the last party thrown by the Alphas. He had greeted me with an extremely long embrace, and I intended to find out if he was interested in me or not. I knew that I was interested in dating *him*.

I had a new dorm roommate by this time, and she wasn't as wild as Pam. Definitely more dedicated to her schoolwork. Mia had been raised single-handed by her mother, who was working two or three jobs back in Talladega to keep her at UAB, so Mia took things seriously. She still liked to party, though.

Mia had told everyone that was her name. Nobody believed her though, and assumed "Mia" was short for something else. Each time, she said, "No, it's just Mia." But once, I saw an official letter from UAB on her desk that had her name typed as "Shamianeequa Richards." When I confronted her about it, she said she didn't want anyone to know what her full name was because hers was another case of a black-mother-gone-a-bit-too-far-with-the-name syndrome—which is a very, very common disease among many black mothers. They still haven't found a cure yet.

Mia and I ran into Langston at the party and step show, and we walked around and spoke to different people we knew. We talked. We danced. We watched the step show, and Langston winked at me near the end, and I fell more and more in like with him. He was the lead stepper, the captain of the Alphas, and wore a pair of cream slacks with a matching cream turtleneck. His cool elegance made him stand out.

After the Alphas had finished stepping and everyone gathered around them to congratulate them all, Mia and I found ourselves talking to another Alpha, Cedric. He pulled us over to where the smiling Langston was entertaining a group of at least five women. I should have known then, but I didn't. I didn't know because Langston pulled me away from the group and begin talking to me alone. Just me. All alone with Langston in his nice cream-colored outfit.

We talked some more. We danced some more. He held my hand, got me sodas, and was the ultimate gentleman. He had been to France and Italy, had taken the same anthropology class, and he liked my Esprit outfit. I liked him.

Two hours after the step show, Langston the Alpha and I went back to his apartment. It was a one-bedroom that he had all to himself, near the campus on top of the hill near the iron Vulcan statue. He offered me something to drink and I accepted. Coke, no ice. I still didn't drink. He had a glass of white wine.

We talked of the Alphas, school, his car. More or less small talk. I could tell his mind was elsewhere as he eased closer and closer to me on his black leather sofa. I had in mind a nice conversation and a little making out. Kissing. I sensed that he had a little bit more in mind. I slid over, put my Coke down on his three-legged glass coffee table and asked where the bathroom was.

"Just down the hall on your left, sweetheart. If you want to, you can come back naked." He reclined back on the sofa and put his hands behind his head.

*Okay, he's just kidding. Good. But wait, I don't think he is. Or is he? Is he testing me? Trying to find out what type of girl I am?*

"Haaaa! You are *so* funny," I said, and turned to walk down the hall.

"Yeah, but what if I'm not kidding? What if I were naked when you got back?"

*What is he, nuts? Just play it off.*

"You're crazy, boy! Stop playing around. I'll be right back." I went on down the hall to the bathroom, closed the door, and leaned up against the back of it like women do in movies when they're being chased by someone and just need to catch their breath a minute. I didn't know what to think. He had to be joking. I thought I should just go ahead, do my business, and get back in there.

I walked out of his potpourri-smelling bathroom and back to the living room. He wasn't on the sofa, and he wasn't in the living room.

*Maybe he went to the kitchen.*

Not there, either.

*Surely he—Just go ahead and check it out.*

I walked back down the hall, and this time turned the doorknob to the room opposite the bathroom and went in. The lights were dimmed, and though I couldn't make out all the things I saw on the wall, I could see that he loved art as well. He had copies of Van Gogh, Picasso, and Renoir. And on the stereo to my left, Luther Vandross' voice was pleading.

*No! Yes!* He had dared to put on Luther, and my favorite song, "Superstar."

*Who is this guy? And where is this guy?*

Well, he was lying across his bed watching me quietly. And oh, he was naked as a jaybird.

What was going through my mind at this moment? Surprise. Confusion. Fear. Not fear because I thought he was going to rape me. Somehow, I didn't fear that. But fear because I didn't quite know what to do. I liked him. I liked him a whole lot. I was attracted to him, too.

I walked over and stood close to the bed. Luther was still singing to me. "Look at you," I said, staring at him. "What are you doing? You're butt naked."

"I'm waiting for you," he said calmly, and held out his hand.

"Langston, I—"

He started to sing, and pulled me down onto his bed. He knew this song by heart. He had a wonderful, sexy voice. He had me, too, and he knew both things.

We started kissing, but I tried to speak. "Langston, I haven't...ummm..."

"Are you a virgin, honey?" He was staring into my eyes, waiting for me to answer.

"No, I'm not a virgin. But I haven't..."

"What's wrong?"

"I haven't...had too much experience...."

"It's okay, baby. I'll teach you everything you need to know." He kissed my forehead. "How many relationships have you had, sweetie?"

"Just one," I whispered. "And it was a bad one."

"So you're saying that you've just made love to one guy?"

"Yeah."

"He must have been incredibly stupid to let a girl like you get away. No matter, though. His loss is now my treasure. I'm so glad I found you, Cassie."

"Really? You mean that?" I sputtered. "I mean, we just met. But I really like you."

"Of course I mean it. I've been thinking about you since the last Alpha party. I can't stop thinking about you, Cassie."

"Really?"

"Really. You're exactly my type of girl."

"Yeah, but I'm just a sophomore. You're a senior. Man! You can have any girl on campus."

"I don't want any girl on campus, honey. I want you. Only you. Don't you want me?"

*Shit, Shit, Shit. What to do, what to do?* Normally, I wasn't a cursing gal, but this guy had me in a sticky situation. Yes, I wanted him. Yes, I was crazy about him. Yes, all the girls would be so jealous if he were my boyfriend. Yes, he looked just as good naked as he did in his cream-colored outfit.

He repeated his question. "Don't you want me, Cassie?"

"Yes. Yes, I want you. But not only for one night." I didn't care what Luther was begging for.

"You won't have me only for one night. I promise you."

"Promise?"

"Promise."

He unbuttoned my shirt and took it off slowly and evenly without skipping a beat in the song, and I let myself be engulfed by Langston Hughes Williams III while listening to Luther Vandross on his queen-sized waterbed outfitted in black satin sheets.

# Chapter 18

Langston took me back to the dorm the next morning, *after* he made me scrambled eggs and bacon. I was amazed that he could cook too. This guy really had it going on—and always the gentleman.

In the car, I looked over at him and smiled. He reached over and kissed me on the cheek, and then told me that I was cute.

"I have a lot of studying to do today, but I would love to see you tonight," he said as I was getting out of his Jag. He parked on the side of my dorm, but I hadn't noticed that he hadn't used the drop off/pick up ramp in front. I was distracted by happiness that I was seeing him, and that he wanted to see me again that night.

"Okay," I said. "You want to have dinner?"

"I don't know. I have a lot of things to do, and I don't know how long everything's going to take. Let me get back to you, all right, sweetheart?"

"Okay. No problem. Give me a call." I closed the door, mind working at full speed.

"Aren't you going to give me a kiss?" he said, raising his eyebrows.

I leaned in over and kissed him. He pulled me closer and held the kiss longer. Maybe my mind was working overtime. After the kiss, I gave him a warm smile, and kept hearing his, *"See you later sweetheart,"* long after he drove away.

\* \* \* \*

Of course Mia grilled me on our whole night together. I gave her all the details because I trusted her. She was happy for me and said that Langston really liked me. She could tell. I said that I hoped she was right.

Langston and I saw each other for a couple of more weeks, but it turned out to be only during the week. That weekend, he called to say he was doing something with his parents and couldn't see me again until Tuesday. I was with him on Tuesday nights, late. I saw him again Thursday nights, late. He picked me up at the dorm around 9 p.m. and brought me back around midnight each time. I wanted to talk. I wanted to go to the park. I wanted to go to the movies. He wanted to drink a glass of white wine. He wanted to get naked and lie in his black satin sheets.

After the first week, I started to doubt the "relationship." He kept assuring me that we would do things when he had more time. I believed him. He asked me to just be patient. I was.

The following Saturday, after having lain in his satin sheets the past Thursday night, Mia and I went to the mall with Cedric, the other Alpha. Langston was there, but he wasn't alone. He was walking with his arm around a tall light-skinned girl with long, straight, jet-black hair. She had extremely long legs and was very graceful. She was dressed just as elegantly as he was, in a navy blue skirt, matching sweater, and black heels. She was nothing short of beautiful from what we could see.

Mia and I stopped dead in our tracks and watched them walking ahead of us, stopping from time to time to kiss each other. Cedric wanted to disappear, but he couldn't. One reason was because he was in love with Mia, the second because we both had him jacked up.

I was furious. I was hurt. I was embarrassed because Mia and Cedric knew I had lain on the black satin sheets. "What the hell is going on, Cedric?" I asked. "Wait, I should just go over there and ask Langston."

Cedric did look sad for me. "Look, Cassie, he told me he and Vanessa broke up. I thought it was over. Especially when he said he wanted to meet you."

"Vanessa?" Mia and I said in unison.

"Who is Vanessa, Cedric?" I said, barely stopping the tears that threatened to betray me at any moment.

"Well...she goes to UA. They have, or they *were* together. For like five years. I thought it was over. I guess she took him back. I don't know, Cassie. I swear I don't."

"But you're going to find out for her, aren't you?" Mia snapped.

"Yeah, yeah, of course. Of course. What do you want me to do?" Cedric was wringing his hands. He was apparently in a very bad position. I didn't care. My situation was worse.

"You're going to ask him flat-out what the deal is with Vanessa," Mia replied. "If we ask him, he'll lie. If you ask him, he won't. You're his frat brother."

"Isn't it obvious, though? Look at them." My voice was betraying me already. The tears would come next.

Mia hugged me tight. "Don't you worry about it, Cass. We're gonna find out about him. Her, too."

I had no response for her, because I already knew the answer to the question. It was simple. I had been betrayed. Again.

\*   \*   \*   \*

Back at Cedric's place. There had been a decent time interval since we saw Langston and Vanessa. We left the mall right after seeing them and went for food. They ate at Captain D's. I picked at my fish and ended up leaving with it in a Styrofoam box. I couldn't believe I'd fallen for Langston's lies, and I knew it would only get worse with the confirmation that I was sure to get in the next few minutes, after Cedric made his phone call. Brother to brother, frat to frat, and my heart broken just like that.

"Cedric, can you call him? Can you go ahead and get it over with?" I said.

"Ummm...Yeah, Cassie, I—"

"Just do it, Cedric. Don't worry about me. Just do it, okay?"

I walked to the phone and dialed Langston's number, gave the phone to Cedric, and put the speakerphone on.

"Hello?"

"Hey, Langston. Hey, man. It's Ced."

"What up, frat?"

"Nothin' much, dude. I thought I saw you in the mall today, man. Was that you?"

"Yeah, man. I bought some niiice pants, man. Why didn't you come over and holla at me?"

"Man, you looked like you had your arms full," Cedric said, forcing a laugh.

"Yeah, yeah, yeah. That was Vanessa, man. She came in Friday night."

"Yo', man, I thought you guys was through."

"Man, you know she couldn't stay away from me." Langston laughed and I cringed.

"I had no idea, dog!" Cedric said. "How long ya'll been back hooked up?"

"A while now. She came back to me right after she so-called dumped me. That's been like, what? Six months?"

Cedric let out a long breath. He was clearly disappointed, but not half as disappointed as I was.

"What about Cassie, man? I thought ya'll were pretty tight there."

"Cassie's great, man. I like her a lot. But you know, Vanessa is Vanessa. Vanessa's my girl. Cassie and I are just, ah, friends. You know? But I'm going to keep seeing her."

"So dude, you just playin' with the girl's feelings. You know she likes you, man." Cedric looked at me and raised his hands in the air. I put a hand over my mouth.

"I like Cassie, too. I told you that. And I'm still going to hang out with her. She just can't be my girl, that's all. Vanessa is."

"Does Vanessa know about Cassie?"

"Are you crazy? That's why she broke up with me in the first place."

"You need to tell Cassie the truth, man. That ain't right what you doin', frat."

"Look, you keep your mouth shut, frat. I'll deal with it. I'll take care of it."

"You gone tell her?"

"Yeah, yeah. Why are you so interested for anyway?"

Cedric hesitated, and then rebounded. "'Cause I'm the one who hooked ya'll up. Plus, like I said, you know Cassie a nice girl and all."

"Look, I gotta go, man. I'll holler."

"All right, dude. Take it easy."

"Yeah, bye." Langston sounded as he always did—confident and coaxing. Only Cedric, Mia and I had gotten our blood pressure raised by their conversation. I was sure Langston had already forgotten it.

\* \* \* \*

The following Tuesday night, Langston was downstairs at the dorm, waiting for me. I had just come from French 102. And oh, I'd been ignoring his phone calls since the call with Cedric. When I walked into the lobby, I pretended I hadn't seen him and kept going toward the elevator. Unfortunately, it was on the eighth floor. I had to wait, and that was just enough time for him to catch me.

"Cassie! I need to talk to you."

"Oh. It's you. I'm kind of busy," I lied, looking up at the elevator. *Sixth floor. Darn.*

"I've been calling you since Sunday night. What's up?"

"You tell me."

"No, you tell me."

Now he was really starting to piss me off. "I know about your little games," I said through gritted teeth. "I'm finished with you. Why don't you go home and call someone else?"

"What are you talking about?"

He pulled me away from the elevators toward the back entrance, much to the disappointment of the girls who were taking an awful long time to get their mail out of their mailboxes behind us.

"I'm talking about your girlfriend," I hissed. "The one who goes to UA. Don't make me say her name."

Langston looked plain dumb and I was plain furious.

"Who? Who told you I had a girlfriend? Wait, I know who it was. It was that Chicago ho. It was Tracy, wasn't it? None of it's true. She's mad at me and trying to get even. And that baby? I don't care what she told you, it wasn't mine."

Now it was my turn to stand there and look plain dumb. It was amazing to me how smooth he was, how smooth he was still. How calm. How collected. How gorgeous in his black slacks and matching turtleneck.

*Snap out of it.* I did know a girl named Tracy who lived on my floor. She was from Chicago, and was pregnant last semester. And then she wasn't. I remembered something about her being "talked into" an abortion.

"Let me get this straight. You're denying that you have a girlfriend named Vanessa who goes to UA? Are you denying it?"

All of a sudden, Langston had that old familiar look on his face, a face that would become that "old familiar face" to me only years later. At this time, that face was like a look of surprise, or of puzzlement. Now I clearly understand that face is the look of one who has been caught, but refuses to go down with the ship. The person who is caught, in the moment of confrontation, starts asking himself how much the other person knows. He starts wondering how much he should confess to, admit to. Lie about. And then finally, the one who has been caught must absolutely do something most despicable, even being totally aware of his guilt, if he is to get himself out of the situation: Turn it around. And this is what Langston did.

"You don't trust me, do you? I'm trying to build something with you, but I can't do that if you don't trust me." He was closer now, rubbing my shoulder, staring deeply into my eyes before continuing.

"I really care about you, Cassie, and I'm falling for you. I thought you were falling for me, too. But hey, if you're going to listen to these petty people in the dorm and anyone else who wants to keep us apart, then that's too bad. If you want to ruin a good thing just because you have trust issues, then that's just really too bad. I thought you were a stronger woman than that. I don't know. Maybe it's our age difference. I'll see ya'."

And then he walked out.

As I said, I didn't recognize the game yet. I knew he hadn't answered my question, and I knew that he was probably guilty. But there was something inside me that didn't want to let go, even though I knew I had to. Some part of me wanted to believe that he could be mine, and mine alone.

It's not that I wanted to be dogged out. What girl does? But then again, what is it that keeps us running back for more?

\*     \*     \*     \*

Another Saturday night, another Alpha step show. Langston was as sexy as ever leading the Alphas. I hated to admit it, but he was. At the beginning of the night, he paid an enormous amount of attention to me, but I was still overcome with pain. I didn't talk to him and tried not to look at him…that was, until I saw him later that night with the leggy girl called Vanessa. Then I was overcome with rage and wanted to smash his cane.

"Don't worry about it, Cass," Mia said, pulling me away from their lovey-dovey scene.

"Damn, he lies like the best of them, doesn't he? How dare him!" I tried to force a laugh.

"You've won, Cass. That girl is stupid. She doesn't know half of the stuff that boy does here at UAB. Consider yourself lucky you're out of it now. She's still walking around calling herself his girlfriend."

She was actually right. I felt better. I'd been used, sure, but I was free. I had the knowledge. Vanessa didn't. Yes, I did indeed feel better, all of a sudden lighter. Yes, I had escaped.

Or had I?

\*   \*   \*   \*

One week later, and something just didn't feel right. What was it? The answer was simple: Langston. I hadn't escaped after all.

I waited until Mia came back from class, and told her that we had to go to the free health clinic. She understood and didn't ask too many questions, being the good friend she was. We grabbed our hats and dark sunglasses and left.

*Damnit! I just can't win*, I thought on the way. *Oh no, I shouldn't curse, but I can't help myself right about now. Forgive me Lord.*

We entered the STD side of the clinic. A white nurse behind a desk looked at us condescendingly and asked us to fill out a registration form. Mia pushed the form toward me, and I noticed a slight look of relief in her eyes. I couldn't really blame her, though, could I? Who'd want to be in this embarrassing position? I shouldn't have been there. *We* shouldn't have been there.

One hour later I had seen the doctor, paid my six-dollar student fee, and was waiting for the results. Finally, the doctor called me back into his office and started explaining what would upset my whole day, not to mention my whole week.

"Cassandra, you have contracted a sexually transmitted disease. It is quite minor and treatable however. Here's a prescription that will take care of it. You need to be careful though, Cassandra. You're very young and you have your whole life ahead of you. Don't mess it up by getting yourself sick. Take care of yourself. Use protection, or next time it could be worse. It could be life-threatening. It could be something that medicine can't cure. Do you understand? Remember to always protect yourself."

He was a white doctor, perhaps sixty, with graying hair, sitting back in his leather chair examining my face with his hands clasped together. I saw kindness and genuine concern in his eyes. He saw fear and total humiliation in mine.

"Yes, I understand." I took the prescription and stood up, and proceeded to apologize as if this man were my father. But he wasn't my father, was he? As I shook his hand and left his office, for one odd second I wished he were my father. Or that my father, who was back in Stockdale, oblivious to this, to me, to what or who I was, was like this doctor who had showed more kindness and compassion and concern for me than Will Taylor ever had.

Ten days later, I was entering the campus bookstore and lo and behold, there he was, the STD villain, Langston. It was more than I could stand not to talk to him. I walked up behind him. He was admiring a rack of fraternity tee-shirts, but he saw me before I could speak first.

"Cassie, darling. How are you?" He was as elegant as usual, but all I could see was the huge bottle of antibiotics sitting back in the dorm hidden behind my human sexuality textbook, ironically enough, in case any visitors came to our room.

"Well, let's see, Langston, how are *you*?" I said, keeping my voice light. "Is there anything wrong? Is there anything you should be telling me that you haven't already?" Maybe he'd confess. Of course, I was dead wrong in still thinking that he had at least one shred of decency in him. "I'm asking because I was at the doctor recently," I continued, glancing around to make sure no one was within earshot.

Langston looked at me with concern. "Cassie, are you okay? Are you still sick? I know a lot of my frat brothers have come down with bad colds due to this crazy weather."

If I hadn't been intimate with him and him alone, well, I would have thought he was telling the truth and totally innocent. I looked back at him, dumbfounded, unable to ask the direct question of whether or not he knew he had an STD when he passed it along to me and God knows how many other girls on campus.

When I didn't answer, he said, "Bye, Cassie. You get some rest and take care of yourself, girl. And call me sometime."

With that, he turned and strode toward the bookstore's entrance. He was still within hearing range when I saw him wave at a girl and say, "Well hello, hello, hello. Aren't you looking fine today, Shareeta. When are you going to come over and see me, girl?"

Oh well. It's like my grandmother always said: You can take a devil out of hell, but you can't make him do right for nothing in this world.

# CHAPTER 19

▼

It was about two weeks before Christmas. Long over Langston and my antibiotics, I decided to render a visit to my cousin Whitney, who was from Stockdale but lived in Kentucky now. Whitney was cool, and actually looked like *the* Whitney. Houston, that is. She danced and sang romantic ballads, just like the other Whitney. She was a very passionate person who often fell in love fast and hard. When she loved you, she loved you with her whole heart. But when it was over, it was over. At only twenty-eight, she had dumped no less than a dozen guys since high school, and these were supposedly "serious" relationships.

Most recently, Whitney had been living in Kentucky with her latest boyfriend, a lieutenant in the US Army. His name was Ricky, and he was stationed at Fort Campbell. They had met in Jefferson at a nightclub one weekend, when he'd gone home with a buddy to visit his parents. A month after they met, he asked her to move to Kentucky with him.

I looked up to her because she had escaped Stockdale on numerous occasions, living in Ohio, Texas, Florida, Illinois, and even California once. What marveled me was that she didn't have a college degree, but she didn't work at the chicken plant, either. She had a cosmetologist's license, but rarely seemed to actually do hair; she was too busy moving around.

I wasn't too enthusiastic about going to Kentucky and thought it a rather long way away, but Mia convinced me it could be a great weekend escape. So, one Saturday morning, we were off.

After driving for hours, Mia and I finally reached Tennessee. In hindsight, I realize why the drive seemed so long. I'd been dreading thinking about it, but by the time we got to Nashville, I couldn't help it: My father was finally back home in Stockdale, and I wondered what the climate was there. I knew I'd have to pay him a visit soon, but I didn't want to go.

Yes, after years of dying to see and be with him, I didn't want to anymore. It was too uncomfortable, even to think about. I didn't know what else to say to him. And even if I thought of what I wanted to say, maybe it was just too late. He seemed as though he didn't know what to say to me either. From Kelly, I'd learned that he'd already found a girlfriend and was living with her. I have to admit I was disgusted, hearing that. He didn't seem to be in dating condition, much less shacking-up condition the last time I saw him, yet he was.

But my real question and source of pain was this: How could he have already formed this type of relationship so quickly, when he and I, father and daughter, had none? I didn't want to see Mama just yet either. I was certain she knew everything and thought of me as a traitor.

When we passed through Nashville, I was happy that Mia was asleep so she couldn't see the new worry lines that had sprung up on my face. I almost got another speeding ticket getting out of Nashville, because Nashville hurt my head.

Two hours later, we pulled up to my cousin's place in Kentucky. Whitney lived in a small but nice two-bedroom apartment just five minutes from the base. Her boyfriend, Ricky, whom I'd already met once before in Stockdale, pulled up just after we did. I recognized him by his red Alfa Romeo.

Whitney had apparently told Ricky we were coming. "Hey! You guys made it, huh?" he called to us with a voice still flavored with a Chicago accent, where he was from originally.

He was dressed in his Army fatigues. I could see Mia salivating, and I understood why, since he was about six-feet-two, light-skinned with sandy-red hair and sandy-red freckles to match. Whitney once confided to me that his grandmother had actually been white, but she didn't hold it against him. I guess being in the Army gave him his toned body, and it looked good in fatigues. You know what they say about men in uniform? It's true—excluding men in jailhouse uniforms. But I'll get to that later.

"Hey you!" I said, getting out of the car and going over to his. He was already out.

"Heyyyy there! Did you guys find us okay? I told Whitney I'd come and get you if you got lost." He looked at Mia as she opened her door.

"Oh, this is Mia, my roommate," I said. They shook hands, and their handshake lingered a second longer that it should have. Earlier, Mia's sudden attraction to him was cute. Now, it was worrying me.

Ricky broke the trance and hoisted a bag onto his shoulder. "Come on up."

"You need any help?" Mia said.

He grinned. "Nah. We have to march miles and miles with a lot more stuff than this, sweetie."

Mia and I exchanged looks and smiles. I knew we were both thinking the same thing: *Go Army! Go Whitney!*

My cousin opened the door before Ricky could get his key in good and stood there looking at us. Or should I say, looking *down* on us. She was two inches shy of six feet without heels, and incredibly slim, which made her look even taller. She was wearing a pair of Levi 501s and a white sweater. Her café au lait complexion was the same as mine, but she, like Ricky, had freckles. She hadn't changed her hairstyle since the last time I saw her. It was still a reddish, shoulder-length, curly weave. As I stood there looking back at her and smiling, all I could think of was *Whitney, Whitney, Whitney!* Houston, that is. She smelled like her usual perfume—Anais Anais. I loved that smell on her, even though I couldn't pronounce it, and neither could she.

After a tour of the apartment and a glass of cherry Kool-Aid, she and I went down to my car to get the rest of our bags. We left Mia sitting on Whitney's tan-checkered sofa, talking to her mother on the phone confirming our safe arrival, and Ricky taking a shower. I didn't call Mama; I didn't want her to know I was out of town again in the Honda. Especially since my infamous trip to Atlanta, I didn't want to risk her having crazy ideas of taking the car away from me.

"I'm so glad to see y'all," Whitney said as she pulled one of our bags from the car. "Dang, what did y'all bring, girl? This bag is heavy."

I closed the trunk. "We're glad to see you too, cuz. It was a long way. But you *know* we had to bring something to wear to go out."

"At least you brought Mia. I have to make the trip all by myself when Ricky doesn't go home with me. The worst part is going through Nashville. Did y'all have a lot of traffic coming through there?"

She continued talking, obviously excited that we were there. But she lost me as soon as she said "Nashville." In Nashville, I'd had a memory attack involving Will Taylor. So Nashville was still making my head hurt, and I wanted to forget about it at least for two days.

"Of course we're going out," she was saying. "You know they have a club on the base...."

I didn't know what she'd said before that, but I just said, "Okay, sounds good," and tried to refocus on the conversation.

We were headed back up to the apartment when she turned around with a smile. "Ricky is glad y'all came, too."

"Really? That's nice. Mia and I were saying how lucky you are."

"Don't I know it? Girl, ain't he fine?"

I grinned at her. "I told you when I first met him. Yes, he is," I said, and we went back into the apartment.

Mia was off the phone and Ricky was out of the shower. They were sitting on the sofa talking about UAB when we drifted back in carrying the bags. Apparently, Ricky knew some people who had graduated from our university.

"You need any help, honey?" Ricky asked Whitney, getting up.

"Nah, we got it, don't we, Cass?"

I grinned at Ricky. "Yeah, even though we don't run miles and miles."

Leaving him chuckling, we took the bags into the guest bedroom and put them on the floor.

"Now, let me see what you brought to go out in." Whitney was already trying to figure out which bag was mine, so I opened it and starting pulling out my clothes to show her. I wasn't really keen on going to clubs, but Whitney loved clubbing and dragged me along every chance she got. And her father was a preacher too. If only he knew.

"I got this at Rich's on sale," I said, showing her a black sweater and a matching black and white skirt.

She looked at me with her hands on her hips. "That's pretty. What shoes are you wearing?"

"These black boots I have on," I said, pointing to my feet.

"Cool. I'm going to wear some Levis and a cute little red top that I got at the mall."

"What shoes are you wearing?"

Before I finished the sentence, she dashed out of the room and came back two seconds later carrying a pair of brand-new cowboy boots. In her hand was a matching brown hat.

I hated the whole cowboy look, but I didn't want to hurt her feelings, so I managed a lukewarm, "Wow."

I hadn't seen that she was carrying another package in her hand.

"And this is what I'm wearing underneath." She opened up a wrinkled pink and white Frederick's of Hollywood bag, which contained one pair of tiny white panties and one tiny white bra.

"Okaaay," I said.

"Look at the panties, girl. Notice anything?" Whitney's face held a mischievous grin, and she turned them over and over in her hand.

"No, I don't see anyth—Wait a minute. There's a big hole between the legs, girl. You have to take those back."

She laughed. "Girl, they are made like this. They're crotchless panties!"

"Yuck! How are you going to wear those?" It was out before I could stop myself.

"These are the latest thing, girlfriend. You better get you some."

"No way. You keep those to yourself."

"I know *one* person who's gonna like them!"

We both fell down on the bed laughing. We laughed so hard and long and loud that Ricky and Mia came to the room to see what was going on. Whitney had to hide the panties before he could see them, and sent him out of the room telling him that it was a "girl thing." We filled Mia in on the joke, and we all laughed until we cried, the three of us, lying on the bed, laughing about the invention of crotchless panties.

# Chapter 20

Before going out it's nice to have a good meal, to help absorb all the alcohol you drink. That's what we were about to do. That wasn't the case for me, though. I knew I wouldn't be drinking. I was just hungry.

Whitney was a great cook, because she learned from her mother. She was the oldest of four children. Since her parents each worked two jobs, it was Whitney's duty growing up to cook. She was a specialist in good ole' Southern food—black-eyed peas, cornbread, cabbage, fried chicken. This is what she was cooking as our before-the-club meal on this particular Saturday night.

Mia and I were at the small wooden kitchen table that separated the kitchen from the living room, looking at the magazine pictures of various stars Whitney taped on the fridge. These included Prince—she had a huge crush on him—the actor Michael Douglas—she said he was super-sexy—and Keith Sweat—she loved his slow songs. As I stood there listening to how sexy she thought Michael Douglas' character was in the movie *Fatal Attraction*, I couldn't help but think that sometimes Whitney reminded me more of a teenager than a twenty-eight-year-old woman—except for her crotchless panties, of course. She sure was a lot of fun, though. That was, until she started asking me questions about two people I didn't want to talk about.

"Babe, can you turn that down a bit?" she called to Ricky, who was in the living room across from us watching reruns of *The Incredible Hulk*.

Then, she turned to me and got serious. "So, Cass, I heard about ya' daddy bein' back in Stockdale."

Well, there it was. She just had to bring it up.

"Yeah," I said. "Are you making a salad to go with this food?"

She grabbed a bowl from the overhead cupboard and kept right on talking as if I hadn't said a word. I glanced at Mia for support, but she was looking over at Ricky, who was laughing at something on TV.

"Mama saw him the other day at Wal-Mart," Whitney said. "Said you look just like him. Always have. He was with Mr. King's daughter, Waneisha. Folks say they shacking up, girl."

"Yeah. What kind of salad dressing do you have?" I asked, opening the refrigerator. Now, I loved Whitney to death, I just didn't want to talk about Will Taylor. Also, she talked to her mother a lot, who in turn talked to my grandmother a lot, who in turn talked to my mother a lot. I didn't want whatever I thought or felt or had done to become news all over Stockdale.

"Well, have you talked to Blake lately?"

Another subject I'd just as soon forget. "No, and I don't plan on it, either. What are we having for dessert?"

She walked to the fridge and pointed to an apple cobbler, then closed it back. Deprived of any way to ignore her, I headed back to the table. She kept talking.

"I thought Blake was the love of your life, girl."

"Yeah, so did I. But he's not, as you can see."

"He sure is fine, though! Dang!"

"Yeah, he looks all right."

"When did y'all finally break up?"

"I don't even remember exactly."

"Does he have a car now?"

I returned to my chair and looked at Mia again. She still had her eyes glued on the living room. "A car?" I said. "I don't know. Mia said he rode to Birmingham with Mr. Monroe."

"Who's that?"

"You know, his high-school counselor."

"But he ain't back in school, is he?"

I chuckled. "I seriously doubt it. He probably just bummed a ride off him. Mr. Monroe has people in Birmingham, I think."

Whitney nodded. "So it's over between you and Blake?"

My annoyance had gotten high enough to spoil my appetite. "Didn't you already ask me that? Now, when are we going to eat?"

She shrugged. "Hey, I'm waiting on y'all."

Grateful that the inquisition was finally over, we dug in.

\* \* \* \*

We ended up at Chaos, a nightclub in downtown Clarksville. Seeing the full parking lot, we weren't surprised at the long line to get in. The sign above the door, when we finally could read it, said, "NO ID, NO ENTRY. NO EXCEPTIONS." I checked my bag, and then checked it again to make sure I had mine. I did.

Once inside, the smoky-gray atmosphere made it hard to tell exactly how many people were there. But you knew it was packed due to the sweaty arms and bodies that excused themselves as they brushed past you. To my wonderment and surprise, the club wasn't an all-black club. There were Asians, Puerto Ricans, Mexicans, white people, Native Americans, you name it. No segregation, at least not noticeable.

I swiveled my head around to take in all that lay before me, and smiled. The soldiers with their military crew cuts walking around with their confident swagger, the frat boys drinking beer and laughing at each other's jokes, the "regular" guys nuzzling together to talk about some girl on the dance floor—everyone was doing their own thing and yet the same thing, but everyone was together. There were huge disco lights hanging from the ceiling just over the dance floor, and the tiny, square floor itself was surrounded by a wooden fence-like structure on which people were holding onto, dancing, or leaning over to scope out the crowd. Behind the wooden barrier was a tiny path that circled the club, and small round tables were on its perimeter. On the dance floor, in the center of the room, partygoers were doing the electric slide.

"Do you see anything you like, Cass?" Ricky said, laughing.

I whirled around. "Why do you say that?"

"Because, I see that."

"You see what?" I said back, smiling.

"Okay. I won't harass you just yet. Now, what can I get you ladies to drink? Mia?"

Mia had been quiet since we arrived in Kentucky, but I hadn't really had a chance to find out what was going on with her. I'd never seen her spiff herself up so much, though. She was wearing her white silk blouse, a black leather mini-skirt with a matching cropped black leather jacket, and black high-heeled boots—an outfit I knew she wore only when she wanted to really turn heads. A short, dark-skinned guy standing to her left and wearing a red bandanna on his head just couldn't stop looking at her. He didn't seem to be the only one.

"I'll take a...sex on the beach." Mia said, grinning.

"Sounds like fun." Ricky said, grinning right back.

"Does it? You should try it."

"Maybe I will."

Whitney didn't seem to notice; she was bobbing her head to the music and looking over at the dance floor. I was eying both of them with my eyebrows crinkled. They continued looking at each other as if neither Whitney nor I existed.

"Okay, so that's one...no, two sex on the beaches," Ricky said, and finally turned his gaze away from Mia. "Whitney? Cass?"

"I'll have a Corona, babe," Whitney said.

"Nothing for me, Ricky. Thanks."

"What do you mean *nothing*, Cass?"

"Cass doesn't drink, Ricky. I told you that," Whitney answered before I could.

"Don't worry about it, Ricky, I'll be the designated driver," I said, trying to assure him that I wasn't missing out on anything. I believed in predisposition.

"She won't drink, like always," Mia said, laughing.

"Just like ole' times, huh Cass?" Whitney was already doing the cabbage patch in place.

"Yeah, I guess so. Let's move." I was tired of standing in the same spot. I wanted to see who was out and about.

Ricky nodded, and Whitney said, "Okay. Hon, we're gonna follow you to the bar. Go ahead."

Ricky led the way and we followed. When we got to the bar, Whitney and Ricky started talking to the bartender, someone they knew. It gave me a chance to talk to Mia a little. She was acting like Nikki from *The Young and the Restless*—all mysterious, glamorous and completely crazy.

I pulled her arm to get her away from the bar a little, though I doubt they could have heard us with the thumping speakers just behind the bar and the happy screams coming from the dance floor. The DJ was only inciting the crowd with music. Nobody was fighting, at least not yet.

"Mia, what's up with you?" I said.

"What are you talking about?"

"Don't make me read you. You know what I'm talking about." I glanced over at the bar.

"Nothing. Why are you asking me?"

"Because you're acting mighty strange."

She pasted an innocent look on her face. "Really?"

"Really. Do you have anything to tell me, girl?"

"Yeah. After they get the drinks, let's dance."

She wasn't going to admit anything, but I had a strange feeling her behavior had something to do with Ricky. She was batting her eyes, as Grandmama loves to call it, and laughed at everything he said. Whenever she was close to Whitney, she cast her eyes to the floor.

My detective brain was starting to smoke when she and the rest of the gang pulled me out on the dance floor.

\* \* \* \*

We all danced until Whitney said, "I have to go pee. Who wants to go with me?"

"I do." I looked at Mia. "Are you going?" I somehow knew what she was going to say.

"No. I'm all right."

Whitney gave an apologetic shrug and waved her hand at the music blaring from the speakers. "Even though this is my baby singing, I've got to go. Come on, Cass."

Whitney pulled me by the hand and we hurried off to the girl's bathroom, leaving Ricky and Mia in the middle of the dance floor, smiling and grooving to Prince's "If I Was Your Girlfriend." Freaky indeed.

\* \* \* \*

Ten minutes later, we were almost ready to leave the bathroom. Whitney had thoroughly checked her eyeliner, mascara, lipstick, and weave.

"Nope, not a track showing," she muttered, flipping the left side of her hair back. "That girl know she can do some hair. You should get yours done while you're here."

"It's not for me, Whitney. Besides, I don't really have time on this trip. But let's gooooo. It's getting hot in here."

I was headed for the door when three girls wearing weaves bigger and longer than Whitney's came into the bathroom. They were all dressed alike in the Miami-bright color of yellow—yellow pants that fit like tights, gold blouses that hung off their bare, dark shoulders, and gold platform sandals.

Maybe they were a band, you're wondering? Maybe they would sing? Nope. From snippets of their conversation, we learned that Rave was having a sale and they just couldn't say no. They should have. The triplets were a little too bright for December. They sure hurt Whitney's eyes. I could tell by the way she was rolling them.

"Those girls must be from Hopkinsville," she said. "Umph!" She turned up her nose as we walked past them. "All I know is that they'd better stay away from my man."

Unlike Whitney, I wasn't worried about the girls from Hopkinsville. I was worried about the girl from UAB.

Three hours later, we had danced, laughed and had a pretty good time. One of us had had one Corona too many, but the others were still standing. It was I who drove us home, because I'd stuck to sodas all night as usual. Rickey and Whitney got in the back of my car, and Mia and I were in front. I liked the fact that I was the only one fully sober. I had always liked that feeling. It made me feel proud. Successful. Happy. Happy that just maybe I wasn't going to turn out like Will Taylor and end up living in a ghetto wearing clothes that were twenty years old.

Suddenly, the fun and excitement made an exit right out the front window. My stomach lurched, and I could feel the ice pick-like needle of pain that signaled another headache.

There was only one thing to do. I had to go back to Stockdale. No matter how it saddened me or angered me to think about him—to think about *them*, actually; Blake was still there, too—I had to make a trip home. We would leave Kentucky early in the morning. I had something that needed to be dealt with, pronto.

# Chapter 21

"So did you have a good time, Mia?"

"I sure did. I wasn't even ready to leave yet."

"Sorry about that," I said, "but I need to get back so I can make a trip to Stockdale."

"Why would you want to go to Stockdale when all the fun is up he-ya?" Mia said, laughing and clapping her hands together. She'd been in a great mood the whole time we were out with Whitney and Ricky. She'd danced with Ricky several times, and I saw them talking a lot out on the dance floor. Whitney didn't seem to mind their newfound friendship at all, but it worried me.

"So, what did you think about Whitney's hair?" I said. "She tried to convince me to get mine done before leaving, but I told her I had no time." I reached out and adjusted the volume on the radio.

"Hey! That's my favorite part, girl! Hold up!" As she spoke, Mia readjusted the volume, then belted out Babyface's lyrics.

I looked over at her and grinned. "Yeah, this song is great. I love his whole album."

"And Babyface is sooo fine, girl. He could sing to me any day."

Finally, Mia had given me a way to bring up the subject. "Yeah, he's a cutie. Speaking of cuties...Ricky is a really cute guy, too. I told Whitney. He's so nice, too."

And then I waited.

"Girl that man is fine with a capital 'F'! Tall, light and handsome."

I had to laugh. "You guys got along pretty well."

"Who wouldn't get along with him?" Mia answered, smiling.

"Yeah. He must be well-liked by his platoon too."

What was I saying? I was losing the thread. But then, she spoke again.

"Well, all I know is that he can order me around any day. I might even have to sneak back up here to Kentucky. Hey now!"

I swerved the car back onto the road and turned my head to glare at her. "I knew it! You like Ricky, don't you?"

"What? Why?"

Her answer seemed innocent, but I couldn't be sure. "Admit it. You might as well. I saw you two talking and laughing and dancing at the club."

"So what? I can't talk to the man?"

"The man is *my cousin's* man, Mia."

"Oh, so now you gonna have an attitude because I talked to your cousin's man?" The humor was draining out of her voice and replaced by something else. Something I didn't like.

"Whether or not I have an attitude depends on what you and Ricky talked about. So what *did* you talk about, Mia?"

"UAB. The weather. The Army. And oh, he slipped me his number at work, plus his beeper number before we left."

"What?" I started looking for a place to pull the car over.

"It's not my fault, Cass. Whitney needs to check her man. I can't be responsible if he calls me."

"What? Are you insane? You gave him the number to the dorm, too? What are you doing? What are you thinking? Are you just going to sit there grinning like a chess' cat? It's not funny!"

"If you shut up for a second, I'll answer you," she said, crossing her arms and staring out the window. "Cass, I'm sorry to have to tell you this, but Ricky doesn't love Whitney. He told me. He's bored, Cass. He's even thinking of breaking up with her, and I mean soon."

Another swerve. "Really?" I said as soon as I got the car straight again.

She shrugged. "That's what he said. He said they moved too fast, way too fast. Said he's not ready to make that commitment."

"Mia, he's already made that commitment! They live together. And why is he telling you and not my cousin? Whitney has a right to know first. He is *so wrong* for that."

"Right or wrong, that's what the man told me."

"Okay, fine. But you can't just step in there and steal her boyfriend. She's my cousin. You spent the night at her house. She cooked for you. She took you out to have a good time. Please tell me you aren't going there."

Mia looked like she was going to scream and cry at the same time. "How can you of all people sit there and judge me like that?"

"What? Judge you? I'm not jud—"

"You, of all people."

"What do you mean, *you of all people*?"

"You know what I mean. Just drop it, Cass. Let it go, okay?"

"Tell me!" I yelled. I was so frustrated by then, my eyes were starting to water, and I was regretting my decision to not stop the car before now. I started looking for a likely spot again.

She turned in the seat and her eyes bored into the side of my face. "Okay, here it is. What makes you so special? You're the one who stole your own cousin's boyfriend. Remember a guy named Blake, Cass? Remember him? Remember your cousin Tasha? Remember her? At least Whitney isn't my cousin!"

Mia's eyes were moist and her voice was trembling. I had never felt so much anger toward her, nor ever seen her so angry with me. The left side of my brain felt like someone had taken a pickaxe to it.

I saw a place to pull off, let up off the gas and aimed for it. As soon as I put the car in park, I started to speak, but Mia cut me off.

"Yeah I said it," she continued. "There it is. You asked for it. You ain't in no position to judge me. Whitney is your cousin, and she cooked for me and I did spend the night at her and Ricky's apartment. But I like him. And you know what else? I think he really likes me too. I *will* see him again if I want to."

Fumbling for words, I began, "But you—"

"But you what, Cass? What did you do to Natasha? Wasn't Blake her man before you started going with him?"

"Yeah, but—I mean no! That was totally different. Totally. They weren't even together."

"Sure."

"They were *not* together!" I was shouting now.

"Sure."

"It's true! Tasha liked him but he didn't like her."

"That's what Blake told you, but how can you know for sure?"

"Because, I *know*."

"Look, Cass, whether you want to believe it or not, you stole Natasha's man. Your cousin's. Even if she only liked him, she saw him first."

Mia's words hit me like a bulldozer. "Look, Mia. This is *not* about me. This is about you and Ricky. Not me and Blake. And anyway, you see how that turned out. It's over. Take my advice: Don't fool around with Ricky. This time Whitney's really in love. I can tell. Don't do it."

I looked over at her, fighting back tears of pain, hurt and frustration.

"Cass, I love you, girl. You know that. All I'm saying is please don't act like you've never fallen for someone hard before. I understand about you and Blake. I really do. You should understand about me and Ricky. And how can you be sure Whitney is so in love this time anyway?" She put her hand on my shoulder.

"Because I can. Whitney is one of my favorite cousins. She'll hate me if you go after her man."

Mia jerked her hand off my shoulder. "So you're just worried about yourself? Is that it?"

I sighed, willing my head not to explode before I could get home. "No no *no*! I'm worried about you too. I could give you ten good reasons not to fool around with Ricky. All I'm asking you to do is wait. See what happens with him and Whitney. At least then you can find out if he's for real, and then go from there. And you won't have to worry that your jumping in too soon caused a disaster."

"Did you wait with Blake?" Her voice was icy. And in that instant, I knew that the battle had been lost, at least for now.

"Okay. Have it your way, ma'am." My tone was as cold as hers.

"I will. I'll have it any way I can get it." She closed her eyes, leaned back into the seat and eased her head up against the headrest.

There was no more to say. I started up the car and drove through Nashville with a heart heavier than it was when we came through the first time, on our way to Kentucky. But this time I wasn't thinking about my hippy father all dressed out in his old clothes. No, I was all cloudy inside thinking about another misery: I had taken my best friend and roommate to my favorite cousin's house, and she had fallen head over heels for my cousin's man.

But already, I was planning for the next battle. Should I warn Whitney? Could I? Perhaps talk to Ricky? Try talking Mia out of it again?

An old Chevy blew its horn at me for driving too slow in the fast lane. I got over into the slow lane. A moment later, I figured out what the noise was that had been banging around in my head. It was the noise of conscience. Mia could have been right about me. Maybe I *was* just a hypocrite, maybe even worse than Mia. Maybe I'd already paid for that mistake. Maybe I hadn't.

The revelation was too much. I decided to exit the interstate and get some Advil. Maybe that would stop the jackhammer still working on my brain.

I had just pulled off the highway when I saw the sign above the exit ramp: "Pulaski, Tennessee." What was it that was so familiar about that?

And then, it came to me.
Pulaski, Tennessee. Birthplace of the KKK.
Just great.

# Chapter 22

I was so mentally exhausted when I got back to UAB that it was two weeks—Christmas break—before I actually made it to Stockdale. Mia and I were hardly speaking by then, so I didn't know if anything was going on with her and Ricky. I'd only spoken to Whitney once, just to let her know we'd made it back to UAB, and I was loathe to call her again, fearing bad news.

Now, mine and Mia's roommate status was an ongoing nightmare, calmed only by the fact that we were in classes all day. Whenever she came back to the dorm, I was already asleep with the covers pulled high over my head, or she was. On Thursday, she spent the night at a friend's place, so I didn't see her before leaving that Friday for Stockdale. Which was fine.

When I hit the Stockdale city limits, the weather changed. It was cloudy and raining. Appropriate. I felt gray all over too. When I arrived at the railroad tracks that separated the white part of town from the black part, I was already thinking about turning around. But I couldn't. I had to see Will Taylor. Had to talk to him. I had to see Blake too, and that weighed on me like two tons of old bricks. Even though it was over between us, I had to know if I was indeed the hypocrite Mia had accused me of being. I had a sneaky suspicion that I in fact was.

I got home, but no one was there, just a note on the table that read "Gone to Jefferson" in Mama's timid handwriting.

Jefferson. Not a bad idea. Blake would probably be home. He wasn't in school, and according to Kelly, he didn't have a job lined up anywhere.

First, I had to see my grandparents. I knew they would be happy to see me, and I would definitely be happy to see them. No, I *needed* to see them. Since before I could remember, they were my rocks, my stability in a world that turned upside-down too often.

The moment I entered their house, I was immediately drawn into the sight and smell of turnip greens, cornbread, baked chicken, rice, macaroni and cheese, and deviled eggs. Grandmama could cook. She always could and always did.

Granddaddy was sitting in his old green leather chair on the left side of the living room as usual, and Grandmama was content to sit on the right side of the room in her tattered green-fabric-covered chair, watching the Atlanta news. She always kept a comfy crocheted blanket slung over the top because she was always cold. It covered her now. Granddaddy, the devoted churchgoer and deacon he was, was preparing his Sunday school lesson. They saw me at the same time.

"When did you get in, girl?" Granddaddy asked me. He was dressed as elegantly as ever with his gray slacks, white starched shirt, and brown suspenders and shoes. He topped off his outfit with a Braves cap. I smiled when I noticed it.

"I just got here," I said, raising my voice so his hearing aid could pick up what I said. "I stopped at Mama's first, and then came on over."

"Ya' mama home?" Grandmama asked.

I shook my head. "She's gone to Jefferson to pick up Auntie."

"Umph! That ole gal. She was supposed to come by here and check my pressure."

"She'll probably stop by on her way back," I said, trying to take the pretend scowl off my grandmother's face. *Pretend* because, no matter what my mother did or didn't do, my grandmother adored her.

"All right. You tell her when you see her that I'm awaitin' on her."

"I will. I'll come back by later on tonight."

I turned the corner and started for the door, but stopped when I heard Granddaddy say, "Ya' heard about ya' sister, didn't you? Ya' mama's just sick about it. I'm not afraid to tell you that I am, too. What in the world was that girl thinkin'? I don't know, Lord Jesus."

Grandmama passed me on the way to the kitchen. "Yeah, that sure is a mess she done gone and got herself into. How mercy. Y'all come on and eat now."

I followed her into the kitchen, and Granddaddy came in a minute later.

"Mess?" I said. "Kelly?"

Granddaddy laughed. Whenever he laughed, it was a beautiful thing. But this time, it was a little scary. "That's ya' sister, ain't it, girl?"

But then, he saw the bewilderment that was surely on my face by then. "Ya' mama didn't tell you?" As he spoke, he took a place at the table and started drinking some water.

Grandmama was still standing at the counter, and I pulled up a stool beside her. "Nobody told me anything. What happened?"

"Honey, ya' sister's expectin'."

"What?" I almost yelled.

"Chile, ya' sister gone have a baby."

"Oh noooooooooooooo." I let it out like a long cry that wouldn't be denied. My stomach lurched again, but so much worse than it ever had. I gripped my chest and almost tore at my heart to stop it from beating as fast as it was.

Nobody was laughing or even talking now. Sadness spilled over into the room and engulfed it. Sadness and dire disappointment, feelings of what could have been, or what would have been.

It was my grandmother who spoke finally, treading through the icy stillness of the room.

"Yep. Yes sir ree bob. That girl, that girl."

"Lord have mercy," was all Granddaddy added, picking up his Bible and turning the pages.

"Who...Well...When?" It was so hard to broach this with them. Something like this could totally destabilize a churchgoing, church-raised family like ours.

"You know who," Grandmama said. "That little white boy she been sneaking out to see. I told ya' mama to pray for that girl and stop her from doing it. It's too late now, sister."

"Sneaking out? Kelly?" I just couldn't see it. Not Kelly. Not shy little Kelly.

"Girl, ya' mama didn't tell you nothin'? That fass-tail girl been sneaking out e-v-e-r-y night to see that boy. Now she spectin', five months already."

"Oh my God!" I put my hands over my eyes as though I could block it out. I couldn't.

"Yes, Lordy. Ya' mama's just sick over it and ya' granddaddy can't stop shakin' his head."

And I couldn't either. I drove all the way to Jefferson with the radio on as loud as it would go, trying to blast out the noise that was totally occupying my head. It did no good. My little sister, my sweet and innocent sixteen-year-old sister was pregnant. She was so shy. So nice. So *good*. I knew what had forced her to sneak out. I wasn't surprised about that. She was deeply in love with Jimmy, and Jimmy was white. But her being pregnant? That, I wasn't prepared for.

The headache came back, and I grabbed my temple with one hand. *It's my family's fault! That's it.* And more specifically, my mother's. She was the one who wouldn't let her date Jimmy openly. *If they allowed him to come over and see Kelly like other kids did, none of this would have happened. Kelly wouldn't have been sneaking around and she wouldn't be pregnant now! Dammit.*

Still, I knew I couldn't put the blame on my family or mother alone. I even fancied that I had let Kelly down, too. My incident with Langston, the STD villain, taught me much about the value of protection—not just from creeps, but from getting pregnant as well. I should have shared more of what little knowledge I had with her. Then maybe she wouldn't be in this predicament.

I was still pondering the ifs and what-ifs when I suddenly realized I was pulling up in front of Blake's house. Bad habits die hard. I sat there for a long moment, then reached for the door handle, muttering, "Time to add to my current headache."

## Chapter 23

When I knocked on Blake's door, a child, a little girl of three or four years old, answered and let me in.

"Hey. You're so cute," I said. "Is Blake here?"

"Yes, ma'am, he here. He in the room with my mama."

I looked toward the bedroom and then back at her. "He's in the room...with your mama? Blake is?"

"Yes, ma'am. I'll go git him for you." And then she ran off, screaming for him at the top of her lungs, "Daddy, Daddy! There's a lady here for you."

I ran off screaming too, but in the direction of my car.

*That damn Blake!* I thought as I drove. He never ceased to amaze me, and not in a good way. After all I'd found out on that day, the news of him not only being a loser, but a teenage parent too...well, I guess I wasn't all that surprised. I was more surprised that I hadn't thought of it sooner.

I hit the Stockdale city limits and decided to deepen my woe. Just get it all out of my system in this one messed-up day. Why not? I drove to where my father was living with his girlfriend. Did he know about Kelly being pregnant? Did he know he was about to become a grandfather? Would he even care?

Unfortunately, or maybe fortunately, he wasn't available either. Definitely unfortunately, his girlfriend was. She opened the screen door and bared two gold teeth.

"Hey honey!" she said. "Why don't ya' come on in here? I ain't seen you since you was a little bitty girl."

I tried smiling but it froze on my face. I tried to speak but my tongue froze too.

I'd seen Waneisha only briefly here and there in Stockdale, and usually in the less-savory areas. In addition to her gold teeth, she wore a platinum-blonde wig that made her ebony skin stand out. The rest of her features stood out as well. A broad nose, big, almost-black eyes and large, permanently red lips. She wore dirty jeans that were much too tight on her curvy frame and a low-cut black shirt. From underneath it, I could see the fraying thread of what used to be a white bra.

I finally managed to speak. "Hey, Waneisha. I— It's good to see you too." *Why am I lying to this woman? I can't believe he's with you. I can't believe he's even in Stockdale.* "So, ah…you're here and my dad's not?"

"No, but me and yo' daddy are havin' us a good time together. He really is a nice man."

*Yeah, I'll bet he is. So nice he's just coming back here after all these years.*

"But wait a minute, girl. Hug my neck here."

I started backing out of the screen door and off the porch immediately, almost falling trying to get away. "I'll give you both one when I come back," I called out. "I have to get home now and see if my mama's back."

I'd rather eat a snail than hug her…or maybe not. But I did want to leave, and leave I did.

Having *not* had the two encounters I wanted was probably better for me than I realized. I still couldn't stop thinking about Kelly, and how being pregnant was going to change her life forever. I knew that an abortion was out of the question. When you grow up in a Southern Baptist church, you can forget it. The discussion would never even get that far. Of course, there *are* certain people who will turn their backs on all that a Southern church deems as holy. In our very choir, we had a girl who was reputed to have had so many abortions, she could never have children. And she was only seventeen. At least Kelly wouldn't suffer that particular fate.

\*     \*     \*     \*

There was an unfamiliar car parked in our driveway. An unfamiliar and *expensive* car. The silver BMW 325 looked liked it had just been driven off the lot.

Before I could get out of the Civic, the front door of the house flew open and a tall, thin woman wearing a blue sweater and black denim mini-skirt came running down the stairs toward me. It was Whitney, and she wasn't alone.

"Hey cuz! Surprise! You didn't know I was comin', did you?" As she spoke, she was hugging my neck and laughing. The smell of Anais Anais floated around both of us.

"Hey girl! I am *so* glad to see you. I *needed* to see you." I closed the car door and leaned against my car.

"Yeah, I heard. I was talkin' to ya' mama. I'm shocked, girl."

"Me, too. I haven't had a chance to even talk to Mama about it yet."

Someone was coming down the front steps of the house. Actually, two somebodies. One, I recognized, one I didn't.

"Whitney, who's that?" I whispered to her.

"You've forgotten about Ricky already?" She threw her head back and laughed.

"You know I know Ricky. But who's that?" I pointed in their direction.

"Oh, that's just John. A friend of Ricky's. He's taking him to Atlanta tomorrow to catch his flight home for Christmas."

Before I could ask her another question, they were at the car.

"Hi there, cuz." Ricky took me in his arms. I clumsily hugged him back. I still hadn't forgotten about him flirting with Mia.

He let go of me and introduced me to John. John extended his hand. "It's nice to meet you...Cassie, is it?"

"Hey," I said, taking his hand. "Where are you from?"

"New York."

"New York? Really? Which part?"

"The city. Manhattan."

"Wow. That's so cool." And it was. I'd never met anyone from New York City.

John Fitzgerald was twenty-five years old, a little over six feet tall with a toned, military body like Ricky's. He had what I like to call an Irish tan, which means no tan at all. His intensely blue eyes reminded me of the color of water. They bore long black lashes and thick eyebrows. Even his dark brown hair was pretty, as were his perfect white teeth and thin lips. He was wearing a pair of jeans, a white sweater and a jean jacket. John was like nothing I'd ever seen, and I couldn't take my eyes off him. And I was pleased to note I wasn't the only one doing the staring.

Before long, we were sitting in O'Charley's Restaurant in Jefferson. Whitney was telling us a story, but I can't even remember what it was about, and I doubt that John could either. When Whitney headed off to the ladies room, I think we were both glad. Ricky announced that he needed to go too, and then we were really glad.

"Thanks for wanting to come out tonight." John said, touching my hand.

I looked at him and feigned resisting, but it was only a ruse. There was something about him I found powerfully attractive and sweet at the same time.

"Believe me, I was happy to escape," I said.

"Yeah, I heard about your sister. I'm really sorry. But hey, it's not the end of the world, is it? She's healthy, isn't she? Everything will work out just fine."

"Thanks. I hope you're right." There was something about the way he spoke that soothed me, but soothing or not, I didn't want to talk about Kelly.

"So tell me," I asked, "are you excited about going back home for Christmas? I bet you have a girlfriend who's dying to see you again."

"Whoaaa. You don't waste time, do you?" He gave a sexy laugh.

"Nope. Sure don't," I said, reassured by the fact that he was laughing. He was having a good time and I knew it. "So, what's the answer?"

"The answer is no," he said, still laughing.

It was hard to believe this honey didn't have a honey already. Before I could follow up, he changed the subject. "Would you like to catch a movie with me after this? I was thinking about seeing that new Michael Douglas movie. Everyone says it's good. The one with—"

"Glenn Close. Are you asking me out?"

That nice, sexy laugh again, and then a nod. "I'm leaving early tomorrow, but I'd really like to spend some time with you before I go. Just the two of us."

I don't know what got into me, but suddenly I just felt like singing some Grover Washington Jr.'s "Just the Two of Us."

"You are so funny," John said, laughing.

I returned with a smile, "So are you. So are you."

When Whitney and Ricky returned from the bathrooms, we were still too busy looking and smiling at each other to even care that this had probably been a setup all along.

# Chapter 24

▼

*Fatal Attraction* is now a classic movie, and rightly so, yet I don't recommend it for a first date. But, that was the movie John was intent on seeing.

Glenn Close had just scared the heck out of us for two hours, but John seemed bothered by something more. After we'd gotten back into his car, I found out what it was.

He took a deep breath and looked out down at his hands. "Cassie, I have to tell you something."

I waited.

"Remember when you asked me if I had a girlfriend, and I said no?"

"Yeahhhh."

"The truth is...I...I do have someone." He was looking at me now, but I wasn't looking back.

"I'm sorry I didn't tell you before. I...I didn't tell you because I really liked you. I mean, I really *like* you. Shit. I'm trying to be honest here, and none of this is coming out right. Would you look at me?"

I wouldn't. I didn't know if I was going to cry. I hoped not. But I *was* disappointed. Today's woe was not yet over.

"Okay. You don't have to talk. I'll talk. I've been with this girl since high school. We're still together. Officially. But the truth is, it's been over for me for a long time. I'm going to tell her this weekend."

I spun my head around to face him. "Look, you...I might be from Alabama, but I am *not* that slow. Why are you telling me all this? It doesn't really matter, does it? Go back to your girlfriend in New York, because I can't. I just can't."

I was so exhausted by the day's bad news that I couldn't stop the flow of tears welling in my eyes. I turned back around to face the window, forcing myself not to cry in front of this stranger.

"Cassie, come here. Come here. I liked you from the moment I saw you. I'm going to call it off with her. I should've a long time ago. There's nothing there, nothing. I swear, I'm not lying to you, I'm not. I haven't even seen her in months."

"Months, yeah right. Big deal." I kept staring out the window.

"Cassie, look at me. Please. I'll prove it to you. I'll call her and break it off officially, on three-way if you like. Tonight. I'll make it right."

I didn't want to hear any more, but yet I couldn't stop myself from asking the question. "If it *has* been over…if it's so over, why are you still together? And why are you telling me all this?"

"We've been together since we were sixteen. First love. Our parents are friends, they hang out. We're like a big family. The truth is, I'm sure she feels the same way. She doesn't call unless I call her. We hardly see each other. I think we've been afraid to call it off, that's all. Please, please, *please* trust me. Give me a chance to prove it."

I'd had quite enough for one day. Not turning around to look at him, I said in the most neutral voice I could muster through tears, "Take me back to O'Charley's so I can get my car, please."

\* \* \* \*

Whitney and company were staying at her parents' house, ten minutes away from mine. After telling Mr. Fitzgerald how to get there, I'd cried all the way home. What else could possibly happen to ruin my day?

I didn't have to wait long to find out. When I got back home, there was yet another strange car parked at the end of the driveway, right next to our black mailbox. It was completely dark outside, country dark, and I couldn't make out anyone inside the car. I pulled into the driveway, thinking, *It's probably someone who almost hit the mailbox.* That happened a lot. Our mailbox was close to the road, and almost every weekend, someone who'd had a few too many sideswiped it.

I was counting how many times it had been hit and nearly destroyed when the passenger door of the mystery car opened and out he popped, then moved toward me so quickly, I didn't have time to react. Before I knew it, Blake was standing at my car door.

I didn't know whether to unlock the door and get out, or just sit there looking at him through the glass. Finally, I decided on a compromise, and rolled down the window a little.

"What are you doing here and what do you want?" I barked at him.

"Hey, Babygirl. I heard you was in my 'hood today. I just wanted to come by and holler at ya', you know, wish you a very merry and all that."

"Who told you I was at your house today?"

"Uhh—"

"Don't 'Uhh' me. It was your daughter, right? Your daughter!" I had screamed that, then remembered we had Christmas company. Quieter, I said, "Your daughter, right? She's cute. I bet she looks just like her mama too."

"Girl, I was gone tell you 'bout Kanisha. I just—"

"Who's Kanisha? The mother or the daughter?"

"Actually, both. Her mama named her after herself. I told her it was stupid but she—"

"Look, Blake, I don't want to know your family business. Get out of Stockdale and leave me alone. Go back to Jefferson to *your family*."

"Why you trippin', girl? You know I loves ya'."

He grinned. I could smell beer on his breath, or maybe some two-dollar white Thunderbird wine. I wasn't sure, but he stank of it.

"Look Blake, it's late," I said. "My family's asleep, and I want to go to sleep. So leave. Don't make me blow this horn. It's over between us, and you know it." I started rolling up my window.

"Wait wait wait, girl. Look, I did have a child with Kanisha. Okay? Well, actually two. But it's...you know, finished between us. She just the mama of my kids, that's all."

"You have *two* kids? Oh my God!" *How old are they? Why didn't you tell me before? I can't believe you.* "Just go home!" I yelled at him. "Get out of my yard. This is your last warning."

My cheeks were flushed and I was hot all over. My fists were balled up, and if freed from my seat belt and the car, I could have beaten him with my bare hands. Easily.

"So that's it, huh?" he said. "You don't have time for a brotha now, do ya'? Fuck it! If that's how you gone be, damn." He took his elbow off the windowpane and started toward the car he'd come in. "That's cool, Miss Taylor. Miss UAB, shit. Miss Perfect, hell. You can take yo' shitty attitude and keep it."

I stayed put in my car until he was back inside his. Although I was as mad or perhaps madder than he was, I didn't want a tougher confrontation. I didn't know how many people were in his car, it was pitch black, I was alone, and Blake was drunk and angry that I'd turned him away.

"She don't want no part of me, man," he shouted at the car he'd arrived in, and then someone pushed open the passenger-side door. Blake held onto the car door and tried to get inside the car. Someone reached over and pulled him inside, and I heard a male voice say, "Man, I told you not to be comin' over here messin' with this chick anyway. Shit. Let's go over to Elbow's house. You know 'bout this time they got some nice paper rolled up."

The driver started the car and drove away, but it was five minutes before I had the strength to get out of my car, unlock the front door, sneak into my room and get under the covers.

I thought I'd been successful until I heard Mama's soft voice at the door to my room.

"Who was that outside at this time of night?"

"It was Blake. It was nobody."

"What did he want?"

"Can we talk about it tomorrow? I am just too, too tired, and my head is splitting."

"Umph." She turned around and sailed off in the direction of her own room.

I closed my eyes and tried to sleep, but the image came of my father's laughing girlfriend, Waneisha, standing on his porch asking me for a hug, her gold teeth shining in the dark. Maybe I should have taken the hug.

## Chapter 25

The next morning, I looked at the clock and remembered: It was Christmas Eve. I needed more time to get in the spirit. I needed more days, more explanations. Blake had not one kid, but two. Two. *God help me. Help him. Help us all!* The real sting was that he had a relationship with this Kanisha while we were still together. How dare he. Why did he have to keep hurting me over and over? Why did I let him? He had to be cut off, completely. Completely.

But for now, life had to go on. I blew out a long breath and crawled out of bed.

While I was trying to eat my Frosted Flakes, I also remembered that my sister was pregnant. Though it was a beautiful, sunny day outside, inside my head hurt like a tornado was passing inside it. I wanted answers about many things from many places, and I had to get them, or my head would maybe *literally* explode. With all that was happening, I had the insane thought that something really *would* burst. I put my fingers on my forehead to see.

Mama came in just as I was finishing my self-examination. I turned the cereal box around to face me so I could pretend to be busy.

Too late. "Whitney called a little while ago and asked if you were up yet," she said, getting a pack of bacon out of the fridge.

"Whitney?" I hadn't yet thought about her, or Ricky, or John Fitzgerald. Darn. Something else to think about.

"What'd she want?" I said, annoyed at the way I had answered my mother. "Have they left for the airport yet?"

"She said they were on their way, and she'd call you when they got back."

Her bacon was sizzling and her eggs were soon to follow. "Who was that guy they had with them yesterday?"

"Who, the white guy?" Of course the question was coming sooner or later.

"Yeah, the white guy," Mama said, turning over her bacon strips and mumbling, "I know I don't need this bacon."

"That was John. He's a friend of Ricky's, and that's who they're taking to the airport."

"Oh. I thought Ricky was flying home."

"No, Ricky's spending Christmas here with Whitney."

"Okay. Well, his friend—"

"Whose friend?" My aunt Betty had awakened. Maybe it was because she was a high school principal, or maybe not, but she had a habit of breaking in on other people's conversations.

Mama smiled at her. "I guess you smelled this bacon, didn't you?"

"No, I didn't, Sis. I've been awake for a long time. Who were you all talking about?"

"Whitney," I offered. My mother went on cooking breakfast.

"Oh, that white guy who was with them yesterday?"

"Yeah, him," my mother said.

The bacon was done and Aunt Betty fixed herself a toasted bacon sandwich. She was leaving the kitchen, and I thought I had escaped further questioning, when suddenly she spun around. "Whose car was that parked in front of the mailbox last night?"

Mama and I looked at each other. She said nothing, so I knew it was for me to explain.

"That was Blake."

"Your ex-boyfriend? What in the world was he doing here at that time of night?"

"It doesn't matter. I don't think he'll be coming back."

"I hope not. That boy is trouble and nothing but," Mama said, exchanging glances with Aunt Betty.

I let out a long sigh. I wanted this conversation to be over.

"What?" Mama said.

"Nothing."

"Tell him to stay away from here, especially at that time of night. We already have enough to worry about without having to watch out for him too."

I turned Tony the Tiger's box around to read about my free prize. *Hmmmm...a pack of stickers...*

"I hope you understand, Cassandra," Mama said. "We already have your sister to worry about. Concentrate on school!"

I came back around. *Sorry, Tony.* "Where is she?"

"Where is she? She's down at that boy's house. She's gone. And she can stay down there as far as I'm concerned."

Mama was no longer cooking. She was facing the kitchen sink, tears in her eyes.

Aunt Betty slipped out of the room. Mama started wiping the counter down, her usual method of stress removal: housework.

Neither of us said a word, but I knew I'd get more answers from the horse's mouth. I was going to pay a visit to my sister and her beloved Jimmy.

# Chapter 26

"Is Kelly here?" I asked Jimmy's mother, who answered the door wearing worn-out flannel pajamas. She wasn't quite as friendly as she'd been the last time I saw her, but then again, I guess the stress was getting to her too.

"Yeah, she here. You by ya'self?" She peeped over my shoulder to make sure I was indeed alone.

"Yeah."

"Okay. Come on in. She and Jimmy in the back."

I followed her down a narrow hallway lined with brown carpet that was as tattered as her pajamas. She stopped in front of the last door on the right and knocked softly.

"Jimmy. Kelly. Cassie here." Then she turned around and left me standing at the door.

Kelly opened the door looking half-asleep, which surprised me. She didn't say anything, so I spoke first.

"What's up?"

"Just trying to get some rest, that's all."

I couldn't bring myself to look below her face. I didn't want to see her stomach. I didn't want to face the fact that my sixteen-year-old sister was pregnant. But I forced myself.

"You sure aren't showing much."

"Yeah, I know."

"When are you coming back home?"

"She ain't coming back 'till we can see each other without sneaking around."

Jimmy appeared behind her, looked at me with his small, pale chest drawn up and his arms folded across it.

What could I say? I said the only things I could. I told them I'd talk to Mama, that she would then talk to the rest of our family.... They'd all see the light.... Everything would work out in the end... etc. etc. In short, all the words of encouragement I could muster.

The sad thing was, I wasn't sure at all about anything I told them. The even sadder part? I don't think they believed it either.

*   *   *   *

From there, I drove to Jefferson. I needed to clear my head, think things over, and get out of Stockdale for a minute. I turned on the radio and commanded myself to sing along with George Michael, who was steadily telling me that I needed to have faith! Problem was, I was losing all of mine. There was a terrible storm brewing, within the very hearts of my mother and family, and sooner or later it was going to blow up directly in my face. Why? Because *I* had helped Kelly to see Jimmy. *I* had supported their relationship. Because *I* was too liberal a thinker. And let's not forget that I'd brought my father into town. They still hadn't forgotten that, or forgiven me for it.

*Humph! Mad at me...figures... And I'm not even the one pregnant.*

After going through the drive-through window of Taco Bell, I headed back to Stockdale. I didn't want to take any chance of running into Blake. Taco Bell had been one of our favorite haunts. It would be just my luck to see him.

With that thought in mind, I risked getting another speeding ticket getting out of there and back home.

When I did get home, I walked into the house to the sound of a ringing phone. I put my Taco Bell bag on the table and reached for it.

"Hey, girl, this Whitney."

"Oh, hey. What's up?"

"Nothing— Stop, Ricky! We just got back from the airport. This boy! Stop bitin' me!"

I glanced at the Taco Bell bag. "Whitney, call me back, I—"

"No, no no! I have a message for you and I promised. Hold on."

I could hear her telling Ricky to shut up.

"I'm back. Listen, girl. Someone is in love with you, girlfriend."

I wondered how she found out about Blake coming over last night. Then again, this was Stockdale. But I had to say something. So I said, "Who?"

"John, girl! Who else?"

She didn't say Blake's name. Maybe I'd misheard. "Who?"

"Have you forgotten about John Fitzgerald already? If you have, I'm surprised."

"No, I haven't forgotten about him. Why?"

"Well, he wanted me to tell you bye—"

"Bye? Okay. Uh, huh." I was disappointed. That was the message? So I was right about him anyway.

"…and that he is going to call you when he gets to New York."

"What?" My ears pricked up like my old German shepherd, Tinsel. "Wait. I didn't give him my number. He doesn't have my number."

"Yes, he does. I gave it to him."

Dead calm on both ends, and then she said, "You mad?"

"Nah. Thanks."

"Ha Haaaaaa! I knew it. Cassie, Cassie, Cassie. Give that man a chance. He's crazy 'bout you, girl."

"Well, he probably won't call anyway." I reached over and tried to grab my Taco Bell bag. It was just out of reach.

"Why you so negative? I am sure he gone call you. I am *sure*."

"Okay, Whitney. We'll see. I'll keep you posted. But right now, I have to tackle this bean burrito. It's already cold."

"You and your bean burritos, chile. Well, call me after he calls you. I'll be home. Bye."

I hung up and grabbed my bag, halfway opened it up, then threw it in the trash. Thinking about John Fitzgerald made my stomach shiver. Taco Bell or not, there was no way I could eat that cold burrito now.

* * * *

I crept around the house all day, keeping to my room as much as I could. I wanted to avoid any type of serious conversation with Mama. It seemed she was doing the same, though. I hadn't told her yet that I'd seen Kelly. There was never going to be a good time to bring that subject up. I knew I had to find a way, though. Sooner or later, Christmas or not.

I couldn't believe it was Christmas. This would be the first year that we weren't all together. We'd never been apart, except for my father of course. He'd always been missing. But Kelly wouldn't be here.

Something had to be done, but what? I was contemplating this very thought when Mama poked her head in my room. "You've been down to Jimmy's?"

Damn Stockdale and its news sources. "Yeah. Who told you?"

"Mr. Culpepper came by taking up donations for the church, and he said he saw the Honda at his apartment."

I liked Mr. Culpepper. He was a nice old man. Funny. But he told everything he could, whenever he could.

"Was Kelly down there?" Mama asked.

"Yeah, of course she was down there. She has nowhere else to go."

I immediately regretted taking that tone of voice with my mother. I didn't talk to her that way. But everything was getting to me, and I wasn't myself.

"Cassie, nobody told her she had to go down there."

I was on the verge of tears, and if they came, I'd let them. "Well, what happened, then? Nobody said anything to me. You didn't even tell me about her."

She sighed. "We had a big fight, and Kelly…I told her that even though she was pregnant, that didn't give her an excuse to keep seeing Jimmy. She got mad and said she was moving out, and left."

"You didn't try to stop her? Or at least think about allowing her to see Jimmy?"

"Well…she's only sixteen, Cassie. She—"

"She's pregnant and in love, Mama. Can't you people see that? Can't you accept that? Accept Jimmy? That's all they want. This is just like what happened to Heather! And look where *she* is."

I had balled up my fists and was ready to strike the walls. The tears were coming fast and furious now, and I didn't care.

"This has nothing to do with your friend," Mama said, her voice almost failing her. "You shouldn't bring that up."

"Yes it *does* have something to do with her. She wanted to be with Max and her racist parents wouldn't let her, so she drove herself off a bridge! And she was pregnant too!"

"Cassie, this is Stockdale. Life is…people are different here. I could very well lose my job over Kelly and this boy's relationship. It was hard enough to get a job teaching here. You know that. Can you understand what I'm trying to say? This is a town of good ole' boys, and you know that."

"Why do we have to care about what other people think?"

"That's the way it is. That's just the way it is. I don't like it and I never have, but that's how it is."

"It doesn't have to be. I'm not going to live with this crap forever." I collapsed on the floor beside my bed and let the sobs come. Poor Kelly. Poor Jimmy. Poor Heather.

Mama left me there to wallow in my sorrow, which was fine by me. I preferred it that way.

\*     \*     \*     \*

I don't know how much time had passed, but I'd long stopped crying and gone to sleep, only to wake up two or three times, when I finally decided to get up off the floor for good.

It was night by then, and almost time to go back to bed. When I looked at the clock, I realized I'd been lying on the floor for almost four hours, wallowing in self-pity and pity for others.

I'd just gotten up and sat down on the bed when the private line in my room, the phone I had shared with Kelly, started ringing. I was sure it was her calling. Perhaps this would give me a chance to convince her to come back home.

"Hello? Kelly?"

"Noooo…this is John."

I knew perfectly well which John, but I said "John who?" anyway.

He laughed. He laughed again, and I felt better already. He had a great laugh.

But then I remembered: He also had a great girlfriend. I forced a more serious tone. "What's up?"

He stopped laughing. "Cassie, I want to explain some things—"

"I think you've already explained, John. By the way, how's she doing?"

"She's doing just great…."

I was just about to hang up the phone on him. He kept talking though.

"In fact, she said she's doing better than she's been doing in a long time. Cassie, it's over. We broke up today. It's finished." And then he waited.

"What? What are you talking about?"

"Remember I told you that I thought she felt the same way? That she wanted to break up too? Well she did. I was right."

I'd heard him, but I had trouble digesting what he was telling me. "What are you talking about?"

"Cassie, When I arrived at JFK, she wasn't even there to meet me. I got home and she'd left a message on the phone asking me to call her. It turns out that she's in California for Christmas."

"Oh. Too bad."

"No, it's not. She's in California because she went home with a guy she met at work. It's over, Cassie. She's in love with someone else and just didn't have the guts to tell me before."

"Are you kidding me?"

"No, I'm not kidding you. Shall I put my mother on the phone so she can confirm it for you?"

As ridiculous as it sounded, I decided to call his bluff. A moment later, I heard him call out, "Mom!"

"No, no no! Don't you do that," I yelled. "I can't talk to your mother!"

"If you don't talk to her now, you can ask her in person. She'll confirm it. Whatever it takes."

I couldn't speak. I could barely think.

"Cassie? Are you there?"

"Ah. Yeah."

"I want to tell you something. I'm crazy about you. And I want to see you again. Soon."

"I...I...ya..."

"Just say you'll think about it."

"I—I will."

"Here, take my number here in New York. Call me collect."

"That's not necessary. I—"

"Please Cassie, I insist. Any time of day or night."

"Okay." I took the number down.

"Merry Christmas, Cassie. Call me soon."

"Okay... Okay, bye." And I hung up the phone before he could say anything else.

I quickly dialed a number. *Come on, come on, come on!*

"Hello?" Groggy voice on the other end of the line.

"Whitney? It's me. I just talked to John."

"Told you he'd call."

"He...He said he's crazy about me. It's over with him and his girlfriend!"

"I told you! Why didn't you believe me? Ricky and me both knew that boy was crazy about you. All right Cassie!"

"Yeah, we'll see."

"Girl, you always thinking about the worst. Why you gone spoil it?"

"'Cause Whitney, trouble seems to be following me around lately."

"Not this time. But call me tomorrow though."

"Will do one-two. Bye." It was corny, the "one-two" thing, but I was feeling better. I was feeling special. I was feeling lighter. I was feeling like dialing another number.

So I did.

After four rings, I was ready to hang up. And then someone answered. Another groggy voice on the line.

"Hello?"

Female. *It's his mom! Oh, no! Should I ask for him, hang up, what?*

And then I heard a click.

"Hello?"

Male voice. Alert. *It has to be John.*

I finally made up my mind to say something.

"Hello?"

Luckily, that was all it took.

"Mom, it's for me, thanks."

"Okay, son." *Click.*

"Cassie! I can't believe you're calling!"

"Is it too late? I'm so sorry. Did I wake up your mom? Please tell her I'm sorry if I—"

"No, no, don't worry about any of that. I'm so glad you called."

"Why?"

"Because I was afraid."

"Afraid of what?"

"I was afraid I said too much when I called you and that I'd scared you off for good."

"Nah. Not yet."

He laughed, and so did I.

"I miss you," he said. "I didn't get to spend nearly enough time with you."

"Yeah, I know." I was twirling the phone cord around my fingers. Yes, he had a sexy voice. He sounded sincere. But there was still the ex-girlfriend. Oh, and whether he was telling the whole truth.

"Cassie, are you there?"

I don't know how long I'd been in my daze, but I suddenly came back. "Yeah, I'm here. When do you get back from New York?"

"I can come back tonight if you want me to."

"Yeah, right," I said, laughing.

"I'm serious. You just say the word."

"For real, when are you coming back?"

"Well…when I bought my ticket, I'd planned to stay until after New Year's. But now…I've decided to cut my trip short."

"Are you sure?"

"I'll be back the day after tomorrow. Wanna pick me up at Hartsfield?"

# Chapter 27

That's how my relationship with John P. Fitzgerald began.

I ended up going back to UAB and trying to concentrate on school, and ended up concentrating on one thing only: John. I didn't have time to worry about Kelly anymore. Mama seemed to accept her living with Jimmy, or pretended to accept it to keep the Stockdale gossip down. But people close to the family knew what the real deal was.

Meanwhile, I was busy burning up my tires driving back and forth to Kentucky to see my new and steady boyfriend from New York. When I wasn't driving there, he was driving to UAB. By the time spring rolled around, we were more than madly in love. We were joined at the hip.

And then, something happened. We were in Birmingham when he told me. He'd met me there for the weekend, and we'd just come back from dinner at Red Lobster. He'd been quiet during the whole meal, unlike himself.

"Cassie, I have to talk to you," he said, sitting down on the sofa and pulling me down with him.

I turned off the TV that I'd just turned on and looked at him, my eyebrows coming together.

"Cassie, I've received my orders."

"Orders?"

"Yeah. It means that I have to change bases."

I started to stand but he pulled me back down again. "Listen, Cassie. I'm being transferred from Fort Campbell."

Alarm. He was hesitating. More alarm. Maybe it would be Washington. Maine? Iowa?

*Iowa? God, no!* I cleared my throat and said, "Where to?"

"South Korea."

"South Korea?" He couldn't keep me from standing up this time.

"Honey, calm down."

"Calm down? You just told me you're going to South Korea! How can I calm down, John?"

"Because—"

"Because what? How long do you have to go for?"

"A one-year tour."

"One whole year? But *I* have to calm down?"

"We'll work it out, I promise. I promise. It doesn't change anything between us."

"Yeah, not now, but…" How could this be happening? I had just spent the best four months with this guy, and now he was leaving for Asia!

"Everything will be just fine. Trust me." He stood up and held me. I let him. But I didn't believe a word of what he was saying, just let the tears roll off my cheeks and onto his shirt.

\*    \*    \*    \*

After John returned to Fort Campbell at the end of the weekend, I immediately took to my bed. Mia and I were back on speaking terms, forgiving each other for our past argument about Whitney's man Ricky. She was trying hard to console me about John's leaving, but it wasn't working. All I wanted to do was stay in bed with the curtains closed. I was too heartbroken at the thought of him going away for one whole year. I'd seen girls at the dorm in long-distance relationships, and they never worked out. And their guys weren't even in Asia. Some of them were just one state over. I didn't see any other alternative. I hated to even think it, but I'd have to break up with him before he left. It was the only way I could avoid a whole lot of heartache later. The problem was, that was the last thing I wanted to do. And I doubted I even could.

While I was lying there in all my misery, he called me.

"Hello, you. I really need to see you. Can you come up? I'd come there, but I have to work."

"Today's Wednesday, John. I have classes tomorrow." I hadn't been to class all week. He didn't need to know that though.

"I know, sweetie, but this is soooo important. Can you make an exception this once? For me?"

I propped up on one elbow. "What's wrong? Are you…Are you leaving sooner than you thought?"

"No. nothing like that. I just need to see you and talk to you. In person."

"I see…."

I heard voices behind him, then he said, "Listen honey, I have to go. Think about it and call me back later tonight. I love you. Bye."

He hung up before I could get another word in.

Of course I was stressed. I was always stressed. I think I've been stressed my whole life. But at that moment, I was especially stressed. What on earth could he possibly have to tell me in Fort Campbell, Kentucky that he couldn't tell me on the phone? And he had never, ever asked me to miss classes before, even when I'd volunteered.

*Maybe he's going to break up with me!*

I heard Mia in the bathroom, brushing her teeth. "Mia?" I yelled.

"What?" came her gurgled response.

"You need anything? Groceries or whatnot?"

She came out of the bathroom. "No. I'm okay. Why?"

"Because I'm about to head to Fort Campbell. I have to see John."

He wasn't expecting me until at least tomorrow, but I saw no reason to wait.

\* \* \* \*

I left UAB as soon as I had enough gear ready for a long weekend. It ended up being only a small overnight bag, a novel, and the last set of snapshots we'd taken together. Mia, as befuddled as I about why John asked me to meet him, hadn't wanted me to go. On the other hand, she shared my curiosity. She made me promise to call her as soon as I found out.

When I hit I-24, I felt better, and worse. Better because I was almost there. Worse because my mind started drifting off again and landed on my father. And like too many times before, I found myself reanalyzing the situation. *How could he have lost himself in Atlanta for all those years, without contacting us, without us even knowing where he was? Did we not count? Do we count now?*

It was a riddle I feared I would never solve, no matter how many conversations I ever managed to have with him.

After a while, I put it out of my mind and just tried to concentrate on my driving and my gas tank. Especially the gas tank, which was teetering quickly toward empty. I was a student, and barely had enough money to get to Fort Campbell. All my credit cards were maxed out, and Mama wasn't giving me any more money. In fact, we were barely speaking. She was mad at me for siding with Kelly, and I was mad at her for siding against Kelly. I wasn't even sure they knew about John and me. No, that wasn't true. Whitney couldn't hold water, much less news. She eventually leaked everything she knew, whether it was supposed to be a secret or not. And my relationship with John, under the current stress of my family, was somewhat just that: secretive.

Once I hit the Clarksville exit, I knew I was home free; I still had some gas left. Hondas are great for that. After being waved through the gate by a bored-looking MP, I pulled up in front of John's barracks.

The only problem was, he wasn't there.

After fifteen minutes of waiting for him in my car, all kinds of thoughts hit me. What if he had to go into the field unexpectedly? What if he decided to go to UAB instead of waiting for me? What if I didn't get to see him at all? How would I get back home? Would Mia be able to scrounge up some money and wire it here? Was there even a Western Union here?

Then God answered my prayers. I saw his car pulling into the parking space right next to mine, let out a long sigh, and opened my car door.

"I am *so* glad to see you," I said. "I was worried I'd have to sleep out here."

That's as far as I got before he grabbed me and hugged me tight.

He was still in his BDUs, and he smelled like Army.

"Cassie, thank God you're here and that you made it okay," he said. "*I* was the one worried."

"What do you mean, worried? You didn't even know I was coming." I stood back to look at him. "Wait a minute. Did Mia—"

Before I could finish, he grabbed me again and kissed me. I didn't resist, and clasped my hands around his neck, tightening my embrace. Some guys walking by started making catcalls, but we ignored them. Nothing was more important than this moment. Well, except for the next few moments.

"Cassie, don't be mad," he said when he pulled away. "I got out of duty and was going to come to UAB. After I told her my plans, Mia told me you were on your way."

"Okaaay."

"Let me run upstairs, grab a quick shower and change first. I promise I'll be back down in five minutes. Will you wait for me, honey?"

He was so cute. So nice. So sweet. Of course I would wait for him.

I didn't have to wait long. I'd had just enough time to touch up my Clinique when he reappeared, carrying a sports bag, and leaned in the car window that I'd rolled down for him. He smelled like soap and cologne now. Calvin Klein. Obsession. I loved that scent. I loved him.

"Where are we going?" I asked.

He winked at me. "Just follow me, sweetheart. I promise you won't be disappointed."

He pulled off in his silver BMW and I followed in my little blue Honda, and felt my stress begin to leave me. I was so glad I was going to be spending some time with John. So glad indeed.

We headed back in the direction of the interstate and onto Wilma Rudolph Boulevard. John pulled into a Holiday Inn parking lot, jumped out of his car and came over to mine.

I was already smiling and opened my car door.

"Just hand me your bag if you want, honey," he said. "I'm going to get a room."

"All right. But then what are we doing?"

"Dinner? Huh? Would you like to eat, Miss Taylor?"

The truth was, I hadn't eaten very well since the last time I'd seen him. Mia tried to bribe me with all kinds of Taco Bell burritos and the like. It hadn't worked. But now, I had an appetite all of a sudden. "Dinner?" I said. "Oh, yeah!"

"Good," he replied. "I'm going to check us in and I'll be right back. You want to just ride in my car and leave yours here?"

I grinned. "Oh, so you don't want to take the Honda?"

"No, we can take the Honda," he said, chuckling. "I've got no problem with the Honda."

*       *       *       *

We had dinner at our favorite place, Red Lobster, conveniently tucked away in a back corner of the restaurant, gazing into each other's eyes and wondering what the other one was thinking.

"Cassie."

"Yessssss…?"

"Cassie…I asked you to come up because I wanted to talk to you about our relationship."

*Uh, oh. Here it comes. He's going to do what I couldn't do: break up with me.*

"Cassie? You there?"

"Uh, huh," I managed, convinced this was going to be the end.

"Cassie, I think you know how I feel about you. I mean, I'm crazy about you. I have been since the first time we met. I—"

"You what? What, John?" I just wanted him to get it over with.

"I love you and I want to be with you. I love you and I want to marry you. Please say you'll accept this...what I picked out for you. But if you don't like it, we can—"

"Be quiet! What is it? Where is it?" I saw him struggling to pull something out of his jacket pocket. When I saw it was a small, velvety-blue box, I helped him.

He opened the box. There, inside, was a ring with a small round diamond staring back at me. I was speechless.

"Cassie. I'm asking you to marry me," he said. "If you don't like it, they said we can pick out another one. We just have to—"

I leaned over and stopped his mouth with mine. That was my answer: No, I didn't want to pick out another one. I was nineteen years old, and I'd just become engaged.

But wait a minute. I'd just become engaged to a guy who was going to Asia for one whole year.

He saw the look on my face. The questions. The anxiety, the fear, the doubt.

"Ah...that's the second thing that I wanted to ask you."

"What?" I whispered, looking at the small diamond still sparkling in the box.

"You know I have to leave soon, but...I wanted to ask you if you would come with me."

I looked up immediately "Come with you where?"

"You know."

I actually scratched my head. He couldn't mean what I thought he did.

"Cassie, I'm asking you to come with me to Korea."

"But I—"

The waitress came and plopped down our Admiral's Feasts, but those clam strips I wanted so much weren't so important anymore.

As soon as she left, John said, "I know it sounds ludicrous, I do. But it's possible, Cassie. My buddy Steve—"

"Wait a minute. You're serious?"

"Of course I'm serious. Listen. Hear me out."

I leaned back in the booth, my ears wide open.

"My buddy Steve used to be in the company, and he got stationed over there. Six months later, after he'd been there for a while, his fiancée went over to be with him. They've been living there for months now. It can be done."

So he *was* serious. Totally.

"But you're asking me to quit school," I said.

"Not quit. Just postpone it a bit."

"Postpone school?"

"School will always be there, Cassie. I promise. I want us to be together."

"I want us to be together too," I whispered. "I don't want you to leave." I looked down at my plate, knew it was futile, and pushed it away.

"I don't want to leave either, baby. But that's what Uncle Sam wants and I have to oblige."

"I know."

"If I had a choice, I wouldn't go. Unfortunately, I don't."

"I know."

"Come with me."

"I…"

"Come with me, Cassie."

Our waitress came back over. "Is everything all right with ya'lls food?" she said, and rubbed her palms against her amazingly white apron.

John looked up at her and said in his northern accent, "Yes, it's fine. But can we have some to-go boxes?"

Her face signaled that she noticed his accent, but she didn't comment on it.

"Ya'll *sure* the food's okay?"

"Yeah, it's great," I said. "But we have to go. We've run out of time, that's all."

She walked off, shrugging her shoulders.

I looked back at John. He was staring at me. "So? What do you say, Cassie?"

I gave him a small smile. "I say, let's get the check."

✱   ✱   ✱   ✱

We drove back to the Holiday Inn, went immediately into our room, and plunked down on the bed. For a minute or two, we didn't speak, but just looked at each other. John took the ring out of the box and put it on my finger. I couldn't stop looking at it. I couldn't stop smiling either.

"So," he said, holding my hand and looking at the diamond on my finger.

"So," I said, looking at it too.

"Do you like your ring?"

"I love my ring. I love you, too."

"I can't believe we're engaged!"

"Me either!" I said, fighting the urge to shout it.

"I love you too, baby," he said, caressing my neck. "I really *really* do. I don't want to be away from you."

And then, I said what had to be said. "I love you so much. Don't go."

"I have to. You know that. Come with me."

"I want to, but…Korea? Let me think about it."

"Is it school?"

"Yes. And that's the only reason. I'm afraid that if I stop I won't get to go back. Getting a degree is very important for me. I don't want to work at the chicken plant."

He laughed; I had expressed that concern to him before. "I know. But…if you stop for now, I promise you'll get to go back. I need you."

"Oh, I need you too. You gotta believe me."

"I do," he said, took me into his arms and kissed me.

I'd wanted to make love to him from the first moment I saw him, whether I'd realized it or not. But given the reputation of Army guys, I'd tried to be careful. I'd taken things as slowly as I could. We'd kissed and done some heavy petting, but tonight, things were going to the next level. No, that's not enough to describe it. Our passion was now finally exploding.

He pushed me down on the bed and began undressing me. All I could think about was that he was going to be leaving me, going off to Korea for a whole year. How would I talk to him? Could I even dare think of quitting school to follow him?

In a rush of lust and want and need and love, I pushed him over, got on top of him, and gave him the deepest kisses my mouth could give.

And then, I stopped.

"What's wrong, Cass?" John said, searching my face.

"Do you have protection?"

His face broke into a smile. "Of course."

"I hope you don't mind, but—"

"No, you're right. We'll wait until later for our little Cassies."

That was part of my question, sure. I didn't need to tell him about Blake or Langston or the free health clinic experience. Besides, I was totally healthy. And I trusted John more than I'd ever trusted the other two. I was simply living by my new motto: "No Glove, No Love!"

# Chapter 28

After a long weekend of lovemaking, restaurants and movie-going, I forced myself to drive back to UAB. It was so hard to leave my new fiancé. I cried. He cried. The whole weekend had been an emotional rollercoaster. Happy, because we were now engaged. Sad, because he had to leave for Korea. Sad because I didn't know if I could leave with him.

But I wanted to.

As soon as he'd asked me, my heart had already said yes. The problem was my head. Getting a college degree had been drummed into me from the time I was a little girl. My grandparents told me that I was at a disadvantage in the world. That I was a woman. That I was a black woman. That I would have to work ten times harder than others. That, in short, I needed and must get a college education. And besides, I wanted one.

But I loved John, and I was an adventurer. Going with him to Korea would be a chance for me to see more of the world. Asia! What a place to start! I'd barely been out of Alabama. Sure, I'd been to Georgia, Florida, Louisiana, mostly all of the southern states, and even once to Washington DC to visit Aunt Betty. But Asia? That was one place I hadn't yet dreamt of. And seeing it with John? Just being with him? It was so tempting. I honestly didn't know what I was going to do.

When I finally made it back to UAB, I had a headache from thinking about it so much. I got to my room to find Mia sleeping over her human sexuality textbook.

"*My* teacher was great, but *your* sex class must be really boring!" I called out, slamming the door behind me.

She woke up and forgot where she was for a second. "Girl, you scared me," she said, pushing herself up against the headboard.

"That class must not be interesting," I said, laughing. "You're sleeping."

"It's interesting all right, but Professor Adams is a robot. We've gotta read six chapters for tomorrow."

"Dang." I put my bag down and looked through my mail.

"Speaking of sex class. Girrrrrl. Did you do it? Did you?" She got off the bed and came over to me, her arms folded across her chest.

"I can't tell you. But I can tell you this!" I flashed my hand in front of her.

"Oh my God! Cassie! Is that what—? Oh my God! You're engaged?" With every word, she jumped up and down.

"Yes! He proposed! I'm getting married!" I said, jumping up and down with her.

"Girl, congratulations! When? When do I need my bridesmaid's dress?"

I stopped smiling. "Well, I'm not sure yet. He still has to go to Korea. And he...he wants me to go with him."

"What?" Then, she saw my face. "Oh, Cass. It'll work out."

"Will it?"

"Girl, it *will* work out. Think positively. Think about it girl: He loves you. He done already gave you a rang. And—Wait, I almost forgot. Your grandma called a few minutes ago and she wants you to call her ASAP."

That pulled my attention away from my ring. "Grandmama?"

"No, your other grandmother."

\* \* \* \*

I adored Big Mama, my father's mother. When I was younger, she used to slip Kelly and me five-dollar bills when we went through the devotion line to shake hands. But I hadn't spoken to her in a while, so I bit down on my lip and breathed deeply as I dialed her number.

In a shaky voice, she told me that my father had been taken to the hospital in an ambulance. It was serious.

We hung up. I needed to get over to Stockdale. It was Sunday night, and I didn't have any classes until Monday afternoon. I figured I could get over there and back just in time.

The irony of it all was that I'd just driven from Fort Campbell, Kentucky, where I tried desperately not to think of my father. I had yet to have a decent conversation with him. And now, I was running to his rescue. When did he ever come to mine?

But one thought stuck out in my head: *If he should die, I'll never know why he left me, then ignored me all those years.*

I didn't know why I was going, what I was going to do once I was there, or if he would even care I was there. But I headed straight to Alabama Medical Center, Room 616.

I walked into the room without knocking to find Will Taylor stretched out in the bed, eyes closed, wearing off-white pajamas that looked three sizes too big for him. He was as big as a gnat. A small gnat.

I didn't see her right away, but when she spoke, I immediately knew who she was.

My grandmother was sitting in the corner, reading the *Jefferson Star*, and the surprise in her voice betrayed the smile on her face.

"Well, Cassie. I didn't know you was comin'." She got up and gave me a hug.

"Hello, Big Mama."

"When you'd get here?" She sat back down and picked up the newspaper that had slipped out of the chair and onto the floor when she hugged me.

"I just came in." I said, glancing around the room. We were alone. The three of us.

"I know Will'll be glad to see you when he wakes up. Here, take a chair, Cass."

I didn't want to, but I did. "You here by yourself?" I asked, trying to make small talk.

"Yeah, Kenny's gone to get us somethin' to eat, and he'll be back in a minute."

From talking to Big Mama on the phone, I knew she wasn't referring to her boyfriend, also named Kenny. *This* Kenny was my uncle, her daughter's husband. Nice enough guy, but I didn't want to be there when he got back. They would try to force me to eat something...and to talk.

"Well, since he's asleep, I guess I'll come back tomorrow." I said, getting up.

"Don't rush off. He ought to be wakin' up soon. He been sleep for a while."

"I—I don't want to bother him."

"Chile, you is the one that saved him. Bother him? If you hadn't gone to 'Lanta and found him when you did, he'd be dead as a doorknob. This boy needed to be home so somebody could see 'bout him. He done 'bout dranked himself to death, and those people up there wasn't his family. They weren't seeing 'bout him."

I looked at him, my heart thumping. "Why is he here?"

"They gone dry him out. Get him back on his feet."

"He's all right? Just drunk? I mean, I...I thought he was dying or something—"

"He gone be just fine. But he gone die if he don't give that liquor up, is all."

Will Taylor woke up and raised his head, and looked dead at me...and smiled.

"Hey, sugar pie."

I walked out of the room without saying a word and headed straight for the elevator, feeling like the biggest fool in Jefferson and Stockdale put together. I had run all the way to the hospital, and for what? To stare a drunk man in the face? Why? Was I supposed to save him? Stop him from drinking? Help him? He was a grown man. He didn't need me. He needed Jesus. We all did.

At that point, sitting in my car wishing I'd stayed in Birmingham, I didn't know if I should drive back over to school, or go to Stockdale. It was late. Stockdale was much closer, and I'd done enough driving for one day. I chose Stockdale. It turned out to be the wrong decision.

When I got there, Mama was watching TV and surprised to see me. What was I doing home? Wasn't it late to be driving all the way from Birmingham? And didn't I have classes tomorrow? I knew it would be wrong to lie, and also pointless. I'd seen at least three people at the hospital, and they'd seen me. She would find out one day or another that I'd been there. That I had visited Will Taylor. Stockdale had no community secrets.

But still, it wasn't easy to break open that dam by telling her. "I, uh—"

"I asked you a question, Cass. What are you doing coming home so late?"

I was nineteen years old, and she was still questioning me as if I were fifteen. I put my overnight bag on the floor beside the kitchen table. She was still sitting on the sofa with her arms folded, looking at me and waiting for an answer. So I gave her one.

"Big Mama called me at the dorm."

"What did she want?" she said, muting the TV.

"She was calling to tell me that Will Taylor was in the hospital."

Silence. I watched her face. There was no surprise on it. She already knew he was in the hospital. Of course she did. This was Stockdale.

"You drove over here at this time of night for this? To see that man at the hospital? It's too late to be out on the road. And especially for something as foolish as this."

I said nothing, just stood there and listened.

"Listen Cassie, things have to change, starting right now."

Okay it was late, but she was overreacting a bit now. "What changes?"

"Changes. First of all, if you can't keep yourself at school, then I'm going to have to take the Honda. You've been running around too much in that car as it is."

I stood there looking at her, with my arms folded across my stomach, wishing I had driven back to UAB instead of coming home to Stockdale, and to this.

Mama continued her speech. "And I'll tell you another thing. I don't want this Army boy around here either, Cassandra. I know you've been up there to see him at Fort Campbell, and that needs to cease too."

"What?" I almost screamed. "You are not talking about John, I know."

"Yes, I am. And I don't want him around here either."

"Why not?"

"Because we already have problems with Kelly. Have you forgotten? I don't want you getting into trouble, Cassie."

"What are you talking about?" I asked, looking at her, not believing a word of what I was hearing. "Is this about you putting people's opinions above our own happiness again, Mama?"

"Cassie, until things change, and someday I hope they will, I will do whatever I think is best for this family."

"But if we don't change, and help things change around Stockdale, they never will!"

"I'm not having this conversation tonight, Cassie. Stay at UAB, or else I'm going to take the car. Now that's it."

I picked up my overnight bag, the one I'd just set down on the floor, and headed out the door.

It was late, too late to be driving, but I didn't care. I just wanted to get out of there. I'd been a fool to come to Stockdale tonight. My father wasn't worth it. It didn't matter though. I now knew what I had to do. What I was going to do.

*Korea, here I come.*

There was no way I would let them keep me away from John. The thought of it was just insane, impossible.

\* \* \* \*

During the last months I had with him before he had to report to Korea, I stayed at UAB and didn't go back to Stockdale, except to show my face every once in a while at church. I wanted to keep a low profile. I was planning my next move, and didn't want them to know about it.

After much discussion, John and I decided it would be best for him to go ahead of me and set things up in Korea. When the time came for him to leave, I didn't cry or kick and scream, because I knew I was going to be with him. Nothing and no one would stop me as they'd stopped my high-school friends, Heather and Max, or as they'd tried to stop Kelly and Jimmy.

At the last minute, I did feel a wave of guilt about Mama, and how worried she'd be. The guilt compelled me to call her. To tell her I was leaving to be with John in Korea. In four hours.

"Cassie, you can't be serious. Are you? What about school?"

"Yeah. I am. I've got my ticket and I'm going to the airport in a bit."

"You know those Army guys, Cass, they—"

"Mama, we're engaged! I have a ring!"

"A ring? You still can't drop out of school, Cassandra!"

"I'm going back to school later, I promise. Mama, I gotta go now. I'll call you when I get there, okay?"

"Are you flying from Atlanta or Birmingham?"

"Birmingham. You can pick up the car whenever you want to. Mia will have the keys."

"Uh, huh."

"I'll call you when I get over there tomorrow. But I really have to go now."

We said our goodbyes, and I headed out the door to my future.

# Chapter 29

Mama was in complete shock.

But so was I.

I had just called my mother and told her I was headed for Korea to be with my fiancée. And I was. I had up and left. I had up and quit school. I had left my Honda Civic in the parking lot of the dorm. And I was gone.

It was my first time flying, much less going out of the country. I didn't know if what I was doing was right or not, but it felt right. It felt good. They hadn't succeeded in keeping me from the man I loved. I would no longer have to keep a low profile, sneak around. I would no longer have to pay enormous phone bills to speak to John. I was going to be right by his side.

After nineteen hours of flight, I got off the plane in Seoul, South Korea.

"Oh my God! Thank God you're here, John," I said after spotting him in the crowd. There weren't many westerners waiting. His American looks combined with his jeans and sneakers made him easy to find.

"Cassie, I missed you, girl. I missed you so much!" he said, taking me in his arms and lifting me off the ground. I could barely stand when he put me back down. My knees were like Jell-O from sitting so long on the plane.

"Are you tired, honey?" he asked, guiding me toward luggage claim.

"Yeah. Mostly I'm relieved to be off that plane! I didn't tell you this before because I didn't want you to worry, but…that was my first time flying."

He stopped walking and took my arm. "You've got to be kidding."

I smiled at him. "See how much I love you?"

"I love you so much, Cassie."

"I love you too." I grinned at him. "Nineteen hours' worth."

And we both laughed.

* * * *

The first thing I noticed about Seoul was all the lights. There were neon signs everywhere. I'd never seen anything like it before in my life, as if the whole city was lit up and there wasn't a dark crevice anywhere.

John ushered me into a waiting taxi and we headed for the city where his Army base was located, leaving the glitzy capital behind. I snoozed on his shoulder during the forty-mile trip, waking every now and then, terrified at how fast the taxi driver was driving. After what seemed like only a quarter hour, we were a mile outside Tongduchon, the home of Camp Casey. Camp Hovey, the camp next door, was to be our home.

The taxi pulled up to a darkened building that looked like an abandoned house. John spoke a few words in Korean to the driver and handed him a wad of bills. The taxi driver helped unload my two suitcases, then quickly sped off into the black night, leaving us standing there with the luggage.

"Cassie, here we are," John said, picking up the suitcases. But I didn't know where "here" was. I didn't see anything that looked like it could be our apartment.

"This is it, just up ahead," he said, nodding in the direction of the abandoned house.

We'd had conversations about where we'd be staying once I got here, and he'd only assured me that he had done the best he could, and that we would be staying in this particular apartment only temporarily until he could find something better. At the time, I was just happy we were going to be together. Now, I wondered. The building I was looking at didn't look like an apartment.

But it was. Sort of.

John took some keys from his pocket and unlocked a big brown door, then pushed it open. It clanged against the building's cement interior and we entered a courtyard of sorts.

He reached up and switched on a light hanging from the ceiling. It was like a house behind this door, but with several doors. I counted five. I looked around but saw nothing else except for the closed doors in front of me.

John walked toward one on the right. The last one. I followed him hesitantly. He didn't speak and neither did I.

Until he opened the door.

"Cassie, this is it!" he announced, putting the suitcases on the floor. "I hope you like it enough."

"Yeah, of course," I said. But I couldn't see anything.

"Welcome to our home, honey," he said, and finally flipped on a light switch.

We were standing in a large room. There was a full-size bed near the door, and to the left, a tiny, tiny kitchen area with a small refrigerator, a single sink, a stove with two burners, and maybe three feet of counter space. That was it.

Many things were missing, but the first thing I noticed was a bathroom. Where was that?

John must have read my mind. "I know it's a lot different than what we're used to at home. That's why families aren't 'allowed' to come here. The standard of living is much lower here. But I tried to find the best hooch I could for us."

"Hooch?"

He nodded and smiled. "This is called a hooch here. Let me show you around." He walked out the door, and I tagged along behind him.

"These other doors you see here? These are our neighbors."

"Those are other apartments?"

Another nod. "There's an American guy in that one. He's married to a Korean girl." He pointed at the door next to ours.

"You see the door over there that's slightly ajar? Where the light is coming from?"

"Yeah. Barely," I said, looking to the far left. I hadn't noticed that door before.

"Look." He walked over and opened the door. The room held a shower in the back, and nothing but a small sink in the front. There was a sliding door separating the two areas.

"This is the bathroom, Cassie." John was looking at my face, waiting for a response. I tried to remain calm, but somehow I knew the answer already before I even asked the question.

"Are you saying that this is the bathroom and shower for us?"

"Yes. For us, and for the other hooches as well."

"You mean, for us and all the other people who live inside this building? What, five families?"

"Yes. I'm afraid so."

"But…"

"I know, Cassie. It's not ideal. But they keep it really clean—"

"No, that's not what bothers me. It's clean enough, but where is the toilet? You said that this is a bath—"

"There *is* a toilet, Cassie. That's it."

"Where?" I said, looking around, not seeing anything at all resembling a toilet.

"There." He pointed a finger at the floor. "It's a squatter. You have the front there, which is called a hood. You need to face the hood and stand over the rest of the squatter, with your feet on both sides of it, beside or just behind the hood. Drop your pants about halfway down, and after you're done, just pull the chain to flush it."

I looked down at the foreign white object in the floor. "You have got to be joking."

"Unfortunately, that's very common here."

"Yes. Unfortunately."

"One last thing, Cass. Don't put toilet paper in there. It goes there in that pop-up trashcan."

"Yuck! That's gross! How can you—?"

"I got us this hooch just outside the gate on purpose," he said quickly. "Our gym's just inside the gate to the camp, complete with showers and toilets. Many showers and toilets. Regular toilets."

I still didn't know what to say, so I just shook my head. I had lived in the dorm before, yes, but this was something all together different.

"If you prefer to shower over there," he said, "you can go inside the camp whenever you want."

"Uhhh…"

"Cassie, please say something other than *uhhhh*."

I looked at him, saw his worried face. "I love you?" I said, and walked over to hug him. I must have loved him, to find myself now living in a Korean hooch about to share a tiny shower and squatter toilet with several other neighbors.

Isn't love grand?

Suffice it to say that it is.

\* \* \* \*

Although my culture shock had officially started, I still found it possible to be happy that I was reunited with John. Just going to sleep in his arms was worth the whole journey.

But our reunion was short-lived. The next morning he had to go to work at Camp Hovey. I walked with him to the gate, just to see where it was. He'd told the truth; it was only about fifty feet from our hooch. That comforted me a bit.

Daylight made it possible for me to see my new neighborhood for the first time, and as he stood beside me, I looked around. The street outside our hooch was lined with other buildings similar to ours, a few stores, and…that was it. The huge gate to the Army base seemed to be the main attraction. In the far distance, on a hill, I could see buildings that looked quite modern, almost like ones at home. I asked about them.

"Those are the American apartments," John said.

"What's that?"

"Apartments built like western apartments. They're nice. I've got a buddy who lives up there."

"You have buddies everywhere," I teased.

"They're very hard to get, though. There's a waiting list like nobody's business."

I nodded and gave a last, longing glance at them. "I see."

"I'd better get going, honey," he said. "I'll see you later on, okay? I'll be back for lunch."

"Should I prepare something? I saw a fridge in our *hooch*," I said, smiling.

"No, you get some sleep. I'll bring something for lunch. Burger King?"

I gasped. "You have Burger King over here?"

"We sure do."

"Yes! Whopper Jr., baby!"

"Done." He kissed me and reluctantly said goodbye.

I quickly walked back to the building, opened up the front door and went inside, and then unlocked the door to our hooch. At first, I sat on our bed and looked around me. The morning sun was coming in through one of the room's two windows. The room wasn't as bad as I thought. It was extremely clean, and the sunshine poured inside. The bed was brand-new, and so was everything else in it.

I looked in the refrigerator. There was a six-pack of Coke, a pack of sandwich meat, a couple of Granny Smith apples, a large bottle of water, a small carton of orange juice and a pint of milk. I looked into the tiny kitchen's lone cabinet and found three cans of chili and one can of corn. There were also three boxes of Frosted Flakes—I smiled when I saw that; he knew my favorite cereal—one loaf of white bread, a bag of Lay's Potato Chips and a jar of mustard. He'd told me about getting American products at the commissary: the base grocery store. Apparently, he'd been there before I arrived, and I was so glad he had. It was nice to see some familiar things in that little cupboard.

There were some plastic plates and cups on the counter, and I picked up one of the cups and poured myself some orange juice. After drinking it, rinsing out my cup and placing it in the sink, I got back in bed. I was looking forward to seeing John for lunch. I wanted to unpack and prepare for it, but the jet lag was too much for me. I intended to lie down for an hour or so—but that hour turned into several. It was eight a.m. when I got back in bed, and I didn't wake up again until after one o'clock, lunchtime. But it wasn't hunger that woke me up. It was noise. Lots of it.

# Chapter 30

I found out rather quickly that the noise I heard was rain, but not your normal rain showers. This was brutal. This was a *monsoon*.

John had sort of warned me about it, but I hadn't paid attention. I didn't think it would happen. Could happen. But it did. And it kept happening. The problem was that John wasn't there, and he wouldn't be for a long time.

When he didn't show up at first, I was sure it was due to the flooding rain outside. When four o'clock came and he still wasn't there, I decided to eat lunch without him, and did, looking out the window, watching all the flooding going on.

By six o'clock, I began to panic. Where was he? What was he doing? Had he forgotten about me?

To make things more complicated, I had to use the bathroom. Big-time. I'd pretty much been holding it all day, and it was beginning to really bother me. I had to go. And like it or not, with all the rain coming down, I had to use the squatter. I had to leave our hooch and go to the bathroom. But just in case, I gave John another hour to come home.

He didn't.

Before I could cry or figure out my next move, I knew I had to get to the bathroom. I couldn't think until I'd used it!

I made sure I had the key to the hooch, opened up the door slowly, and looked around the courtyard. It was empty. I closed the door to our hooch, locked it, and walked over to the toilet as quietly as I could.

It was locked! *Damn it!*

I could hear water running inside, and guessed that someone was taking a shower. I turned around, hands in my black Esprit pants pockets, and started walking back to the hooch.

Then, the water stopped.

A couple of seconds later, the door opened. There stood a Korean lady in a towel, looking at me, slightly smiling.

"I be out in one second. Please. One second," she said, standing there in the doorway with a small green towel barely wrapped around her.

Holy cow. Culture shock city, baby.

"Okay," I stumbled. "Thank you." And I started walking rapidly toward my hooch.

"Hey. You new lady, no? Lieutenant woman?"

I turned around. So she knew who I was. But who was *she*?

"Yes, I am," I said, walking back toward her.

"Nice it is to meet you. I Cho. I married with friend of Lieutenant John."

"Oh. I'm Cassie. Nice to meet you." I wondered if I should extend my hand. Not wanting her towel to fall down, I decided against it.

"I live in hooch beside of you."

"Okay," I said, looking in that direction.

"You all-white wit' monsoon?" she said. "You got food, no?"

"Yes, I'm fine. Thank you. Ah…when will it be over?"

"Oh, hard to say. Days maybe." She reached inside the bathroom and pulled out a multicolored robe that had been hanging on an old nail.

"When will they get back?"

"Get back?"

"Yes. When will the men—your husband and John—come back here?" The rain was coming down again, so I had to shout the words. I pointed at the floor. "When will they come back here?"

This lady had become my ray of hope. But only for a second.

"Oh, that's could be one day, two day. When the flood stop, they let them off base."

I could have fainted. The monsoon. Korea. I was all alone in a hooch thousands of miles away from home. Ouch. Cho must have understood the expression on my face, the weariness in my eyes.

She came out of the bathroom and shooed me in. "You use toilet and then you come home for ice coffee. Go."

She closed the door behind me. And there I stood, looking at the squatter. The trash can beside it full of toilet paper. It took everything I had not to cry.

At least it was clean.

I forced my legs to move, placed my feet in the designated spots, and did what you have to do on a squatter: I squatted. I squatted and willed myself to get it over with. The problem? Nothing came out.

For maybe the first time in my life, Stockdale didn't seem such a bad place after all. Back at home, it was the Fourth of July. They'd be firing up the grill. Someone in the neighborhood would be setting off some firecrackers. And me? What was I doing? Spending the Fourth of July standing over a squatter and wondering how in the world I was ever going to make it through this.

After I'd spent more than my fair share of time over the squatter, I went back to the hooch and threw myself down on the bed. I knew that Cho was waiting for me, and that I had to make an effort. The alternative was lying there listening to all the rain, imagining a million and one more things that could go wrong.

It was too much. I got up, found a scrap piece of paper in my bag and left a note on the bed just in case John came back while I was at Cho's house drinking iced coffee.

He didn't come back, though. In fact, it was late the next day before he made his way back to the hooch. And when he did, I was waiting for him.

"Where have you been? Oh my God!" I said when he opened the door and walked in soaked to the bone.

"Oh, Cass. I've been trying to get here forever. I'm so sorry. Are you okay, honey?" He grabbed me up off the bed and held me against his wet BDUs.

"I'm okay. I was so scared. I was so worried. I had to use the bathroom!"

I was shouting, thinking back on the horror of it all.

"Oh, honey. I'm so sorry. They wouldn't let us leave the base. Security reasons. I tried to, really I did."

"Okay. But when do you have to go back?" I said, about to cry just thinking of being alone again. Cho had been nice, but I didn't want to spend days over at her hooch drinking iced coffee.

"I'm not going back, baby. I got someone to cover for me. He'll send word if they start looking for me."

"Oh, thank God. Thank God," I said, hugging him tighter.

"It's okay. I'm here and I'm not going anywhere."

\* \* \* \*

A few days later, the rain finally let up, and we were able to go outside and explore the camp a little. Once we'd walked inside Camp Hovey's gate, we stopped at a bus stop. This bus was the transportation for getting around the camp as well as getting over to the next base, Camp Casey, about a mile away.

Camp Hovey had, among other things, lots of trees, Army buildings and barracks, a gym, a few restaurants, an officer's club and an NCO club. Camp Casey however, had more restaurants, more buildings, more barracks, a post exchange, called a PX, a commissary, hospitals, dental clinics, and a Burger King—our current destination. It was clearly the larger and more energetic camp. With the bus, it was easy to get from one base to the other. However, with each new thing I saw, it was clear to me that families might not really belong here. It was a rough place to live, much less raise a family.

Inside the Burger King, I noticed another black woman sitting near the rear of the restaurant. I jabbed John in the arm and made him look at her. Apparently, my thoughts of being the only American woman around, much less a black American woman, were wrong. I was instantly optimistic.

I agreed with John to hold us a table. It was getting pretty busy with guys coming in for lunch. I chose one close to her, this black woman, on purpose. She was probably American, too; not only was she on an American Army base, but she was reading a *Cosmopolitan*. She stood out in this place of BDUs…but so did I, because she noticed me too.

I'd seen her looking at us more than a few times as we ate our burgers. A couple of times, she'd smiled. After we'd eaten and were getting ready to leave, she got up and walked directly over to our table, never losing eye contact, swaying her hips and wearing a huge smile on her glossy lips. All the men were watching her, and even a couple of female soldiers, too. I couldn't blame them. The woman wore a tight pink tank, skintight white capris, and her feet were shod in hot pink sandals with four-inch heels.

"Hi, I'm Tonia," she said, extending a manicured hand tipped with pink nail polish. I noticed that her toes were painted pink, too.

I gave her my hand and introduced myself, then John.

She helped herself to a chair, then said, "Are you new here? Because I ain't never seen you here before."

"Yes. I've only been here a few days," I said, staring at her pink earrings. Her lipstick was pink too.

"Chile, it's so good to see another sister in this place. I've been here for almost a year with my husband, and I've only met two or three."

"Wow. That's a long time," I said, genuinely surprised.

"It sure the hell is," she said, laughing. She turned to John. "What company is you with?"

Up until now, he hadn't said much. "I'm in the 1st Battalion, 9th Infantry."

"Okay. My husband is with the 1/503rd Infantry."

"I see," John said, looking at me. That was the cue. He was ready to leave. But I wasn't.

"Where do you live around here?" I asked, ignoring the look in his eyes.

"I live on top of the hill in the American apartments," Tonia said, tossing her hair back off her shoulders. "They're the closest thing to home, girl." She looked at John, then at me. "You live in a hooch?"

"Yeah, just outside the gate," I said.

"Well, come and see me sometime girl. I do hair, too."

And for the first time, I really looked at her hair. It was a weave, but a good one. It was curly and hung halfway down her back.

I had to ask. "Did you do your own hair?"

"Oh, yes ma'am. I changes it every week just about. I get bored, and go to Seoul to buy the hair." She dug into her bag, a brand-new-looking Louis Vuitton but with various ragged strings dangling from the handles.

"You do perms too?"

"Girl, I do everything. I'll do yours for free. What else have we got to do around here? *He, he, he.*"

She had a funny laugh. Almost cartoonish. What some people would call a blonde laugh. In fact, she was rather ditzy-acting herself. But it didn't seem to be her real personality, or at least, not all of it.

She gave me the phone number to her American apartment. A phone? There was no phone in our hooch, or in any of the other hooches in our building. My first phone call to Mama had been from a phone inside the camp.

Tonia also told me I could use her phone whenever I wanted, as well as her washing machine, dryer, and television. I was starting to feel better about my situation now. So much better, in fact, that I didn't notice how quiet my fiancé was being.

∗  ∗  ∗  ∗

After looking around a bit more on the base, John and I got back on the bus and headed back to our hooch.

"Cassie, I don't want to ruin it or anything," he said, "but just be careful with that hot pink girl."

"What?" I said, distracted by the scenes rushing by outside the bus. "She's nice, isn't she? At least I know one person here other than you."

"I know, and I want you to have friends. Just be careful, that's all."

I pulled myself away from the window and turned to him. "Why?"

"Because. Did you see her? She looks like trouble. She walks like trouble."

I gave him a teasing grin. "So you were watching her walk, huh?"

"Everybody in the place was watching her walk. But you know what I mean."

I nodded. "What you want to say is that she was very fass, wasn't she?"

"*Fass*? Is that one of your Alabama words?"

"Yep. Was she fass or not?"

"Okay. She was *too* fass," he said, and punched my arm gently. "I love you, Cassie. I'm so glad you're here."

"Me too, John. Me, too!" I said, and hugged him, giggling.

I *was* glad I was there. And I was glad that I might have made a new friend who'd help me get over this culture shock.

# Chapter 31

One night, about three weeks after I'd seen Tonia for the first time, John and I ran into her in the street outside our hooch. We'd noticed her right away from the way she switched her hips from side to side, as well as her head-to-toe, red-as-fire clothing. We would have noticed her no matter what because, up until now, we hadn't seen any other black women around the bases. This time, though, Tonia wasn't alone. She and the man with her spotted us about the same time we spotted them.

"Hey, Miss Cassie! I've been trying to find you, girl," she said, and ran over to me and hugged me like she was my new best friend. She *was* my new best friend.

"Hi, Tonia. I've been meaning to call you." I really had, but just hadn't done it yet.

"Girl, this is my husband, Abraham." She giggled. "First Sergeant Abraham Jackson."

"Tonia. Just say my name, girl. Just say Abe." He extended his hand and shook ours. After he let my hand go, I had to wiggle my fingers around a bit.

But then again, everything about him looked strong. First Sergeant Abraham Jackson, a.k.a. "Abe," was black and from Mississippi, the same state as I later learned Tonia came from. He was nearly six-and-a-half feet tall and must have weighed over three hundred pounds. And he had muscles everywhere. His complexion was jet black, but he had light brown eyes. Almost bald, he still wore a little fuzz, though.

"Why don't you guys come to the party with us?" Tonia said, still giggling.

"You guys are more than welcome there," said the giant beside her.

"What party are you talking about?" I asked.

Tonia laughed. "My birthday party, girl. Didn't I tell you?"

Was she *this* ditzy? I'd only met her once, and had never spoken to her since. To be polite, I said, "Oh, I must have forgotten." Now *I* was the ditzy one, and the look John gave me proved it.

"Girl, come on here." Before I could protest, Tonia had my arm and was leading me down the street. Abraham and John could only follow. We walked for only a couple of minutes before we wound up in front of a dark-looking dive with a sign on the front that said, "America."

How appropriate. As we walked in, that's exactly what we saw: Americans. They were in their casual clothes, some sitting at the bar, some at booths. Some playing pool. Some throwing darts. All of them were drinking.

"This is it, girl," she said casually. "Tonia's birthday mixer."

Two "party guests," both soldiers, came over to Abe and Tonia. "Hey there, First Sergeant!"

"Hey there, ya'll," Tonia said, smiling and signaling the waitress.

She ordered a rum and Coke, then sat in a booth, still giggling, and looked around at the five or so guys who had now joined them. I saw her wink at one of them, and to my surprise, the guy winked back. Abe was too busy laughing at a joke another guy had just told to notice.

When I looked at Tonia, wondering what to do next, she smiled, got up, came over to John and me and put an arm around each of us. Then she said, in a whisper that was barely audible above all the loud rock music playing, "That's Rico. He's my boyfriend."

John and I stood there with our eyes wide open. I knew he was probably thinking the exact same thing I was: *This girl is crazy.*

I thought I'd misheard her, but for some reason, I knew I hadn't. Still, I had to ask, "Did you say he's your—?"

"*He, he, he.* Funny, ain't I?" Tonia said. She had her rum and Coke in her hand. *Maybe that's it, she's drunk.* "Oh…that's a good one," I said.

"But he *is* my boyfriend," Tonia insisted, looking over at Rico, who was sitting right next to her husband, and winking at him again.

"But didn't you say that Abe was your husband?" John said, putting his hands on his hips.

"Yes. He is," she whispered. "Abe is my husband, but Rico is my boyfriend. You see, Abe…he's a lot older than me. Try twenty years. He was always accusing me of runnin' around. I got tired of him accusin'."

John cleared his throat, then said, "So you—"

"So I went out and got somebody else. But I'm keeping him too. *He, he he.*"

"And does he know it?" I whispered. "He's sitting right there."

"Are you crazy, girl? He would beat the shit out of me."

John looked at me and I looked at John.

"Cassie, I need a drink," John said. "Go with me to the bar?"

Telling Tonia that we'd be back in a few seconds, we left her sipping her rum and Coke. After a moment, I saw her reclaim her seat across from Rico and Abe.

"That girl is nuts, Cassie. I don't like it," John said, and ordered a beer for himself and a Coke for me.

"Yeah, she's crazy. Can you believe it?"

"She's a regular troublemaker," John said, and glanced in her direction. "Let's leave after this, all right? I don't want to be here when the first sergeant finds out his wife is rubbing another guy's leg under the table right beside him."

I almost spit my Coke in his face. "Holy smoke! Are you kidding?"

"Check it out." John said, jerking his head in their direction while downing some of his Heineken.

I looked, then said, "Oh, my goodness, she really *is* crazy."

Just then, Tonia looked over at us and winked again.

\* \* \* \*

A few weeks later, John came back to the hooch and told me that he had to go to the demilitarized zone, also known as the DMZ, the frontier that separates South Korea and North Korea and located about eleven miles from the base. I'd heard enough about it to know that it was an ugly place, an unsafe place, ripe with propaganda. The thought of him going there depressed me. Even worse, he didn't know how long he'd have to stay there.

We hadn't seen or heard from Tonia and Abe since her birthday party, and I didn't know any other people in South Korea. Except Cho, but she had gone down to Pusan to visit her family and I had no idea when she was coming back. John had seemed happy Tonia hadn't contacted us, so I was surprised when he said, "Why don't you look Tonia up while I'm gone?"

"Me, see Tonia? I thought you hated the girl."

"She's something else, no doubt about that. It's true I have tons of reservations about that girl. But she's one of the few American women around here. And I don't want you to be here all by yourself. Call her. Maybe you guys can go shopping or something."

Having lunch, gossiping, and did he say shopping?

How could I say no to that?

One week later, John was gone and I was knocking on Tonia's American apartment door with an overnight bag in my hand. We'd called Tonia and Abe and told them about John going to the DMZ, and when they suggested I stay with them, John thought it was a good idea and I'd be safer up there. So up there was where I was.

When I walked in, I immediately understood why they were called "the American apartments." There was a huge kitchen with American-size appliances, two bedrooms, a dining room, a living room and a real, working telephone. Tonia had decorated everything herself, and in red: red sofa, red curtains, red chairs and even a red rug.

"Make yourself at home, Cassie. This will be your room." As he spoke, Abe took my bag and put it in a neatly arranged bedroom with a brass bed, white curtains, and a television set. "You guys want some fresh lemonade? I'm about to finish making some." With that, he headed for the kitchen.

"Yeah, babe, that's nice," Tonia said, winking at me. "He spoils me rotten, girl. Do you like your room?"

"Yes, it's really pretty. You did a good job in decorating."

She shrugged. "That's all I have to do around here, girl, besides shop and do my hair! *He, he, he.* We're gonna go out later, okay?"

"Okay."

"Here you are, girls." Abe handed us each a glass of icy lemonade. He'd squeezed the lemons himself, he was telling us, when the phone rang.

"We'll, I'll be damn," I heard him say. "I thought we weren't leaving 'till tomorrow morning. I'll be down there. Just give me a few minutes."

Abe got up and went to their bedroom. Five minutes later, he came out fully dressed in his BDUs and boots.

"Girls, I gotta go to work. We're leaving for the field." He gave Tonia an apologetic smile. "I won't be able to cook those egg rolls for you tonight. Cook 'em when I get back, though." He bent down and gave her a kiss on the top of her head. "I'll probably be back in four or five days this time. Ya'll be safe and be good."

I felt like saying, "Yes sir, we will."

He walked out in a hurry and slammed the door. Tonia walked straight to the phone, picked it up and dialed a number.

"Hello? I need to speak to Sergeant Gonzalez, please." She tapped her right foot, looked at me, and giggled. Then, "Hello? Rico? Hey, baby. It's Tonia. Abe gone. Can you come over?...Now!...Okay...All right...See you in a few, baby. I miss you too. Bye."

I'd crossed the room, but it was too late. The line was dead, and Tonia was already headed for the bathroom looking for her Fashion Fair. "Are you crazy, girl?" I called after her. "What are you *doing?*"

But what she was doing, of course, was obvious.

When the doorbell rang I almost screamed, but managed to hold it in. Tonia came out of her bedroom almost immediately, smelling like vanilla, not paying me any attention whatsoever, and opened the front door.

"Hey baby. I'm so glad you came," she said, and took Rico in her arms. They kissed long and hard before he was even inside the apartment. My nerves were so bad that I had to use the bathroom, and it wasn't going to be pretty.

After they finally let each other go, he came over to me.

Now, I'd be lying if I said he wasn't fine. Rico was about five-feet-nine-inches tall, slim and nicely muscled, with dark brown eyes that were almost black and matching hair. This Rico was a 'Rican from Puerto Rico. He loved to say that, and from what I gathered, people, especially Tonia, loved to hear it.

"Cassie, hello," he said. "Nice to see you again."

"Yeah, I…nice to see you too…. Look I'm gonna be over there…" I pointed to the bathroom. I had to get in there. My guts were going to spill out any moment, any second.

Tonia nodded. "Okay, girlie. We gone be in my room if you need anything or need to know where anything is."

"You'll be where?" *Did she just say she's taking this guy to her and Abe's bedroom?*

"*He, he.* Girl, look at him." She lifted up Rico's arm. "Now you *know* I got some business to take care of in there. *He, he, he.*"

"I love you, woman," Rico said, kissing her on the back of her neck.

"I love you too, baby," she cooed back.

Insane! I was surely in a madhouse. I knew it. She knew. He knew it.

I was just thinking of getting my overnight bag and getting the heck out of Dodge when I heard something. We all heard it. And my blood ran cold.

The sound was a key in the lock of the door of their apartment. In other words, Abe was back.

They figured it out a second before I did, because when I turned to yell at them, they were already headed for Tonia's bedroom.

*Not the bedroom!* I was prepared to scream. Now it was too late. Abe was opening the door.

"Tonia, I forgot my wallet, girl. Got all the way down there and tried to get in the gate and didn't have one piece of ID on me." He slammed the door, turned around, and looked directly at me. "Hey, Cassie. Where's Tonia?"

My fear couldn't be contained a second longer. It was impossible. I looked down to see if it had already started: the evacuation of said fear.

"Honey, what happened?" Tonia strode into the room, smiling, still cooing.

"Girl, I left my damn wallet."

"Oh, babe. That's terrible. I'll get it for you." She sashayed across the living room and into the bedroom. A second later she came out with his wallet, placed it in his hand, and asked for a kiss.

"What you girls up to?" he said, after he'd bent down and planted one on her lips.

"Babe, I was just getting ready to take Cassie shopping. I'm ready. I'm waiting on her to get ready." She looked at me and smiled, her red lipstick still perfectly intact.

"Yeah, I'm going on to the bathroom....That's where I was headed," I added, trying to get my feet to actually go there.

"Okay. You girls be safe now, Tonia."

"Okay. Bye hon'."

"Bye-bye." Abe was gone. Again.

As soon as the door slammed shut Tonia ran to her bedroom, opened the balcony and looked out. For the first time I saw alarm on her face.

Then suddenly she broke into a smile and started waving.

*What is she waving at? And where's Rico?* I ran to the balcony, all the time looking around for him. Finally, I bent my head over too. I found him five stories down below, blowing kisses up to Tonia.

"How did he—?" I sputtered. "What did he *do*, Tonia?"

"He jumped, Cassie! Isn't he something? My Puerto Rican baby."

"He jumped?"

"Yeah. That's our escape plan. They don't call him Superman back at the barracks for nothing, *he, he he.*"

I headed to her American-style bathroom and stayed in there for about an hour. Part of the time was to eliminate the fear I'd been experiencing, and part of it was because I didn't know what I'd say or do once I came out. But out I knew I had to come. When I did open the door, Tonia had changed clothes again and was waiting for me.

"Girl, I thought you'd done fell in. *He, he he.*" She got up off the sofa. "You need to get ready so we can get out of here."

"Where are we going?"

"Downrange. We gone do some shopping, *he he, he.* But first, let me do something to your hair."

I wanted to ask what "downrange" meant, but I was more concerned about the other thing she'd said. "Do something to my hair?"

"Yeah. Let me put a couple of tracks in there. You'd look so good with a little more length. Like mine."

"I don't know about a weave, Tonia. Plus, I don't have the hair. We'll have to wait—"

"No, we don't have to wait. I got everything right in there." She pointed to her room.

"Oh. Okay."

She saw my hesitation. "What's wrong, girlie?"

"You tell me. What's up with Rico and Abe?" I stared at her and waited for an answer.

"Let's just do your hair and leave, and I'll explain everything on the way downrange, okay? But don't be mad."

"I'm not mad. I'm just worried. You are crazy."

"*He, he he.* I know it."

\* \* \* \*

An hour later, my new weave and I were inside a taxi with Tonia. I'd never worn a weave before, but I liked my new glamorous look. I couldn't, however, delight in it just then, because I was too busy praying that God would allow me to see my family and the United States again. The driver had already barely missed a bus, a bicycle, and a woman pushing a cart. He was the driver from hell. But afterward, I learned that they all were. Korean drivers are hell on wheels. Really.

I tightened up my grip on the back of the seat, and Tonia laughed. I knew she was enjoying herself. I couldn't help but laugh, too, when I saw her trying to reapply her red lipstick while the driver threw us both back and forth.

Finally we arrived downrange, and much to my surprise, all in one piece. The driver was smacking on gum and tapping his hands on the steering wheel. Tonia gave him the fare in Korean *won*, then tipped him five American dollars.

"Thank you. Thank you, beautiful lady," he said with a thick accent.

She smiled at him. "*He, he, he. Ahn-nyong-i kah-se-yo. Ahn-nyong-i-kay-se-yo.*"

"Bye-bye, American girls," he said, and off he drove.

"I didn't know you spoke Korean," I said in wonder.

"You gotta know a little bit, Cass. Do you have any dollars? Always keep some dollars on you too. That goes a long-long way here."

She reached in her purse and came out with a wad of dollar bills. "Take this."

"I can't take—"

"Girl, just take it. Here."

I hadn't reached out my hand but she'd stuffed it down in my bag.

"And there's more where that came from too. A lot more. *He, he, he.*"

We were walking toward a place called "Club Studio 54" when I started noticing my surroundings. Going downrange was really going downhill. Everything around us looked nasty, greasy, spooky, and ironically, lively. From Tonia, I learned that this was Tongduchon's shopping and entertainment district. The soldiers called it "the ville" as well.

The clubs and restaurants were all Americanized, with names like "Manhattan Club," "American Night," "California Club" and "Las Vegas." The streets were lined with hawkers selling everything from tailored suits and shoes to brass beds. If you wanted a fake Louis Vuitton or Gucci bag, you could have them in spades. There were scarves, vases, linen, towels, beer, water, food, hats, sunglasses…and women. When we got inside Club Studio 54, the first thing I saw was the many made-up Korean girls who stood at the door as we walked in. Red lips. Red cheeks. Red eyes. All of them wore mini-dresses with high-heeled shoes.

When we walked into the club, it was as if we'd been announced. Everything stopped. There were at least thirty soldiers inside, all staring at us. What were they thinking? Later, I'd find out: *Real American girls. Wow.* American girls in South Korea were indeed a rarity. Tonia already knew this. She lived for this.

We chose a side booth in the front of the club, near the small, circular dance floor. There was a DJ spinning R&B music. More Korean girls, and a few girls of other nationalities that I wasn't sure of, were at the bar talking to a group of soldiers. And the girls were for sale. Tonia explained that the girls belonged to the bar, and that the "mama-san" standing in the corner ran things. Sex went for $50 for just a few minutes and up to $160 for a full hour. If a soldier messed around and fell in love with a girl—and that happened all the time—he could buy her from the mama-san for a few thousand dollars, depending on the negotiations.

I was a long way from Stockdale.

While staring at the girls and wondering what type of hell their lives must be, I decided that I needed a drink, even though I didn't.

As though she'd read my mind, Tonia hailed a waitress wearing a black micro-mini, saying, "It's time to celebrate your first trip downrange."

The waitress bounced over to our table. "Hi. You want rum and Coke?"

"*He, he, he.* You know it. Two."

"Okay ma'am. Two rum and Coke tonight."

"This is my friend, Cassie. Cassie, this Hyun."

"Hello," I managed.

"You American girl, too?"

"Yeah."

"That very good. Two rum and Coke." Hyun skipped off, bobbing her head to the music, something about Bobby Brown's prerogative.

Then, it hit me. I turned to Tonia. "Wait a minute, did you just order me a rum and Coke?"

Tonia nodded. "Yes, you need one."

"Rum and Coke? I don't want that."

"You'll love it. Watch," she said, and began singing with Bobby.

I'd been sober my whole life. I had an alcoholic father. I wasn't going to let that happen to me. But one drink wouldn't hurt, would it? Yes, it would. I was in South Korea. I was engaged. I had a new best friend. I was far away from Stockdale. But maybe Bobby Brown was on to something. I could do what I wanted to do, too. I was free. But I'd still just drink a Coke instead.

"Two rum and cokes." Hyun sat the drinks down on the table. Tonia paid her on the spot as expected.

"Yo' boyfriend," Hyun said to Tonia. "He come with you tonight?"

*Does everyone in Tonguchon know that Tonia's having an affair?* I wondered.

Tonia took a sip of her drink, then replied, "Which one? *He, he he.*"

"Hahhhh. She so funny," Hyun said to me, then waited for me to agree.

"I don't think he's comin'," Tonia said. "He had to be Superman again tonight. But it don't matter. I'll see him tomorrow. Maybe. *He, he he.*"

"Haaah. She very funny girl, no?"

I shook my head in agreement, but thought, *Funny? Maybe. Crazy? Definitely.*

"Give me another one, Hyun," Tonia said. "Tonight we celebratin'. Bring Cassie another one, too. It's her first time downrange." Then she looked at me as though just realizing something extremely important. "I can't believe this is your first time downrange. And you been here two months?"

What could I say? It was true. And maybe I realized now why John hadn't been in such a rush to bring me. This place was no rose garden.

"First time?" Hyun said. "Okay ma'am. Haa, haa." Then she strode off, still bobbing her head to Bobby Brown.

"Tonia, you are so crazy."

"I know. *He, he, he.*"

"Now tell me about Abe before you get too drunk."

# Chapter 32

"Abe and I met when I was seventeen. He was thirty-seven. We've been together now for four years. We got married as soon as I turned eighteen." Tonia stopped, took a sip on her drink, looked around for the waitress, and then continued. "I loves him. I really do. And I know he loves me, in his own way…."

"What does that mean?"

She shrugged. "In his own way is his own way."

"What?"

"Well, he loves me. Sometimes he doesn't show it the way he should, but I know he does." This time she was downing her drink.

I asked the obvious question. "What are you doing with Rico, then?"

"I am *crazy* about Rico. That's my baby."

"I know. But you're married!"

She shrugged. "So. So what? I am entitled to some fun, too."

"Yeah, but then why did you get married?"

"Because I wanted to. I told you I love my husband. I do."

"Then how can you cheat on him with Rico?"

"Because…Because I can."

"Okaayy…"

"Cassie, you don't understand."

"Well, make me," I said, tugging on my new tracks to make sure my weave was in tight enough. After all, I didn't want any hair falling out onto the floor.

"Cassie, I was faithful to Abe for three years straight, but he didn't trust me. Even before we got here to Korea, he didn't trust me. Then, once we got here and he saw all the attention I was getting from the GIs, he went crazy. I wasn't doing nothin'. But he didn't believe me."

"What happened?"

"He started giving me black eyes, hell."

"What? He beats you?" I picked up my rum and Coke, but then put it back down. I wouldn't crack.

"He's better now. He got some help at the base. I turned his ass in a couple of times, *he, he*."

"Noooo."

"Yeah. But back to what I was sayin'. He was beatin' me for somethin' I wasn't doin', so I figured," another shrug, "I might as well have some fun. Shit, if he gone beat me, might as well be for a reason."

"But you shouldn't be getting beat at all, Tonia."

"Cassie, you know, sometimes he—" In mid-sentence, she got up and went toward the bar. I thought I'd said something to offend her, but she turned around, smiled and said, "I'll be right back, Cass. I'm gone check on our drinks."

I watched her adjust the denim dress she was wearing and strut off. She passed several tables where soldiers were sitting. All eyes were on Tonia. I saw her toss her long black hair back. She even went over to one table and hugged two dark and handsome guys. *Friends of Rico's, maybe?* I thought, then sighed. *Maybe they're just friends of Tonia's.*

To distract myself, I looked around and took in the rest of the club. It wasn't a big place, but it was packed. Huge globe lights hung from the ceiling. It reminded me of the old TV show *Solid Gold*. The DJ wore baggy shorts and a Hard Rock Café–Houston tee-shirt.

I turned to look at the tables behind me, and that's when I saw him.

He was staring directly at me and smiling. From what I could tell, he had a good tan and blonde hair. He was wearing a black tee-shirt that said "*Catch The Wave*" and jeans. Something gold hung around his neck.

I realized I'd been looking at him a few seconds longer than I wanted to, so I turned back around to face the DJ. Just then, Tonia came back with two rum and Cokes. But there was a problem according to her: I hadn't even drunk the first one.

"Tonia, I told you. I don't drink."

"Then let me get you a glass of wine, or something, girl. I can't just let you sit here parched all night. Hyun!"

"Noooo. I'm gonna get a Coke later on. Just finish telling me about Abe."

"What else can I say? He beats me. I see Rico whenever I can. End of story."

"Are you going to stay with him?"

"With Abe? Hell, yeah!" She reached for the rum and Coke I hadn't drunk.

"But why?"

"Because he takes good care of me. That's why. I mean, Rico is all that, but he can't afford Miss Tonia."

"Oh, so it's all about the money then?" I said, turning the corners of my mouth up and slightly rolling my eyes.

"Look, missy. You can't understand my life in one day. And speaking of lives, you need to rethink yours."

"What?" I almost stood up. "What are you talking about?"

"You don't need to get married yet. You only twenty years old. You too young."

"What? *You're* young. You were younger than me when you got married to Abe."

"Yeah, and look where I'm at."

She had a point. All I could do was stare down at the table.

"Cassie, I am telling you this as your friend. We have so much in common, girl, I know it. Don't get married yet. There are too many fine ones out there. Trust me. You are not ready." She downed her third rum and Coke.

"I *am* ready. I love John more than anything else in this world."

"I know you do. But you are not ready for marriage. And you know what? I'm gone prove it to you." She stood up and signaled at something behind our table.

I didn't turn around to see what she was doing. I figured she was calling the waitress back for more drinks.

Tonia sat back down, giggling.

"Are you getting more?" I asked.

"I've ordered something, all right. But it ain't what you think it is, girly, *he, he, he*."

"What—?"

"Hello, ladies."

The blonde guy who'd been sitting behind us was now standing at our table. From this closer vantage point, he was a little less than six feet tall and had green eyes, perfect white teeth and a square jaw. In fact, except for his short blonde hair, he looked just like Ridge Forrester from *The Bold and The Beautiful* soap opera.

Thing is, I always did have a crush on Ridge Forrester.

"What's your name, sweetie?" Tonia said, smiling at him.

"Hunter."

"Hunter?" Tonia and I asked in unison.

He smiled and looked at me. "What's yours?"

I was trying to determine an accent. I couldn't, but I knew he wasn't from the South.

Tonia put her hand out. "Oh, this is my friend Cassie. I'm Tonia."

He took it and shook it, then reached for mine. But when I gave it to him, he kissed it instead of shaking it.

Tonia leaned over and whispered to me, "*He, he, he.* Looks like you got yourself an admirer, Miss Cassie. That's why I called him over here. He been staring at you all night."

She looked back at Hunter. "You wanna sit with us?"

"Sure." He slid inside the booth and faced me. "Where are you from, Cassie?"

"I'm from—"

"Guys, I'm gonna go to the bar, I'll be right back," Tonia cut in, and off she went.

"Sorry. I'm from Alabama," I said, and looked around, my stomach jumping. *What if John walks in? What if some of his buddies are here? But after all, I'm just talking, right?*

I really needed something to drink. *Coke, water, orange juice—*

"California. Have you ever been to San Diego?"

I shook my head. "Not even to California. Not yet."

"You should go with me someday," Hunter said, flashing his beautiful teeth again.

"Look, Hunter. I'm...uh..."

"Why are you here?"

"Here?"

"Yeah, here in Korea. Do you teach school?"

"No. I'm engaged to a soldier." It came out nervously. I didn't know why.

"Don't tell me that. You can't be."

"Why not?"

"You're way too beautiful to be getting married."

*Here we go again.* "What?"

"When you walked in, every guy in here was looking at you and thinking the same thing I was."

"What's that?" I asked, slightly leaning toward him.

"Damn she's fine. Just beautiful."

"That's because I'm one of the only two Americans in this joint."

He started laughing, and reached over and grabbed one of my hands. "What does this guy have that I don't?"

I laughed, incredulous. "What?"

"I'm serious. How can I steal you away from him?"

Still laughing, I said, "I've heard about Army guys' reputations, but you're good." I had to admit I was flattered. He could see it, and I think it egged him on.

"Cassie, I'd love to take you home with me."

"Hold on, now."

"Really. You'd love California."

"Oh. But what would your mother say about you bringing a black girl home?"

"Why would you be worried about that?"

"I guess...I guess it's because I'm from—"

"The South, right?"

"Yeah."

"Guess what? She wouldn't say anything at all."

"Yeah, right."

"Really."

"You could bring home a black girl and your mom would be okay with that."

"Yes, of course."

"Okay." He seemed to be serious.

"Besides..."

"Besides what?" I asked.

"My stepfather is black."

"Ohhhhh," I said, slumping down in the booth a little. Clearly, this guy wasn't from Stockdale.

※　　※　　※　　※

Hunter and I talked about everything from surfing in California to life growing up in Alabama. He wasn't just the pretty boy I thought he'd be. He was interesting. His parents had divorced when he was a young, just like me. His mother had remarried an African American. Hunter joined the Army because his stepfather was a retired Army man. They got along, and he considered him his "real" father. Sweet.

I wasn't about to go into any details whatsoever about all the crap I'd had to deal with and was still dealing with about Will Taylor. In fact, I found Hunter's face and smile so appealing, I just wanted to talk about him, not me.

Hours went by but we didn't notice. Once during our conversation, Tonia came back to the booth, saw how engrossed we were and left again, wearing a smile. But she had no reason to. I was still just talking, that's all. Hunter was being a friend, and maybe I needed that. This is what I told myself. But I couldn't help the fact that I was madly attracted to him.

"Cassie. Sweet Cassie," he said. "I have to come back to this point. Why are you getting married?"

"Because I love my fiancée, that's why."

"Okay, but if you ever change your mind—"

"Thanks, but I'm sure."

I looked around for Tonia. I needed a distraction. I wanted Hunter to stop questioning me about my marriage plans. It didn't seem right. John was at the DMZ, and…well, there I was downrange talking to a gorgeous blonde guy. Besides, we needed to be getting back. What if Abe forgot something else? I shuddered to think that huge man, who seemed so sweet, could actually be beating on this girl.

Tonia was nowhere to be found. I excused myself from Hunter and told him I had to go in search of her.

I checked at the bar and even asked Hyun if she'd seen her. No luck.

I went to the bathroom. She wasn't there either. Several guys grabbed my hand and tried to pull me over to their table as I made my way back to where we'd been sitting. Some of them were very attractive. But I was on a mission to find this long-lost girl. No time for more temptations. I'd had my fill for the night.

I asked Hunter if he'd help me look for Tonia, and he agreed in an instant. We went outside. We didn't see her anywhere. Well, at least not at first.

It was Hunter who finally spotted her, or a tiny piece of her, across the street from the club. The rest was being overshadowed by a huge man. They were entangled and doing some serious kissing. I'd never seen the guy before, and guessed that she probably hadn't either. *What about Rico?* was my first thought, then, *What? Am I insane? What about Abe, her husband?*

Before I could stop myself, I hurried over to her and grabbed her arm. Hunter was right on my heels.

I looked from her to the huge soldier, and back to her again. "Tonia, what are you *doing*?"

"Hey, litt'el sis," she said, slurring her words, and turned to the man. "This is—"

"Tonia, we need to go home. Now." I turned around. "Hunter, can you help me get a taxi?"

"Of course." He started waving and trying to get one to stop.

"Tonia, come on," I said. "Let's go."

She gave a sloppy shake of her head. "No, Cass, I promised Lieutenant Mancini I was going home wit' 'im."

"No, you are going to get in this taxi and go home to your husband," I said, trying to stare down the huge person in front of me.

"Oh. Sorry about that, ladies," he said, and backed away. "My bad. No hard feelings, right?"

"Don't gooooooo!" Tonia squealed.

The taxi pulled up beside us just as she went limp.

"Hunter, help me get her in," I shouted. "Help me."

He grabbed one arm and I took the other one and pushed her into the back of the cab.

"How are you going to get her in the house?" Hunter said. "Let me go with you."

Before I could answer, he was already getting in the other side of the taxi, placing Tonia in the middle.

I gave the driver Tonia's address and sat back looking at her, shaking my head. When I looked back up, Hunter was smiling at me. He reached over and gently rubbed my shoulder. I smiled back.

Tonia seemed to be fast asleep, but then she looked up and started laughing hysterically. I jumped. Hunter and I looked down at Tonia, then at each other. This girl was crazy *and* crazy-drunk.

"Tonia, what on earth are you laughing at?" I said, wondering how many rum and Cokes she'd actually had.

"You, Miss Cassie, *he, he, he*!"

"Me?"

"Yeah. I's tol' you you ain't ready to git married."

# Chapter 33

What could I say to that? She *was* drunk, of course. She didn't know what she was saying. At least that's what I told myself. The truth is, I hadn't thought as much about John as I should have when talking to Hunter. Still, I convinced myself that Tonia was out of her skull and that I hadn't done anything wrong.

After we got to Tonia's apartment, I went inside to make sure Abe wasn't back. I didn't go alone, though. Hunter escorted me in, brave soul that he was. But then again, he hadn't ever seen Abe.

Once the coast was clear, we dragged Tonia inside, plopped her down on her bed, and left her there to sleep off her poison.

That's when the awkward moment took place. I'd seen that look in Hunter's eyes all night. He wanted something from me, something I couldn't give him. And anyway, I had to get him out of the apartment before Abe surprised us and gave us all black eyes.

"Hunter, thank you for—"

He crossed the room and put a finger to my lips, and just stood there gazing at me.

I tried again. "Thank you for—"

This time he moved in a step closer and put his whole hand over my mouth, sending chills down my spine. To my surprise, his hands were so smooth, so soft. He was so gentle, and his green eyes were outrageously beautiful.

"Cassie, you don't have to thank me."

"Yes, I do," I mumbled.

"I loved being with you. Let me see you tomorrow."

"Hunter, you know I can't. I—"

"Just as friends, Cassie. Just as friends."

I started scratching my head. It didn't itch, but I didn't know what else to say or do. I did want to see him again. That fact couldn't be denied, as much as I tried to fight it.

"Let me see you again tomorrow," he said.

"I...I don't know, Hunter."

"Then at least call me. Say you'll call me tomorrow."

"I can't do that, either," I said, smiling.

"Why not?"

"Because I don't have your number."

Only one day hanging out with Tonia, and I didn't know what I was doing anymore. There I was, happily engaged to a wonderful guy, and yet I was taking another guy's phone number and promising to call him the next day. And, I had a new weave and was wearing Tonia's red lipstick. Crazy!

After securing a hug from me, Hunter left me to go back to the base. I didn't know what I felt for him, if anything, but I was grateful that he'd been downrange with me tonight, and that he'd helped me bring Tonia home.

✶   ✶   ✶   ✶

When Tonia woke up the next morning, the first thing she talked about was Hunter. When was I seeing him again? Wasn't he gorgeous? Weren't his eyes like none we'd ever seen? She posed so many questions and what-ifs and whatnots that I had a headache way before lunch.

"Okay, so if you have a headache, I've got a cure," she said. "Let's go shoppin'."

"What? Again?"

"What are you talking about, *again*? We didn't even go yesterday."

It was true. Due to her little encounter with Rico, a.k.a, Superman, and his flying performance off the balcony, we'd ended up going downrange late.

That night we were going to be late again, because Tonia wanted to eat lunch, then stop at the PX, post office and commissary. Not only did we have matching hair now, but Tonia bought us matching outfits and insisted on us wearing them that night. She told me I didn't have a choice: We were going back downrange later that night to have some more fun.

I really wasn't that keen on going back, but what else did I have to do? Go back to my lonely hooch and sit by myself? Or sit by myself at Tonia's apartment, hoping and praying that her husband wouldn't come home and ask me where she was? No way! I was hanging with Tonia, reluctant or not.

When we got back to her apartment from the errands, there was something else bothering me—aside from the matching outfits, and even more than the plan to go clubbing again. It was Hunter. I'd been thinking about him and I wanted to call him. Something told me it was wrong. I'd wished I could call John at the DMZ, but it wasn't possible. I guess I just needed someone, and he was…available.

I picked up the phone twice and hung it up twice before I had the courage to go through with it. Finally, on the third try, I let it go through. Someone answered on the first ring. Too late to turn back now.

"Hello? May I speak to Corporal Scott?"

"Hey, beautiful."

"Hunter?" *Really* too late to turn back now.

"I'm so glad you called, Cassie."

His words made my nervousness evaporate. "What were you doing, waiting by the phone?" I said, laughing.

"As a matter of fact, I was," he said, laughing too.

"So…"

"So…?"

I laughed again. What was I *doing*?

"So…can I see you tonight?"

"What?"

"Can I see you tonight, Cassie?"

"Well, Tonia and I are going downrange again. Unfortunately."

"I'll meet you there."

"What?"

"I said I'll meet you there. Wait a sec…Hey, Jones, turn that music down!" Then, he came back to me. "Sorry. I was saying that I can meet you downrange…that is, if you want me to."

There it was. The bait and the hook…and I fell.

"Is he comin', is he comin'?" Tonia said, jumping up and down behind me. She'd already changed into our twin outfits for the night: black pants and a black-and-white-striped shirt.

"Yes. He's c-o-m-i-n-g,'" I said.

"Hot damn! Cassie got herself a pretty-boy boyfriend. Girl, come on in here and get yourself ready. You gotta look *extra* good tonight."

I was starting to think that this was such a waste of time—hanging out with these new people. And after what had happened last night, dangerous as well. "What about Abe and John?" I asked her. "Don't you feel bad?"

"Forget about them, girl. Have fun while you can. Besides, you know what I told you last night, don't you?" She put one hand on her hip. "You ain't ready to get married."

"But I am. I love John. And I *am* getting married to him."

"Then hanging out with Hunter won't change anything 'bout that, will it?"

"Nope. Not at all."

But I realized I was already excited about seeing him again, and that couldn't be a good sign at all.

# Chapter 34

Downrange. Club Studio 54. Round two. It was much busier than the night before. This time it was Friday night, and all the soldiers were out. As soon as we got out of the taxi and started walking the greasy strip, they were scoping us out from head to toe.

When we walked into the club, it was as if we were the only two women left alive on earth. The looks and stares and smiles were that intense. Heads turned from all over the place, even if the guys were with other girls. We owned the club, and Tonia knew it. She basked in the attention, and had us walking all around the club pretending to look for a table when she knew all along that we were going right back to the same booth we were sitting in the night before: her table.

There were so many good-looking guys looking at us looking at them, I began warming up to the attention too. Nothing like this had ever existed in Stockdale. There were blondes, brunettes, redheads—mostly white or Latin, and nine out of ten of them were absolutely gorgeous, or at least very cute. The few African-American guys seemed more interested in the Korean girls, and didn't pay much attention to us. Maybe they were just exploring their different options as well. Maybe they came from towns like Stockdale, too.

Before Tonia had the chance to order her precious rum and Coke, Rico had found us and brought two over to the booth. They kissed as if they hadn't just seen each other yesterday. I couldn't help but remember that she was passionately kissing that guy named Mancini last night too. But for some reason, I thought she really had intense feelings for Rico, and that she wouldn't mind having some type of future with him if she could free herself from Abe. I made a mental note to ask her about it as soon as we were alone.

Two hours later, Tonia had consumed four rum and Cokes and Rico was keeping up with her. Between all their kisses and gyrating on the dance floor, Rico managed to tell me how much he loved Tonia and wanted to be with her. She, however, was keeping mum on the subject of the future, and I didn't understand why.

What I *did* understand was that I was being stood up. Hunter was nowhere to be found. By the time this realization set in, I was feeling mighty guilty about meeting up with him in the first place. I'd go back to Tonia's apartment and write John a long letter. Yes, that's what I needed to do.

I leaned over to explain to Tonia that I wanted to leave. I couldn't believe it when she said they were ready to leave too. We got up and headed for the door.

Tonia had already exited the club with Rico when I discovered that I'd left my bag. I turned around, dodged several people, returned to the booth and got it. Halfway back to the door, someone grabbed my hand from behind. I turned around, ready to shoo off another would-be suitor. It was Hunter.

"Cassie, where are you going? Don't leave."

"Oh, hi. You made it. Too bad. I have to go now."

"Cassie, don't leave yet. I've been looking all over for you."

"Hunter, I've been here for over two hours."

"I just got here about fifteen minutes ago. I'm sorry. Stay."

I glanced toward the door of the club. "I can't. Tonia's already outside waiting for me."

"Let's just go and get her then."

How dare he show up here now, and looking so good too. This time he was wearing a tee-shirt that read *"Surfers Do It Better"* and black Levis. He smelled good, too and I knew that smell. John wore it too. *Obsession. Damn it!* "Hunter, I'm tired. I have to go."

I started walking off.

"Cassie," he said, stopping me and spinning me around. He pulled me over to the side of the bar and put his arms around my shoulders. "I know you're mad. I do. I'm so sorry I'm late. I was back at the barracks and I had to get ready for work tomorrow before I could come down. That way, it would all be done and I could spend as much time with you as you'd let me."

"What were you doing, shining your boots?" I said. I crossed my arms and fought a smile.

"Actually, I was. And a lot of other stuff too," he said, showing me his perfect white teeth.

"Well, I still have to go. I'll call you though." I turned to leave. It really was the best thing.

"Are you leaving because you don't want to see me? Just tell me that."

His look changed. He was totally serious now, his gaze piercing me for an honest answer. "Just tell me you don't want to see me, and I'll leave you alone."

I took a step back, raised my hand to my mouth, and said, "No, I do want to see you."

Hunter started coming toward me. I stopped him. "But I can't."

I left him standing there and joined Tonia and Rico outside. They had already hailed a cab and were waiting for me, meter running.

I raced to the taxi and got inside. The last thing I saw was Hunter standing outside the entrance to the club, watching our taxi drive away.

# Chapter 35

Downrange. Club Studio 54. Day three. It was Saturday night, and the soldiers were out in full force again. Why I was there again, I can't say. Yeah, I could give you the same reasons I gave for being downrange on day two. But that might not have been quite true now. Maybe I was into all the attention I got. Maybe being in this place that was so amazingly different from Stockdale was my drug. I didn't need beer or whiskey or Tonia's rum and Cokes to get high: I was getting high off all the attention from white guys who would never dare give me a second look back in Stockdale...not necessarily because they didn't want to, but because they didn't have the guts to go against society's rule. Stockdale's rule. The black and white rule.

Tonia had given me a lot of flack about Hunter. She'd spoken about him all night long and all day long too. She couldn't imagine letting a magnificent-looking white boy like that get away. Coming from Mississippi, which she said was just as bad as Alabama, she'd sleep with Hunter just to prove she could, if she could. This was one of the reasons she never ceased to amaze me: her audacity.

I, on the other hand, tried to forget about Hunter. He was clogging up too much of my brain. Because of him, I hadn't even written the letter to John yet. I'd gone back to the apartment that night and actually cried because I felt so bad, so confused, and so alone even though Tonia and Rico were in the room right next to me.

And now we were back at Club Studio 54, where Tonia was yakking away to Hyun, who was standing beside our table listening to Tonia's latest amorous adventures. Not really interested in hearing what I already knew, I looked past Hyun at a pretty Korean girl who was grooving to Keith Sweat's "I Want Her" out on the dance floor. She was wearing sexy, skin-tight clothes, all black. I wasn't the only one looking at her—half the men in the club were, too. I sang along; after all, I had that album.

The Korean girl was changing positions now, and maybe I'd get a look at her lucky dance partner—lucky, seeing as half the guys there were vying for her attention. When she finally gyrated to the left, I got a surprise I hadn't been waiting for.

Hunter saw me at the exact moment I saw him. Two other people saw him too: Hyun, and more importantly, Tonia. I panicked and grabbed Tonia's hand, which, at that moment, was flying high to wave at him.

I asked Hyun to bring me a rum and Coke. She and Tonia both looked at me with blank expressions. Then Tonia snapped out of it. "You heard her, bring us two rum and Cokes. Wait a minute, make those doubles! Cassie's man is out there dancing with another woman! We might have to do some ass-whupin' tonight, Hyun!"

I shushed her, then hissed, "Don't talk so loud and crazy. First of all, he is *not* my man."

"Well, he sure is lookin' over here. He tryin' to get your attention too."

"Well, he sure is dancing pretty close to that girl too, isn't he?"

She grinned. "Is Miss Cassie jealous now?"

"Noooo. He can do whatever he wants to. See this ring? I'm engaged!"

"That ring don't stop you from having feelings though, do it?"

At this, I said nothing, just looked back at the dance floor and caught Hunter's eye again. He seemed neither smiling nor frowning. But damn, he looked so good, yet again. It would be better for me to escape. Get out clean and clear. Maybe this would be my last night going downrange. I could go back to my hooch and just read or something, and wait for John to get back from the DMZ.

Suddenly, the lights went down low, and I snapped back to attention. Everything was quiet, and then the DJ continued his love for Keith Sweat. This time, it was one of my favorites, and Tonia and I both let out an "Ohhh, no, he didn't cry," at the same time. But yes, he was. The DJ was playing "Make It Last Forever," and it was just too much. Way too much.

I told Tonia that I had to change positions. I got up and started for the bathroom. That's when he caught me again.

"Cassie, dance with me." Hunter stood directly in front of me. "Dance with me, beautiful."

"Hunter, I don't have time."

"You don't have time for what? For me?" he said, taking my hand.

"I'm on my way to the bathroom. Let me go." I tried to free my hand but he held on, and then noticed the mean look I was giving him and backed off. He rubbed my shoulder instead.

Another soldier approached me and asked me to dance. Hunter didn't like the competition. I didn't like the other soldier.

I tried letting him down easy. "Thanks, but not now."

He didn't buy it though, and smelled like he'd been drinking with Tonia, who had surely consumed my rum and Coke by now too.

"Come on, sexy lady. You know you want to dance with me." The soldier was getting boisterous, and I was getting uncomfortable.

"The lady said no, man," Hunter said. "Leave her alone."

"What the fuck, Blondie? I ain't talking to you, man."

"Dude, you need to chill out. The lady is not interested, it's just that simple."

"Boy, I'll fuck you up. You'd better back up."

"Look dude, you're not touching her, so just get out of here."

I grabbed his hand and starting pulling him away. "Hunter, let's go. Come on. Let's just go."

"Yeah, that's right. Run, you pussy," the drunkard yelled.

Hunter stopped and tried to turn around, but I kept leading him back to the booth where Tonia was still downing drinks.

So much for Making it Last Forever.

Back at the booth, Tonia couldn't get over the fact that Hunter had almost been in a fight over me. He was a real hero in her eyes. She leaned over and told me several times that he was perfect for me, as though she'd never even heard of John, my fiancé. I guess my own behavior reflected the same thing. Here I was chilling in a club in South Korea on the Tongduchon strip being admired by several American soldiers—and one very handsome blonde one in particular—and I was following Tonia's motto: I was going with the flow.

Since there weren't any drinks left at our table, I called Hyun, who was now our favorite waitress, and ordered one for myself and one for Hunter. At that point, I still wasn't convinced that I'd actually drink it. However, I was tried of analyzing and thinking and questioning my entire life: I was going with the flow.

When the waitress came back with the drinks, Hunter held up his glass and proposed a toast. "To Cassie. I adore you."

It was my first taste of alcohol.

INXS came on, and I had to dance. I downed my rum and Coke as though I were a pro and pulled both Tonia and Hunter up on the dance floor with me. Of course, Tonia had at least four or five guys after her that night, so she danced with us only for a second.

Hunter and I moved to the beats. We had the same rhythm. He danced in such a cool way. He was already too sexy…and then he started singing. We were already in perfect sync, but then the DJ went one better: He put in Al B. Sure. I didn't know if Hunter knew the song or liked it, but "Nite and Day" was another of my favorites.

I didn't have to ask him if he wanted to slow dance with me. As soon as the song came on, I knew I was staying out on the floor. Hunter looked into my eyes, pulled me close to him, and we started rocking to the music. This boy looked so good and just smelled so good. I was inhaling him like I couldn't get enough. And he was letting me.

Hunter kept stopping and looking at me during the song. He asked me if I was all right. I said I was, and that the rum and Coke had had little effect on me. I was lying. I didn't want him or anyone else to know that the room had started revolving slightly. I had to play the part. I was going with the flow.

His sweetness made me bolder. I started singing to him, and this was no singing in the church choir. I suddenly became Al B. Sure's new sidekick, and he sure was killing me. He was killing us both.

"Cassie."

I raised my head off Hunter's shoulder and looked at him.

"Cassie."

"Huh?" My feet stopped moving and I looked hard into his face.

"Look." His voice was even lower this time.

I looked around for Tonia. Surely it had something to do with her. But she was right beside us, dancing with Rico.

"Oh, you know Rico, don't you?" I said. "It's okay."

"No, Cassie. Look. Someone's trying to get your attention."

I followed Hunter's pointing finger and saw Hyun standing on the edge of the dance floor. I walked over to her, pulling Hunter along with me. When we got to the edge of the dance floor, Hyun didn't say a word, just pointed toward the exit. Again, I diverted my eyes and followed the end of her long, perfectly red-polished fingernails.

What I saw turned my stomach inside out. John was standing there, looking at me with a face I'd never ever seen him wear before.

*Oh, shit.*

I looked down at the floor, as if that could change something, and then looked back up. It wasn't a nightmare. He was there. And I was busted.

I bit my lip and looked at my partners in crime. "I'd better go, guys."

"Cassie, I'm coming with you," Tonia said, placing herself in front of Hunter.

"That's okay. Don't worry. He's not going to beat me," I said with a sheepish smile.

"Are you sure you'll be okay? Damn it!" She stomped her foot.

I couldn't tell if she was mad because John had shown up and spoiled her night, or because she wouldn't get to continue teasing me about Hunter. But it didn't matter. "I have to go. I'll talk to you tomorrow."

"You promise?"

"I promise. Hunter?" I looked at him.

"You know you don't have to go if you don't want to," he said. "You—"

"Just who the hell are you anyway?"

I'd moved too slowly. John was approaching. His face was flushed and his eyes were moist, as if he had been or would start crying at any minute. The worst thing was the way he was looking at me. As if I completely disgusted him. As if I had literally stabbed him through the heart.

"Hi," Hunter said to him. "I'm just a friend, dude."

"Why don't you get your own fucking woman, dude?" John barked. "Did you know she's engaged? Huh? Did she fucking tell you that, surfer boy?"

"Look, I told you, I'm just a friend of Cas—"

"Shut up! Don't you even pronounce her name. Do you hear me?"

Rico intervened. After telling Hunter he'd better get lost, he started ushering the rest of us outside. I turned around and saw Hunter take a step toward us.

"No. Don't," I said. He stopped moving, and I headed out of the club.

Outside, John was ranting and raving about Hunter. Who was he? Where did he come from? How long had I known him? Rico tried to get him to calm down, which only further enraged him. "You are on thin ice yourself, my man," John growled at Rico, and stabbed his finger first at Tonia, then me. "This fucking girl is married, and this one is engaged. So leave them the fuck alone!"

Then, his eyes narrowed. "You'd better fucking hope that First Sergeant Jackson doesn't hear about this shit. Yeah, that's right. You'd better take care of your own ass. And you, Miss Tonia, you stay the fuck away from Cassie. You're a bad influence, girl. Look at what you've done. Look at her lips. Look at her hair, for Christ's sake."

Tonia tried to react, but she was too drunk. All she could do was plead, "Please don't tell Abe. Please don't tell him!" between choked sobs.

Rico grabbed her arm and they went back inside the club, both obviously shaken up.

John's looked softened a bit, and he held out his hand to me. "Are you going to stay here, Cassie? Or are you coming home with me?"

I could see that he couldn't and wouldn't hold it in any more. His rage had turned into raw pain, *all because of me…and Hunter…and fucking downrange.* These were my last thoughts as we got inside a taxi heading to our hooch.

## Chapter 36

We didn't say a word to each other during the ride home. John wouldn't even look at me, and I was too afraid to look at him again. Once we reached our hooch, I went in ahead of him while he was paying the driver and turned on the lights. I took my earrings off and attempted to wipe off the red lipstick I'd borrowed from Tonia. But then, he'd already seen it anyway.

He walked into the hooch, closed the door, sat down on the bed and put his face in his hands. I thought he was crying, but I wasn't sure. My guts churned. What had I done? This guy, whom I really loved, was suffering. I went over to the bed and sat down beside him, tried to reach out and touch his shoulder.

He raised his head and looked at me. "I just want to know one thing, Cassie."

"Yes?" I answered slowly, and stared down at the bed. I knew what he was going to ask me.

"Did you sleep with him? Did you sleep with that guy?"

My head jerked up. "Nooooo. I didn't sleep with him."

"Don't act like I'm asking you a fucking ridiculous question here," he shouted, got up off the bed and began pacing.

"Please don't shout, and stop saying 'fuck' every three seconds, John!"

"What the fuck do you expect, Cassie? I get a chance to ride in for two days, *two days*, and I'm so excited about seeing my fiancée. Only when I get here and knock on the door where she's staying, she's not there. Tonia's fucking nosey neighbor tells me to try downrange. Now, I'm fucking exhausted, going to every fucking club down there trying to find you, and when I do, you're fucking slow dancing with somebody else. How the fuck am I *supposed* to react?"

I looked down again. "I was just dancing. He's just a friend!"

"You can't be friends with soldiers, Cassie. That guy only wants one thing. One thing!"

"Not all guys are like that, John."

"Baby, trust me. I'm in the Army. I know how they think." He knelt down in front of me and lifted my head to look at me. Then, his eyes narrowed. "Wait a minute. Have you been drinking too?"

"I just had one drink, that's all."

"One drink? But you don't drink!" He threw his head back and sighed. "That fucking Tonia!"

"I'm sorry. Look, I am. I didn't mean to hurt you. I love you."

"Do you?"

"Yes! I love you! I love you so much."

"Then how could you do it, Cassie?" He lowered his face to mine. The rage was gone, but the raw pain was back in his eyes.

"I don't know.... Maybe we should...I don't know. Are we...*Am* I too young?"

"What are you talking about?"

"I don't know. That's what I'm trying to tell you. I don't know!"

"Then why did you come all the way over here? Huh?"

"I came here for you. I came here to be with you. I do love you. I'm sure about that."

"Then prove it to me."

"What?"

He breathed a ragged sigh, got up and began pacing again. "One of the reasons I hitched a ride in was because I couldn't wait to tell you something. We got our papers back."

"Our papers?"

"Yep, our marriage application. We can get married now. The government gave us the okay. And...I thought you'd be just as excited as I was. I made us an appointment to go to Seoul to do it. It's already set up. The day after tomorrow."

"We can get married the day after tomorrow?"

He nodded. "That is, if you still want to. Do you, Cassie? Do you?"

His eyes begged me to say yes. I knew I loved him, I was sure about that. And I'd gone there engaged and planning to marry him. I couldn't let him go.

I nodded. "Yes. You know I want to marry you."

He came over and lifted me off the bed. "Cassie, I don't want to be without you. Please don't ever do anything like that again. I love you. I love you, baby." He kissed me.

"I love you too. I'm so sorry. Please forgive me. I love you." We fell down on the bed and I started tearing off his BDUs. He didn't smell like Calvin Klein's Obsession. He smelled like Army, and I loved it. He stopped me long enough to take his boots off, and then we made love with more passion than we had ever before.

Figures. Jealously does funny things to people.

*   *   *   *

A few hours later, I fell asleep thinking about getting married in two days. But although I really loved him, part of me couldn't help but wonder if I'd given him the right answer.

The next morning, I told him I needed to go on base to call my mother. I'd been in Korea for two months, and this was only the second time I'd talked to her by phone since I left. I told him I wanted to let her know I was getting married. Actually, I wanted to ask her opinion about it.

He walked me to the phones and waited outside while I talked, eventually going inside the PX to buy a few supplies to take back to the DMZ with him. As soon as he left, I cut the small talk and told Mama what was going on.

"That's crazy," she said.

"That's crazy?" I repeated.

"Yes. You need to get back in school. You should have never left."

"Yeah, but I'm…I'm just twenty years old. I can always go back to school, Mama."

"Really? What if you get pregnant and end up like Kelly? Have you thought about that, Cassandra?"

"But I love John. And he knows how important school is to me. I'm telling you, I *am* going back."

Mama let out a long, exasperated sigh, then said, "I can't talk to you anymore right now. Here's Kelly."

I couldn't figure Mama out. Love didn't even matter to her. All she ever worried about was school, school, school, and she didn't trust me enough to believe that it was important to me too.

"Hey girl! Do you want to say hello to your little nephew?"

I woke up and almost dropped the phone. "When did you have the baby? What is it? Why didn't you tell me?"

"We sent you a letter with pictures of the baby. You didn't get it?"

"No! Send me another one, with a picture. So it's a boy?"

"Yeah. His name is Jimmy. He's *Little* Jimmy."

"Wow! I can't believe you're a mommy. Where's big Jimmy?"

"He's in Florida on a new job. As soon as he gets us a place, I'm going down there. It's so much better than Stockdale, Cass."

"I know. Almost any place seems better than Stockdale—"

I glanced at the door of the PX and saw John inside, at the cash register. "Kelly, we have to hurry because I don't have much time left."

Okay, one more thing. Blake's been calling here. Collect. From jail."

"Oh yeah? Too bad. Don't tell him anything about me. Look, I gotta go."

"One more thing. Don't come home. Don't come back to Stockdale."

*Click.* We were disconnected. No more time on the payphone.

For the entire day, the only thing that kept reverberating in my head was Kelly's last sentence: *Don't come back to Stockdale.*

\* \* \* \*

The next day was my wedding day. It had been two days since the drama happened downrange, and John and I were on our way to Seoul. We'd made love several times, and it had felt right. I felt more in love with him than ever before. But still, something was off. Something was bothering me. No, more like some *things.*

I couldn't get Kelly's words out of my head: *Don't come back to Stockdale.* What did she mean? Should I call back? Would she be there?

But there was no time.

I decided to let go of it all. It was too much to worry about. I leaned back in the taxi and closed my eyes until we got to Seoul, and soon, we were walking to the City Hall, where we would be pronounced man and wife.

We were almost there when we came across a group of student protestors. What were they protesting? Americans being stationed in South Korea, of course. And we had to pass right in front of them.

John squeezed my hand and we walked faster, but not fast enough. His Army haircut was a dead giveaway. One of them turned around and signaled to the group, then turned back and yelled, "Hey, you American GI! Go back to America."

Others joined in, yelling, "Go home, Yankee!"

We were hugely outnumbered. We started jogging, then running. There had to be at least thirty of them. My heart wouldn't stop leaping out of my chest. I looked back to see if they were following us. They weren't. But my legs had given out. I was sweating and out of breath. I wanted to stop, and John wanted anything but.

"Cassie, we have to hurry," he said. "Come on. The place is going to close in fifteen minutes."

"I can't, John. I'm too tired. I won't make it," I panted.

"You have to make it. Come on! If we don't make it today, I don't know when I'll be able to get back down here."

"If we don't get married today we can do it another day."

"Are you serious? You can do this, Cassie. Come on."

He started running again. Every couple of steps, he turned back to look at me, to see if I were coming.

What could I do? I looked back at the protestors; they'd stopped chasing us, but were still watching us, and still agitated. I couldn't go back in that direction.

Then I remembered Kelly's words: *Don't come back to Stockdale.* So I grabbed my side and started running again, and caught up with John. My only thought now was whether the city hall would be closed when we got there.

# Chapter 37

▼

It wasn't. We were the last ones to enter before the guard locked the door, but enter we did. John handed the secretary our paperwork, paid the fee, and she put a stamp on it.

We were pronounced married by the Republic of South Korea, Seoul, on September 19, 1988. I was twenty years old, and the whole process had taken less than ten minutes.

I was now a married woman.

The shock didn't come until later. We left the city hall, made sure the student protestors weren't a menace, and made our way back to the taxi stand. John was exceedingly happy that we'd pulled it off, and kept calling me "Mrs. Fitzgerald." His only regret was that we couldn't go on a honeymoon right away; as soon as we returned to the base, he had to report back to the DMZ.

After he had left, having given me plenty of kisses and advice, the first thing I did was not follow it—I went to see Tonia. I had to talk to someone about what had happened. Had to confide in someone that I was married.

I could hear music coming from inside, but even though I rang Tonia's doorbell over and over again, no one answered. I'd just decided to leave and come back later when the door swung open violently and a voice growled, "Who the hell is ringing this doorbell like that?"

It was Abe. He jerked opened the door, his face dripping with sweat or tears, I couldn't tell which, and his eyes were red and bulging. "Cassie. What do you want? Now's not a good time to be comin' round here."

"I…uh…is Tonia here?"

"Yes, she is, but she's busy right now." He started to slam the door, but a hand caught his from behind and stopped him.

"Cassie, don't go," Tonia shouted from behind him. "Call the MPs. This ape bastard won't let me go."

I couldn't see her, but I could hear her loud and clear through her sobs.

"Abe, open the door. Open it now!" I yelled. She was hurt. I could tell. And I remembered what she'd told me about him beating her.

I tried to put my foot against the door, to block it from being closed. Both our actions were in vain. Abe was too big and way too strong. Neither Tonia nor I could stop him from slamming the door in my face.

I knocked on the door as hard as I could, then rang the bell and shouted, "Open this door or I'm calling the MPs!"

Tonia's neighbor, a middle-aged Korean woman who was married to a GI, opened her door and threatened to call the MPs herself if we didn't quiet down. She was the same one who'd told John he could find us downrange, but I didn't have time to tell her to mind her own business. In fact, I was glad she'd opened her door. Maybe Abe had heard her threat, too.

He had. Five minutes later, he jerked the door open and stormed past me, carrying a gym bag.

I stood there, stomach quivering, too scared to go in and too scared to leave. But I had to know what had happened to Tonia. I eased the door open and walked inside, leaving it open. I shuddered to think of what I might find. What was in that gym bag Abe was carrying? Was he murderous? Had he chopped off her head and shoved it in there? *Okay*, I told myself, *time to stop watching horror movies.*

"Tonia? Tonia? Are you in here?" *Of course she's in here,* I thought. *Abe's the one who left, silly.*

"Cassie, I'm here. I'm in here."

*Here* was the kitchen.

My knees were shaking so badly I could hardly walk. *The kitchen? This is bad. Has she been stabbed? Is she in there bleeding to death?*

I let out a sigh when I saw her standing at the refrigerator with no blood dripping from her body. But when she closed the freezer door, I saw that she hadn't come out of their altercation completely unscathed. The left side of her face was twice as big as it should have been. With trembling hands, she placed the ice cubes she had retrieved from the freezer inside a washcloth, then placed it on her eye, which was already turning black.

"Oh, my God! Tonia! Shit!" I ran over to her and took a closer look at her face. Not only did she have a huge black eye, but her lip was busted and bleeding as well. "What the hell did he do to you?"

Instinctively, I balled my hands into fists and ran to the balcony to look outside to see if he was still there. I wanted to apply a few punches to Abe myself. I was so furious, I momentarily forgot how huge he was and how he could pulverize me with one punch—just as he'd done Tonia.

"Cassie, he gone girl. He ain't comin' back no time soon."

I ran back into the kitchen. "How do you know?"

"'Cause I threatened to call his company commander if he didn't leave and go stay in the barracks." She rubbed the ice from her eye, to her lip, and back again.

I headed for the phone, wondering where she kept her phone book. "We need to go see a doctor," I called over my shoulder. "And we need to call the MPs."

"Cassie, don't."

"Don't what?" I said, whirling around. "Don't what? Look at you!"

"Cassie, I'm fine. It looks worse than it is," she winced, "even though that bastard really fucked me up this time."

"*This* time? And what about next time? What about the times before?"

"Cassie, my head hurts. I don't want to talk about it. Can you just find me some aspirin? Look in that drawer."

I got her the aspirin, but I was far from finished. "Why did he do this to you? What happened?"

"Shit. Can't you guess?"

I felt my eyes go wide. "Did he find out about Rico?"

Another wince. "Yes-sir-ree-bob."

"How? How did he find out?"

"I don't know. I just don't know. I was askin' myself if John had told him."

"No way. And anyway, John's been with me the whole time during the past two days." *It couldn't be John*, I thought. *He wouldn't have done that.*

Her face went still, and she looked away. "It don't really matter. He knows."

"Shit."

"So, you been with your fiancée for the past two days, huh?" Tonia said, walking out of the kitchen and into the living room to sit on her red sofa. She turned back around. "On second thought, let's stay in the kitchen and fix ourselves a couple of drinks."

"No. That's the last thing we need. We need to go to the doctor. We have to."

I forced her to put some clothes on and hailed a cab. The driver kept staring at us through his rearview mirror, but said nothing.

When we finally reached the Camp Casey hospital, one look at Tonia, and the soldiers waiting to see the doctor moved aside. The doctor, a scrawny soldier with graying hair and tiny wire-rimmed glasses, came in to examine her. The look on his face was grim.

"Would you like to tell me how this happened to you?" he said, turning her face from side to side.

"I fell," Tonia answered, nonchalant.

"Fell where?" He wasn't buying it, and I was glad.

"Off the balcony of my apartment."

"Off the balcony of your apartment?"

"Yes. I was bending over looking down and I lost my balance."

"I see. Dangerous thing to be doing, huh?"

"What really happ—" I started, but Tonia stomped my foot and gave me a look that stopped me in mid-sentence.

The doctor peered at me. "Yes?"

I remained silent and shook my head. "Nothing"

When he left the room, saying something about going to find Tonia's paperwork, she grabbed my hand and rushed me out of the hospital.

"He wasn't going to get no paperwork," she shouted as we got back into the cab. "He already had my paperwork. He was going to call the MPs!"

I thought it would have been good if he had.

"Cassie, I've gotta tell you something."

"What is it now?" I couldn't take much more, not tonight.

"Abe didn't do this to me."

"What?" I hadn't expected that. Apparently neither had our taxi driver, because I could have sworn I saw him raise his eyebrows too.

"Abe didn't hit me."

"Then how in the hell did you get like this?"

"He was gone hit me. I know it. But instead of just lettin' him, I ran."

If I'd said it once, I'd said it a hundred times: This girl was nuts.

"I ran and jumped off the balcony."

"You did what?"

"But I fell all wrong—on a rock or somethin'....Hell, I don't know....And this is what I got."

"You *are* crazy. What's wrong with you?"

"I thought I could do the Superman thing like Rico, but I fucked it up. I...I just didn't want Abe hittin' me again, that's all."

"So you risk hurting yourself or damn near killing yourself?" I yelled at her. "That's no better, Tonia!" My head started to throb. There was just too much drama. *She* was too much drama. "I'm going back home."

"Cassie, don't be mad at me."

"I can't help but be mad at you. Whether he beat you this time or not, you still ended up getting hurt. Look at you! And what if you hadn't jumped? Maybe you'd *still* look like this."

"Cassie, you're the only friend I have. Try to understand. I *will* leave Abe. I will."

"When, Tonia? When?"

"Soon. I'm already working on it."

She finally convinced me to spend the night with her, because she was still afraid of Abe. We talked until she went to sleep, and I stayed there watching over her for most of the night. In the wee hours of the morning, I finally fell asleep myself, but only after having barricaded the door—just in case Abe did come back.

## Chapter 38

Two days later, we couldn't even tell that Tonia had been "beaten up." With plenty of ice and rest, we'd managed to get her to looking herself again, and with the evaporation of her "wounds," the old Tonia was back and in full form. The first thing she wanted to do was go downrange.

I didn't. I wouldn't.

Because of my obstinacy, she yielded and decided to throw a party at her apartment. I really wasn't in the mood for it and just wanted to go back to my hooch, but one thing remained for me to do: I still hadn't managed to tell Tonia I'd gotten married.

The first person she invited to her little party was Rico, but he didn't come alone. He knew about what had happened. Tonia told him that she and Abe were officially separated, and that he was now living in the barracks. But Rico wasn't taking any chances, and came to the apartment with two of his friends as backup. The friends came with their Korean girlfriends. I wasn't surprised that she invited Rico, and by now, I didn't care. I was so exhausted over all the drama that if Abe had come back and caught Tonia again, I was going to jump over the balcony myself.

There was music, hot wings, beer and cheap wine on the menu. Everyone was having a good time. Except me. I missed John. I wanted to see him. I wanted to talk about our marriage. I wanted him to tell me that we'd done the right thing and that we'd live happily ever after. None of this was possible, however. He couldn't be reached at the DMZ. I was almost ready to cry. I didn't want to be there at Tonia's anymore, but I didn't want to be at home alone in my hooch either. I was trapped.

The doorbell rang in the middle of Rick James' "Super Freak," and everything and everyone became silent. Rico's two friends, the backups, stood up. *Dear God, please don't let that be Abe*, I prayed, getting up off the sofa too.

Tonia crossed the room and shouted, "Who is it?" Everyone else strained their ears to hear the voice on the other side.

"Oh, okay. Great!" Tonia said, pulling the chains off the door.

"Tonia, who is it?" I called to her. "Who's—?"

And in he walked. I stood frozen while she made the introductions. Everyone was overfriendly. I'm pretty sure they were relieved that the newcomer to the party wasn't Tonia's three-hundred-pound husband.

I stared at Hunter with my mouth wide open. It had been almost a week since we'd seen each other. Tonia had called him and invited him. She must have done it when I was taking my shower. Damn her! Little did she know that she was just adding further complications to my already-complicated life.

Hunter, for his part, smiled and nodded in my direction, his hands pushed into his jeans. After the intros were made, he came over to me immediately. I heard Tonia in the background saying something about mood music, but I tried to ignore her. I would deal with her later.

"Cassie, I'm so happy to see you."

"Hey, Hunter."

"How are you? Are you okay?"

"I'm fine, just tired."

"What happened? I was hoping you'd call me."

"Sorry. I've been…busy." I looked over at Tonia, who was fiddling around with a cassette. Soon, an Atlantic Starr ballad began playing.

"I missed you."

I smiled but kept my eyes on Tonia. I'd missed him, too. All of a sudden, it was clear to me that I had missed him. But I couldn't tell him.

I looked over at Tonia and wondered what she was up to. She held her glass up to me and started singing something about someone taking crazy chances to be alone together. I watched her with Rico, and decided it was more about her, and them, than me.…

Or was it? There was no doubt about it—the song was getting to me. I felt myself cracking. All the pressure, the questions, the drama from the last few days grated at me. I made both of us a drink—Tonia's infamous rum and Coke mixture—and downed it. I made another one and downed it, too.

I took Hunter by the hand and led him into the spare bedroom, which had become my second home. I closed the door behind us and leaned up against it, still holding his hand.

I couldn't hide it anymore. I had to tell Hunter. I had to tell someone.

Atlantic Starr had finished lamenting over their secret lovers and was now singing us a different tune. Damn Atlantic Starr! My church had always been right: This type of music could really get you in trouble. I fought to ignore them. I had to get it out.

"Hunter, I did something," I started, surprising myself at the way I'd begun, as if I'd stolen money out of the collection plate at church.

"Don't say anything," he said, taking a step closer to me. He smelled like his signature fragrance. Obsession. And I was now facing a startling reality: I *was* obsessed. I wanted him. I knew it. He had been that little thing that made me uneasy on the way to Seoul to get married.

"I have to say something, Hunter. It's important."

"Okay, what is it?"

"I got married. I'm sorry, but I did." The tears fell freely now. I couldn't stop them. "I got married a few days ago in Seoul. I'm so sorry."

"Cassie, it's okay. Calm down, I'm here. It doesn't make a difference." Hunter took me in his arms and caressed my hair.

"I'm not a bad person. I love John, but I…I…I can't stop thinking about you."

"Cassie, I care about you."

He cupped his hands around my face and I held his hands in mine, and for the first time, with Atlantic Starr still singing far away in the living room, we kissed.

My heart was all the way in it.

We kept kissing and kept kissing and kept kissing until I pulled him down on the bed on top of me. Tonia had slyly placed condoms in the nightstand drawer next to the bed. I fiddled around in there with my one free hand until I found one. I passed it to him. Then, we were ready. I couldn't contain what I felt for him anymore. In that moment, the knowledge that I was married wasn't enough to stop me. I loved John, I was certain of it. But now I realized I'd fallen in love with Hunter too.

Is it possible to love two men at the same time? Even though I didn't want to be, at that moment, I thought I was living proof that it was.

* * * *

The morning after. Hunter had left along with all the other guests, and Tonia and I were in the kitchen eating a bowl of cereal. No doubt, she couldn't wait to question me about what had happened between Hunter and me. But this time, she let me lead the way.

"Tonia, Hunter and I—"

"Girl, I knew it. Did ya'll do it? What was he like?"

"Yes. We did it…and it was amazing."

"Amazing? Girl, do tell!"

"I don't know. It was just…so passionate, so…it was the best sex I have ever had."

I couldn't stop myself from smiling when I thought back on it. Then my smile turned into a big frown, and the next thing I knew, I was crying, thinking, *I'm an adulterer and I'm going straight to hell.*

"Cassie, what's wrong? What's wrong with you?"

"Oh, shit, Tonia. I made love to Hunter because I've messed around and fallen in love with him too!"

"That's okay. You'll decide…. It's all right."

"No! It's not. You don't know."

"Know what, girl?"

"I'm married! I'm a married woman now!"

"What?" she screamed, and clanged her spoon down in the bowl.

"That's what I came up here to tell you the day you and Abe were fighting! John and I got married that day!"

"Oh, fuck. Why didn't you tell me?"

"All that was going on…everything…I was waiting for a good time."

"Shit. Well, hey, don't worry 'bout it."

"But now I'm an adulterer!" I cried even harder.

She reached out and put a hand on my heaving shoulder. "Two dimes, Cassie."

I looked at her. "What?"

"Two dimes in a bucket. Know what that means?"

I shook my head.

"Two dimes in a bucket means fuck it." She shrugged her shoulders and said it again, "Fuck it."

Easy for her to say. If only Reverend Sanders could've seen me then.

# Chapter 39

One week later, and the guilt was eating away at me like termites in a newly framed house. I had to confess my sins. Not to a priest—I wasn't Catholic—but to John. I was a good Baptist, or at least I used to be, and I wouldn't be able to sleep until I'd made some real decisions, and confessions.

Apart from that, Hunter wanted an answer. He wanted to be with me all the time, fulltime. He was nearing the end of his tour in Korea and wanted me to go with him to California, where he'd be stationed next. I didn't know what I wanted yet. All I knew was that I had to see John.

Luckily, there was a trip scheduled for the few family members there who wanted to visit the soldiers at the DMZ. With the rest of the wives and girlfriends, I got on the bus and headed north to the 38th Parallel. I knew it wasn't the best place to tell John I'd cheated on him, but it couldn't wait.

When I finally arrived and saw all the barbed wire, I felt that I was entering a prison. There were guards everywhere, and everyone carried their weapons with them. It was dusty and dirty. There was hardly anywhere to go or sit. We found a makeshift restaurant, but it was already crowded. We ended up just sitting on the bus that had brought us up. John was so happy to see me, I almost lost my resolve to tell him.

"I missed you, baby," he said squeezing me again.

"I missed you, too."

Was it a lie? Not really. I had. Yet seeing him made my stomach hurt. I was anxious, panicky. In spite of my feelings for Hunter, I was starting to feel regret. *I shouldn't have done it....*

"Cassie? What's up? Where are you?"

Back to reality. Too late for what-ifs.

"John, we have to talk."

He took my hand in his. "What's wrong, honey?"

"I…I've done something. I think I've made a mistake." I bit my lip. That sure was a funny way of putting it.

"What's wrong?"

"I—I met someone…and…we hung out. I—"

I felt my hand being dropped back into my lap. "Tell me what happened."

"I'm not sure if we should have gotten married. I don't think I was ready."

"Who is it? The blonde surfer guy?"

When I didn't answer, he knew he was right. "Motherfucker."

"I'm sorry! I do love you! I do, but…"

"Go with him." After saying that, he got up and walked toward the front of the bus.

"What? Where are you going? We need to talk."

"Go with him, Cassie."

"John, wait!"

He turned around, and when I saw the tears streaming down his cheeks, my heart stopped beating.

"It's over, Cassie," he said, and stormed off the bus.

I cried all the way back to Tongduchon.

I was twenty years old, hadn't even been married two weeks, and there I was already getting divorced.

I desperately needed to find Hunter. After I got off the bus at Camp Casey, I went directly to his barracks. The CQ told me Hunter was in his room and he let me go up. My tear-swollen eyes probably softened his heart a little.

I knocked on the door, but he didn't answer. I went back down to the CQ and asked him if he was sure Hunter was there, he assured me that he was, and I went back up again.

This time my knock was answered, but it wasn't Hunter who opened the door. It was the Korean girl I'd seen him dancing with that night on the dance floor. The one all the guys were salivating over. The one dressed in all black. Only this time she wasn't wearing all black. She wasn't wearing anything at all except a towel.

I heard the shower running in the bathroom and pushed my way into the room. For a moment, I tried to tell myself that maybe it was Hunter's roommate, here with his girl. I was wrong. Hunter came out of the shower dripping with water, and his face changed colors when he saw me. The Korean girl was gathering her lacy panties off the bed. I watched her, holding my stomach as if I would throw up, and looked back at Hunter.

"Cassie, what are you doing here, I thought you were going to the DMZ."

"I did, but I'm back. I guess I'm bothering you, aren't I?"

"It's not what you think."

"Really?" I yelled. "Really? *Really?*"

The Korean girl scooted out the door, carrying her shoes in her hand.

"I trusted you," I screamed at him. "I threw it all away for you, and look at this shit!" I waved my hands in the air.

"I'm sorry. You were married.... I didn't know if you were going to leave him or not.... I didn't think you would."

"Sorry? Well, I am too, Hunter!"

"Cassie, wait!"

"Fuck you!" I said, walked out of his room and slammed the door.

I ran out of the barracks and back to my hooch, where I collapsed on my bed. I could find no comfort anywhere. I was alone, and I had only myself to blame.

# Chapter 40

A few days later, as much as I hated it, I was on a plane back to Stockdale. I'd called my grandparents, who'd called Mama. My plane ticket was waiting for me at the airport. As long as I assured them I was coming home to go back to school, there was no problem in sending for me. Beside, there was nothing left for me in Korea. I had to go back.

Tonia had passed by the hooch and tried to convince me to stay, then move with her back to the States, but I had no further interest in Tonia. I had accepted my guilt, but she really *was* a bad influence. Hunter had sent word by her that he still loved me and wanted us to be together, but I didn't want to hear that either.

When my plane landed in Atlanta after a five-hour layover in Salt Lake City, I wasn't surprised that no one was waiting for me at the airport. My family was notorious for not being at the airport on time to pick people up. But on this day, the last thing I wanted was to be left waiting.

I found a place to sit. Mama, the person who was supposed to pick me up, was already an hour late. I sat there people-watching, asking myself how I'd ended up back there. But deep down, I thought I understood how it happened. The saddest thing of all was that I still loved John, whether he loved me anymore or not.

I was still caught up in those thoughts when I heard someone shouting my name. I looked up and laughed, glad to see her and my mother a few steps behind.

I hadn't seen my cousin Whitney in months.

We hugged and spoke all the way home. I had barely heard from her since I'd been in Korea. She'd had some problems of her own. Ricky had left her for someone else. Who? She didn't know because he wouldn't tell her. I prayed to God that it wasn't my old UAB roommate, Mia.

Mama didn't have much to say to me. She was clearly disappointed that I'd wasted time going to Korea; I could tell by the way the corner of her mouth was turned up when she looked at me through the rearview mirror. Once we got back to Stockdale, the only thing she had to tell me was that Kelly had gone to Florida to be with Jimmy, and that she was glad I'd finally come to my senses and was going back to school. Figures.

Whitney spent the night with us, and I told her everything that had happened. She was nice enough to help me take my weave out, and cried with me when I told her that all I was waiting for next was the divorce papers from John. She seemed to think there was still a chance John and I might reconcile. I didn't.

The next day, newly weave-less, I paid my grandparents a visit. Grandmama and Granddaddy were thrilled to see me back in Stockdale. I myself, having seen the city again in daylight, felt sick to my stomach just being there. Stockdale, with all its airs and racial division. Stockdale, city of segregation and racism. Stockdale, where all the blacks still lived on one side of the tracks and all the whites lived on the other. I no longer could stand living in Stockdale, or Alabama period. But, I was back all right, and just the reality of it, mixed with the fried eggs Grandmama was cooking, made me run into my grandparents' bathroom and throw up.

While I was washing my face, I overheard them talking. "She didn't have no business being over there anyway....needed to bring her tail back here...need to be in school somewhere...*umph, umph, umph.*"

I couldn't blame them. What they were saying was right. I *did* want to get back in school. I needed that. Now, I realized that was my only way out of Stockdale and the South for good. Having this plan was the only thing that was saving me from pulling all my natural hair out at the roots.

I came out of the bathroom, pretending to hear nothing, and talked to them for hours before I finally got up the courage to ask them for help—financial help. I needed money to get my own apartment, and to get back in school. I couldn't live with Mama anymore. I didn't want to. I needed my own place and space, no dorms. Besides, I was mad at Mama for being mad at me. I'd take care of myself. I would stay there just long enough to finish my degree.

Granddaddy didn't say anything when I asked for help, just dropped his head down on his chest. My grandmother, however, got right up from her chair, put her sewing down on the stool beside her and went to her bedroom. When she came out, she was carrying her checkbook. How much did I need? I wasn't sure yet. So she wrote me out a blank check, signed her name on the bottom and handed it over to me. "Now get back in school, gal."

I walked out the door and got into my car, the check still in my hand. Grandmama stood behind the screen door watching me turn the car around. I gave her the old two-horn blow, and smiled and waved. What would I ever do without her?

\* \* \* \*

At least it was easy to find an inexpensive apartment in Stockdale. The furniture wasn't a problem, either. I had gotten some from Mama, some from my grandparents—a sofa here, a chair there. It didn't matter. I didn't care so much for decorations, or anything else. I got my old Honda back from my grandparents' garage. It had over a hundred thousand miles on it, but it would do. It was good to be back in the driver's seat.

It was too late to start the fall session, but I kept myself busy during those two or three months by getting moved in and settled. I started going back to church and found my religion again. I confessed all my adulterous sins and prayed that God would rescue me from the pit that I had come from—South Korea—and the pit I had fallen back into—Stockdale.

I chauffeured my grandparents around like in the good old days, when I was still a teenager at Stockdale High. We visited relatives all over Alabama, including Montgomery, Bessemer, Loachapoka, Notasulga and Roanoke. They paid me each time, even though I tried to turn it down. Deep down, it was just an excuse for them to help me.

Although I didn't want to be there, it was comforting to be with them again. They even went with me to UAB to do all the paperwork to have my grades transferred to Jefferson State University. That had been our deal: They would help me finish school, but only if I were closer to home…where they could keep an eye on me. Ironic that I ended up going to the one school I had avoided when I finished high school because I wanted to get as far away from Stockdale as possible. At the time, Birmingham seemed so far away.

\* \* \* \*

I wrote out my plan of attack to leave and studied it closely. I applied for financial aid, and went back to cleaning houses for white people in our community. My objective? I'd save whatever I could from it after paying all my expenses, and as soon as I had my degree, I'd leave Stockdale and all its prejudices behind me. I hadn't exactly made up my mind where I was going, but I had a few ideas. It was looking like either the West Coast, the East Coast, or maybe even Europe. I dreamed of going to Italy…or France.

I didn't even think about having another rum and nothing. My drinking days, as brief as they'd been, were over for good. I can't say that I blamed my actions on drinking, because I hadn't had that much in Korea. I just knew it wasn't for me.

I started a journal about everything that had happened so far in my life, and spent hours on the phone talking to Kelly and hearing about her new life in Florida with Jimmy and their baby boy. I'd finally seen him, and he was just as cute as I'd imagined. I was amazed at how almost everyone in my family had now accepted, or at least tolerated Jimmy, simply because they loved Little Jimmy. The love of a child had changed them. Maybe there was hope for the people of Stockdale yet.

But then again, I knew better. This was only my family. There were still a lot of people to convince who believed a person could only love and be with someone with the same skin color. In other words, we were still years and years away from realizing Dr. King's dream that people would be judged by who they *were*, and not by the color of their skin.

I went to see Heather's mom and dad, who still had her pictures everywhere in the house. I placed a flower on her grave and told her a little about what had happened to me, and wondered if, somewhere, she could hear me. The dreams I used to have of her had finally stopped, but I still missed her a lot. She would have been a good friend to me now, when I needed one terribly.

Other than that, there weren't many people left in Stockdale that I'd gone to school with. They were all off at college, or had joined the military, or had gone on with their lives in other ways. Some were working long shifts at the chicken plant or one of the other plants, and hardly were seen around town. I was thankful. The last thing I wanted to do was play catch-up with old high-school buddies and discuss my life thus far. I wasn't proud of it. But I kept telling myself I could straighten it all out, if I could just get my degree.

I tried not to think about Korea, Hunter, or Tonia, but I still couldn't stop thinking about John. I hadn't gotten any divorce papers from him, and figured that he was just waiting until he came back from Korea to file. I'd sent him a few letters to say how sorry I was and how much I missed him, but he hadn't written back yet.

By the time winter rolled around, I was ready and even a little bit excited to be back in school. I took lots of English classes and studied Poe, Dickinson, Browning. Sometimes I found the words so painful, it was all I could do to not burst into tears during class. I discovered Walt Whitman and fell in love with *Leaves of Grass*. Like a literary hermit, I came home every night to my apartment from the library. When I wasn't reading books of poetry, I wrote poetry. Most of the poems were for John or about John. There were some about Hunter too, and they were all scornful.

When I wasn't writing or reading or doing homework, I was trying to sleep. Sleep was the only thing that saved me from my more depressing memories. And even then, it wasn't guaranteed I wouldn't dream about John, Hunter, Tonia or even Will Taylor, whom I was running into more often that I wanted.

One Sunday I came out of church and saw him leaning on the Honda, waiting for me. I said goodbye to everyone, waited until the last of the members had gotten into their cars and then rushed over to see what he wanted.

"Hey darlin'. I sho' is glad you back in town," he said, and reached out for my hand.

I stepped back from him. "What are you doing here? Church is already over."

"I just wanted to see you, that's all."

"Why?"

"'Cause you's my daughter, that's why."

He looked like he'd fall if he stopped leaning on my car, and I realized that he was dead drunk.

I shook my head and looked at his '70's jeans, reminded of the first time I ever saw him. "I'm your biological daughter. That's all! I don't even know you, and you don't even know me. But I do know one thing: You need help. You've got a problem."

"I'm sorry I left ya'll, baby. I really am."

"Why did you? Why did you stay gone? Why won't you tell us?"

"I just…I just…"

"I can't keep wondering about you, and why, and what for. Kelly and I—"

"Yeah, I heard ya' sister gone to Florida with that honky."

"What did you just say?" I spoke between gritted teeth.

"She ran off with that white boy, didn't she?"

"You have nothing to say about her, and you have nothing to say about Jimmy. You weren't there for us. You left. You're just like the rest of these crazy people here in Stockdale, all worried about the wrong things. My God!"

I started crying and let out a long sigh, my knees shaking.

"Cass…"

"Who do you think you are, coming here? I wish I had never gone looking for you." I covered my face with one hand and cried harder.

"I didn't mean no harm, sugar, I'm just sayin'," he said, and tried to hug me.

I jerked away. "You weren't here when we needed you. Don't you see that? Kelly hates you!"

He chuckled. "Now don't go exaggeratin' now, honey.…I's gone—"

"Just leave us alone!" I shouted, taking my hand away and pointing at him. "Go back to Atlanta. Go hide in your liquor, just go somewhere!"

I walked around and got inside the Honda, cranked it up and drove off, my chest aching. I was the one who brought Will Taylor back to Stockdale, but he would never be a part of my life. Kelly was right. It was just too late.

I cried over Will Taylor for two days, then forced myself to stop thinking about him. I had to stick to my original objective: finish college and get out of Stockdale.

\* \* \* \*

For three semesters straight, I took more classes than I could handle to hurry and finish my degree. Summer semester, 1990, I was almost through—only one more semester to go. After the fall semester, I would leave Stockdale for good.

That's when the news broke.

## Chapter 41

When Whitney told me that Blake's brother had been killed in a racial incident over the weekend, I was flabbergasted. It was early August, and I was on my way to register for my classes. "What?" I yelled into the phone, and threw my car keys down. "He's dead?"

"Yep," Whitney replied. "Girl, he was shot to death over a white girl. Stole some white boy's girlfriend, and the white boy said he'd rather kill 'em both than to see them together. Said he couldn't stand to see her with no nigga."

There it was again. The n-word.

"How do you know all this, who told you?" I said.

"Well, you know I'm dating that policeman, right? Since I moved to Jefferson?"

"Noooo…what policeman?"

Her voice lowered. "It's kind of on the downlow."

"Why? Is he married?"

"He's white."

I gave a bitter chuckle. "Oh. That explains it. Same old dirty South."

"Anyway, he got the story from number one, the suspect, and number two, Blake himself. You see, Blake's already in jail. Been in jail. And when they brought in his brother's killer, they were trying to decide how they were gonna proceed, seeing having them in the same jail could be dangerous and stuff."

My legs gave out and I sat down.

"They finally shipped the white boy off to another jail, 'cause they figured if Blake didn't get him, some of his friends in lockup would. Just a mess girl. Just a mess."

"You're telling me."

"Luckily for her, the white boy missed the white girl. She all safe and sound, hiding out somewhere from her parents, 'cause they didn't even know she was going with a black boy."

"I hate this damn place."

"Huh?"

"Nothing. Sorry."

"So you goin' to see Blake or what?"

"Going to see Blake? What for?"

"All I'm doing is passin' the message. He wants to see you."

I sighed. "If you see him or send word by your ghost of a boyfriend, you can tell him that I'm sorry about J.R., but as far as seeing me? He's the last person in the world I want to see."

But he was also the first person I saw the following day.

That night, all the nightmares I used to have about Heather came back. I would have one, wake up, go back to sleep and have another one. Heather was drowning; so was J.R. Heather was with Hunter. Heather had survived and had a baby named Max. Heather, Heather, Heather. Dear Heather, who had probably driven her car over a bridge in rebellion.

The cycle was continuing. People couldn't date whom they wanted because of skin color. People were still using the n-word, and people were actually shooting others over an interracial relationship. I couldn't help but think about J.R. and what a funny character he'd been. He and Blake were really close. And Blake must be going nuts.

I finally decided to at least pay my respects, if nothing else. Another person had lost their life because the person they loved had a different skin color. Besides, Blake was my first love. We'd gone to the prom together. He was the first boy I'd ever been intimate with. Even though our relationship had ended badly, I guess I still felt something for him, if nothing but the feeling one gets over a bittersweet reminiscence.

But, to go and see him in jail? It was the first of a series of horrible decisions, but I didn't know it then.

\* \* \* \*

Later that morning, I found myself at the city jail asking to see him.

"He'll be right out," a guard said, and pointed to a chair in front of a thick glass window. I saw a telephone on the wall and felt like I was in the movies, only

I wasn't. And in a few seconds, I'd be picking up that phone and speaking through it, but facing him through a pane of glass.

The weirdest thing occurred to me: I didn't even know why he was in jail in the first place.

After a few minutes, Blake finally came out. He wasn't the Blake I'd known in high school. Not at all. Almost all of his hair was gone; the huge bald spot started in the middle of his head and went all the way to the back. He was also much thinner, sporting none of the muscles he used to have. His face was all sunken, and his eyes hollow with dark circles underneath.

*My God, what has happened to you?* I thought. I dared not say anything aloud. He wasn't wearing the mischievous smile I'd expected him to, either.

"Hey," I said into the phone, wanting to smile but unable to.

"Hey, what up, now? I didn't think you was comin'."

*Neither did I.*

"Yo' cousin got you the message, huh?" he said.

"Yeah. Look, I can't stay. I just wanted to tell you I'm sorry about J.R."

He was missing several teeth, and the ones that remained were stained and rotting. I was ready to go.

"Yeah, that's some fucked up shit, ain't it?" Blake said, sniffling.

"Yeah," I replied, looking around at the small room and then back at the glass window.

"And you know what the most fucked-up thing about it is? These mutherfuckers talkin' 'bout they ain't gone let me go to his funeral. Now ain't that some fucked-up shit?"

"Yeah. I hope you get to go." I got up. I had to leave. I felt like I was suffocating in there. "Give your family my respects, all right?" I placed the phone back onto its hook, then turned to walk away.

I heard tapping on the glass and hesitantly turned back around.

I didn't want to, but clearly, he was grieving. I walked back over, sat back down and picked up the phone.

"Yeah, Cassie, I wanted to tell you that you still lookin' good, baby."

*Oh my God. That's all I need.* "Why are you here, Blake? What did you do?"

He gave a little chuckle and relaxed back in his chair as far as the phone cord would allow him, then said, matter-of-factly, "I got in a little trouble. Stole some shit. Nothin' big. But I'm gittin' out in less than a month. How 'bout you and me git back together when I git out?"

The thick glass between us wasn't enough. As he had, but for a far different reason, I leaned as far back in the chair as the telephone cord would allow.

"Girl, you know I been thinkin' 'bout you ever since we broke up. What was that, two, three years ago?"

"It was a long time ago. Look, good luck with everything and take care of yourself."

"What about gittin' me some cigarettes, girl?"

I hung up and walked out. This time, there was no way he could call me back.

# Chapter 42

Hunter? I couldn't see that he was bad for me. It wasn't obvious in the beginning. But Blake? I had known he was trouble already, so I can't tell you why, three weeks later to the day, when he showed up at my apartment, I let him in. In retrospect, I can only say that I still had those high-school feelings for him. Perhaps because he was my first love. Perhaps I was just too sentimental. But more than that, I honestly felt sorry for him.

I felt sorry that his brother had been murdered. I felt sorry because he said he didn't have a place to stay and just wanted to crash on my sofa, at his "only friend's place," until he could get back on his feet. I felt sorry because he was an African-American brother who couldn't catch a break and had no help in the world whatsoever. He didn't have a loving family like me, no grandparents to take him to Sunday school and church every week. But I also thought I could save him, and everyone except me knew that couldn't happen.

The initial deal was that he'd stay there just until he got a job. Then he'd move out. Mama was against it, Granddaddy said that I was shacking up again, and the pastor at church came to speak to me about it after church one day. But I assured them all that I was just helping the guy out and we weren't together in that way.

They still thought it was an incredibly bad idea, but Blake said all the right things—that he wanted to change, that he had stopped drinking, that he even wanted to go to church with me in Stockdale.

I thought he could do it. I thought that he could make something out of his life. I even encouraged him to go back to school and get his GED and then go on to college. He nodded in agreement each time. He was a good fooler, and I was a better fool.

He stayed in my apartment all day long when I was away at school, when he should have been out looking for a job. But with each passing day, he gave me another excuse. *It's too hot. It's too sunny out there. It's going to rain today. It's too far to walk.*

Knowing that the sooner he found something, the sooner he'd be out of my hair, I even brought home listings from the job bank at school. On my day off from classes, I drove him to the unemployment office. But he always had something negative to say. Whenever I'd complain, he'd start crying and say how much he missed J.R. and that he had no one in the whole world.

After he'd been there for about a month and a half, his old high-school counselor, Mr. Monroe, started coming by, supposedly to take him looking for jobs. I was happy he was getting some help, especially from his old counselor. One day Mr. Monroe drove up, blew the car horn, and Blake rushed out to get into his car. As they were driving away, I waved at Mr. Monroe from the balcony. I'd always thought it was nice of him to be a mentor to young men and boys.

What an idiot I was.

\*   \*   \*   \*

After a while, sometimes when I went to bed, just before locking my bedroom door, Blake asked if he could go to bed with me. I always told him the same thing: "You are only here as a friend." I could do him this favor of letting him stay with me because I was so hurt and angry over his brother's death—a prime example of why I hated Stockdale, Jefferson, and all its surrounding areas. And yes, we had history together. But Blake kept telling me he was going to win me back.

I had to get him out.

He was still hanging out with Mr. Monroe, and I was hoping he'd help him find a job and a place of his own soon. He was cramping my style. The fall session was almost half over, and I was approaching the end of my degree. As soon as I marched down the graduation aisle, I was out of Stockdale. One way or another, Blake had to leave.

One night, I told him so.

"You have to find a job," I said. "If you can, maybe you can try to take over my lease."

He just nodded his head and kept watching TV.

"Are you listening to me?"

"Girl, I heard you."

"I'm leaving soon, so you'd better get your stuff together."

I guess it was a mistake to fill him in so much about my plans, because everything started going downhill from there.

He asked to use my car to get us a pizza for dinner at Domino's. He said he'd worked all day for Mr. Monroe, had a little bit of money, and wanted to pay me back for some of my food he'd been eating. I was surprised, pleased at his thoughtfulness, and tired of eating beef noodle bake. He grabbed his coat and left.

I took a shower while he was away. I stayed in there much longer than necessary, doing my customary job of fogging up all the mirrors. When I came out, he still wasn't back. I did some homework, then tried to study for an important math test I had the next day. Still no sign of him.

I finally got so hungry, I ended up having leftover beef noodle bake anyway. He still wasn't back. Had he been in an accident? Where was he? Where was my car?

At two o'clock in the morning, he knocked on the door. I had gone to sleep on the sofa. I snatched open the door, shouting at him from the moment I saw his face. "Where were you? Do you know what time it is?"

"Heyyyy, baby," he said, stumbling into the house and dropping the keys on the floor. I picked them up and then looked at him: He was as high as the last kite I flew back in elementary school.

"Are you crazy?" I yelled.

"Hey now. It's cool, baby."

"You're getting out of here tomorrow, do you hear me? Tomorrow!"

"What I do?"

"What did you do? You left here seven hours ago. Count them, seven. In my car!"

"I been gone that long?"

I wanted to slap him, but I decided to go outside and check the condition of my car first. Since he could hardly walk, I didn't see how he'd been able to drive back.

When I got downstairs and looked at the body of the car, it was intact. I opened up the front door and looked inside. Everything was fine there too. I was just about to shut the door again when I saw two things. One was a plastic sandwich bag full of marijuana lying near the emergency brake. And the other thing? A used condom lying on the passenger seat.

I ignored the condom but grabbed the bag, raced back upstairs to where Blake was sitting on the sofa trying to take off his shoes, and did exactly what I wanted to do before: I slapped him, and hard.

After he'd gotten over the shock, he coolly sat back and pulled out a cigarette while I stood there with my hands on my hips, glaring at him. I could feel sweat dripping down my back.

"You are getting out of here tomorrow, and I mean that." I threw the bag at him.

"Girl, please. I ain't goin' nowhere. Not yet, anyway."

"Oh yes, you are. You are getting up out of here."

He looked at me, seeming befuddled. "What's yo' problem, girl?"

"You know what my problem is, Blake? You. You don't work. You don't want to work. You're eating all my food. You're draining me. You're a drunk, and you left a used condom in my car and a bag of marijuana in there for *me* to go to jail. I want you out!"

"Oh, is that what you trippin' off of? I'm sorry 'bout that. The weed? Yeah, that's medicine, shit. But the condom, you're right. That *is* rather funky. I'll take care of it tomorrow, 'K?"

"Why is it in my car? Answer me!"

"Well, you sees, I was with some of the fellows, you know, reminiscing about J.R. and all.…We drank some beers and whatnot…had a few smokes…yo', that weed is tight as hell, too. You sure you don't want me to light one up?"

He saw the evil look in my eyes and continued. "Anyway, some broads came by and you know, we was goin' for some more beers and shit, she wanted to git with me and I wanted to git wit her, so we got with each other."

"You had sex with this girl in my car. And you smoked weed in my car."

"I had to! You ain't puttin' out shit. A brother's gotta get his thang on, ya' know."

I grabbed my head in disbelief. "We are not together, so no, you are not getting any sex here. But that doesn't mean you have to be sexing women in my car!" I spat the words at him.

I wanted to slap him again. I moved closer to do it, but held myself back. Seeing that I wasn't coming any closer, he stretched himself out on the sofa and put his hands behind his neck.

I ran into my bedroom and slammed the door, thinking, *What in the hell have I gotten myself into, and how am I going to get this disaster out of my apartment?*

\* \* \* \*

The next day, Blake did exactly what I expected him to do. He cried and blamed everyone in the world for his problems, including me. I was already having a hard time at school, having saved my weakest subject, math, for the last semester, and I had all my other classes. I had a math test that morning and I was sure I'd failed it as soon as I left the room. The problem was, I couldn't afford to fail it. As it was, I was hoping to make it out of the class with a C.

Two days later, Blake did something that completely surprised me: He went out and got a job cutting off chicken heads at the chicken plant. He even offered to pay me for letting him stay with me, if I'd only do it for a little while longer until he could save some money.

I couldn't take Blake being there anymore, but could I honestly throw him out?

I tried. I told him I was happy that he had a job now, but that he had to get out. Then I got the few things he had together, stuffed them in his gym bag, and threatened to call the police if he didn't leave.

We finally compromised—I'd give him a lift. To get him out of my place, I did just that.

The first place we went to was to his mother's house. Unfortunately, no one was home. Next, we went to a couple of his friends' houses. No one had room for him, or they were just a heck of a lot smarter than I was. Then he decided to play his trump card: the guilt card.

"Just let me out here," he said.

We were passing in front of the Greyhound bus station. "I'll just bunk out here," he continued. "I hope I'll be able to get to work tomorrow—that someone won't cut my damn throat in the middle of the night or some shit like that."

I pulled over and stopped the car. He got out, dreadfully slow, as if he were marching into war to die at any moment. But instead of walking forward, he just stood there sighing and looking around.

I told him to call his mother again, to see if she was back home, that maybe he could stay with her. He laughed and said, "Yeah, right. She was probably there all along but just wouldn't open the damn door."

I thought he was bluffing. "Let's just call her and see."

"Okay. You wanna call her? Let's call her. I'll even dial the number for ya'."

I needed someone other than me to help him. I got out and we found a pay phone.

"Good luck," Blake said cynically from outside the phone booth. I ignored him.

After several rings, a sleepy-sounding woman picked up. Bad start already.

"May I speak to Miss Reynolds, please?"

"Who is this?"

"This is Cassie, a friend of Blake's."

A few moments later, Blake's mother picked up.

I did the small talk—asked her if she remembered me. Of course she did, and how was I? I was just fine, and I was so sorry about J.R., etc., etc., etc. Then I went to straight to the point of why I was calling: Could she come and get Blake?

"No, I cannot." Whereas she had been semi-nice, even chatty, now there was silence.

"He can't stay with me anymore," I said. "He can't... You can't help him?"

"No, I cannot." Same answer, same tone.

"He's found a job, but he needs some help."

"I cannot, I'm sorry."

"Okay then. I guess I'll try to contact Mr. Monroe," I said, hoping that would get a rise out of her, with him being connected to the school and the community.

She let out a long sigh on the other end of the phone. "Leave Mr. Monroe alone, honey. He's got enough problems of his own."

"Excuse me?"

"Please don't call here anymore, either."

The line went dead. Blake's mother had hung up in my face without even saying goodbye.

How I wish I had driven off and left him there, but I didn't. I want to blame this on the church. I did, after all, have the pastor's Sunday sermon running through the back of my head. *Am I my brother's keeper? Yes! I am! Am I charitable? Yes, Lord, I am! Do I, the Christian that I am supposed to be, help others in need? Yes, Lord! I do!*

As though he had been in church and heard that sermon himself, Blake turned around, and I saw tears running down his face. Oh, he was so *good*.

"Cassie, I know I fucked up. I know I did," he said. "But if you will just give me another chance...I got a job now.... I'm tryin' to git my shit together. I don't got nobody else.... I'll pay you.... Please let me stay with you 'till I can get my own place. Please, Cassie, please. Don't leave me here like this."

He was clutching his bag to his chest as if they were only possessions he had in the world. And in fact, they were.

What happened next? I bit. Hook, line and sinker. I didn't want him to end up dead, like J.R. I thought he deserved a chance. He didn't have anybody, and I had been blessed with plenty of people who cared about me...except for Will Taylor. I also knew how it felt to be abandoned, so I guess that's why I did what I did.

"You're only going to stay for one month maximum. You hear me? And maybe not even that."

I reached over and unlocked the car door. He got in and said nothing, just smiled. But it wasn't a smile of appreciation. It was a devil's smile. In that moment, I knew I'd made another mistake.

## Chapter 43

Blake did everything he could to prove me wrong, though. He never asked to borrow my car again. He walked to work every day, and for three or four weeks, he seemed to be working hard and focused. He came back on Fridays, his payday, and gave me fifty or seventy-five dollars, bought food and paid for an electric bill. I told him to keep most of his money though, for his move. I still wanted him out.

In mid–November, when I had one month left of school, Blake returned to being Blake. He stopped giving me any money. He stopped buying food. He was even asking *me* for money, of which I had none that I would give him. And besides, he was the one working fulltime, not me.

First, it was that he'd seen a place but had to pay a deposit on it, requiring him to save more money than he'd planned. Then it was that he had to pay child support or he'd be locked up again. The excuses went on and on. I told him that I was sticking to my deadline: He had to get out.

Finally, one Friday after school, I decided to meet him at work, to see for myself what he did with his paycheck. I waited in my car for him to come out, only he didn't. Several people did, though, and I saw someone I knew—good ole Deacon Culpepper. I called his name and he shuffled over to the car. After we'd said hello and he'd asked about my grandparents, mother, and school, I asked him if Blake was still inside. I thought maybe he was working a double shift that day.

"Blake? He ain't here."

"Oh," I said. Maybe I'd arrived too late or he'd gotten off early. "Has he already left?"

"That boy ain't worked here in about a month, girl."

"What? But—"

"Naw. He worked for about two days and then up and quit."

I bit my lip and nodded to signal that I'd understood. But the good Deacon wasn't through with me. "And I'll tell you somethin' else, too. They say he's on that stuff, so you'd better watch out. You don't wanna be mixed up with someone on that dope. What you doin' hangin' round somethin' like that for, anyway?"

With that, Deacon shuffled away shaking his head.

I sat in the car, staring straight ahead, my fingers tightening around the steering wheel. Not only had this boy used me, but he had sullied my reputation in Stockdale. And he was "on that stuff?" Was it the serious stuff? Heroin? Cocaine? What? Did everyone in Stockdale think I was on whatever it was, too?

I cranked up the car and went back to the apartment. When I got there, I slowly walked up the stairs. For some reason, I knew he'd be there.

He was. I found him sitting in my living room, shirtless, smoking a pipe. Gray smoke was coming out of it, and there was a horribly weird smell. I had no idea what it was. I'd never smelled anything like it before, but I knew it wasn't marijuana.

As it turned out, Blake was actually smoking crack before my very eyes.

I picked up my *Leaves of Grass* book and threw it at him and his whole contraption. He dropped the pipe on the carpet and it broke into pieces.

"You crazy bitch," he yelled. "Do you know how much I paid for that shit?"

"I don't care," I shouted. "Get out! Get out! Get out!"

He lunged at me and I ran to the front door, threatening to call the police. He backed down then and started looking in his pockets, and retrieved two more crack rocks. "Looky, looky, I still got some left. Now."

"Get out, and get out now, or I'm going to call the police!" I screamed.

"You ain't gone do shit, and I'm gone sit here and finish my high."

He went to the kitchen and looked through the cabinets, searching for something else to use for a pipe. I ran to the phone and picked it up. There was no dial tone.

"Oh, I forgot to tell you, yo' shit's turned off. I think 'disconnected' is the proper word," he said, taking on a fake British accent and laughing. "Remember when you asked me to pay your phone bill for you a couple of times? Well, I had to use that money, darlin'. That's why yo' shit is now off."

I looked at him, aghast. "But…But I didn't get any notices. I didn't get any disconnection notices." I backed up toward the front door.

"'Course you didn't. I threw that shit away. But fuck 'em. Fuck the phone company. I guess they didn't like all those calls I was makin' to my homies out in California, either."

Leaving him braying in laughter, I ran out the front door and to Miss Ethel Mae's house, banged on the door and yelled, "It's me, Cassie from next door. Can you call the police for me?"

The neighbor, an elderly lady who sang in the choir with me at church, opened her door immediately.

"Cassie, what is wrong with you? Are you all right? Come on in."

I went inside and let myself be sat down by her. Her voice and hands were trembling from either concern, or fear, or both, and I already regretted coming there.

"I have to use your phone," I gasped as soon as I could speak. "Please. It's an emergency."

"Chile, go, it's yours." She pointed to the kitchen counter. But instead of calling the police, I called Whitney. Thank God, she answered on the first ring.

"Whitney, it's Cassie. I need you to come over to my place right now."

"What's wrong, girl?"

"Whitney, just come. I'll explain when you get here. Please hurry."

"Okay, I'm on my way."

"And Whitney?"

"Yeah?"

"Can you bring your boyfriend?"

"My policeman?"

"Yeah." I struggled to remember his name, then said, "Yeah, bring Terry."

"Okay, now you're scaring me."

"Just do it."

I hung up and sat there, looking at the phone. Miss Ethel Mae came over and patted me on the back. Her gentleness made me give way to tears. What on earth was I thinking? Why was I so gullible? I was so close to my degree, yet so far away, and now this. Miss Ethel Mae held me in her arms the way a grandmother would do—as if she had understood everything. Considering what Deacon had said to me, she might have.

Whitney and her white policeman arrived twenty-something minutes later. She made the quick round of introductions and he awkwardly shook my hand. I thought it was bold of him to come out of hiding, to reveal to anyone that he was her lover. This was Stockdale, remember. If the wrong person—and that could be anyone—saw them together, their little secret would be over.

I went back to my apartment with them, not knowing what my next step would be, just aware that the stakes were now higher. Blake was poisonous. Everything about him was descending or had already gone down, and he was pulling me down with him.

When we got inside my apartment, Terry checked the bathroom, but Blake was gone. So was his gym bag with the few clothes he had. For the first time in days, I felt a little relief. He had finally left, and on his own. I sat down and buried my face in my hands for a long time.

Whitney and Terry continued to search the apartment. I just sat there, numb and afraid, unable to stop my legs from shaking well enough to trust them to follow them around.

After we were sure we were alone, Whitney sat on the sofa beside me and gave me a hug. But her boyfriend was still in police mode. "We need to check to see if he took anything with him, Cassie."

"His bag is gone," I offered.

"Is there anything of yours missing?"

I looked around and immediately saw what had been off when we first re-entered my apartment.

Blake had taken my TV and VCR. But he hadn't stopped there. All the money from my wallet was gone, along with my radio and the gold chain that had once been on my dresser. So was the engagement ring and wedding band John had given me.

Terry wanted to file a report. I didn't. It was too much. There had already been too much drama. Did everyone in Stockdale have to know what a fool I was? I just wanted to finish school and get out. They tried to talk me into it, telling me that Blake was crazy and dangerous. Terry, who also worked at Stockdale's jail, knew it from witnessing Blake's behavior there.

They helped me clean up the apartment and sweep up the broken crack pipe. Whitney opened all the windows to get the smell out, and insisted on staying with me until my nerves settled. She still wanted me to file a report, to press charges against Blake. I wanted no part of it. If he needed those things to leave, so be it. I could always buy another TV and VCR once I got to my new place, couldn't I? Besides, those would be two less things I'd have to pack. I'd write those things off as a going-away present and another lesson in life. What I didn't know was that the lesson wasn't over yet.

\* \* \* \*

One week of school left before my final exams, and I was convinced that Blake was following me. I never saw him, but I felt something overshadowing me at different times. *But why would he do that?* I asked myself each time. I hadn't seen or spoken to him since he'd left with my things, and I was sure he wouldn't show his face again. Perhaps he was even on the run or hiding out, afraid the police were looking for him. Yet as much as I tried to convince myself it was my imagination, something was bothering me, a bad feeling I couldn't shake.

I reasoned it was the anxiety of school finals, of graduation, of moving to a new place and finally being able to leave Stockdale. I'd secured a job for after graduation, far away from Stockdale, and everything was falling into place. Still, I kept looking over my shoulder everywhere I went. Whitney had stayed for a week. I felt silly needing her there, and was relieved when she asked if I wanted her to go back home. With one week left to go, I needed to be packing and getting everything ready to move.

The day of my math exam, I said prayers on top of prayers and went in fully motivated. I high-fived another student when I came out. I knew I hadn't made an A or even a B, but I did well enough to pass. That was the end of it: I was ready for my college graduation.

Two days later, my confidence became reality. I'd done it! *Nah nah nah boo boo!* I was getting my bachelor's degree in English! Even more, I was leaving Stockdale for a whole new adventure. Blake wasn't going to bring me down after all.

Remembering that saying, "Pride goeth before a fall," I forced myself to come back down to earth. But it wasn't easy. I only needed a C in math, and that's exactly what I got. Lucky C, oh me, I was home free!

On graduation night, the whole family turned out to see me in all my glory—my grandparents, Kelly and Jimmy, Whitney, some other cousins, uncles and aunts, the pastor and entire deacon board (and let's not forget about the Motherboard). And yes, even my father came to see me graduate.

I spoke to him and clumsily thanked him for coming. He pulled me close to him and hugged me, telling me how proud he was of me. I didn't know what to say after that. When he let me go, I fought off tears and watched him walk off to find a seat. Mama watched him too. I don't know what she was thinking, but I was content: Will Taylor had finally come to see about me, whether I wanted him there or not.

After I practically skipped down the graduation aisle and waltzed up on stage to accept my degree, all my folks, except my father, took me to Piccadilly for a celebration dinner. It was the best I'd felt in a long, long time.

We were having such a good time, I couldn't bring myself to tell them my plans of leaving Stockdale. I was sure Mama suspected it, although she said nothing during dinner. Besides, I didn't have to leave until a week later. I told myself they'd understand, and even be happy about my new life and job offer.

We all stuffed our faces with roast beef, roasted chicken, macaroni and cheese, green beans, cornbread, sweet tea, red velvet cake, apple cobbler and ice cream, and told jokes and laughed it up. Finally, the party broke up. In the parking lot, I thanked everyone for coming and gave them all big hugs.

Whitney wanted to do something else, maybe go dancing or just hang out.

"I'm going to go on home," I said to her after she'd pleaded with me one last time.

"I could come by later if you want me to."

I smiled at her. "I thought you had a date with your policeman."

"Yeah, Terry and I have plans. But…if you need somebody…"

"I'm fine, girl! I'm just happy and excited that it's over."

She smiled. "Okay then, I'll come over tomorrow."

With a final "Bye girl and congratulations again!" she got in her car and drove away.

I was just about to get into my car when Mama came back over. She'd already given me a hug, so it surprised me to see her. Everyone else had gotten in their cars, and my grandparents were waiting for her.

"Cassie, I know this could probably wait until tomorrow.…"

And then I knew. She was on to me. I tried to play it off anyway.

"What couldn't wait until tomorrow?" I asked, hoping I was wrong.

"Are you leaving? Are you leaving Stockdale?"

*Bam.* There it was. She had me.

I didn't answer her, and when I didn't, she walked over and gave me a long hug. "When I was young," she whispered in my ear, "I always wanted to leave Stockdale too."

I pulled her arms from around my neck and looked at her in astonishment. "What? You never told me that."

She nodded. "It's most certainly true."

"Why didn't you, Mama? Why didn't you get away from this place?"

"Because I met and got married to your father. That's why. And besides, Mama and Daddy are here, so—"

"I know, but—"

"But *you* don't want to stay here, do you?"

I looked down at my shoes and then back up at her. She put her arms around me and hugged me again, tighter this time. When she finally let me go and we looked into each other's eyes, I saw that she completely understood: I would never be happy in Stockdale.

\*     \*     \*     \*

Still wiping tears, I got into my car and put a cassette in. This time, Hall and Oates. It was old, but I didn't care; I loved it. I fast-forwarded to my favorite song, "Sarah Smile," and sang along with them.

I thought about my family and how they'd react when I told them I was leaving again. I knew it would be hardest on my grandparents. I would really miss them. I thought about Heather and what she would have become, had she lived. I thought about Korea and John, and how much I had really loved him. As happy as I'd been a few minutes earlier, I was now panting and crying like a child. It was as if the dam had been opened and all the sorrow and pain I'd experienced during the past few years was being released.

Through heavy, heart-achy sobs, I sang on with Darryl and John, though, and by the time I reached my apartment I had pretty much put myself back together. After "Sarah Smile" ended, I'd ejected Hall and Oates and put in M.C. Hammer. "Pray" had gotten me back on track, and I felt like a whining sap no more.

I pulled into the parking lot at the apartment feeling psyched, eager to continue packing my things. Inside, I threw my keys on the table, as usual, and placed my graduation robe and diploma on the table beside them. I turned on the lights and looked around. A few weeks before, each time I came home alone, I'd gone over my quarters with a fine-tooth comb. But, uplifted by how well the night had gone, I didn't even think about checking closets or looking under the bed.

I pulled off my dress and got in the shower. It felt so good to be under the hot water. I decided to go ahead and wash my hair, pamper myself a bit with a new conditioner I'd picked up a few days earlier at Wal-Mart. I stayed in the bathroom until I had put the conditioner in twice, rinsed it out, and completely dried my hair with the blow dryer.

I guess that's why I didn't hear the front door open.

According to the clock sitting on my bedside table, it was 10:59 p.m. I looked at the electronic display of red light until the numbers changed.

The thought came suddenly: *It's 11:00. Do you know where your children are?*

I chided myself for thinking about that, but for years, that slogan from the Atlanta Child Murders had stuck in our minds. A shiver passed down my spine. This was definitely not a night to go there.

To block out the horror that had taken place in Atlanta, I quickly revived the images from my graduation and Piccadilly, and pulled a pair of navy blue cotton pajamas, my comfort pajamas, from my dresser. Since I'd stayed in the bathroom so long, I'd decided to pack the next day instead. But then, I remembered my diploma, still in the living room. I couldn't help it. I wanted to look at it once more. There was still a part of me that had a hard time believing I had finally completed college.

I walked out of my bedroom and into the darkened living room, and knew that I wasn't alone.

# Chapter 44

▼

Blake was sitting in a chair near the door. Except for the faint light passing through the living room window, I could hardly make him out. But it was him. I wondered if perhaps he might be asleep, but then he moved his hand.

"Good evening, Miss Cassie. Miss College Graduate."

I said nothing, just stood rooted to the spot, my mind racing a thousand seconds a minute.

"Now I guess you think you real better than me, don't ya'?"

"Blake, what are you doing here? It's late," I said, as nicely as I could muster.

"Yeah, it is," he said, rearranging himself in the chair. I saw an empty liquor bottle on the coffee table in front of him. He noticed that I noticed.

"Cassie Taylor, meet my friend, Jack Daniels," he said, and grabbed the bottle and tried to get one last swig out of it. "Fuck! That shit already gone. You got any liquor in here, girl?" He threw the bottle across the room into the kitchen. It hit the refrigerator and crashed into pieces. The sound of it breaking made me jump. I turned around to look at the mess.

"Blake, you need to leave, now." I reached over to turn on the light, but he startled me with a crazed yell.

"I wouldn't do that if I was you, girl."

I stopped in mid-action. "Just leave now," I said, "and we can talk tomorrow."

"Well, Cassie, you know it's like my ma-man A—Apollo Creed said, baby: There *is* no tomorrow. You 'member that? There *is* no tomorrow. Fuckin' Rocky wouldn't have got nowhere without my man Apollo, shit."

While he was in his *Rocky 3* reverie, I headed toward the door. I had to pass him on the way out, but if I could just get outside, I could go next door to Miss Ethel Mae's apartment.

Blake got up from the chair, brandishing something long and silvery in the dim light. I blinked. I was staring at a butcher knife, and Blake was pointing it right at me.

"Oh, my God!" I said, grabbing my mouth and backing up.

"That's right, baby. You better fuckin' pray." Blake jabbed the knife in my direction. "What, you wanna run out of here and call the police again? That what you was plannin'?"

"No, I—"

"I, I, I, my ass. Sit *yo'* ass down."

I didn't move. Couldn't move. Just stood there.

"Sit yo' ass down before I make you." He started advancing toward me, so I backed into the kitchen, took a chair from the table and sat down.

When Blake retook his chair by the door, I started thinking of what I could do next. There was no phone. Thanks to him, it had been disconnected.

He kept the knife in this hand for a few minutes, just staring at me with an icy look on his face. I had a hard time meeting his gaze.

After what seemed like hours, he put the knife on the table in front of him, leaned back again in the chair, looked at the knife and at me, and then back at the knife again, as if to gauge whether I could grab it or not. I was thinking exactly the same thing. I was sitting about six, maybe seven feet away from him. It would be close.

My best bet was to run out of the apartment, or into my bedroom and lock the door. *But he's too close to the front door,* I thought. *And he might catch me before I actually get into the bedroom.*

I had to wait it out a little bit, try to talk him into leaving. Maybe I'd be able to convince him that this whole thing was needless.

Suddenly he moved, and I twitched. He reached in his coat pocket and took out something. From the small amount of light, I could tell it was a bag of some sort, maybe plastic, and another object. He felt around in his jeans pocket and took out something else after that. I watched him in horror, wondering what he would cook up next. And then I knew. He had taken out a crack rock and was lighting it up. He might have been out of alcohol, but he still had a need to get higher.

He took a few puffs. He seemed distracted, so I turned around to look at the clock on the stove. Out of nowhere, he ran over to the chair in which I was sitting and bent down near my face. *Does he have the knife with him? Did he leave it on the table?* I was too afraid to look in his hand, and too afraid to look on the table.

"Here girl, take a puff of this." He put the smelly pipe close to my lips. "Go ahead, try it, Mikey. You just might like it." He laughed at his own joke.

"I don't want any," I said, pushing his hand away.

"Naw, 'course not. Miss Goody Two-Shoes." He walked back over to his chair and sat down. I just sat there, looking at him, eyes glaring. The knife was still on the table.

"That *is* you, right? Miss Goody Two-Shoes?"

"What do you want? Why are you here?" I yelled, my eyes starting to water, my hands balled in fists at my side.

"Girl, don't you raise yo' voice at me. Who the hell you think you is, anyway?"

"I want you out of here, or else," I said, trying not to breathe in his poison.

"Or else what, goddammit? Huh? Who you gone call? Ghostbusters?"

Again, he broke into a laugh at his own joke. I pretended to laugh at his joke too, and then suddenly stopped, sickened by the fumes coming from his pipe. This made him even angrier. He got up, picked up the knife and threw over the coffee table with his other hand. I rose up from my chair and backed into the tiny bar separating the kitchen from the living room. He followed.

"Who the fuck do you think you are, huh?" He was in my face again, brandishing his weapon. "Still afraid of knives, though, I bet."

I stood with my arms folded against my chest, trying not to show my fear, and moreover, trying not to cry. I was backed up in a corner against the kitchen bar. He was standing so close to me, I dared not try to run. At that moment, I knew he was certainly capable of stabbing me. I could see it in his eyes. I could hear it in his voice. But I still thought I had a chance. And besides, this couldn't be happening to me anyway, could it?

"Blake, what's wrong? Tell me," I said, as soothingly as I possibly could. I forced myself to reach out and stroke his cheek.

A tiny crack came in his tortured face. "Fuckin' everythang girl, just everythang."

"Well, talk to me. Talk to me, Blake. You know…me and you. Just sit down, let's talk."

"I know we's go way back, girl. Shit, I thought for a moment it was gone be me and you." He retook his chair, but he pulled it within inches of me first. The knife was still in his right hand, the pipe in the left. We were now only about three feet apart. I couldn't make a run for it.

"See, Cassie, you think you know everythang, right? But let me tell you somethin', you don't know nothin'. You got all your degrees—"

"Blake, I only have one de—"

"Shut up! That's what I'm talkin' 'bout. Shut up and let me finish this."

I flinched at his words and vowed not interrupt him again.

"You see, Cassie, not everyone grew up with a silver spoon in their mouth."

I started to disagree, but I stopped myself, let him continue his tirade.

"Not everyone's mama is a big-time school teacher. Not everyone's granddaddy is the head of the deacon board. You see what I'm sayin'?"

I had no idea, but I let him talk anyway.

"You have had people all around you yo' whole life," he continued. "Real people. Peoples who cared about you, fo' real. I didn't have nobody, and I still ain't got nobody."

This time, I had to interject. I thought I had all the answers. "What about your mother? I'm sure she loves you."

"See, that's yo' first mistake. That's yo' first mistake right there. My mama don't mean shit to me. Never has, never will. You know why?"

I shook my head to signal that I didn't.

"Because I never will mean shit to her. That's why."

I shook my head and looked down at my bare feet. I guess he was waiting for me to look up again, because when I did, he continued his explanations.

"My mama is a slut, Cassie. She was when we was growin' up, and she still is right now."

"That's not nice to say about your own mother, Blake."

"When the fuck is you gone wake up, girl? The woman is a fuckin' prostitute. If that don't make you a slut, then what do?"

"I'm sorry," I said, and meant it. "I didn't know she—"

"What the hell you sorry for now? Huh? Did you make her ruin my life? Nah. So keep your apologies to your damn self."

I leaned my elbow against my knee and put my forehead into my hand. It didn't help much to stop my body from shaking.

"Shit, if you think *that* shit'll give you a headache, wait 'till I finish," he yelled. "See Cassie, I know exactly what yo' problem is. You underestimate people."

I sighed at the irony of that. "Just tell me this," I said. "How did you get in here?"

"See, that's a prime example of what I'm talkin' 'bout. Girl, I done broke into so many liquor stores and houses, I could have broken into this place blindfolded. Now quit interrupting me." He jabbed his knife in my direction. "My bitch-ass mama, you know what she did? She done gone and got herself some kids by a white man that we can't even call Daddy in public."

This was getting more and more insane by the minute. "What?"

"My dear old mama, that's what."

"What are you talking about?"

"See, you runnin' round here talkin' 'bout yo' daddy this and yo' daddy that. Well I's got a daddy too, Cassie."

"I thought he was—"

"Dead? Yeah, me too. 'Till a couple of days ago. My mama…see, she been keepin' this shit from me."

"I'm sorry. I mean—"

"Yeah. And you know I'm just feelin' fucked up, ya' know? I ain't got nobody. J.R. gone. Mama ain't worth shit…. You tryin' to up and run off, sayin' you don't want no part of me. And now this mutherfucker talkin' 'bout he wish I could have knew sooner, but it don't matter cause he can't see me no more noway."

I was listening intently, but he'd just lost me. Who else, according to him, was making his life hell?

"Blake what are you talking about? *Who* are you talking about?"

And all the while, I sat wishing that I could have just gone back to those two seconds when I'd decided to go and visit him in jail. Damnit! Isn't it a crying shame that hindsight is 20/20? I hate that.

"I'm talking 'bout him, you know. *Him*." His voice had quieted down, as if there were other people in the room listening. But there weren't.

"Who, Blake?"

"Mr. Monroe. Do I need to spell it out for you, girl? He my fuckin' daddy. Can you believe this shit? All this fuckin' time…"

"Oh, my God! Mr. Monroe is your *father*?"

Blake nodded. "Shit, he and I was down for all these years, and now all a sudden we got to chill out and shit right when I'm learnin' he my old man."

"I-I can't believe it." And that was the truth.

"Shit, me neither. I got a cracker for a daddy."

"He's not a cracker, don't say that. Why can't he see you?"

"Girl, why don't you wake the fuck up? He married and got three or four white kids with his white wife. That man ain't got no time for me."

"Why didn't your mother tell you before?"

"She couldn't, hell. That white man's wife and her family done already run her out of town once." He jabbed the knife up and down on his knee.

"Holy shit. Holy, holy shit." I clasped a hand to my mouth, thinking, *So that's why Blake's mother was always gone and he and J.R. were living with his grandmother.*

He saw my shock and said, "Ha, haaaaaaa! You wasn't 'spectin' *that* shit, was ya'?"

I said, "Oh my God," but in my head, I kept repeating it over and over again.

I was sure I was going to throw up, and there was nothing for it. I tried to resist by closing my eyes, but when I did, images of the two of them together made me quickly reopen them again.

"But, he's married," I sputtered. "Mr. Monroe's married."

"So what? He still messed around and fell for my mama—a black woman. Sucker. But tonight I went to see him, and he lays this shit on me...that he gone always love me and shit, but his wife is gittin' suspicious and shit. Talkin' 'bout he don't want to lose his job and all."

"Stockdale, Stockdale, Stockdale!"

"What? What you talkin' 'bout? Well, fuck it. Fuck him and fuck that. If he wanna cut loose, let him."

I still wanted to throw up, but more than that, I wanted Blake to get out. "Will you please leave now?" I asked him. How I hoped he would, that maybe he just needed to get this all off his chest, and then he'd go. But I was wrong.

"We ain't really got to the business of why I came, now have we?"

I bit my lip. What next? And then he told me.

"I need some money, Cassie. I need some money to git outta town with."

So *that* was what the visit was about. I said the first thing I could think of: "What?"

"Yep. I need *cash*, darlin'."

"Okay, let me turn on the light.... I can see what I have."

He let me get up and walk over to the light switch, my knees still shaking the whole way in fear that he'd go even crazier than he already was. I switched the light on, and got my first clear look at him. He was wearing raggedy Army fatigues and mud-caked boots. He looked skinnier than he'd been the last time I saw him, and the black circles under his eyes were even darker. He was a complete and total mess.

He let me go through all the trouble of getting my purse, taking my wallet out, and handing him twenty dollars before he started laughing, a laugh that sent chills all over me, a laugh that reminded me of Vincent Price's laugh in Michael Jackson's *Thriller* video. Come to think of it, Blake could have very well been a creature in that video.

When he stopped laughing, he said, "Girl, I don't want no chump change. I came fo' somethin' else. Come on now, where you hidin' it?"

I turned my eyebrows up and shook my head. "What are you talking about?"

"You know what I want. I want that money you been stashing away all this time."

"What?" My heart started thudding in my chest.

"I wants yo' gittin'-out-of-town money…and I wants it now."

# Chapter 45

Thank God, oh thank you, Jesus for letting my grandparents believe in savings accounts. "I don't have any money here, Blake. It's at the bank."

"Don't bullshit me!" he bellowed, then jumped up out of his chair, grabbed my purse and dumped everything out on the floor. "Where is it? Where is it?" He tossed each thing aside—Clinique compact, lipstick, pocket camera, graduation program...and empty wallet.

"I told you, it's at the bank," I said, backing myself into that same corner near the bar, then thinking better of it.

Too late. He advanced on me, looking me dead in the eyes. I was shaking and breathing hard enough for the neighbors to hear me next door, and how I wish they had. When I looked down at his hand, hesitantly, and saw that he still had the knife, I breathed even harder.

Then Blake did something unexpected. He started laughing again. But this time, it was more like his usual laugh. "That's aw'right. We'll just hang out, and go to the bank in'a mornin'."

The problem had solved itself, hadn't it? Perhaps. But then, as though I'd be happy to say yes, he told me he needed my car to leave town with as well.

It was enough to drive me over the edge. Give him my hard-earned money? My "gittin'-out-of-town money," he called it, but what *I* called my "leaving Stockdale for good" account?

No way. Excuse my French, but there was no way in *hell*. This insanity had to end. *Now.*

My legs stopped shaking, my heart and head stopped pounding, and my mind cleared. I don't know where the courage came from, but when it did, I made a run for the front door.

I had just put my hand on the doorknob when Blake grabbed me from behind and pulled me back.

"Stoppppp!" I shouted, and he tried to put his hand over my mouth. I bit down hard on it.

We struggled for what seemed like hours. I expected to feel the knife blade at any moment, but he had dropped it during the battle. I didn't find that out until later, though. When he finally got me on the floor and rested his full weight on me, I was still kicking and screaming.

"Girl, shut up! Shut up!" He was still trying to cover my mouth, but I continued, screaming, "Help! Help!"

He was doing a pretty good job of stopping my yells, though; it all came out muffled.

He was on top of me. When I looked into his eyes, all I saw was a black, emotionless pit. It was at that moment I figured I was really in trouble.

His hands quickly moved from my mouth to my throat, and he began choking me with the frenzy of a madman. Which he was.

I continued struggling against him and tried to remove his hands from my neck. I couldn't. It's true what they say about crazy people: They are *insanely* strong. I had the proof right there in my living room.

I was losing the battle and I knew it. I could hardly keep my eyes open and I was coughing and gasping. I tried begging and pleading with him, but I could hardly make a sound. I felt tears streaming from my eyes. For a second I thought about Heather. *Will she be there to meet me if I die tonight? And where is "there," anyway? Have I been good enough to get into Heaven?*

I tried to say the Lord's Prayer, but couldn't remember the words. The illogical thought came to me: *How awful! All those years in Sunday School...*

I had to plead with him one last time, with my eyes if nothing else, and forced myself to look at him. But instead of meeting his cold stare instantly, my eyes looked past him to an end table.

That's when I saw it. My airline ticket. Literally, my ticket to freedom.

And that gave me the strength to keep going.

I tried again to pry his hands away from my throat. No luck. He was still sitting on top of me, not saying a word, just choking me to death as if he were shopping for shoes.

I felt around on the floor with my hands. Nothing.

I kept grasping, and my hand hit something hard. I grabbed it, recognized what it was. *Will he hear the noise? Doesn't matter.* Now, if I could only get it to work.

*T-chick. T-chick.*

*Please God, don't let today be my day.*

Dying feels just like going to sleep. Coherent thought was a struggle. But my fingers kept working.

*T-chick, T-chick.*

The sound stopped.

*Is it still on? Does it even work?*

I felt heat, and my mind screamed, *Yes!*

I moved my hand up to his shirt. My finger was already starting to burn, but that was nothing compared to the pain he was inflicting on me.

It was only a few seconds before the pain became unbearable, and I had to release the object. But that was good enough: Blake's shirt was on fire.

He turned up his nose a little, sniffing the air like an old hound dog. Then he looked on the floor beside my body and saw the cigarette lighter. *His* cigarette lighter.

Before he could choke me anymore, his flesh started burning. That was the last thing I smelled before I drifted off.

\* \* \* \*

Later, I learned that the fire itself was small. But Blake was high and delusional. He ran out of my apartment, screaming, and fell off the balcony. He made so much noise that Miss Ethel Mae heard, and she immediately called the police.

When they were carrying me out of my apartment, I glanced over at the end table.

"Wait a minute," I choked. "Give me that envelope. Please, give it to me. It saved me."

Miss Ethel Mae had no idea what I was talking about, but picked up the envelope and carefully placed it in my hands before we left for the hospital.

\* \* \* \*

I let out a long sigh, then looked out the window through the flaky blue clouds. It felt so good to be flying high. I had made it. I was free.

"They loaded Blake up as well," I said. "He had second and third-degree burns to his torso. After he gets out of the hospital, he'll be going to jail for a long, long time. He's out of my life forever."

"Amazing. What an *incredible* story. What an *incredible* life you led."

I smiled at the gentleman beside me. "Yeah. You must think I'm completely nuts, huh?"

He said nothing, just shifted his weight in his seat, and to my surprise, said, "No. I zhink you are wonderful, zat you have life, *mais* full life, running through your veins."

"You're teasing me, right?" I said, looking at the kindness in the stranger's eyes. He smiled, but before he could answer, the captain came in over the intercom.

"Ladies and gentleman, we are now starting our descent in to Paris. Temperature on the ground is…"

"Now, what were you saying?" I asked, intrigued by his reaction to my tale.

"I was saying zat you are a very beautiful person. You deserve to be happy. You *will* be happy in zhe life. Of zhis, I am sure."

"So…Jean-Luc, right?"

"*Oui*." He was still smiling.

"That's what Frenchmen tell all the foreign girls, right?" I smiled back at him.

"Let me show you what a Frenchman does. Better, let me show you what a *friend* does. How about dinner tomorrow night near La Sacre Coeur?"

"La what?"

"La Sacre Coeur. If you say yes, I will tell you all about a poet zhat I am sure you will like. His name is Baudelaire."

"Who?" I asked, embarrassed because I hadn't yet read this particular writer.

"Charles Baudelaire. It's okay if you do not know him. I will tell you all about him. I am absolutely sure zhat you will love him, Cassandra Taylor."

And I did.

# Author's Note

Stockdale is a fictitious place. Although there are probably hundreds of similar small towns all across the southern part of the United States, the city itself does not exist…

But it used to.

I wrote this book and choose to call it *Stockdale* in honor of my grandmother, the late Mrs. Beatrice Stockdale Heard, who was born and raised in Talladega, Alabama. Her ancestors, and therefore my own, are descendants of what was once the Stockdale Plantation, in Stockdale, Alabama. Again, the city no longer exists, but the old Stockdale farm does, and is currently owned and inhabited by a very nice lady who is of no relation to the Stockdale family, but who has become my friend due to this whole adventure.

While it might be an ironic coincidence that Cassie, the main character of this novel, deals with segregation and racism during the story, and the original Stockdale was indeed a working plantation supposedly founded around 1843 by a James Seeds Stockdale who owned many slaves, it is only that. Had my grandmother's name been something else, with no ancient plantation associated with it, I would have probably used it. However, things as they were and are, I guess it just works out nicely that it was Stockdale, and that there is this tremendous history associated with it.

Besides, I like the name. I hope *you* liked the story. I'd like to think my grandmother would have.

Sincerely,
Priscilla Lalisse
August 2005

For more information about *Stockdale* the novel, and the original plantation, visit www.priscillalalisse.com.

978-0-595-37244-7
0-595-37244-9

Ingram Content Group UK Ltd.
Milton Keynes UK
UKHW010633130323
418477UK00001B/247